Ellie's Window

Surrender – Book One

To my dear friend,
very dear friend,
thank you so
much for your
loving ...
Love & Joy
Darrell

Published by Mindstir Media

1931 Woodbury Ave. #182 | Portsmouth, New Hampshire 03801 | USA

1.800.767.0531 | www.mindstirmedia.com

Printed in the United States of America

ISBN-13: 978-0-9903626-4-7

Library of Congress Control Number: 2014940215

Ellie's Window

Surrender – Book One

written by
Sandy Snavely

MINDSTIR MEDIA

Dedication

To My Bud:

The man who knows me best and loves me still.

The man who has filled my life with adventure.

And the man who listened attentively to every word of this story.

You are, and always will be, the love of my life.

Acknowledgements

Ellie's Window is an example of what God can do through broken people who are willing to receive hope from His heart and help from our friends. I have many to thank for seeing me through from start to finish.

First always in my heart and life - Annette, the daughter who never ceases to fascinate me with her gentle spirit and enduring love. Dean, the son who surprises us with his brilliance and blesses us with his respect. Kim, the woman who married our son and found a permanent place in our lives. Morgan Elizabeth-Anne, and Jakob Ellis, - my precious ones who thrill my heart every time they call me *Nane, (Nahnee)*. Wacky. Wild. And Wonderful. We are family!

To my group of encouragers - Nancy Alcorn, Tia Collins, Phyllis Bennett, Jeanie Burgin, Celeste Delaney, Bernice Gadbaugh, Jacquie Guthrie, Mary Kinoshita, Bonnie Knopf, Kelly Kramer, Diana Martin, Shirley Monroe, Dena Stuerhoff, Alice Tate, Sheala Pritchard, and Sarah & David Van Deist- knowing you knew what I was doing kept me from quitting in the middle.

Thanks also to Angela Hunt - your books, your ability to teach writers how to write, and your email friendship, has made me a better writer. To Paula Wiseman - thank you for letting me into your heart and life through email, blogs, and phone calls. Ellie's Window is now in print because of your encouraging counsel. To Dannette Mondary - my dear niece, who answered all my medical questions and cheered me on to the finish line. To Chip Mac Gregor - thank you for not liking the first draft! I hope the final meets with your approval. To Connie McClellan, thank you for hovering over every word and lingering over every concept so the final edit would be nearly perfect. You're a great friend. And finally, thank you to Kay Sass, Public Affairs and Emergency Management Coordinator at City of Dover. You made Dover come alive with sights, and sounds, and stories, that you just can't get from Google. Can't wait to see you again."

Table of Contents

Then those who feared the Lord spoke with each other, and the Lord listened to what they said. In His presence, a scroll of remembrance was written to record the names of those who feared Him and always thought about the honor of His Name. Malachi 3:16 NLB

Chapter One

June 23, 1954

1:45 AM. Awake again. The persistent longing to bury her nose in the cool softness of her pillow was too compelling to resist, so she gritted her teeth and gave it another go. Audrey blew the bangs off her forehead as the bulging weight of her front side pulled her back to her backside. And this must be why whales don't sleep upside down. She breathed in as deeply as her lungs would allow while random thoughts clicked to the ticking of the clock on the nightstand next to her bed.

Tick: Is that man really sleeping or is he snoring just to annoy me?

Tock: Why can't someone invent a mattress that adjusts to the size of my belly?

Tick: Whoa baby, what are you doing in there?

Tock: I wonder how long it's been since I've seen my toes.

Tick: Okay Mommy, hold on, here comes another one.

Tock: Wow that was huge. Do I dare wake him? Again?

Tick, tock, tick: O-o-o-h yes, I think I do. "Charles, are you awake? Honey, I think this could be it."

Tock, tock, tock: "Charles Wesley St. Clare! I'm really sure this is it. Please wake up. Now!"

Charles' lanky frame propelled him out of bed faster than a cork out of a bottle of champagne as his feet shuffled across the carpet in search of his slippers.

Audrey struggled to push her mammoth self to a sitting position with one hand while turning on the lamp with the other. "Honey," she exhaled as her eyes squinted through the light, "I don't think your large hairy foot is going to fit into that small pink slipper. Yours are next to the chair, why don't you wear them instead?" Her nostrils pinched together as the rumblings of pain were gearing up for another hit. "So, I hope you're ready to have a baby because I'm pretty sure I've discovered the difference between false labor and the real thing."

Pressing her lips together she tried to remember where she might have put their, *what to do when the baby's coming* checklist, but her mind was just too scattered to concentrate on anything but breathing. Another spasm of pain seized hold of her abdomen with superhuman force.

"Charles, we need my suitcase from the closet. Not the big black one but the smaller one with the leather straps. It's all packed and ready to go. And we need the diaper bag, I think it's downstairs next to the door. No, wait, I put it in the back of the car yesterday. Or maybe that was last week when we *thought* I was in labor. Then I moved it back to the door downstairs. Ow!" Audrey wrapped her arms around the mound of baby that was working very hard to squeeze the stuffing out of her.

"Are you alright?" Charles asked. "How close are your contractions? Should I call an ambulance? What if we can't get to the hospital in time?"

"Good grief, Charles," Audrey answered through panting breaths, "*whew, no I don't need an…ho-o-o-o* that really hurts."

"That's it, we're leaving *now!* I'll go get the car. You just stay put and work on keeping that baby in there until we get to the hospital."

Never one to take orders unless the word *please* was involved she rose up from their bed in militant protest, "But, Charles, I haven't even combed my hair and I'm not going anywhere in this ratty old nightgown. I want to wear the new one your mother gave me at my shower. *Whew-w-w!* And I think it would be good if you put some pants on."

From the look on her husband's face Audrey felt as if she had suddenly sprouted antlers off the sides of her head. "I can't help sounding irrational, Charles, so could you just humor me until we get to the hospital?"

Charles wiped a fountain of sweat off his forehead. "Audrey, you're in labor! No one cares how you look or what you're wearing."

"Trust me," she said as she hobbled her way to the flowery printed chair in the corner of their room. "It will only take a minute. Now hand over the gown. It's in my top drawer, and then grab my hairbrush and my toothbrush from the bathroom." She fixed her hand into the small of her back while her eyebrows pushed creases into her forehead. "It'll take us thirty minutes to get to the hospital, that will give me, *whew-w-w-w*, plenty of time to take the fur off my teeth and get the knots out of my hair before…Oh, hurry Charles, Squeaky is not a happy baby."

She smiled painfully as she watched Charles open the top drawer of their dresser while digging through the tangled mass of unmentionables. When he finally found the nightgown he tossed it to her and then headed to the bathroom muttering a host of things she didn't want to hear just before giving birth to their first child. But five years of praying, two miscarriages, and dozens of rabbits that didn't die, had only made Audrey more determined to make sure her story ended better than it began.

The warmth of Charles' arm around her waist as he walked her down the stairs filled her with a deeper love for him than she ever thought possible. He deposited her on the hand carved wooden bench next to the door, picked up the diaper bag that was exactly where she thought it might be, and dashed outside with his keys pointed toward their car.

A twinge of nostalgia bruised his ego as Charles' hand grabbed hold of the chrome handle on the aqua blue station wagon in their driveway. It had only been a month since he'd left his sporty two-seater, the pride of his profession, sitting like a bewildered puppy at Lucky's Auto Dealers, while he drove home in something far better suited for midnight runs for formula, trips to the dentist, hauling squirrelly teeny boppers to the movies, and if fate would allow, a few more deliveries to the labor room in ratty old nightgowns.

He tried to keep a mental count of Audrey's pains while navigating their way by starlight from Bowers Beach to Dover. It all seemed to be happening too fast. Weren't first babies supposed to take their time? His white knuckles dug into the steering wheel while warm beads of sweat dripped through her auburn hair curling it into stringlets that hung limply over her slender shoulders. The grooming supplies she insisted on bringing with her sat like useless friends on the floor near her swollen feet. It didn't matter; she had never been lovelier than she was right now and he had never felt more helpless.

Charles took great pride in upholding his family's long honored tradition of remaining tearless while in the presence of their women. Tonight would be no exception. Besides, it wouldn't be prudent to cry like a girl when the girl sitting next to him was about to accomplish feats of heroism unmatched by any man since Adam. He swallowed hard and kept on driving while the veins in his throat pulsed in sync with the thumping of his heart.

Another groan announced the coming of another contraction. Resting his hand gently over hers he spoke as comfortingly as he knew how, "We picked the perfect time to travel. There's no one on the road but us. How are you doing?"

Audrey glared back at him, "Well, I'm thinking I'd like to bite down on something fleshy right about *now!* And I'm thinking we forgot to put fresh food out for Basil. And, let's see, I'm thinking I'd like to go home and do this tomorrow when we're feeling more prepared to have a baby."

Labor and logic would not be shaking hands any time soon. Best to play along with her by denying the obvious - the baby was coming whether she felt ready or not. "Okay. So, how about when we get to the Emergency Room I ask an orderly to come and lend you a nice boney hand to gnaw on. And, Honey, as for Basil - we dropped him off at Mother's yesterday with his rug and sloppy bear. He's probably stretched out across her bed chasing tennis balls in his dreams and having no idea he's about to become a very big brother to a tiny little who knows what."

Charles tapped his foot on the brake ever so carefully while turning left onto Clapham Road, which would become Main Street, which would become State Street. Why one name for one street wasn't enough for the two adjoining towns never ceased to baffle him. "Now, what was that third thing? Oh yeah, you can't wait to get to the hospital so you can wear one of those fancy-schmanzy nighties with the cute little ties in the back." Her eyes rolled in disapproval. Clearly there was nothing he could do or say to make this evening bearable.

The streets of Dover lay snuggled under a blanket of quiet. Ahead Charles could see a row of moonlit trees lining the circular driveway leading to the hospital entrance, their branches outstretched to protect the weak and weary, and those whose nerves have gone bump in the night.

"And here we are," he said, while parking the car as close to the front steps as he could possibly get. "Admit it, Sweetie Pie, - I'm still your hero! You stay right here while I go get you a wheel chair; there's no point in wasting your energy trying to hoist yourself up those stairs."

As he popped the door open Charles remembered what was at the top of their elusive list, "You know neither one of us thought to call Doctor Cohen. Let's just pray he's not sunning himself on an island somewhere in the Caribbean." Ooo, not helpful Charles, not helpful at all. The last thing she needs is to worry about her doctor not being here when she needs him. When we need him. "Never mind, every thing's going to be alright. I'm sure the nurses know where he is and how to get hold of him." Lord, let it be true. "I'll only be a minute. Do you think you can wait that long?"

"Just don't dawdle, Charles. If I find you've been chatting with some cute nurse while I'm - Oh dear! You'd better get going. And bring a towel back with you."

So much for that plushy new interior.

The mingling scents of aging plaster and rubbing alcohol assaulted his nostrils as Charles walked through the hospital doors. Two nurses, in crisp white uniforms with matching crowns perched neatly on their hair-sprayed heads, whisked passed him without so much as a nod of recognition. His inner boy wanted to stand in the middle of the lobby and howl for help.

"Young man, is there something I can do to help you?" A plumpish wom-an with red hair, and a husky voice, barked from behind the long counter under a very large sign that read, "Reception Desk." Right. I guess obvious is only obvious when you're looking in the right places.

Wasting no time, Charles rushed to the desk and demanded the nurse's immediate attention. "My wife's in labor. She's in the car out front and she needs a wheelchair! Now!"

"And what is your name, sir?" the nurse asked.

"Charles St. Clare. But -"

"And your wife's name?"

"Audrey St. Clare. But -"

"Try to stay with me young man. This won't take long. And your doctor's name?"

"Doctor Cohen," he said, "and you'll need to call him right away."

"I'll get to that in a minute, Mr. St. Clare. Now where's your wife?"

"She's in the car. I just told you that. She's in the car." Charles began mouthing his words as if they were separated by exclamation points, "and she's in a lot of pain and she needs a wheel chair so I can get her out – of – the – car – right now!"

The nurse was a tank - armed for battle and prepared for anything that might threaten her tidy little world of lists, rules, and procedures. She reached for a clip board and a pen. "Let's not get testy, Mr. St. Clare. I'm going to give you some forms that need to be filled out. In the meantime, I'll send an orderly to go and get your wife. Now where is your car?"

Lowering his voice to a growl he placed both hands firmly on the cold Formica counter and leaned in for the kill. "It's the only station wagon you'll find parked right in front of the front door!"

"You know, Mr. St. Clare, you're going to have to move your vehicle out of the driveway as soon as we bring Mrs. St. Clare inside. That's not a park-ing space. Now, take these forms with you over there and I'll call the doctor." Her pointy finger traced an invisible line from Charles' nose to the far side of the counter, where several rows of blue Naugahyde chairs sat waiting for their next victim. "How far apart are her contractions?"

Charles counted his fingers while fumbling for an answer. "Two, maybe three minutes. Maybe five."

"I know this is taking time, Mr. St. Clare, but you'll thank me for it later. Now, when did they begin?"

His mind was quickly going blank. "About an hour ago. Maybe two. I don't know. I was asleep."

"Mr. St. Clare," a hint of a smile curled into her pudgy cheek, "your wife and baby are going to be just fine. You just go sit down and I'll call for one of our nurses to meet her at the door and bring her upstairs. Our job is to help her deliver her baby, but your job is to give me all the information I need to make that happen. Now, can you do that for me?"

Cranky Nurse - 1.

Frantic Husband - zip.

Charles slumped into the seat where he could keep watch on the front doors. That familiar surge of anxiety, the kind that reached down into the pit of his stomach and twisted around his backbone, reminded him all over again, that he wasn't a man who took well to taking orders. He had been running his father's firm since his Masters in Architectural Engineering was placed in his hands. His secretaries did what he told them to do. His contractors followed his directions. His clients asked him for advice. And now here he was, being whipped into submission by a woman with way too much starch in her bonnet.

Charles tried to focus on the questions in front of him but the words just popcorned off the paper. What's going on out there? Why did I let a perfect stranger go out to help my wife while I sit here with this stupid clipboard? At last the doors flew open.

The dark-skinned orderly was whispering into Audrey's ear as he wheeled her into the lobby. Does she have to make friends with absolutely everyone she meets? Charles tossed the clipboard down on the empty seat next to him and ran to her side.

Her face looked pale against the green hospital walls. "Well, Daddy-to-Be, have you been behaving yourself while I've been gone? You haven't been beasty with that nice nurse over there, have you?"

How does she do that? Charles knelt down close to those eyes that always had a way of melting his mood. "I've been an angel with horns. Now let's get this show on the road." With that said he nudged the orderly aside and took control of the wheel chair, nodding his head in the direction of the elevator, "Is that where we need to go to get to where we need to go?"

"Yes sir, we'll be headin' up to the second floor. But the nurse isn't here yet. Can't go nowhere unless she says so."

"Really? Watch me."

The metal doors slid open as a fortyish woman, with a stethoscope hanging off her neck, smiled compassionately in their direction. Charles nearly ran the chair into her as she attempted to exit the elevator. "I'm Charles St. Clare, and this is my wife, Audrey. She's in labor."

"Well, I can see that. I'm Nurse Wilson, but you can call me Connie. I was just on my way down to get you. So, how are we doing tonight?"

"We're doing just fine," Audrey answered. "My pains are coming" she winced as she drew in a short breath, "really fast and my water broke in the car just before this nice man, Leonard, came to get me."

Nurse Wilson's manner was comforting with just the right hint of authority. "Now, Mr. St. Clare, I'm going to need you to let go of the wheel chair and give it back to Leonard here so we can get your wife settled in upstairs. I know it probably seems silly to you, but the hospital has certain rules that just need to be followed. I'm sure you can understand how important that is, can't you?"

Visions of grade school flashed through his brain as Charles reluctantly released the wheels to the orderly. Just before the doors were about to close, a white-sweatered arm with a clipboard attached to the end of it, pushed through the gap while a white-polished shoe, tied neatly with thick cotton laces, held them in place. Her words scratched through the air like metal across cement, "You forgot your forms, Mr. St. Clare! Now take these upstairs with you and give them to the nurse at the desk as soon as you're finished."

The bright lights on the second floor blasted through his senses as Charles followed Leonard and Nurse Wilson as they escorted Audrey to the counter that was littered with stacks of manila file folders. A woman with blue curls springing out in all directions from under her nurse's cap smiled at them while putting the phone back onto the receiver.

"Are you the St. Clare's?" Her vibrato matched the age of the building. "Doctor Cohen is on his way. Now, Darlin', we'll get you settled in a room while your nice man here fills out those admittance forms. By the time you're tucked into bed your doctor will be here to deliver your baby."

"I'll be going with my wife, thank you."

"Mr. St. Clare, we'll bring you to her room as soon as we get her prepped for delivery. That way you can finish the paperwork and make whatever phone calls need to be made before your baby arrives." The old nurse wasn't as frail as she looked.

Phone calls? Somehow it hadn't occurred to him that his mother had been waiting a lifetime for this moment. Charles was an only child and his mother's only child was about to add a little bundle to her family album. *How could I forget to call my mother?*

His last nerve was fraying at the edge as he watched the nurse wheel his wife down the hall. Somehow it never occurred to him that having a baby would require pens, and paper, and rules that would divorce him from the most important moment in their marriage. But there was no pushing against procedure. Forgetting as quickly as he remembered to call his mother, Charles sunk into a seat near the nurse's station and began scribbling answers across the admittance forms with a deranged sense of purpose.

Ten minutes later he pounded a period at the end of the last question. *There! Done! Now all I have to do is hand it over and I'm home free.* Charles rushed to the counter just in time to catch the attention of the desk nurse as she shuffled her way back to her post.

"Well, Mr. St. Clare, looks like you've finished your job quite nicely. And such lovely penmanship. Good thing you're not a doctor, you know they're just notorious for their chicken scratches. It's beyond me how anyone can read a single thing they write. Now, would you like to use the phone to call your family?"

Just as Charles' blood pressure was about to hit the red zone, Dr. Cohen walked out of the elevator looking a bit too chipper for a man roused out of bed at O-Dark Thirty AM. "Well, Charles, looks like this is it. It's been a long time coming hasn't it? Hey, I'd ask you how you're doing, but from the looks of your hair I'd say you're doing just about as well as any first time father's allowed to." Dr. Cohen patted Charles on the back. "Don't worry, by the time number five comes along you'll be an old hand at it."

Samuel Cohen's short stature was packed tight to the ring of grey hair that circled his shiny scalp. When it came to delivering babies, he had built a reputation as the best of the best. "Now, I'm going in to check on Audrey. You wait here and I'll come and get you when it looks like she's ready for visitors."

Visitors? I'm a *visitor*? When do I get to be the second half of this event? There were three words Charles learned to hate that night at Kent General Hospital - sit, wait, and paperwork. These were the times when men turned twelve. Time to call mother.

Esther answered on the first ring. As she listened to the panic in her son's voice, she went bluntly to the point. "Now Charles, women have been having babies for hundreds of years, so quit your fretting. Your Audrey is a tough little thing. She's going to be just fine. I'll be there as soon as I can. See you soon, dear. And Charles, try to keep a hold on your patience - you know they'll charge you more if they have to sedate you."

Everything about the room felt strange to her as Audrey climbed into the stiff white sheets of the hospital bed. She looked around imagining how much friendlier it would be if the walls were painted in something other than green and if the windows had curtains on them instead of the fading roller shades that were torn in several places. Maybe lace. Or something floral. A chair that wasn't covered in blue plastic cracked with age. A night-stand with a homey lamp. A room that looked more like - home.

Redecorating her world was something Audrey had turned into an art form since she first discovered how messy life could be. She'd spent half her childhood cutting out pictures from her mother's magazines to hide the holes in their walls left by her father's fists and turning her mother's beer bottles into flower vases. And then there was the day she got in trouble for painting a bright yellow sun on the window next to her bed just to make her feel happier on the inside. Her mother thought it was a useless waste of paint and time. But her grandmammy loved it. "I swear, little Audrey, you could paint a pig pretty if you had half a mind to." Her grandmother, Eleanor Mae Hamilton, was the light of her life taken too soon.

"Audrey? I see you're all tucked in and ready to get busy delivering that baby. We have a few things to do before Doctor Cohen comes in."

"I'm ready," Audrey said. "In fact I'm more than ready. I really don't know what I'm looking more forward to, getting rid of this constant pain, being able to bend over to tie my shoes, or holding my baby in my arms."

"I think you'll be happy with all three. So let's get started."

Once Nurse Wilson had finished doing all those things that left Audrey feeling more like a lab rat than a mother-to-be, Dr. Cohen walked in with a huge grin on his face. "So, how's our patient doing?"

Before Audrey had a chance to answer, Nurse Wilson took over. "Her contractions are between three and four minutes apart, she's dilated to six centimeters, her heart rate is steady, the baby's heart rate is 140, and her water broke about twenty minutes ago. She thinks her labor might have begun around nine PM. The pains were somewhat erratic until midnight, and then they started hitting hard every four to five minutes. Evidently Mrs. St. Clare was feeling shy about making another unnecessary trip to emergency so she decided to wait until she was sure the pains were for real. They were."

"And, hello to you too, Connie." Dr. Cohen was happy to see his favorite nurse standing next to his favorite patient. There wasn't a delivery partner he trusted more than Nurse Wilson. "Okay, let's take a look, shall we, and see what's happening." While he poked and probed into areas where no other man had been except for Charles, Audrey relinquished her dignity to her much loved doctor as she drifted back to the last day of her first trimester. It all felt superbly inspired at the time; she would choose a girl's name, Charles would choose a boy's name, and when their baby finally made its way through the chute he, or she, could at last be called something other than Squeaky. Being quite sure it was a boy, Audrey was anxious to hear the name Charles chose for his son.

"Well Audrey", Dr. Cohen's voice snapped her back to the present. "Your baby is moving into position for delivery. You're at six centimeters right now, but we'll be looking for you to get to at least eight before we can take you into the delivery room. Now, I'm going to need you to rest here for a while and I'll be back to check on you again soon." Dr. Cohen peeled off his rubber gloves as he and Nurse Wilson stepped into the hall just outside room 212.

Audrey strained to listen as Dr. Cohen spoke quietly to his nurse. "Mrs. St. Clare has a pretty high threshold to pain which leads me to believe that her labor has been going on for longer than she thinks it has. I'd like to pretend this is going to be an easy birth but she's been a high risk pregnancy from the beginning. My gut tells me we're probably in for a long day. Go ahead and finish up her prep work as quickly as possible so we can get her husband into her room. And Connie, let's not be stiff about hospital policies, just give him as much time with his wife as you can."

3:10 AM. The desk nurse put the receiver down before rescuing Charles from his endless pursuit counting the floor tiles in the waiting room. "Mr. St. Clare, your wife is ready to see you. She's tired, but she's doing well. Just be as calm as you can - she's got a ways to go before your baby makes its appearance. You'll find her in room 212, just down the hall on your right." He would have kissed the old saint but there wasn't time. His wife was having a baby.

Charles flew to room 212. One look at Audrey and he could almost hear his father's voice sounding up from the grave, "Charles, women need their men to be men so they don't have to fight over who gets the hanky." So, he squared his shoulders and stiffened his upper lip before entering the room. "Hey, baby, how are you doing?"

"Oh, Charles, this is not at all what I expected. I don't know what I expected, but it just isn't how I thought it would be. My hair must be a fright." Audrey raked her fingers through the tangled curls that lay sprawled across her pillow. "I feel like I'm turning into Lucille Ball on a bad day. How are you doing? Did you call Esther? I hope she'll be able to make it here before Squeaky gets a name. Speaking of names, do you remember what you decided to call our little boy?"

"Oh no, you're not going to bamboozle me into spilling the beans before we hear him holler. Nice try though. Besides, I think it's going to be a girl and I don't think she'll be any too pleased to know what we've been calling her all these months. Now, if you can stay quiet for a single second, Audrey, I need to tell you something."

"Okay, Charles, I'm all quiet. For a second. But you better hurry because I'm getting woozy. I think they drugged me."

Feeling like a sophomore at a sock hop, Charles cleared his throat as he placed his index finger softly over her lips. "Audrey, I love you. I love you no matter what your hair looks like. I love you no matter what you're wearing. And I love you no matter how much you babble while I'm trying to get an 'I love you' in edgewise. I'm so ..."

"Aughhh!" Audrey grabbed hold of the bars of the bed leaving Charles' rare moment of sentimentalism dangling in the space between them. Nurse Wilson moved in quickly to her patient's side, leaving Charles to feel like an observer in someone else's story.

"Audrey, I need you to not push when you feel a contraction. Yell all you want to, but don't push."

"But it feels like I need to," Audrey cried. "Doesn't the baby know when it's time to come out?"

"Yes," Connie said, "but the baby's never done this before. That's why I'm here. So, you're going to need to trust me. Now, I'm going to let Charles keep track of your pains for a while and I'm going to see about getting you some ice chips and an extra pillow." It wasn't everything, but at least it was something. Something he could do that mattered.

The sun began to peek through the window stealing all traces of night away. There are times when time moves as slowly as a slug on a summer day and there are times when time dissolves into timelessness, as if it has no meaning. This was surely one of those times.

Charles looked over his notes:

5:00 AM - after making it to seven centimeters, Audrey drifted off to sleep.

5:15 AM she's awake again.

6:00 AM a new supply of nurses take over. Audrey's contractions coming every three minutes. No sleep possible.

7:20 AM Audrey's hungry and wants to go home.

7:30 AM She's asleep – again.

7:33 AM Contractions still coming – no sign of the baby.

8:37 Audrey is dilated to a whopping eight centimeters!

8:40 Again I'm sent out of the room and left out of the birth of our baby while my wife rides away on a gurney.

The delivery room felt pitilessly cold as Audrey examined the smattering of tools lined up on a metal tray. Why does everything on that tray look like a weapon? Swallowing her fear Audrey pushed her feet against the stirrups for what was about to become the wildest ride of her life.

A sheet hung over her knees like a large white tent blocking her view of her doctor's face. Nurse Wilson buzzed back and forth like a woman on a mission. And Audrey felt alone with a headful of questions.

"Doctor Cohen," she whispered through short breaths, "I know having a baby is supposed to be painful, but is it supposed to be this painful?"

She felt the warmth of her doctor's hand patting the side of her leg as he did his best to reassure her that she was not alone. "Every birth is different Audrey, just like every baby. But you're doing great. Your baby is face down against your spine, which is just what I was hoping to see. You've dilated to almost nine. Depending on how long it takes for you to get to ten is anyone's guess, so Audrey, when we tell you to push - give it all you've got. But not until we say so."

"I don't care what the rules are, Doctor Cohen, I need Charles. I need him. Please let him come in. I promise he'll behave himself. We've waited too long for this and I can't imagine doing it without him."

Samuel Cohen's impressive family tree had been well rooted in the fine art of proper protocol, which is exactly why breaking archaic hospital rules, for the sake of his patients, energized his passion for change. "I understand, Audrey. And I agree. So, how about I send one of the nurses to go and get Charles suited up for delivery? From the looks of things I think we can make it until he gets here. Just save your energy. And, don't push."

"I promise, besides, I'm so tired." A few moments of sleep interrupted her pain.

Soon a man wearing a green hat, with matching gown, mask, and booties, stood over Audrey's bed gently stroking her forehead. "Hey, sleepy head, how are you doing?"

Her eyes opened slowly as the man she loved came into focus. "Oh, Charles, I was dreaming we were standing on the shore just outside our house when a thick layer of fog came rolling in, covering our feet, and rising up until we could hardly see each other. I was crying out for you to come closer, but you couldn't hear me. Then all I could see was your shadow fading away. I'm so glad you're here. Don't leave me." Audrey reached out and filled her hand with the hand that always fit perfectly in hers.

Audrey and Charles ebbed and flowed their way through one pain after another while the morning hours slipped into obscurity. The urge to push their baby out of hiding was becoming more and more difficult to resist. Nevertheless, one thing remained certain - when it came to birthing a baby, two were better than one.

11:16 AM. Audrey was unusually quiet behind her veil of white.

"How are you doing, Audrey?" Dr. Cohen asked. "Are you with me? Before she had a chance to answer, she rose up from the bed heaving a guttural scream that echoed through the walls of the delivery room.

Dr. Cohen was quick to comfort his patient. "It looks like this is it, Audrey, go ahead and start pushing!" Audrey bore down as hard as she could then fell back in defeat while tears, mingling with sweat, soaked the pillow under her head. He motioned for Nurse Wilson to come closer. "Get me a fresh read on the baby's heart rate."

After moving the cup of the fetoscope slowly over Audrey's abdomen, Nurse Wilson put the instrument back in its place and moved in close to Dr. Cohen's side. Her eyes narrowed with intensity. Connie knew to tread softly when speaking her mind to a physician, but Samuel Cohen was different than most doctors, and for this she was most grateful. "The baby's heart rate has dropped from one thirty six, thirty minutes ago, to one twenty one. I'm afraid this baby isn't going to be able to hold on much longer."

"You're right," he answered, "but, she's too close to risk a C-section now. The baby's head has fully crowned, but it's going to be a pretty tight squeeze. Let's get the forceps ready."

"Audrey, I've given you a local anesthetic but you're still going to feel some significant pain. I want you to hold on to Charles as tightly as possible. And Charles, your job is to keep Audrey still until I have the forceps in place. We're near the finish line."

Dr. Cohen slipped the forceps, ever so gently under and over the baby's head, cradling it between the spoons. The force of labor rallied Audrey's energy and before the instruction to push could be given, Audrey grabbed a fist full of sheets and wailed so loudly that her husband nearly fell to his knees. Then silence.

What followed the baby's birth would replay in Charles memory through a thousand nights of uninvited flashbacks. The baby they had so faithfully prayed for entered the world limp and lifeless. Dr. Cohen quickly cut the umbilical cord and thrust the child into a waiting nurse's hands. "Get her to the nursery STAT." With barely a chance to catch his breath Audrey's hand released her grip on Charles' as she slipped into darkness.

"What's happening?" Charles cried, "Where are you taking our baby? What's wrong with my wife?"

Dr. Cohen's hands moved steadily as he removed the afterbirth and began repairing the episiotomy, and the tear that followed its path. Then peering over his glasses for a brief moment, he looked squarely into Charles eyes and spoke to him with protective firmness. "Charles, Audrey has worked harder than any ten men could have done. She's exhausted. Your baby is in good hands. They'll be doing everything they can for her. Now, I want you to head up to the nursery and stay near your daughter while I tend to your wife. And Charles, if you're a praying man I suggest you start now. Your family needs all the help they can get."

Charles' feet slushed heavily across the floor while leaving the delivery room. This can't be happening. This isn't real. Oh God, why? Help our baby! Help my wife! I don't know how to do this! I don't know how to do this! Help me!

As he approached the nursery he saw a young man, barely old enough to grow whiskers, handing a cigar to his father as the tiny blue bundle gurgled and cooed behind the long window where newborns were nestled in a row of tiny white baskets. Anger rose up from Charles' stomach, stinging his throat with the foul taste of bile as he watched from a distance what should have been *his* proud daddy moment.

"Charles." The look on Esther's face gave her son permission to release the pain that had been stalking his emotions since he first entered the delivery room so many hours ago. They enveloped each other in a flood of tears. The sound of his helplessness turned her heart back thirty years to the morning he carried his *broken kitten* into the kitchen and begged her to fix it.

"It was horrible, Mother, she wasn't breathing. She was all blue and still. I don't know how to tell Audrey that our daughter didn't make it. I'm just so glad she's sleeping; it will give me time to figure this all out before she wakes up and wants to see our baby."

Esther grabbed hold of her son's shoulders and spoke with as much clarity as she could muster. "Charles, don't you dare fall apart before you even know what's happening. Listen to me - my granddaughter is in there fighting for her life and she needs her daddy to be strong for her. She's going to make it, Charles! I just feel it in my bones. She's not dead. Do you hear me? She not dead." Burying his face in his hands, Charles sank into the seat next to his mother, grateful for whatever encouragement she could give him and praying she was right. His wife and his baby were going to be just fine.

"Excuse me." The young nurse seemed to appear out of nowhere. "Are you Mr. St. Clare?" Charles looked up at her in dazed oblivion. "Doctor Eleff is with your daughter right now, but he wanted me to come out and let you know that she's breathing on her own and her color is good. Her heart rate has stabilized but we're going to have to watch her very closely for the next few days. Doctor Cohen did a great job getting her to us as quickly as he did. If all goes well we should be able to bring your baby to the window soon so you can see for yourself what an amazing little girl you have."

But before Charles and Esther had time to digest the good news, Nurse Wilson approached the entrance to the nursery. The look on her face was as grave as the sound of her voice. "Charles, Doctor Cohen would like you to come back to the delivery room with me right away."

Charles rose quickly to his feet and followed Audrey's nurse down the hall desperately searching for a way to turn back the calendar to last week, last year, last anytime but now. The doors to the delivery room creaked open. A doctor he didn't recognize stood over his wife adjusting the dials on a machine he'd never seen before. Everything in the air smelled of crises.

Running his hands through his hair Charles turned to Dr. Cohen. "What's wrong with my wife? Is she…" Samuel Cohen turned to face the moment every doctor dreaded.

"I'm sorry, Charles. We've done everything we know how to do. She began hemorrhaging just after you left. There was a tear in the vaginal wall. We've tried to repair it but she's just lost too much blood. The anemia she's been battling hasn't made things any easier." Dr. Cohen placed his hand on Charles' arm, "She's asking for you. There isn't much time. I'm afraid we're losing her."

The room began to spin. Charles reached for something to steady himself but there was nothing but Dr. Cohen's arm to grab hold of. "No, this isn't possible. The baby is doing fine. Just tell her the baby's okay. That's all she needs to hear. She's just tired, you said it yourself. She's just…"

"Charles?" Audrey's voice whispered from behind.

Charles let go of Dr. Cohen's arm and hurried over to the bed where his wife looked as white as the sheets that covered her. "I'm here Audrey." Stroking her cheek with the back of his hand he leaned in close and spoke softly in her ear, "You know you're quite a trooper. Our baby's fine."

"Charles," Audrey continued, as if deaf to his words. "Charles, I'm so sorry."

"Honey, you have nothing to be sorry for. You've done a great job. You've just delivered a baby and she's magnificent, just like her mother."

She slowly traced the sculpted curves of her husband's face as if to preserve its memory while a thin veil of fog began to distance her from all things tangible. "I can't stay, Charles. Please try to understand. I'm just…I'll always…" She smiled faintly as her eyes closed for the last time, "Love. You."

"Stop it, Audrey!" Charles begged. "Stop it. You're tired, that's all. You need to rest. You need to just stop talking for once in your life and rest." He grabbed her hand and held on to it as if he could stop time from slipping into eternity. Oh God, please not now. Not now. Charles felt the chill of her shallow breath against his skin as his head burrowed into her shoulder.

"I do."

"What Audrey? What did you say?"

"I love the Lamb."

"I don't understand what you're trying to say. Say it again. No don't. Save your strength. I love you Audrey. Oh, Sweetheart, just keep breathing. Don't speak - just breathe." The blunt reality of death hovered over them as the woman who had become his reason for living drifted slowly away. "No-o-o-o! Oh, God, where are You?"

"I'm not afraid, Charles. Love her for me."

The children of your servants will live in your presence;
Their descendants will be established before you." Psalm 102:28 NIV

Chapter Two

A gentle rush of Edenic air blew softly through her nostrils, filling her lungs with life while her eyelashes fluttered like tiny wings emerging from a cocoon. The room that had turned cold, and quiet, and dark as night, was invaded by the presence of celestial light. Charles, can you see it? Can you see it? Audrey felt something warm slipping under her weightless spirit, wrapping her up in a featherbed of safety, and lifting her from the place where she breathed her last breath of mortal air.

The walls of the delivery room dissolved into a shimmering veil of dust as the Heavenly being carried Audrey away into the space beyond. How could this be? Though everything seemed to be moving in slow motion her thoughts were spinning with wonder. Death was neither dull nor silent. The swelling sounds of music joined into the percussion of wings beating against the air and drawing them upward while shapes, and colors, and what appeared to be the clashing of swords, dazzled her senses. This was more than an out-of-body experience - it was out of this world. Clearly something incredible was happening in the life of Audrey Rose St. Clare.

A wail of grief split through the air as Kent General Hospital grew smaller and smaller until it was barely a dot in the final chapter of her earthly life. Oh Charles, please let go. Don't be afraid, I'm not going away, I'm just going before. Audrey hoped her words would reach her husband's heart and bring him the comfort he so desperately needed. It's all true Charles. Death has no sting. Believe what you know. Our daughter needs you.

She kissed the air with her thoughts one last time before the clouds between two worlds exploded in a burst of brilliant light. "I will wait for you sweet Anne, your mommy loves you so."

Transcendent beauty surrounded her. Audrey's senses were soaring as the angel carried her through the portal that opened to a world more magnificent than she could ever have imagined. I'm alive. I'm alive! I can see. I can breathe. Whatever is happening to me is not a dream. It's real. Thoughts and feelings and adjectives without nouns to define them emoted from within her. She was an infant learning to comprehend. She was a child learning to speak. But she was a woman; tangible and surprisingly coherent. She was the same woman she had been, yet new.

The Voice of Many Waters resounded through the heavens in words that rained a stream of healing peace over all her insecurities, hurts, disappointments, and the secret doubts that mocked her faith and accused her of believing in fairy tales.

"Welcome Home, Audrey, welcome Home."

She turned toward the Voice and gasped in profound delight. Oh my, He's not a carpenter anymore. There He was in all His glory - the Lamb of God who was slain for the sin of the whole world. His presence filled everything in ways that words could not express. All the pictures she had ever seen of Him were merely kindergarten drawings. He was more delightful than a bride's smile and more stunning than a million diamonds glittering across the sea at sunset. His eyes were blazing like fire, yet they bled with kindness that left her in speechless awe. He was a man and yet He was God. He was the Jesus she had always imagined him to be. And yet He was more.

Audrey stood still, except for the knocking of her knees. She couldn't take her eyes off Him. The young woman who had been so full of words found herself with nothing to say. She simply fell on her face and wept at the sight of His appearing.

"Audrey, do you love Me?"

"Oh, yes, Lord Jesus, I love You."

"Then come to Me and don't be afraid."

Audrey's legs struggled to stand on what felt like a glassy lake beneath her feet. Fearing she might sink she tiptoed two steps forward and then, buoyed by a rush of fresh confidence, she ran into His waiting arms. Her fingers nestled into the softness of Jesus' robe as He pressed a kiss on her forehead. He leaned back just far enough for their eyes to meet while the perfection of His being transformed her into the likeness of His own radiant self.

"Now, sweet Audrey, feel free to drink in the purity of My love for you and let it renew your spirit as you stand with Me at the brink of eternity. Abba and I have been eagerly planning your arrival since before you were born. Come, and let me introduce you to Forever."

As Audrey curled her hand into His she felt the protrusion of nail driven scars covering the place where her name had been inscribed with sacrificial ink. I was made for this. Her eyes pooled with tears. She looked up into Jesus' glorious face and whispered, "No wonder we call You our Savior."

I'm alive and I'm holding hands with Jesus! I'm breathing. I'm walking. The air is so sweet; like a fragrance I've never known before. I've never felt so awake. So alert. So filled to the brim.

"It's because you're Home, Audrey," Jesus answered her thoughts. "This is the place I've prepared for you. But it's only the beginning. There's so much more for you to see. I know you expected Heaven to be filled with those naked cherubs that people paint on Valentine's Day cards, strumming on harps, and playing leap frog with the clouds. Yes, I saw it all. And I loved the way your nose crinkled up whenever the mention of Heaven sent waves of boredom over your feisty spirit."

The laughter in Jesus' voice took Audrey by surprise. Where did she ever get the idea that the Son of God was boorishly proper and spoke in an English accent? But here He was, bantering with her like an old friend who shared a lifetime's worth of private jokes.

"Jesus, how will I ever be able to see it all? How long will eternity be? I just can't fathom it. How will I know what to do first, who to see, where to go. I have at least a million questions. I feel like all of Heaven knows all of everything while I know nothing at all."

A smile beamed across Jesus' face. "It's not a race, Audrey, it's a process. Just think of all your many questions as if they were a banquet where you get to taste and savor every answer one delicious bite at a time. Believe Me, soon you will forget to live by hours, and weeks, and years. Eternity will become as natural to you as breathing. And I have a great surprise for you - your mother, and your grandmother are busy getting ready for a great reunion with their *Audacious Audrey*."

"Audacious Audrey." She gasped in amazement. "I can't believe You just called me that. I hated that nick name, but hearing you say it just sounds different. But, Jesus, you said my grandmother *and* my mother. How can that be? I knew my Grandmammy would be here, but my mother? She never gave any hint at all that loving You or following You ever mattered to her in the least little bit."

Jesus' eyes pierced through Audrey with tender compassion as he motioned for her to come and sit with Him on a bench near a patch of flowering trees. He took hold of her hands and held them gently. "Yes, Rose is here and she's beautiful. What you perceived about your mother was true. She spent most of her earthly life trying to outrun My love for her. But the day came when she couldn't run anymore. I never left her side while she slept through those long months before her death."

"But she was in a coma. The doctors told us that she would never hear or speak again because of the severity of the stroke."

"Doctors can only tell you what they think they know. But I speak of what I *do* know and I knew your mother well. I didn't just walk into her room at the hospital, Audrey - I entered her private world of loneliness and regret. Yahweh chose to use her coma to give her time to be still and become reacquainted with the deep needs of her desperate heart.

Your mother gave her heart to Me when she was four years old. It was a great day in Heaven when she prayed that simple prayer of faith and she loved Me right up until the day she met the first man who claimed to love her more."

"My father."

"Yes, Audrey, your father. He led your mother down a path that turned her into a bitter and angry woman. But it was your Grandmammy's love for her that proved how far My love will go to redeem a wandering soul. She never stopped praying or believing that one day her precious Rose would come back home to the heart of her Abba Father."

"Grandmammy was my best friend in the whole world. I couldn't understand why God would take her from me when she was all I had. When she died I felt completely alone."

"So what did you do?"

Audrey sat quietly as her thoughts drifted back in time. "I remember when the funeral was over, I ran all the way from the graveyard to Grandmammy's house. I stormed into her room and slammed the door behind me so hard that the walls shook. I fell across her bed and sobbed until my face stung with the salt of my tears. Then I saw her Bible sitting on the pillow. She loved to keep it close just in case she woke up in the night and needed a psalm or two to help her go back to sleep. I picked it up and held it to my chest. The cover was taped together and the pages felt as thin and frail as her old hands." Audrey pressed her hands over her heart. "I can still remember how it smelled when I opened it. It smelled like her. I clung to that old Book as if it would bring her back to me. Then the pages fell open to a verse that was underlined in red with my name scrawled in the margin next to it;

'For I know the thoughts that I think toward you, saith the Lord, thoughts of peace, and not of evil, to give you an expected end. Then shall ye call upon me, and ye shall go and pray unto me, and I will hearken unto you. And ye shall seek me, and find me, when ye shall search for me with all your heart.'

"I couldn't bear the thought of never seeing her again so I got down on my knees by her bed and sought You with all my heart."

"Aha!" Jesus said. "Do you see how unsearchable His ways are? In your Grandmammy's death you found life and because you found life you will live forever with her, and with your mother, in the presence of My Father's glory."

Audrey's mind danced with new understanding as Jesus went on with the rest of the story. "When your mother fell into the long sleep of death every one of your Grandmammy's prayers was answered. Rose and I had three sweet months together before she breathed her last breath. During that time we talked and sang hymns of praise, as she released all those things that sin had corrupted during her years of rebellion. And when she crossed over to Forever, she was free of addiction, and the anger that held her in bondage for so much of her life. When she saw her mother, waiting for her, they fell into each other's arms and wept. It's the way family was created to be."

Her heart pounded with excitement. "I can't wait to see them. Thank You for never giving up on her. Or me. But what about my father? Is he here too? Will I have to see him?"

Mercy and Justice flowed together as Jesus spoke. "Audrey, your father was a depraved man. He pretended to be a true believer only when he knew it would buy him what he wanted, and he wanted everything but Me. When My enemy offered Carl the ability to charm the virtue from innocent women, he grabbed hold of it with the greed of a man starved for pleasure. One evening, when he was drunk and blazing with desire, he tried to enter your room, but the presence of your Watcher stood at the door wielding a flaming sword that prevented him from coming through. On that very night your father's eyes were finally opened to the evil of his own soul. He ran out of the house seething with rage.

I met him on the road just before he drove his car over the bridge. In those final moments I offered him one last opportunity to repent and to be set free of the sin that controlled him. But when his eyes met Mine, he shook his fist against the dark and cursed My Name. Carl knew his life was over. He pounded his foot on the gas pedal, and pointed his destiny toward the river below. Your father followed the path of the Evil One and missed the joy of forgiveness and the eternal pleasures of Abba's presence."

Audrey covered her face with her hands. "Oh Jesus, I was so afraid of my father. I couldn't understand why my mother loved him. And I was so angry with her for not protecting me from him. But, You were there the whole time, weren't You?"

"Yes, Audrey, I was there the whole time. I'm the Alpha and the Omega. I'm the Beginning and the End. I have always been with you. In time you will see the reasons why wickedness has been allowed to win temporary victories against the innocent." Jesus stood up and spread out His arms as if to touch the stars with His fingers while He lifted His voice in triumph, "Justice will have its day, Audrey. Sin will be crushed. The Evil One will be destroyed. The earth will be renewed. And every knee will bow before the Name above all Names to the praise of Abba Father."

A shadow stretched giant-like over the path as Audrey and Jesus walked together. "Inservio, come here." A tall and stately being, dressed in white, with hair flowing silvery across his shoulders, accepted the Savior's invitation to join them. There was something about his presence that felt strangely familiar. "Audrey, I want you to meet the one who has travelled with you since the day you were born. And he has been waiting like a puppy in a box on Christmas morning to show you around Heaven. Audrey, meet Inservio, your Watcher."

Audrey laughed out loud. "My Watcher? Like a guardian angel? Really? Oh my, that just answers about half of my million questions."

Inservio smiled back with a knowingness that radiated from within him. He had spent twenty-eight years watching her life's story unfold, standing by her in her deepest hours of need, and meeting her in various forms of human encounters. But today was the day of great unveiling, the day when they could call each other by name and speak of things that had been carefully recorded in Heavenly pages. "We have much to talk about, you and I."

"But you don't have wings. I thought all angels had wings." Audrey patted Inservio's arm, half expecting her hand to pass right through him. Then she patted him again just to be sure he was as real as he appeared to be. He was. "You were the one who carried me away! I felt your arms around me. I was so cold and tired. Then you wrapped me up in warmth like I've never felt before. Did you have wings then? You must have because I felt like we were flying through space."

"I only have wings when I travel, but I can sprout them for you if it would make you happy."

Jesus placed a hand on each of their shoulders, "Well, you two, there is another child of Abba who's soon to arrive. But, before I leave you to your million questions, it's time for you to see the place where Glory begins. Abba's waiting for you. Inservio, why don't you transport Audrey to the Throne and I'll meet you there."

Audrey turned just in time to watch her Watcher's arms press in close to his sides while two massive wings unfurled in graceful beauty from around his body until they stretched out in shimmering beams of transparent color. Once they reached their full height they began to flutter in the air as if searching for a breath of wind to catch them upward. Inservio bowed from the waist waving a hand of invitation to his charge, "Madame, your chariot awaits."

Audrey clapped her hands and squealed for joy as she melted into her Watcher's arms. "I love it here." Together they soared through Heavenly air while choirs of saints and angels, singing psalms of praise, ushered them to the place where Glory begins. Scriptures she had memorized throughout her life on earth hummed through her spirit,

"I go to prepare a place for you and if I go to prepare a place for you I will come again and receive you unto Myself that where I am there you may be also. I am the way, the truth, and the life, and no one comes to the Father but by Me."

Inservio touched down upon a shining surface that surrounded Abba's Throne while Audrey held on to her Watcher's neck as if she would fall right through the foundation beneath them. "It's alright, my friend," he said, "you can let go of me."

"No, I can't. I can't let go. I'm too small. I'm too new. He's God, Inservio, and I'm just – me, Audacious Audrey. What will I do? What will I say?"

A voice resonated behind her. "You couldn't be more safe, Audrey. This is the moment you were created for. Now, open your eyes and behold The Ancient of Days, The God of compassion and mercy! The One who's slow to anger yet filled with unfailing love and faithfulness. He's the One who lavishes love to a thousand generations. He's the One who forgives iniquity, rebellion, and sin. He's My Father. And He's your Eternal God.

Audrey surrendered herself to Jesus' words and turned to behold her God. *Her* God. The One who loved her and saved her through the death of His beautiful Son. The One who preserved her life through the power of His Holy Spirit. The Omnipresent One whose Being permeated every molecule of eternal space. Her *God*. When she saw Him her heart was filled with gratitude and she began to sing with the angels who stood guard, wing to wing, around His Throne,

"Holy, Holy, Holy, is the Lord God Almighty. The whole earth is filled with His Glory."

Audrey fell to her knees and wept with uncontrollable joy, "I'm Home."

Inservio proved to be the perfect companion as Audrey explored the vastness of Heaven asking questions all along the way. "Ah, my friend, you wonder about many things. I think it will take all eternity for you to run short of wonderings."

"Does that pester you, Inservio?"

"It delights me. It always has. If a ministering spirit could have favorites, you would be mine."

Audrey sat crossed legged on grass with her fists tucked under her chin as she watched her Watcher with wide eyed fascination. Everything about her new home stunned her with curiosity. "So, you were with me, weren't you? Tell me about it. I want to hear everything. Isn't it amazing, Inservio, that Heaven is so full of energy? I mean we can talk forever and not get tired."

"Without a doubt," he said as Audrey continued to babble on with all the new things she was discovering in her Eternal Home.

"And I've met so many people. Did you know that I got to visit with Moses and Isaiah yesterday? Can I call it yesterday? Do yesterdays make sense in Heavenly time? No matter. Did you know that Moses has the best sense of humor and Isaiah seems surprisingly young for how old he must really be. My mother and I have become the best of friends. Isn't that incredible? And my Grandmammy is so beautiful! She's healthy and her fingers are all straight and nimble. We're like the family I dreamed about when I was just a little girl."

"The newness never fades away. It will always be just as wonderful later as it is right now." Inservio looked beyond Audrey's rhythmic chatter. "But, my insightful friend, I know there are things you're holding close to your heart; questions that you've been afraid to ask. But you don't have to be afraid, Audrey. You can go to the places where your deepest thoughts are hiding."

A gentle hush fell over them as Audrey allowed the questions in her heart to rise to the surface. She stroked her hand over her Watcher's cheeks as if the warmth of his being would bring back those final moments of her life with Charles. "I remember tracing my fingers over Charles' face just before I slipped away. He was, no, he *is*, the dearest man. I love him so very much and I can't help but wonder how he will ever live without me." Audrey's arms cradled the belly where her daughter had been. "Is it wrong for me to miss my daughter? I never got to see her, or hold her, or tell her how much I love her. She will never know the name I chose for her. Anne."

"Like the books you hid under your bed?" Inservio interrupted.

"I keep forgetting you were there," Audrey said. "From the time I learned to read, Anne of Green Gables became the secret place where I went when life got ugly. It was the place where I could pretend to be happy, peaceful, and safe. And I swore that someday when I had a daughter she would be just like Anne, a red-headed rebel, with a tender heart. All I ever wanted in life, Inservio, was to have a family that would change the direction of my story. Was that wrong? I love it here, and I would never want to leave, and yet I can't seem to stop thinking about the ones I left behind. Does my longing for them displease God?"

"Life on earth is a prelude to Forever, Audrey. Though you may feel galaxies away from where your story left off, you're living in the everlasting epilogue. And, my audacious friend, it's impossible for you to displease Your Heavenly Father. His image has fully perfected you. You can do no wrong here. This longing in your soul is a gift given to you by Abba Father, because, you have a great assignment waiting for you."

Audrey's curiosity pricked at her imagination. "What do you mean, Inservio? What could I possibly have to do that would be of value here? Everything is already finished."

"Finished? Oh no. Perfected, yes. But finished? The joy of Forever is that it never ends. Its beauty and purpose is the perpetual workmanship of Creator God. And everyone who lives here has a part to play in His never ending story. All the gifts and talents you possessed on earth, Audrey, were simply practice sessions for what you were created to do here."

"But I have no gifts or talents," Audrey said. "I was a miserable cook. I couldn't sew a stitch. Plants cowered in fear of me. I failed finger painting.

Whatever I was created for on earth was lost in my inability to finish anything worth keeping. Even having a baby."

"But Audrey, you had the one thing that won the love of all who knew you. You had words. Lots and lots of words. But you wove them together in ways that left everyone around you wanting more. You were born, Audrey, to use those words for the glory of the One who gave them to you. You are a writer, my friend, and Yahweh has a story waiting for you to record on Heavenly pages."

"Oh, Inservio, can it be true? I can't think of a book I ever read that didn't make me long to paint pictures with yummy words that would take people to places they've never been before, and experience things they could never have imagined. You're right. I love words." Her eyes glowed with wonder. "But what will I write about? Who will read what I write? Seriously, Inservio, I do believe I am going to spend all Eternity never being able to understand what's possible here."

"That's the joy of Heaven Audrey. It's wonderful beyond comprehension. And you will have forever to explore all its possibilities. Now, come with me and see for yourself what God has prepared for you."

She should have become accustomed to his ability to sprout wings whenever the mood inspired him. Everything about Heaven fascinated her but what she was about to see would thrill and amaze her beyond her wildest dreams. Inservio set Audrey down in a spacious room lined with large glassless windows where saints were busy peering into space, laughing, whispering, praying, praising, and some even weeping for what appeared to be unparalleled joy.

"Where are we? What are all these people doing here?"

"They're watching," Inservio answered.

"You mean they're all angels?"

"No, not angels," he said, "but children of Abba. They come here to watch their loved ones on earth. Aside from what mortals believe, it has never been the Father's desire to allow death to separate His children from each other - family is His grand creation. These portals join the hearts of those who have gone before to the hearts of those who remain. It is here, Audrey, where you will put to eternal use all those *yummy* words that run circles inside your head. You, Audrey Rose, have been given the Divine privilege of writing your daughter's story as it unfolds before your eyes. Her story will be recorded in Heaven's books as a testimony of Yahweh's faithfulness to His creation throughout all the ages. The Scroll Rooms are just beyond the Place of Portals. There the books, written by the scribes of Heaven, are kept for all the saints to read. And you, my student, are now officially one of them."

The scriptures she learned as a child at her grandmother's knee flowed from her lips.

"*He will show me the path of life, in His presence is fullness of joy, at His right hand there are pleasures forevermore.*'

Oh, such mercy, Inservio. How great is Abba's love for us. I can't wait to get started. Amazingly, however, when you scooped me up into your big strong arms, I didn't have a chance to grab a pen. So, how will I do this great work?"

"Aha, a pen! To think such a brilliant work of prose will be forever missed all because of the lack of proper writing utensils. How very tragic. Perhaps my friend would like for her servant to fly down to Dover and pick up a few supplies to help her get started."

Before he had time to recover from his feeble attempt at humor he found Audrey leaning over the Portals in search of life on Bowers Beach.

Many plans are in a man's mind, but it is the Lord's purpose for him that will stand. Proverbs 19:21 AMP

Chapter Three

July 3, 1954

Esther's hands were covered with mayonnaise, mustard, and pickle juice, as she prepared her famous Fourth of July potato salad. Why am I doing this? The answer echoed back at her. It's tradition. And tradition is all you have to hold on to. That and little Ellie Mae - though the chances of her wanting potato salad with her bottle tomorrow are slim to none.

The sound of a shoe banging against the backdoor snapped her back to life. Esther wiped her hands on the towel hanging off the waistband of her apron as she opened the door just in time to rescue a stack of diapers teetering off the pyramid of baby supplies stacked precariously in her son's arms. Charles' face was tight with tension. She had hoped the sweetness of his new daughter would bring a breath of comfort to his grief but the wall of pain was too thick for a seven-day-old infant to penetrate.

"Good morning, Mother. Eleanor's asleep in the car. I didn't want to wake her up so I left the window open so if she fusses, and I'm sure she will, we'll hear her. I fired that obnoxious nurse yesterday, so I spent the whole night trying to take care of her myself."

"You should have called me, I would have been happy to come and help you. No matter, just bring her stuff in and I'll go and get her. If she wakes up I can rock her back to sleep while we visit. You look truly awful, Honey, have you eaten anything since yesterday?" Charles was deaf to his mother's smothering and Esther had learned that trying to pry open his thoughts before his second cup of coffee was a waste of good intentions. "Coffee's fresh. Grab a cup and go sit down at the table and try to relax for a while."

Esther nearly tripped over Basil, who was sunning himself on the warm cement just outside the back step. "Please don't feel a need to move, Basil, I know a dog your age needs his rest." Basil simply rolled over, slinging a string of drool through the air, as he stretched out his giant St. Bernard paws and resumed snoring.

The beauty of her granddaughter's tiny face gleamed through the window, stinging her heart with both sadness and delight. She could hardly wait to snatch her from her bunting and nibble on her slender little fingers. "Oh, sweet baby, come to Gramma." As soon as the sleeping infant felt the warmth of her grandmother's lips on her cheek she began to nuzzle into her shoulder. "I'm sorry, baby; I've nothing but love to give you. You miss your Mommy don't you, dear? We all miss her. But don't you fret, Miss Ellie Mae, there's a wonderful life waiting for you and nothing's going to keep you from it."

After dropping his load on the counter near the coffee, Charles plunked himself down in the seat at the breakfast nook. Nothing in the home where he grew up had changed much. The pale yellow kitchen still looked like the egg salad sandwiches he hated as a child. Roosters of all kinds and colors peered down at him from the tops of the cupboards, matching the prints in the curtains that lined the windows of the place where he labored over countless essays, and spelling tests, and the masses of blueprints studied by the boy who had been groomed since birth to follow in his father's footsteps. This was the place where he learned to dream big dreams for his future.

Charles stared intently into his cup - his thoughts as dark as the caffeine inside. He never looked up as Esther came into the kitchen, rocking his daughter gently from side to side. "I built that home for Audrey," Charles rambled as if his words were stuck on autopilot, "and the family she risked everything to have. Five bedrooms." He waved the five fingers on his right hand as if to accentuate the absurdity of it all. "She had to have *five* bedrooms. One for us and one for each of our four imaginary kids. 'But Charles,' she'd say, 'we have to have four children. See, one for each hand!' And she wanted a kitchen that would be big enough for all their friends to pile into after school. It was like she was trying to make up for the mess her family made of her life. She never wanted our children to be known as *that family* that lived in *that house* down *that* street. So I built her a home she could be proud of and where we could build a future *together*. Did you hear me, Mother? Together! Was that too much to ask for?" Charles slammed his fist on the table so hard that his coffee spilled across his lap. Esther ran to the sink, grabbing a cloth with one hand while holding her granddaughter protectively near her heart with the other.

"Leave me alone!" he barked as he tore the towel away from her. "I've got it. Just take care of Eleanor. I mean it, Mother, just leave me alone." Charles wiped the hot brown liquid off his legs and tossed the towel in the sink, then stormed out the back door, nearly tripping over Basil in his fury. "Get out of my way you stupid lump of fur." Basil flashed him a disinterested yawn and returned to dreamland while Esther watched her son drive away without so much as a goodbye, see you later, or thank you for being here for me, Mother, I know you're hurting too.

Charles sped out of the driveway, screeched around the corner from Park Street to Lookerman and continued driving through Dover with his foot heavy on the pedal. Visions of Audrey's casket, sitting on display, while friends and family filed passed wiping their faces with tissues, stuck in his throat like a bone from a fish. His hand still smarted with the pain of his outburst in the kitchen. But it was a good kind of pain, the kind that feels like justice. He was angry. He was angry with his mother for giving birth to him. He was angry with his father for teaching him to build houses. He was angry with Dr. Cohen for not saving Audrey's life. And most of all he was angry with Audrey for insisting on having a child even though she knew it would be risky. They could have adopted children, or just loved other people's children while building a life together and growing old *together*. And though he couldn't admit it, even within his own soul, he was angry with his daughter for causing her mother's death. He couldn't look at her without hearing Audrey's voice nagging at him from the grave, "Love her for me."

So he drove to Lucky Auto Dealers to get back at least something of what he lost.

"So, angel baby, where's that fussy little girl your daddy was complaining about?" Esther sunk into the overstuffed chair in the living room. It was the old friend who never failed to be there for her when her heart needed a place to breathe. That old chair worn with age, stained with coffee, tea and tears, held her together through the struggles of life and grief of death. Today would be no exception.

Audrey had been like a daughter to her, yet no one seemed to recognize the depth of her loss. She felt like an extra in a silent movie, mouthing words no one could understand. Audrey's death unraveled everything. Her son was left without a wife, her granddaughter without a mother, and she without the sweet friend who came into her life and filled her empty nest. So Esther held tightly to the baby sleeping peacefully in her arms as the events of the past two weeks replayed through her thoughts until they all converged on that terrible day when they were to bring their nameless baby home from the hospital.

It wasn't that the nursery staff hadn't tried, but every time they brought the birth certificate to Charles he'd backhand their questions and walk away grumbling about funeral arrangements and the never ending flood of paperwork that needed his attention. For five days Esther encouraged him to at least try holding his daughter but when he did, he'd look at the helpless child in his arms as if she were an uninvited guest in his preoccupied life. This was a side of her son Esther had never seen before, and it scared her. On that last day, the day the baby was to be released to come home, he threw the birth certificate across the waiting room. "I don't *have* a name for her, Mother! That was Audrey's job, and in case you haven't noticed, Audrey isn't here! So, come up with something while I go and get the car."

It boggled her mind every time she thought about it. A child's name wasn't something you just picked out of the TV Guide. How could he care so little about his daughter's sense of identity?

She could still feel the pain of it all. How she wrung her hands searching for answers. Until, as if Audrey had shouted it from heaven, the answer came. Eleanor. Yes. Audrey would have wanted her daughter to be named after her grandmother - Eleanor Mae. She wrote her granddaughter's name in the space on the certificate, and then ran to the window and looked at the bundle wrapped in pink. "Hello, Miss Ellie Mae St. Clare, your grandma loves you so."

Clinging to the sweet memory of that moment, Esther closed her eyes and surrendered to the welcoming comfort of sleep as she kissed the silky web of curls that crowned the tiny infant's head. The potato salad would have to wait for a better time to celebrate the nation's freedom.

Charles walked back into his mother's house. The kitchen was quiet. The potato salad sat in a bowl unfinished. Welcome to my world, Mother, it's impossible to get anything done with a crying infant whose only goal is to have your complete and undivided attention. He walked through the rooms until he found his mother curled up with his daughter in the living room chair.

A beam of sunlight sparkled through dust in the air around them creating a surreal beauty that should have softened his spirit. Instead, a wave of envy pulsed through his veins. Charles needed his mother's comfort more than he knew how to express. He wanted the peace she was finding in the new life in her arms. He wanted to go to sleep with Audrey next to him. He wanted life to return to normal. But in a matter of days he had been reduced to nothing but an empty stream of wanting.

"Mother," he whispered as he tapped her shoulder, "we need to talk." Esther's eyes fluttered for a moment then opened to find Charles' face staring down at her. The firmness in his voice confirmed what her intuition suspected - *their* need to talk meant *she* needed to listen. Whispering a prayer for help, she drew the sleeping child in close to her chest as she rose up from her chair and carefully deposited Ellie Mae in the bassinette near the sofa. Gently curling the soft flannel receiving blanket near to the baby's cheek, Esther silently willed for the child to wake up and excuse her from the confrontation she knew was waiting for her in the kitchen.

Charles motioned for her to sit down. "I've given this a lot of thought, Mother, so I need you to listen without lecturing me. I can't deal with being a father right now and I don't know if I ever will. I'm sorry if this disappoints you, but you need to understand that Eleanor needs more than I can give her. I've tried, Mother, I've really tried. But I'm just too dead inside to care for a crying, needy, child. I won't be taking her back home with me. I need to be alone. No, I am alone." Having nothing more to say Charles left Esther sitting at the table in stunned silence as he paused with his hand clutching the knob of the back door. "I've packed up all her things. I'm going to bring them in and then I'm leaving."

The fire burning in her belly rose up with righteous indignation. Her nostrils flaring, Esther marched to the door, pointed a determined finger in her son's face, and shot back like a mamma bear protecting her cub. "You will do nothing of the kind, Charles. You will take your hand off that door and march yourself right back to the table. Now!" There was a certain tone of voice that Charles had learned over the years not to ignore. He marched to the table feeling like he was six all over again.

Now that she had his attention, Esther began pacing the kitchen floor searching for something brilliant to say. She looked out the window above the sink and spotting a shiny new car in the driveway she turned back to her son with her nostrils flaring. "What is that thing in the driveway? Where have you been Charles? What in the world are you thinking?"

"That *thing* is a car Mother," he answered. "I saw no point in keeping the station wagon. Besides, I hated it from the minute I signed the papers. And since Lucky sold my Austin the day after I bought the wagon, he offered me a great deal on a Bentley. Being the sensible one in the family I would think you would appreciate my decision to not drive around in something bigger than I need."

The battle was on. "What you need, Charles, is to give yourself time to *know* what you need. You need to walk through this nightmare and think through what you *and* your daughter need. I'm so sorry to have to be the one to tell you this, Charles, but life isn't all about you right now. You have a baby to consider."

"Obviously, Mother, you aren't listening. I can't even think through how to get up in the morning, let alone how to feed, clothe, and burp a baby! For Pete's sake, Mom, what do you want from me? Look at me! I'm hanging by a thread here. Finding a nurse to take care of that baby isn't working. Even if I find a nurse, all the crying and tension is driving me insane. I know nothing about babies." Charles pointed his finger at his mother, determined to win his point. "You're the one with all the motherly instincts. You're the one Audrey would want to raise her daughter. Good grief, Mom, you'd mother a lamp post if it leaned in your direction. Surely you knew this day was coming. Please don't make me beg. I need your help. I can't do this."

The desperation in her son's voice nearly shattered her ability to stand firm in the midst of his brokenness. He was right. She was a woman who needed to be needed. If it hadn't been for the occasional visits from Basil, and the vulnerability of Audrey, she would have wasted away without someone to take care of. But now wasn't the time to use her son's pain to fill the void in her own life. Esther sat down to face the decision that was best for her, for Charles, and for little Ellie Mae.

"Charles, I know what it feels like to lose what you think is your reason for living. I loved your father more than you or anyone could ever understand. When he died I felt as if my heart died with him. But I had to go on — and so do you." Esther's mind was running on fast forward as she struggled to find a reasonable solution to Charles' dilemma. She loved him too much to give him what he wanted and she loved Ellie Mae too much to allow her to grow up without a father to love her, protect her, and tell her what her mother was like. Without a moment to spare, the answer flowed off her thoughts with impeccable wisdom. "So, my son, here's the way things are going to be. I will keep Ellie Mae here with me until she's one year old. But, you will come here every night after work, and in the mornings on Saturday and Sunday. You will spend time with her. You will feed her, bathe her, rock her to sleep, and take her to church. Then you can go home at night and do whatever you need to do to deal with the grief of losing Audrey. But, if you miss one day with your daughter, I swear to you Charles Wesley St. Clare that you'll find your baby in a basket on your doorstep faster than you can dial the phone to say 'I'm sorry.' Do you understand me?"

Charles sat bewildered by his mother's words. There was nothing for him to do but lay down his weapons and wave the white flag of surrender. "Alright. I understand. But you have to promise me, Mother, that you won't leave me alone with her. Every time she cries I just want to run for cover. When I pick her up my hands feel like huge planks of wood. I don't know what to do with her. When I look at her all I see is Audrey. I can't deal with it. I don't know how to live with all this pain. And I don't know how to make it stop." Charles covered his eyes with his fists to block the tears that refused to stay put.

Esther drew in close to her grieving son. "We'll get through this together, Charles. Trust me. In time you'll find God's love shining through the smile of that little girl who needs her Daddy and you'll discover what everyone who's lost a loved one discovers - life goes on. That's what love does, son, it doesn't give up and it doesn't give in. It just keeps on going."

My heart overflows with a good theme; I address my verses to the King;
My tongue is the pen of a ready writer. Psalm 45:1 NAS

Chapter Four

Ellie Mae sat in her high chair sticking Cheerios between her teeth with milk-soaked fingers, stopping occasionally to plant one or two of them in the bright red curls on top of her head. Charles rushed passed her with his nose scrunched in disapproval. "Really, Mother, shouldn't she be learning how to use a spoon sometime before she starts college?"

"Treasure the pictures, Charles, she'll be grown before you know it and when she is she'll scrunch her nose right back at you while you dribble applesauce down your chin. Life's a circle, dear, what goes around comes around."

Charles buttoned his sport coat while looking for a place to kiss his daughter goodbye. He chose to wave at her instead. Basil, who cleverly sprung to life whenever Ellie Mae had food on her tray, barely noticed his master walking out the door. Esther held Charles' briefcase out to him as he hurried to the car. A wave of contentment brought a welcomed smile to her lips. He wasn't where he needed to be in his journey through grief, but he was making progress every day.

The door barely closed behind him before Charles stepped back into the kitchen. "Mother, remember I have a meeting with the city planners this evening. The Silver Lake Development is set to break ground next month, and if we can't all get on the same page soon the deal will be dead in the water. It was easier for me to spend the night here last night but I don't see that happening tonight."

"It's okay, Charles, you do what you need to do. Besides, Ellie and I have a big day planned. We're going to bake some cookies this morning and then we've got some shopping to do this afternoon. Your daughter's feet are growing out of her shoes and she's going to need something frilly to wear for Easter. By the time we're done she'll be ready for her bath and jammies. You won't be missed. So, you just head back to the beach house after your meeting and we'll see you in the morning."

The meeting went longer than he expected. Tempers flared between those who saw progress as a threat to their quiet way of life and those who feared the status quo would one day be their economic undoing. Charles' nerves were splintering by the time they decided to quit for the evening. There was a time when he wouldn't have backed down until the contracts were signed to his satisfaction. He was getting soft and he wasn't sure if he hated himself for it or if he simply no longer cared about deals, and more deals, and bank accounts with balances that would make his father proud. As he left his office he had just two things on his mind; the comfort of home and the pillow that had his name on it.

The road leading to Bowers Beach seemed unusually dark except for the red and blue lights flashing in the distance just around the curves of Skeeter Neck Road. The coffee and donuts he had for dinner rumbled through his stomach bringing back the unsettling chill that often visited him on nights like this. Beads of perspiration trickled down the back of his neck as his hands tightened around the steering wheel. Get hold of yourself, man. What's wrong with you? Calm down. Breathe.

The mist of the ocean air clung to the windows of his car like a veil of glitter as the windshield wipers swooshed back and forth doing nothing to clear his vision. Then through the haze Charles spotted a police officer standing in the middle of the road with his hand out as if trying to stop the traffic. But there was no traffic, only him and the white and yellow Pontiac lying on its side just a few feet off the pavement. His heart nearly exploded in his chest. He began gasping for air as he pulled to a stop in the middle of the road. No. It couldn't be. Why would his mother have driven to the beach house instead of heading home after shopping? Isn't that what she told him before he left her this morning?

He stumbled out of the car, drunk with fear. The officer grabbed hold of Charles' arm muttering something about an ambulance and that he would have to move his vehicle out of the way. "Leave me alone! Let go of me!" As he staggered toward the car he tripped over something soft. He looked down to find a pink ruffled dress, drenched with blood, rumpled under the sole of his shoe. "No! Oh, God, no!" He tried run but his feet were too heavy to lift. He tried to scream but his voice was mute with terror as visions of the women he loved flashed before him.

"Mother!"

"Ellie!"

"Audrey-y-y!"

Charles woke up with his hands clutching his throat, struggling to fill his collapsing lungs with air. The sheets on his bed were twisted around him in a cocoon of sweat. The room was dark except for the glare of moonlight shining through the mist that shimmered against the window. He looked at the clock on the nightstand next to him. 12:45 AM. He was alone.

The dream was too terrible to remember yet too real to be forgotten. Desperate for relief he climbed out of bed, wandering around the room like a man lost in his own skin. He fell to his knees, confused, drained, and broken. Audrey's words, those troubling words that he stuffed into the recesses of his grief, returned to haunt him, "I do. I love the Lamb."

"God, what are You doing to me? Why are You tormenting me like this?" Charles pounded the carpet with his fists. "When are You going to say, 'it's enough'?" The room was cold but he was too weary to move. As he struggled to free himself from the terrors of the netherworld of sleep he felt a shadow covering over him with what felt like a warm blanket of comfort. Then a voice, like nothing he had ever heard before, whispered through the hollows of his heart, "Charles, do you love Me more than these?"

Charles felt the hair on his arms rising to attention while an indefinable sense of awe stirred within him. For the first time since Audrey's death, he wasn't afraid, and he wasn't alone. The room where he spent countless nights chasing sleep appeared enveloped in a sanctuary of peace. The carpet where he knelt burned beneath him as if it had become holy ground. The voice continued to hover over him, repeating over and over, "do you love Me more than these?" Hot tears ran down his cheeks. He knew what he needed to do. Like a blind man who had just been given the gift of sight, Charles lifted up his trembling hands in a sacrifice of praise.

"I understand. I know what she meant. Oh God, I know what she meant. Yes, I love You more than these. Forgive me. I've been a stupid fool. I do. I love You. I love the Lamb."

The sound of footsteps thumping up the stairs leading to Esther's room sent Basil into a frenzy of protective barking. "Shush, Basil, you'll wake Ellie!" Desperate for rest, she buried her head under her pillow to block the swooshing of the dog's tail whopping loudly against the side of her bed. Then Basil let out an alarming growl that sent her swiftly to her feet.

Charles flicked on the light as he rushed into her room. "Mother, it's me!"

"Charles, it's three in the morning! What in the world are you doing here? Is everything alright?" As her eyes began to focus on her son she could see that something was different about him.

"I want my daughter, Mother. I want to take Ellie Mae home with me. Tonight! I can't wait another minute. I'm so sorry for what I've done to her. To you. I've been a fool. I've been angry, Mother, angrier than I've ever been in my whole life. But I'm done. For the first time since Audrey died, I understand what she meant. I get it, Mom. I really get it."

Esther's eyes filled with tears as she watched the answer to her prayers standing before her in his pajamas and slippers grinning with the same smile he wore the day he came home from school and told her he found the girl he was going to marry. "Charles, come sit down and tell me all about it."

Charles sat on the bench at the foot of the bed as he rehearsed the details of what led him back to Dover in the middle of the night. "Mother, when I heard that question, 'do you love Me more than these?' it was like someone stepped into the blackness of my soul, pulled out the truth, and held it in front of me."

His eyes narrowed, the way they always did just before his point was about to be made perfectly clear. "Mother, Audrey said something to me before she died that I've never told anyone before. It was just too painful to repeat. Even to myself. She said, 'I do. I love the Lamb.' There was something about those words that made me feel like I'd been punched in the gut. I couldn't admit it, even to myself, but I was jealous. It was like she'd fallen in love with someone else and chose to quit breathing just so she could leave me and go to be with Him. It's crazy isn't it? I was angry with her for choosing Jesus over me."

"It's not crazy at all, Charles. It makes perfect sense. You loved her so deeply and you loved her so well. You must have felt like a jilted lover. But Honey, don't you see? She didn't choose Jesus over you. She saw the Lamb and she loved Him more than life itself. What an amazing moment for her and for you. Charles, she wasn't alone in death.

Remember when Jesus asked Peter, three times, if he loved Him? Remember how Peter finally broke down and said, "I do, I love the Lamb." Oh Charles, you only heard Audrey's answer, but she heard the question. How amazing. It's like God wanted *you* to hear her answer so He could ask you the same question. Charles, God has given you a whole new direction for your life; to feed His little sheep. And you're ready, Charles! You're ready to be Ellie Mae's wonderful Daddy."

Charles exhaled slowly as he reached over and took hold of his mother's hands. "Mom, how can I ever thank you? All the way here all I could think about was you and Ellie Mae and how much time I've wasted because of my stubbornness. But I have a plan Mother, and I'm hoping you're going to be okay with it."

Esther sucked in a deep breath as if to prepare herself for what was coming next. "I've known this day would come, Charles. I've prayed for this day to come. And now it's here. I'll pack her things in the morning and we'll get her settled into that lovely room Audrey prepared for her."

"No," Charles said. "You don't understand. I didn't come here just for Ellie Mae. I came for you. I want to bring both of you home with me. Mother, this place has become a tomb of tired old memories. Don't you see? We can sell this house and we - you, me, Ellie Mae, and even this lump of a dog, can all become the family Audrey always wanted. It won't be perfect, but it will be glorious. I promise you Mom. It will be what all three of us need."

The sound of a happy baby giggling in her sleep, echoed through the wall. "I think she likes the idea. And so do I. So, can you live with two strong willed females fussing over you? Oh Charles, I do believe Audrey, her sweet Grandmammy, and your father, are smiling down on us right about now."

Audrey rested her hands on her lap while breathing in the joy of her seeing her husband's heart find the peace she'd prayed for since she first discovered the Portals. "Oh, Inservio, if they only knew. If they could only hear the applause of Heaven."

"Not to worry, my friend. The time will come when every story finds its shout of praise."

He has made everything beautiful in its time. He has also set eternity in the hearts of men; yet they cannot fathom what God has done from beginning to end. Ecclesiastes 3:11 NIV

Chapter Five

October 11, 2011

Charlie's stomach tightened as the familiar sounds of sand and broken shells crunched between her tires and the pavement. There was something about coming home to Bowers Beach that always set her nerves on tumble dry. Charlie loved her mother. She *had* to love her mother. Everyone else did. Besides, what kind of daughter would dare to distance herself from the legacy that flowed through the bloodline of Ellie Mae St. Clare-Mondary.

"So here we go, Charlie-girl, another evening of mother and pasta. You can do this. Just let her babble, pretend you're interested, and before you know it you'll be on your way back home." She turned off the engine, took a deep breath, and leaned her head back against the head rest.

The gulf of separation between them didn't happen overnight. It began long ago, like a pebble worn smooth by the incessant beating of the waves. *It's probably all my fault. Maybe if I'd never gone away to college. Maybe if I'd stayed here I wouldn't have drifted so far away from her and all her uncompromising values. I'm the one who changed. I'm the one who avoids her. And apart from all her bizarre behavior lately, she's never once argued with me, or criticized my choices. She just looks at me with those eyes that pierce right into my soul like a hot knife.*

In spite of all the reasons why Charlie dreaded Monday dinners with the woman who had become more of a stranger to her than a friend, the truth of the matter was - she still needed her mother's approval. So, tonight would be another night of enduring the monotonous droning of what her mother had for breakfast, how far the tide had gone out the night before, the rising costs of groceries and health insurance, and finally ending with the disgusting details her cat's latest hair ball episodes. Princess Leia had a habit of depositing her wads of yuk wherever she had a mind to leave them.

Charlie patted her briefcase lying on the seat next to her as she imagined her mother doing a happy dance in the kitchen, the way she used to whenever she came home with straight A's on her report card. She missed that side of her. *How is it possible for a woman who's read every book in the family library to suddenly start running about three light bulbs shy of lucidity?*

Nevertheless, Charlie was anxious to tell her how, after months of interviews and strategic back slapping, she landed the contract to redesign the interior of one of Dover's most historic buildings. *Keep your expectations low, Charlie. But who knows, maybe she'll be attentive enough to know what I'm talking about. And if she is, who knows, maybe she'll even trust me to bring this eye sore of a beach house up to Grampa Charles' level of acceptability. Could happen. Probably won't.*

Charlie ran her fingers through her auburn hair, bit her lip, opened her car door and marched, straight and tall, up the stairs leading to the back door. The knob turned easily in her hand; too easily. *Sheesh Mother, when will you realize you can't just leave your house open like a farmer's market and expect the world around you respect your right to safety.*

The house felt cold as she entered the mud room, stepping carefully over the assortment of shoes, slippers, and rubber boots that lay scattered around the hand carved bench that had been there since before her mother was born. Her nostrils began to pulse to the beat of her rising temper as she walked through the open door to the kitchen. She turned on the lights. The house felt eerily silent. No water bubbling in the pasta pan on the stove. No news blaring off the walls from the little TV on the counter. Not even the mewing of Princess Leia to welcome her home.

"Mom. Where are you?" A wave of irritation ruffled her nerves as she made her way from the dining room to the living room. *Seriously? If I had known you weren't going to be here I would have had dinner with the girls and headed home for a glass of wine and a nice warm bath.* She traced her finger through the dust on the lamp table next to the sofa. Charlie didn't know if she should scream or cry, or just stomp her way back to her car and meet up with her friends at Frazier's. Guilt niggled at her conscience as she turned on her heels to leave. I should check upstairs. Maybe she's sick. Maybe she's...but before she could finish her thoughts the sudden smack of the French doors slamming against the siding on the back porch, stopped her dead in her tracks. Is there anything she hasn't left open?

The dusk of twilight cast ghostlike shadows over the weathered wood as Charlie edged her way through the open doors. She wrapped her arms around herself to ward off the chill of the evening air then, looking to her left, she gasped as a wisp of gray hair blew sideways from the back of the Adirondack chair facing the bay. "Mother?" Charlie tiptoed around the chair. "What in the world are you doing out here? You'll catch your death of cold." Oh God, what's wrong with her?

Ellie Mae, still in her pajamas and wrapped in her green chenille robe, sat as silent as stone with her eyes fixed against the horizon. Charlie slipped her hand under the sleeve covering her mother's arm. It felt alive. Before she could pull her hand away Princess Leia hissed at her from the afghan on her mother's lap, slapping a paw full of claws across her palm. Panic seized hold of her as she closed her fist around the bleeding wound then plunged her hand into her purse, tickling her fingers through pens, and glasses, and tubes of lipstick, until they landed on the slick surface of her phone. She hit speed dial connecting her instantly to Bernie Mason, their well-loved friend who'd lived next door to them since before Charlie was born.

Charlie felt a special bond with Bernie, whose life was as well rounded as her frame. Whenever she felt the need for a molasses cookie, or a story from the *olden days,* she would run barefoot across the sand to Bernie's house. Her big arms always had a warm hug making Charlie feel like she was almost as lovable as Chester, Bernie's oversized golden retriever. Bernie was a legend of a woman who never referred to her husband in casual terms. She loved the way the words rolled off her tongue with gospel-like inflection, "as Mr. Josiah Mason would always say." Or, "Mr. Levi Josiah Mason was a willow of a man, but his character was as sturdy as a wall of bricks." Or, "Someday child, you will find a man like my Mr. Mason, and you will *run* to the altar to say 'I do', and when you do, you won't be sorry you did."

Over the years the two widows, Bernie and Ellie Mae, not only shared their deepest secrets and girlish dreams; they took care of each other with patient understanding and enduring friendship. And Charlie needed a dose of that now more than ever.

"Bernie? It's Charlie. Something's terribly wrong with Mother. She's sitting in her chair on the porch. She's breathing, but she's not moving. She doesn't seem to even know I'm here. I'm scared, Bernie, I don't know what to do. Please come."

"Don't you fret, Honey-girl, I'm puttin' on my shoes right now and I'll be there before you can hang up the phone. Now hang up the phone and call 911."

"Lordy, Lordy, Lordy, that poor woman must have been sittin' out here since she got up this mornin'." Bernie held Charlie tightly in her arms while the paramedics lifted Ellie Mae from her chair onto the stretcher. After answering what felt like a bazillion questions, Charlie walked alongside her mother to the waiting ambulance as the red and blue lights danced disco-like across the sand.

"Bernie, could you close up the house and maybe carry PL upstairs to Mom's bed? She's kind of freaked right now." The stinging in Charlie's palm was a fresh reminder of how dysfunctionally attached Princess Leia was to the woman who spent her days whispering sweet nothings into the wads of fur that made the aging cat look like something straight out of Star Wars. The vet said it was a deformity, probably triggered by malnutrition before she was born, causing her ears to fold over looking like two little muffins glued to the sides of her head. She would have died under the beach grass if her mother hadn't heard her *wee little* cries for help. But that's what Ellie Mae did, she rescued things like birds, lonely people, discarded furniture, leftovers in the fridge, and poor little abandoned kittens.

Bernie patted Charlie on the shoulder, "You go on now, Miss Charlie, and I'll take care of everything here." Charlie sat quietly on the padded bench near her mother while the paramedics attached electrodes to Ellie

Mae's chest, adjusted the oxygen mask covering her face, and hung a bag of clear liquid on a stand while inserting the needle on the end of the tube into her left arm. The beeping of the heart monitor clashed like symbols against the whir of the sirens, creating a dreamlike concert that Charlie feared might be the finale of a life she had taken far too much for granted.

Bernie huffed her way into the emergency waiting room at Bayhealth Medical Center, a massive structure built over the site of Kent General Hospital, where Charlie's grandmother Audrey died after giving birth to Ellie Mae. Looking much like a woman who just ran a marathon over a gravel road, Bernie stopped near the reception desk scanning the various clusters of people until she spotted Charlie curled into a chair in the corner. *Lord, do You see our girl over there? She's about as helpless as a butterfly in water. Now You show me what to do, and I'll do it as best I can.*

Charlie looked up to see Bernie's sweet face smiling at her through chocolate colored skin. "Bernie, do think mother's dying? Would God take her away before I even have a chance to make things right between us? I should have been better, Bernie. I should have been more patient with her. I'm so selfish."

"Now, Honey-girl," Bernie interrupted, "you just need to quit arguing yourself before you even know what's goin' on behind those big white doors. Your mamma loves you, and in all the years since you've been born she's never been anything but proud of her little Charlie Mae."

Charlie's chin began to quiver as tears trickled down her cheeks. "I keep seeing her eyes staring into that water as if she were waiting for Daddy to come walking across to take her home. I'm so glad she doesn't know where she is right now, because if she knew what hospital we brought her to, it might just throw her right over the edge. This is where they all, except for Daddy, left her. Bernie, why do I keep forgetting that she's lost everyone who's ever mattered to her; her mother, her father, her grandmother and her husband? All she has left is a geriatric cat and a daughter who treats her like a cold she can't get rid of."

Bernie took a deep breath, the way she always did when wisdom was about to erupt in a Sunday morning sermon. "You listen to me, Miss Charlie Mae Mondary, your mamma's life has had as many ups as it's had downs. And you, sweet darlin', are one of her ups. So don't you go thinkin' you know everything that's been written into the pages of your mother's story. Now I don't know what's been goin' on with her lately, but I know this - we can only see what we can see, but the One who really sees knows it all. Ellie is a strong woman, she comes from hearty stock, and her faith runs deep. So we're gonna trust our Jesus because He's never failed us yet."

Unconcerned over who might be listening, Bernie pointed a commanding finger up to the ceiling, and prayed like a woman who lived square in the middle between heaven and earth. "You hear me, Lord? You've never failed us yet. I don't know what You're up to, but I know You love that woman in there more than we do. So You go in there and do Your thing, Lord. Do Your thing. And if You don't mind tellin' us what You're up to, we'll praise You for that. If not I guess we'll just have to praise You anyway. Cause we love You, Jesus. You know we love, You."

"For I know the plans I have for you," declares the Lord, "plans to prosper you and not to harm you, plans to give you hope and a future." Jeremiah 29:11-12 NIV

Chapter Six

Charlie sat in the stiff purple chair running her fingers across the flat surface of her purse and hearing her mother's voice tutoring her from between the pages of happier days. *Now, Charlie, play the **C** major scale slowly. Pay attention to the fingering. Good job. Now repeat it until it feels as natural as brushing your teeth.*

Their weekly piano lessons never ended without a hug, a plate of warm snicker doodles, and her mother praising her daughter's remarkable ability to make even the most boring finger exercises sound musically poetic. Bernie says You never quit listening to us, Lord, so if that's true, I want my mother back - the one who loved music, and poetry, and who never forgot to come in from the cold.

It had been nearly a week since her mother was admitted to the hospital and still no firm diagnosis from any of the doctors who waltzed in and out of her room with little notice of the daughter who needed more than a handshake and a quick hello. Results! She needed results! So she sat in the stiff purple chair, passing the time with her imaginary keyboard, and waiting for Dr. Mac MacKenzie to finish his coffee, or his golf game, or whatever doctors did while anxious family members prayed for good news.

Just as she was transitioning from **C** major to **D** minor, the thirty-plus doctor, with the deep dimples in his cheeks, entered his office filling the room with the fresh scent of soap and aftershave. What's wrong with me? My mother's life is hanging by a thread and all I can think of is how utterly attractive her doctor is. Lord, I'm heading straight to You-know-Where, aren't I!?"

"Good morning, Ms. Mondary." Dr. MacKenzie walked to his desk and sat down in the high backed chair, looking about as serious as a flat tire without a spare. "I've just finished reviewing the results of all the tests we've run on your mother, and I'm sorry to say, the news isn't what I hoped it would be."

Charlie felt a wave of nausea rolling through her stomach as the reality of why she was called in for a private consultation took over her ability to think clearly. So she just sat there, staring into Dr. MacKenzie's blue eyes, hoping he would see how close she was to teetering on the brink of an emotional collapse.

"I know this has been a roller coaster of a week for you, but your mother's case has baffled all of us who've been trying to define the cause for her condition."

"And have you? Found a cause, I mean." Charlie's voice gurgled through what felt like a dam ready to burst.

"Well, Ms. Mondary,"

"Please, call me Charlie," she interrupted, "I don't think I can bear another second of professional politeness. So, if you don't mind, could we just cut to the chase before someone has to come in here and pick me up off the floor?"

"Fair enough, *Charlie*." Dr. MacKenzie clicked a few keys on his computer, then proceeded to deliver what he knew would be a litany of unwelcome information. "Alright, here it is in a nutshell. Your mother has Type 2 diabetes. And, with that, we believe she's been experiencing a series of mini-strokes known as TIA's which have complicated the effects of Early-onset Alzheimer's. Though cases like your mother's are uncommon, they're not unheard of. From all you've told us about Mrs. Mondary's behavior over the last two years, it would seem the interplay between the effects of her mini-strokes, diabetes, and the episodes of apparent disorientation brought on by Alzheimer's has been like a perfect storm, aggravated by hypothermia. We hope to see her wake up soon, but whether or not she's coherent when she does, is doubtful."

Charlie twisted a string of hair around her index finger, a habit she resorted to whenever she felt insecure and overwhelmed. "I'm not sure I un-

derstand what all this means, Doctor MacKenzie. My mother's behavior has
been a bit odd lately, but it's not like she's been chasing pink rabbits through
the streets of Dover in her housecoat. I mean she hasn't lost her mind. She's
just lost her way a little. Maybe she just needs better nutrition and concentrated rest. She spent the whole day outside in the cold, for heaven's sakes,
so maybe the hypothermia has masked her symptoms. Or maybe she's suffering from depression. She's been alone for a long time. Once she wakes
up, I'll move back home so I can help her get her strength back. It's not that
I don't appreciate your medical expertise, Doctor, but it's only been *a week*.
I don't see how we can jump to such drastic conclusions before we see how
she is once she wakes up. What I want to know is what are you doing to
help her *wake up?*"

"I understand how difficult this must be for you, Ms. Mondary,"

"No, I don't think you do," Charlie snapped back. "I don't think any of
you understand what I'm going through. You all get to go home at night and
sit by your cozy little fireplaces with your dogs, and your families, while the
rest of us pace the floors not knowing if we should be planning a welcome
home celebration or a funeral. No, I don't think you really understand at all!"

Charlie watched Dr. MacKenzie's Adam's apple rise and fall before he
responded to her outburst. "First of all, let me be clear - I don't have a dog,
or a fireplace, and believe it or not, when 'we all' take off our white coats, we
go home to lives that are just as complicated as everyone else's. You appear
to be a well-educated woman, Ms. Mondary, so you should know that our
college degrees don't protect us from the uncertainties of life. But, if you
would like to have a second or even a third opinion regarding your mother's
condition I would be happy to recommend a list of qualified physicians for
you to choose from."

The heat of embarrassment burned against her face. "I'm sorry. I'm just
so afraid. I don't know how to think, or what to do, or even who to trust.
You're probably a great doctor, and I know I'm a terrible excuse for a good
daughter."

"Whoa, hold on now," Dr. MacKenzie leaned across his desk and spoke
with deliberate understanding, "Charlie, what's happening to your mother
right now has nothing to do with you. It has everything to do with her

body's failure to grow old gracefully. Sometimes our minds and our bodies work in opposition to each other. And in Mrs. Mondary's case, they've been failing to communicate for quite some time. But this doesn't mean this is the end for your mother, it just means we have a long road ahead of us. Now, though there are no known cures for Alzheimer's, there are treatments and medications that are making remarkable progress to slow down the effects of the disease.

I don't know what kind of a daughter you've been before she entered this hospital", Dr. MacKenzie continued, "but from all I can see, you've been nothing but an admirable daughter to her now." He handed a box of tissues to the weeping young woman sitting across from him. "We have a lot of ground to cover regarding your mother's treatment, but maybe, it would be best for us to take a break so you can go back to the hospital, sit by your mother's side and give yourself some time to look at her in light of what I've just shared with you. Sometimes it's best to let the patient tell you how they feel and what they need. Believe me; patients have a way of communicating even when they appear to be completely non-responsive. I'll be coming by to check in with you this afternoon to discuss where we'll need to go from here. Are you alright with that?"

She quickly pulled three tissues out of the box then held them to her nose and blew loudly. "Ewww! Sorry to be so - indelicate. I'm not usually such a blubber head. This afternoon will be fine." Her hands shook as she hung her purse over her left shoulder, and then clumsily dropped her purse on the floor as she reached to catch the box of tissues falling from her lap. "Obviously, I'm not at all myself today," she snuffled, "thank you for the tissues. Can I take them with me?"

"They're yours to keep."

She smiled back at him, completely unaware of how the color of her hair, the subtle way her nose twitched when she talked, and how the fire in her eyes made his palms sweat. "One more thing, Charlie, there's a chapel at the hospital near the O.R.; I find it a peaceful place to go to when I need to be alone with my thoughts for a while."

"Thank you, Doctor, I'll think about it." Charlie flashed a nervous grin as she shook Mac MacKenzie's hand. "So, I'll see you this afternoon. I'll be in my mother's room watching her breathe. Feel free to interrupt me. I'm sure I'll be coherent enough by then to finish our conversation."

"What's going on with you, Mother?" Charlie combed her fingers through the wisps of hair that were clinging to Ellie Mae's forehead. Her skin was cool and clammy. "Are the doctors right? Are you drifting away from me? I'm so sorry for not seeing it sooner. I thought you were just burrowing into that big house with nothing to do but count the waves and wait for death to come and get you. Remember how you used to always tell me not to judge a book until you've read the last sentence? I should listen to you more. See how much I need you? It's true, Mommy. Wow, I haven't called you that in a long time. I need you. There's so much about me you don't know and so many things I haven't told you. Please wake up. Please open your eyes and let me know you're still here. Please tell me what you need."

The minutes clicked by one at a time until the growling in Charlie's stomach begged for food. But it didn't matter; this was her time of sacrifice and she was determined to stay right where she was, staring into her mother's face and becoming re-acquainted with the woman she'd pushed aside for far too long. Charlie drew in a long sweet breath of remembrance as she studied the thread-like creases forming happy lines around her mother's eyes and felt captivated by the way her nose tipped slightly upward with noble confidence. "I've forgotten how beautiful you are. I remember walking with you along the shore, with your pants rolled up to your knees, and your hair blowing in the wind, and I would tell you how lucky I was to have the most beautiful mommy in the whole world. Where did it all go? How did I forget all the lovely things that made me want to be just like you?"

While Ellie Mae lay still and unresponsive to her daughter's touch, fresh pangs of grief rose up from the deepest parts of Charlie's soul. She reached for another tissue from the nearly empty box sitting on the metal stand next to her mother's bed. As she was about to wipe her nose for the umpteenth time that morning, the silence in the room was broken by the familiar sound of humming; something Ellie Mae always did just before she was about to yawn. "Yes. I knew you could do it. You can do it, Mom. Just open those eyes and prove to the doctors you're still the same Ellie Mae Mondary you've always been. I'm right here with you. Please wake up."

Ellie Mae's body began to squirm under the covers, struggling to escape the confinement of the bed where she had been sleeping so peacefully only seconds before. As the veil of sleep lifted her eyes flashed open with a sudden burst of madness sending icy waves of fear rushing through Charlie's senses. Make eye contact. Just look at her. Make her see you.

She did. And as their eyes met a sound unlike anything Charlie had ever heard her mother make before spewed from her mouth like a scene from the Exorcist. "Whoooo arrrrre you? Arrrr youuuuuu."

"Mother, it's me, Charlie." Charlie leaned in close to her mother doing all she could to hold her down as Ellie Mae's arms thrashed violently through the air until she landed a stinging blow across Charlie's face.

"Noooo," her mother screamed. "Hellllppp. Meeee!"

Charlie grabbed the remote from her mother's bed and pushed the red button. "Mother, it's me, Charlie. You're alright. You've just been sleeping."

Two nurses rushed into the room followed by Dr. MacKenzie. "What's happening to her? She was sleeping so soundly then all of a sudden she was hysterical. I don't understand. You have to help her."

One of the nurses quickly injected a syringe into the tube of the IV fluids. It took only seconds for the wildness in Ellie Mae's eyes to glaze over in a medicinal stupor. Traumatized by her mother's macabre behavior, Charlie paced the floor, clutching her stomach, as she watched the nurses calmly tending to their patient. She turned to Dr. MacKenzie. "What's wrong with her? What happened? I did what you said. I watched her and talked with her and then she woke up and started screaming like she didn't know who I was."

"Charlie, your mother's the only one who doesn't know where she is right now and when she wakes up again she won't remember this incident at all. The fact that she did wake up is what we've been waiting for. Now, I'm going to need a few minutes to check her over, so why don't you head over to the cafeteria and I'll meet you there when I'm finished. We have a lot to talk about."

Charlie stared at the salad on her plate as the events from the past week stirred up a fresh batch of tears, adding salt to the tasteless leaves in front of her. The good thing about hospitals was being able to cry your make-up off without making a ninny of yourself; it was a gathering place for the sick and down-hearted, and people needing a place to let their emotions run free. All that changed, however, when the handsome doctor, who still looked as fresh as a morning shower, sat across the table from her with a steaming cup of coffee in his well-manicured hands.

"I'm sorry, Charlie, there's no easy way to handle what you've just experienced. The good news is that your mother's physical condition is stable. Her blood pressure is good, her lungs are clear, and her body temperature is exactly where it needs to be. And though she's still incoherent, our goal for the next few days will be to get her out of bed for short walks, eating on her own, and making sure her body is able to digest and eliminate food. When those things are in place we'll be able to release her from the hospital." Charlie winced in horror as he continued. "Please know that when I talk about releasing your mother from here, I don't mean sending her back home. I believe it would be advisable for you to seek out a care facility where your mother's daily needs can be monitored and where we can help her, and you, to learn how to manage her disease. Because we have no way of determining what stage of Alzheimer's she's in, it would be highly unwise for her to live at home."

Charlie pushed her plate off to the side and rested her head in her hands; her mind clouded by emotions she couldn't articulate. "I did what you said, Doctor. I watched my mother lying in that bed and I saw her all over again as if for the first time. She was so beautiful. So peaceful. It was like rewinding a movie and watching her when she was young and vibrant and happy.

I believe my mother would want us all to see her as she is - a woman who needs to be loved and respected. She needs..." Charlie's voice broke at the thought of visiting her mother in *one of those places where people go to die.*

It was difficult for Dr. MacKenzie to maintain professional control when all he wanted to do was reach for Charlie's hand and hold it tightly. "Charlie, no one knows how to do this when it first happens to them, but there are experts here who can walk you through the basics of what you need to know about living with a family member who has Alzheimer's. I'll be happy to set up an appointment for you as soon as possible. They will also have a list of places where your mother can receive the care she needs once she leaves the hospital."

A thousand thoughts ran through Charlie's mind as she stared at him. Really? I'm falling apart here. I can't decide what to eat for breakfast. How am I supposed to find my mother a new place to live? "I'll get back to you on that."

As Dr. MacKenzie stood up to leave she flashed him a piece of a smile. He responded by lifting her chin with his hand, "You might want to put some ice on your cheek - looks like your mother packed quite a wallop."

"She's stronger than she looks. It's a family trait. I'll be fine. Thank you."

Whether you turn to the right or to the left, your ears will hear a voice be-
hind you, saying, "This is the way; walk in it." Isaiah 30:21 NIV

Chapter Seven

Bernie watched Charlie pushing the crumbs of her cranberry scone across the china plate that clashed against the red vinyl table-cloth in her modestly decorated kitchen. Beauty wasn't all that important to Bernie, but feeding people was. She kept her fridge and pantry filled with goodies just in case a friend, a neighbor, or a stranger, came by for a visit. Today Charlie looked and felt like all three.

"The *Cleaning Queens* came and cleaned Mother's house yesterday. I saw their van in the parking lot at Carroll's Market Thursday night when I stopped to get cat food, so I jotted down their phone number. The place looks almost beautiful."

"You know your Momma and I have used up a dictionary full of words just complainin' about house-keepin'. There's no joy in doin' it for ourselves. Things that mattered to us when we had someone to share it with just don't matter now." Bernie brushed a few crumbs off the table into her hand. "You know the only place I have a mind to clean is this here kitchen. And that's only because I know you're gonna' be here to share it with me."

"I love being here with you, Bernie. You're my rock. We all love you; me, Mother, and even Princess Leia. You know she hasn't moved out of the bedroom since all this happened. Thank you for coming over and taking care of her. She misses Mother something fierce."

"We all do, don't we, Sugar? We all surely do." Bernie lifted the cozy off the teapot and topped off Charlie's cup with a steaming brew of chamomile and mint. "And you're looking about as puny as a glass of blue milk. You know what I'm talkin' about. That stuff all those skinny girls drink to keep skinny. The last thing your momma needs is for you to be gettin' sick on her. Now finish up what's in front of you. I stocked your fridge yesterday with some fresh vegetables and a couple of containers of soup, so you be sure to eat them up before they're fit for nothin' but the garbage disposal." Bernie pushed the plate closer to Charlie commanding her to take another bite.

"I don't know what I'd do without you. I can't remember when I've ever felt so helpless. It's been over a week and it doesn't seem as if much has changed with Mother since she was first admitted to the hospital. I mean she's awake, but she's not awake. Not really. She just stares into space like she doesn't know who or where she is. When she walks down the hall she doesn't look at anything but the floor. She eats but she doesn't know what she's eating. How is it possible for her to have slipped into this world of nothingness so fast?"

"I know child. Believe me I know. I've never seen anything like it. One day she's pickin' up shells off the shore and the next day she's starin' through the wall like it was a window with nothing behind it. I should have seen it comin', the signs were all there, but I just couldn't accept them for what they were. Pitiful. It's just plain pitiful. You know my knees are clean worn out from prayin', but the good Lord is still listenin'. Yes He is. Still listenin'."

"I want to believe that, Bernie, but right now I don't have the strength to believe much of anything. I just feel lost. I can't even find a place for Mother to go after she leaves the hospital. I've been going through the list of places they gave me, most of them are like glorified hospitals, all spit polished and polite, and the rest are so small that I feel claustrophobic just walking through the front doors. Mom needs to be by the water. She's never lived anywhere else but Bowers Beach. That old house holds every one of her memories in it; Daddy, Grampa Charles, Great Gramma Esther, and even the mother she never knew. There's something about the water that draws her into it. It's like she sees something the rest of us don't see. Does that even make sense, or am I losing it too?"

Seeing the need in Charlie's heart for something to hold on to, Bernie did what she was best at doing – she pulled a metaphor out of the air and handed it to her young friend with tender affection. "Honey-girl, I've watched a thousand waves spread over the sand out there, droppin' their treasures along the shore, then goin' out to find some more. But the sea has a way of speakin' to me in words that only its Maker can interpret." She leaned back in her chair while her thoughts travelled back in time. "Now you know Mr. Mason and I were the first ones in our family to go to college; our degrees are still hangin' in the hallway over there, leadin' to our bedroom. Our heads were filled to the scalp with higher learning. You hear what I'm sayin'? But whenever we sat out on our porch together and watched the hand of God movin' the water around with the swish of His finger, well it just brought us down to size. Still does. It's where I go when I'm lookin' to have a good long conversation with my Jesus and my Mr. Levi Josiah Mason. They always have a way of showin' up when I need them. And I need them all the time."

Charlie knew there was a point coming; she just wasn't sure how long it would take her old friend to get there.

"Now, your momma," Bernie crossed her arms over the broad expanse of her bosom and continued, "comes from a long line of brilliant minds. Hers included. Oh, she's quiet about it, but she's about as deep a woman as I have ever known. But she's been smart enough to know - you can't never know it all. When she sits out there, watching those waves comin' and goin', she's not countin' everything she's lost Miss Charlie, she's countin' up all she's gained. Your momma is a rich woman, and I don't mean in dollar signs, though the good Lord knows she has plenty of them. She's rich in understanding. You just pick up one of her prayer journals and read her heart. They'll give you a window to what she's been seein'. You just remember, Honey-girl, when you watch your momma layin' in that hospital bed all locked up in her own mind, there's more goin' on in her than meets our mortal eyes."

Charlie poured the freshly ground, dark roast coffee into her sleek stainless steel mug. Soon she'd be heading out the door for another day of searching for an adult care facility for Ellie Mae to move into. Temporarily. The thought of never hearing her mother's voice singing in the kitchen, never watching her gush over the beauty of a newly discovered starfish, never finding her asleep in her chair on the back porch with one of Grampa Charles' books in her hands, was more nevers than her heart could bear. It's all temporary Mother. We'll find a place that suits your needs until you're ready to come back home where you belong. I promise!

Princess Leia's soft fur wound through Charlie's legs, bumping her head against her shins and mewing as if she had just woken up from a long winter's nap. "Well look at you PL, you decided all on your own to pad your way downstairs. Mommy would be so proud of you. But as you know, I'm *not* Mommy, so if it wouldn't inconvenience you too much I would appreciate it if you would move your furry little self out from under my feet before you send me sailing across this squeaky clean floor."

Charlie fingered her hands across the sparkling subway tile on the counter as she breathed in the clean aroma of the freshly scoured kitchen. I can't remember the last time this old house smelled this good. I love those women. Note to self: put the Cleaning Queens on speed dial.

She picked up Princess Leia for an eye to eye conversation with the cat she'd never been truly fond of. "Now little PL, in case you feel the urge to burp up your breakfast after I leave, please be so kind as to do it in your litter box. No more surprises on the carpet or the bedspread. It's a new day Miss Kitty, and there's a new sheriff in town, so behave yourself while I'm gone." Charlie put her back down on the floor and ran a gentle hand across the back of Princess Leia's long grey fur. "Ouch, you little stinker! It's not nice to bite the hand that pets you."

Her cell phone began to dance across the counter just as Charlie was wiping the dots of blood off the back of her hand. She picked it up and scooted her index finger across the tiny screen. "Hello. This is Charlie."

A flush of red rushed to her cheeks as she recognized the voice on the other end. "Good morning, Charlie, this is Doctor MacKenzie. Sorry to call you this early, but I wanted to connect with you before you headed out the door. I've just been in with your mother and from all I can tell, she'll be ready to be released from the hospital as early as tomorrow. I need to know how things are going with your search for a care facility."

"They're *not* going," Charlie answered. "I've looked at about twenty different places in and around Dover and nothing feels quite right. They're either not equipped to deal with my mother's condition, or they're just too clinical. I have a few more places to look at this morning, but I'm not very hopeful at this point. I hate to sound hard to please, but this is my mother we're talking about. She's never lived anywhere but here. I'm terrified that she's going to pop into clarity and feel like she's been dropped off like an unwanted pet." Princess Leia's claws began climbing up her leg causing a pause in her conversation.

"Charlie, I know this is hard for you but the truth is I can only buy us another day or two. I appreciate your need to make sure your mother's in a place where she'll feel comfortable in her surroundings without sacrificing the quality of her care. But a thought came to me this morning. Have you looked at Still Waters? It's by a large lake. It's quiet. And the staff specializes in Alzheimer's. I think it's worth taking a look see."

"Look see? Does anyone even say that anymore? You're truly an old soul in a young man's body, Doctor." Her face puckered with embarrassment. "Sorry, my sarcasm sometimes slips off my tongue before I have a chance to close my mouth."

"Good to see you've found your sense of humor. I can send the information to your phone if you like."

"Thanks. That would be great. I'll get back to you sometime today to let you know how it goes, and I'll be stopping in this evening to visit with Mother, though I'm sure you'll be gone by then, sitting by that fireplace you claim not to have." Way to go Charlie. Death by insult. Not an attractive quality. No wonder you're still single.

The rain plunked against the windows of Charlie's car while the swiping of the windshield wipers beat like a metronome without an off switch. Pictures of the places she'd already visited replayed in her mind. Too big. Too small. Too cold. Too smelly. Too impersonal. Too old. Too new. And still the rain kept beating.

Her thoughts were intersected by the voice in her cell phone. "In one hundred feet, turn right. Then you will have reached your destination." The sign for Still Waters sat snuggled into a clump of trees with orange and yellow mums peeking through the greenery surrounding them. Charlie slowed down to a respectable speed as she turned into the driveway leading to the front entrance. Friendly, but not folksy. Big, but not industrial. Well, Dr. Mac you might just have earned your keep today. So, let's go have a 'look see'. She chuckled at the first of what she dreamed would be a long line of private jokes shared between the handsome doctor and the overly imaginative decorator.

After parking her car in one of the spaces alongside the brick colonial structure, Charlie walked up the stairs to the entrance. She stopped to read the sign next to the door, "Please ring bell for entrance to our facility. Thank you." Aha, good security. Check one on my list.

The wood paneling on the walls in the reception area made Charlie feel like she was walking into a library rather than a place where people go on their last stop before heaven. As she examined the furniture and the quality of the carpets, she was greeted by a perky girl with freckles. "Hi, my name is Megan, can I help you?"

Either I'm growing older by the minute or they've hired a twelve-year-old to make their patients feel younger. "I'm Charlie Mondary. I called about half an hour ago about touring your facility. I think I spoke with a woman named..."

"It must have been Jodie. She's on the phone right now, but if you want to sit and wait for a moment, I'll buzz in and let her know you're here. In the meantime let me give you this portfolio of Still Waters. Feel free to have a seat wherever you like. Oh, and there's fresh coffee on the table over there," she pointed her perfectly manicured nails to the left, "It's really yummy."

Yummy! Oh goody, I hope they have some tasty little lollipops to go with that 'yummy' coffee. Definitely twelve. Stop it Charlie. Stop it. Just sit down, read your brochure, and don't be critical. Thank God she's not the doctor. Or the nurse.

"Ms. Mondary?" A petite blonde woman with huge brown eyes, wearing a brightly colored blouse with black pants, and accented perfectly with yellow shoes, held out her hand to Charlie. Things were looking up. "I'm Jodie Pritchard. Sorry to make you wait. Actually I was on the line with Doctor MacKenzie. He wanted to give me a brief run down on your mother's condition. I'm sure this is a tough time for you. Why don't we go to my office and visit for a bit before I take you through our facility."

"Thank you," Charlie answered, "I'd like that."

Jodie's office was warm and friendly with just the right touch of femininity. They chatted over all sorts of things; from the colleges they attended to the professors they couldn't stand. By the time they dove into the specifics of Ellie Mae's condition, Charlie felt as if she'd made a new friend. She was impressed by Jodi's obvious maturity and her deep compassion for the residents at Still Waters.

"Doctor MacKenzie," Charlie explained, "believes my mother is locked in a state of Early-onset Alzheimer's, though I'm not convinced he's completely right in his diagnosis. Nevertheless, it's obvious right now that Mother is just not going to be able to live at home until she comes back from wherever it is her mind has wandered off to. As soon as she does come out of it, this place she's stuck in, I'll be bringing her back to Bowers Beach."

"Bowers Beach? Okay, now I see why it's so important for you to find a place near water; it will help your mother to feel more at home. Charlie, I can't imagine how painful this must be for you. I lost my mother to breast cancer about two years ago. She was only fifty four. There's not a day goes by when I don't think of her. I still wait for my phone to ring every morning. She would always call me and ask me what I needed prayer for, before I began my day. My mother was my best friend and losing her was like losing my right arm. I would think this is even worse for you, because you've lost your mom and yet she's still here. But I love that you have hope she will return from wherever she's at right now. So, whether or not you choose our facility or another one that's better suited for her needs, I'd be privileged to share that hope with you. So, shall we get started?"

Hope. Yes, that's exactly what she needed. "I'd like that. Would it be okay if I left my coat and purse in your office?"

After making their way through every nook and cranny of Still Waters, they returned to Jodie's office. "So what do you think, Charlie? After talking with Doctor MacKenzie, I'm confident that Still Waters is more than equipped to care for both your mother's physical needs as well as her rehabilitative needs. But, are we a good fit for what *you* were hoping to find?"

Charlie took a few moments before answering Jodie's question. "This is so hard. Two weeks ago I was grumbling about having to give up a night of my busy life to spend with my mother and now I would give up a thousand nights just to have her back the way she used to be. Daughters aren't supposed to become mothers to their mothers. It's just so unnatural. But from all I've seen, Still Waters is exactly what I've been looking for."

Charlie took a sip of the coffee she left on Jodie's desk before they began their tour. It was cold. She grimaced and set it back down before completing her thoughts. "I love how each room has its own personality. I love how the dining room isn't like a huge cafeteria. All those little clusters of tables seem so much warmer and more intimate. And I love the large windows everywhere, especially the one in the sitting room overlooking the lake. I must sound like a complete control freak, but I want my mother to able to sit by the water as often as possible. She may not know where she's at, she may not even notice the water at all, but it doesn't matter. She just needs to be as close to familiar as possible. So, yes, I think I've found Mother's home away from home."

Has His unfailing love vanished forever?
Has His promise failed for all time?
Psalm 77:8 NIV

Chapter Eight

"Ms. Mondary," the tension in his voice sent visions of stocks, guillotines, and helpless maidens walking the plank, flashing through Charlie's mind as Mr. Campbell pronounced judgment on the fate of her career. "You've missed three important meetings in the last two weeks. Now, I'm sorry for the difficulties you're facing regarding your mother's health, but surely you can understand the complications your absence brings to this project. I chose you for this job because of your impressive experience in reconstruction design and your understanding of the historic value of our city, but I'm afraid time is running out for you. If you're not at the meeting this afternoon you will leave me with no other alternative but to consider your absence as a breach of contract. Please tell me I can count on seeing you today at three o'clock."

Certain words that ladies should never use nipped at the tip of her tongue. "Mr. Campbell, if you could just give me one more day, I promise you I will be prompt, prepared, and fully on board with your committee. But, we're moving my mother to a residential care facility today and I need to be with her. I'm only asking for one more day."

The silence in the air was so blatant that Charlie tapped her phone to see if she had lost connection. "I'm sorry Ms. Mondary. I can't possibly ask five other people to reschedule their lives for one person. It's been my experience when you have to work this hard to force something to fit into place, it's best to find a new plan. I'm not an ogre Ms. Mondary, I simply have a job to do and part of my job is to know when to cut our losses and move on. Obviously your mother is going to be absorbing much of your time, so please consider the ending of your contract with us as our way of giving you that time. I know this may sound harsh right now, but one day I think you'll see it's the best decision for everyone concerned. Your family has been well loved in this community for more years than I can remember, so please give our regards to your mother for us."

Charlie clicked the red button then pounded her fists against the steering wheel of her car sending her phone flying into the backseat. "Your regards? Who needs your regards! How is this decision the best for everyone concerned? It's not the best decision for me or for Dover. And what happened to all that gushing over how when you found me you found the best woman for the job? If this is the way you show your love for my family then God protect me if and when that love runs out. You, Mr. Campbell and all your stuffy little trolls, wouldn't know talent if it came and painted itself on your backsides. So, just try and find someone to replace me!"

Charlie felt that all too familiar surge of resentment rising up with more *whys* than could be answered. Why did life always kick her in the belly just when she was about to have everything she'd ever wanted? Why couldn't she break free from the phantom bullies waiting in the wings to pull the curtains closed on her success as a designer? Why couldn't she have been a better daughter? Why didn't her mother take better care of herself? Why was she always asking why? As she pulled into the parking lot of the hospital she threw a quick prayer heavenward, "If You're there prove it or I'm done trying to find You, not that I've been looking all that much. But aren't You the One who's supposed to be finding me? Or am I wrong about that one too?"

Charlie followed the trail of invisible footprints leading to her mother's room noting along the way how every plant, every picture, every squiggle of design patterned into the unattractive carpets had become as familiar to her as an old pair of jeans. With the exception of a quick stop to the café for a 20-oz. sugar-free vanilla latte with three shots of espresso, she kept her pace brisk with purpose; get her mother moved and get her own life back on track.

Turning the corner on the fourth floor she collided smack into the right shoulder of Dr. MacKenzie. "Excuse me, Doctor." The formality of her greeting spoke loud and clear as to what kind of a mood she was in. "I didn't see you coming. Is my mother about ready to be transferred over to Still Waters?"

Mac took a step backward as if he might need to assume a defensive position. "Good morning Charlie. Actually, the nurses have just begun preparing her for transport and they have a clipboard full of papers that need to be gone over and signed by you. We'll need to have a copy of the certificate that grants you full power of attorney over your mother's affairs. Did you bring that with you?"

"You told me to bring it, didn't you? I may be rattled and exhausted but I'm not incompetent! My lawyer drew up the papers three days ago. They're all signed, sealed, and notarized. So, if that meets with your expectations, I'd like to go in and see my mother."

Charlie's unrelenting hostility pierced straight through Dr. MacKenzie's infatuation with the young woman whose smile had been keeping him awake at night. "Excuse me, but have I done something to offend you?"

She refused to budge an inch in his direction. "Not everything is about you, Doctor. *Life* has done something to offend me. Does that answer your question or do you need me to draw you a picture?"

"I think I get it. And I'm very sorry for all you're going through, Charlie. I certainly didn't mean to imply that you were incompetent. The hospital just needs to be sure that all their ducks are in a row before releasing your mother from their care. You know, it's going to be a while before she'll be ready for transport, why don't you head over to the chapel and take some time to be alone. It's peaceful there. Maybe you need to give yourself a break."

"A break?" she snapped. "Believe me Doctor, it's going to take a lot more than a time out on a pew to get my life back in order. I don't need a chapel. I need a redo. I need to go back a few weeks and start all over again. I need my mother to wake up and come back into the land of the living. But what I *don't* need is for you to tell me what I *do* need."

A twinge of guilt pricked her conscience as Mac raised his hands in surrender before walking away deflated and defeated. Sorry Doctor, but today isn't the day you get to enter my airspace without permission.

As her car followed close behind the medical van, traveling at the speed of turtle, Charlie's mind whirled with regret over the way she treated the man who had done nothing to deserve her wrath. I'm a terrible person. I'm a porcupine! I'm selfish, self-centered, self-serving, self-protecting, and self-whatever else a self can be. Oh, and one more thing; I'm self-deprecating; which means I'm hopelessly self-absorbed. No wonder Jeff and I never made it past the engagement.

Charlie hated the way Jeffery's name came up whenever she felt overcome by her own inadequacies. Since college he had been the only man who could blast her emotions off into the stratosphere of fun and fantasy and then send them crashing to the ground in a broken mess of disappointment and disillusionment. Note to self: Be much nicer to the nice doctor and don't ever think about Jeffery again! Yeah, right.

The transition between Kent General Hospital and Still Waters was quietly uneventful. By the time she arrived she felt uncharacteristically calm. She even found Megan's effervescent perkiness to be mildly refreshing. But before Megan had the chance to ramble on about her latest blend of coffee, Jodie Pritchard walked into the reception room extending a gracious hand to her new friend. "Hey Charlie, how are you doing?" Charlie barely had time to respond to Jodie's question before her mother was wheeled through the front doors of her new home.

Jodie went straight to Ellie Mae's side and bent down low enough to meet her new patient eye to eye. "Mrs. Mondary, I'm Jodie. I'm so happy to finally meet you. I've heard a lot about you and I'm looking forward to getting to know you. Your room is all ready and I think you're going to love it. Your daughter tells me you love the water so I know you'll be happy to see that we have a wonderful sitting room with a large window overlooking the lake. I'm sure you're going to want to spend a lot of time there."

Jodie turned to Charlie. "So this is your mother. Obviously beauty runs in the family."

Charlie marveled at Jodie's ability to see beyond the obvious. She was respectful without being condescending, something her mother would have appreciated if only she were able to comprehend it. Her eyes pooled with tears as she mouthed a silent thank you. Jodie flashed a quick wink before turning to lead the small procession down the hall to Ellie Mae's new home.

Room 13 B smelled of freshly laundered sheets, while splashes of blue and yellow coordinating fabrics flowed in subtle contrast against the cream colored walls and white wainscoting. A tall glass decanter filled with sand and shells sat perched on a book-shelf near the window while a large white hand-carved starfish hung on the wall above it, providing just the right hint of the sea. Charlie moved around the room then stopped near the bed where an assortment of empty white picture frames begged for something to fill them.

"Yes, they're empty," Jodie said. "I think it's important to keep as much familiarity in our residents' rooms as possible, so if you would bring in some family photos I'll have them copied and sized to fit the frames. Oh, and if there's anything that would help your mother feel more at home, like an afghan, or her favorite books or music - please feel free to bring them with you on your next visit. You just never know what might light that spark of remembering." Jodie then turned her attention to Ellie Mae, "Ellie, I want you to meet Celeste and Loie; they're going to help you change into something more comfortable and once you're all tucked into bed it will be time for lunch. Your daughter and I will be back to check on you soon. This afternoon we'll take you on a tour so you can see how beautiful it is here."

Tears filled Charlie's eyes. "You're amazing, Jodie. You have such a natural way of talking to my mother without treating her like a two-year-old. I have a lot to learn from you."

"There's time, Charlie. Thank God for that. So, while we get your mom settled let's go to my office and chat a while. Thankfully we're all done with the paperwork, so now we can just concentrate on our plan to help your mother find her way through Alzheimer's. I don't want you to feel left out of the process. So, I thought I'd have some lunch brought in while we visit. How does soup and salad sound to you?"

It sounded great. It sounded like a new day might be dawning. It sounded like hope was hovering on the horizon.

It was a long day at Still Waters. Charlie walked up the stairs to the beach house feeling weary to the bone and hungry for comfort food. She opened the fridge and there on the shelf next to the milk was a yellow casserole dish filled with creamy baked macaroni and cheese and a sticky note pressed over the clear wrap with large letters scrawled across it, "Dinner is all cooked and ready to be reheated. Just plop it in the microwave. Prayin' for you Honey Girl. Bernie." Bless you, Bernie.

The phone rang just as Charlie slid next to Princess Leia on the old maroon velvet chair in the parlor balancing a plateful of steamy, cheesy goodness with one hand while placing a tall glass of cold milk on the end table next to her with the other. She picked up the phone on the second ring. "Hello, this is Charlie."

"Charlie, its Mac MacKenzie. I'm just calling to hear how things went with your mother after you left the hospital today. We gave her a mild sedative to keep her calm just in case she began to feel anxious during the move. I hope it helped."

"Well Doctor," Charlie answered while brushing Princess Leia's fluffy tail away from her plate, "it worked like a charm. Mother's resting comfortably. Her room is wonderful and the staff there is amazing. Honestly, I can't thank you enough for recommending Still Waters. I don't know what I would have done if I hadn't found it." Charlie felt her cheeks flush while babbling nervously into the phone. "They have everything Mother needs. Did you know there's a physician on staff who specializes in dementia and Alzheimer's? She just couldn't be in better hands. So, thank you," she paused knowing what she really wanted to say was stuck somewhere between her heart and her mouth.

"No problem, Charlie. I'm just happy things are coming together for you and your mother. But there's something else I'd like to talk to you about, if you don't mind." The long pause following his last sentence gave her the feeling more bad news was coming. When in doubt change the subject. So she did.

"Doctor MacKenzie, you may not have even noticed it, but I was a little tense this morning when I bumped into you in the hall at the hospital. I'd just gotten some really disappointing news, and that, along with everything else, well ... it just kind of threw me over the edge. I guess what I'm trying to say is, I'm sorry. I didn't mean to take it all out on you." She stuffed a forkful of dinner into her mouth just to keep herself from over-talking the subject.

"There's nothing to apologize for Charlie. I didn't take it personally." She was quite sure he was lying through his teeth but it was a gesture of forgiveness she was more than happy to latch on to. "Charlie, I don't do this often. In fact, I've never done this before. What I'm trying to say is, now that your mother has been released from Kent General, I was wondering if - I mean if you would *like* to, sometime when things calm down for you - maybe have dinner with me." Did he really just say what I think he said?

"Dinner?" She choked on her macaroni. "I'm sorry," she hacked, feeling a strange empathy with Princess Leia's hairball seizures. "I just swallowed wrong." Her face twisted with embarrassment. Okay, that was stupid. Like 'I've never eaten macaroni before' and 'I ain't never learned to not eat while I'm talking'. Sheesh, he must think I'm a hopeless dork!

Charlie took a quick gulp of milk to clear her throat, hoping to rescue what was left of the dinner invitation dangling in the air from the handsome doctor whom she feared was kicking himself for dialing her number. "Are you sure you want to have dinner with me? I mean, now that you know what disgusting table manners I have and all. But then again, you're a doctor, so you've probably seen and heard worse, right? So Doctor MacKenzie, are you asking me out on a date?"

"Yes." Another long pause. "I believe I am," he said. "I was thinking Italian, but maybe pasta's too risky for you to swallow. How about Shucker's. They have great seafood and it's not so fussy and formal that you won't be able to choke on your food if and when the need arises." Charlie covered her mouth to hold her laughter in. I think this guy is actually more nervous than I am.

"Sorry, that came out all wrong. Obviously humor isn't my strong suit, that's why I'm a doctor and not a comedian. Why don't I get back to you after you've had some time to settle into the changes that've taken over your life during these past few weeks?"

"I'd like that Doctor. Should I still call you Doctor?"

"How about Mac; it's been my name since before I was born, so I'm totally comfortable with it. Actually, my mother calls me Mackintosh. But that's a whole other subject and I'm sure you're too tired for a boring walk through my family's history. It was good talking to you, Charlie, I'll call you. Soon."

Life somehow felt better as Charlie pressed the icon that ended her conversation. Even PL seemed to be purring contentedly. As she finished her dinner she remembered Jodie's request for photos and familiar items for her mother's room, so she leaned over the arm of the chair and grabbed the small stack of devotionals in her mother's basket under the table. The leather covers smelled of old age, bringing her back to the days when she would press in close to her Grampa Charles' side while he read to her until she fell asleep. "Charlie," she could still hear him saying, "I would never have written these books if I hadn't lost the love of my life and found a greater love waiting for me at the cross. Never go backward from the cross, Charlie; it's where all our stories find their meaning."

The titles nudged her memory with a sweet kind of sadness as she laid the three small books across her lap tracing the faded gold lettering with the tips of her fingers; *Audacious Love, Audacious Faith,* and *Audacious Hope.* The fourth in the series, *Audacious Prayer,* sat unbound and unpublished in a notebook in the bottom drawer of the old desk where her precious Grampa

Charles, spent so much of his time. And though the publishers begged her mother to finish it for him, Ellie Mae never felt worthy to complete what her father had begun. Maybe someday, Grampa.

She opened the covers of Audacious Love and began thumbing through the pages. Hand written notes marred almost every paragraph on every page. It seemed her mother could never read a thing without a pen in her hand. She flipped through the devotional, stopping to read a line or two before flipping further until her eyes landed on November 16.

The hand scrawled note above the date made her blood run cold while the macaroni and cheese began to swim through her stomach. "Why Mother? Why would you have written my name across the top of this page?"

Charlie - November 16
Audacious Love…
Beareth all things, believeth all things,
hopeth all things, endureth all things.
Charity (Love) never faileth. KJV

Her heart was pounding so loud she could barely hear herself think. As if searching for a clue in her grandfather's words she forced herself to continue reading.

There sat our precious Ellie Mae, with Basil's massive head resting in her tiny lap. His eyes were glazed over with age and his fur matted like a woolen sweater left out too long in the rain. Every breath was a labor of love; not for himself but for the child he had protected with his bark and his brawn since the first day he smelled food on her fingers. They were friends, compatriots, companions, and very often partners in crimes of cookie thievery and midnight stories when they should have been asleep. I would have done anything to spare my daughter the pain that was soon to come when his eyes closed for the last time. But as I listened to her sweet voice speaking to her dying friend I realized she was living out what had taken me a lifetime to learn; Audacious Love goes boldly beyond the comforts of self-protecting pleasure. May I invite you into that day when

God's eternal story was being inscribed in the heart of my daughter?

"Oh Ba-silly, you're the best dog in the whole world, but you can't keep your eyes open forever. It's OK for you to go to sleep now, because when you wake up you'll get to see Mommy, and Mommy's Grandmammy, and most of all, you'll get to see Jesus. And you'll be able to run and play, and eat whatever you want to and no one will say 'no' when you want to jump into their laps with muddy paws. I love you, my big puppy, but I'm a big girl now and you're a tired old dog. I'll miss you forever. And remember Ba-silly, Jesus loves you so."

And with those words, Basil released a parting whine as Ellie Mae covered his face with salty kisses. Then she smiled at me and said, "It's alright Daddy, he's happy now."

Charlie wiped the tears off her cheek, remembering how much she'd loved this story and how proud it made her feel to see her mother's name written in a book that would be read by thousands of people. She could hear her young voice asking her Grampa Charles, "Are we famous, Grampa?" "No," he answered, "we're not famous Charlie, we're just very, very blessed." But tonight wasn't about reliving the past. She needed to know why her mother had written her name on the top of this page. Above this particular date. She kept on reading hoping a clue would jump off the page and solve the mystery.

Audacious Love believes beyond all doubts, hopes beyond all shadows of mistrust, endures beyond all our frail strength, and bears the pain of loss, the fear of failure, the disappointment of betrayal, and the faltering steps of those who are young in faith as well as those who are lost in rebellion. Love releases itself, and others, to the will of our Holy God. Audacious Love surrenders all that is mortal to all that is eternal. This is perfection in the making, completion in the molding, and mercy in the mysterious wonder of Love's enduring purpose. May you rest your weary head today, in the arms of the One who will never forsake you, never give up on His plans for you, and never leave you to bear it all alone.

Barely able to appreciate the depth of his words, Charlie's eyes darted back to the scratching of her mother's pen at the top of the page. She stared at what was written until the sight of it was permanently imbedded into her brain;

Charlie, November 16, 1999.

She couldn't have known. No one knew. Just me. And Cheri. And Jeffery. Just the thought of his name made her nostrils flare. But why would she write my name on that particular page with that exact date next to it?

She closed the book and spoke into the night's shadows. "Mother, please come back to the land of the living. Oh God, if You're as merciful as Grandfather believed You to be, please wake up her mind. I can't bear the thought of never knowing what she knew and why she never mentioned it to me."

Dropping the book on the floor next to her chair, Charlie burrowed deeper into the afghan wrapping her arms around Princess Leia. "Oh PL, there are secrets in this house that scare me half to death. If only you could speak and tell me what to do. If only someone could tell me what to do." Princess Leia mewed softly and curled into the nook between Charlie's chin and her shoulder. It wasn't everything she needed, but it would have to be enough for now.

Insomniac, I twitter away, mournful as a sparrow in the gutter.
Psalm 102:7 The Message

Chapter Nine

Every shift of light and every flutter of the leaves on the trees charged through her veins like tiny electric shocks as Charlie drove to Still Waters on the heels of what had been a night filled with nightmares separated by bouts of insomnia. And though she swore to herself that she would never, but never, contact Jeffery again, she did. She had to.

After the fifth ring his voice yawned into her ear, "Yeah, what's up Charlie? Don't tell me you're lonely and needing a little Jeffy time?"

"Don't flatter yourself. This isn't any more fun for me than it is for you. I have something to ask you and I need you to tell me the truth. Seriously Jeffery, if you lie to me I will staple your lips shut before I burn you at the stake."

She could see him grinning that sly fox grin that drove her crazy, and not always in a good way. "You should know by now, Charlie darling, never to threaten a lawyer. We document everything. Now, the least you can do is buy me a good breakfast before you batter me with sarcasm. How about we meet somewhere in - say, about an hour?"

Grasping tightly to the wheel she gritted her teeth while commanding her focus to stay glued to the reason she called him in the first place. "Jeffery, did you tell my mother what we did? I don't need explanations or apologies, I just need the truth. Did you tell my mother what we did?"

The long silence on the other end of the conversation did nothing to calm her fears. "No. Is that the answer you wanted to hear, Charlie? I never spoke to your mother about anything worth remembering. Remember? She never liked me much. I never liked her much. So, we didn't talk much. Now, how about breakfast between two old friends who can't seem to keep their minds off each other?"

This was one of those times when Charlie missed having a land line phone so she could slam the receiver down into its holder and experience the satisfaction of knowing a bad conversation had been properly ended.

The twenty minute drive to Still Waters gave Charlie plenty of time to reflect on her college years, they were after all, the best and the worst times of her life. The best began the day she and her mother hobbled into her dorm carrying large boxes of brightly colored stuff to fill her side of the room with the kind of decor one would expect from a soon-to-become world class interior designer. By the next day her roommate arrived with colors that complemented hers and a career path that would make them great friends and study partners. Their room quickly became a holy huddle in a world of frats and brats, whose identities were shaped by their family's fortunes.

And Jeffery fit that mold to a tee. She and Jeffery couldn't have been more different if they had been born on opposite sides of the globe. He was insufferably spoiled with a serious aversion to work; homework, handy work, and the kind of work that left grime underneath his handsomely manicured nails. Charlie, on the other hand, though never experiencing a moment of want in her life, grew up knowing that the only silver spoon she would ever be handed would come with a cloth soaked in Hagerty Silver Polish. From the gallons of lemonade sold to thirsty summer tourists to the hours of babysitting for packs of rowdy kids, Charlie had learned to earn her privileges and appreciate her advantages.

Charlie found Jeffery easy to resist until the day Cheri woke up with a massive headache that increased throughout the morning until the paramedics came and rushed her to the hospital. Suffering from a severe case of mononucleosis, her roommate's college life came to an abrupt end. The loneliness for Charlie was excruciating and the only one who seemed to understand was Jeffery. And the one who never understood her need for Jeffery was her mother. And from that point on life between Bowers Beach and Boston University became a battle between the platitudes of the prudish and the attitudes of the foolish; a war that Jeffery was only too happy to champion.

Why did I let you change everything in my life? Oh yeah, I remember, it was that charming way your smile curled up on one side when you said my name, and that cute little cleft in your chin that felt so good against my cheek, and the way your eyes pierced into my soul challenging everything I believed in. I'd never met anyone like you before; so suave and so sophisticated and so not like me at all. I was putty in your hands, wasn't I Jeffery? How stupid. I hate the way you re-arranged everything in my life and left me with a heart full of broken promises and secrets that will keep me tied to you forever. You've ruined me Jeffery Allen Luckeroth. You tapped into the worst of me and now I don't know how to find my way back. My mother was right; you're an actor playing the part of a real man.

"O God, I'm such a mess! I have no business even thinking about Jeffery, or Mac MacKenzie, or anyone else for that matter. I should just drive to the nearest nunnery and give up on men altogether."

The halls leading to 13 B were still, with the exception of a few nurses moving quietly from room to room. Good. I need some time alone with Mother. Charlie found Ellie Mae sitting up in bed with the yellow and blue flowered quilt tucked up under her elbows. She was staring straight ahead as if waiting for a forgotten word to appear on the blank screen that had become her mind.

"Mother," Charlie whispered, "I see you're awake. I need to talk to you." She moved the striped muslin chair near the window over to the side of her mother's bed and lifted Ellie Mae's hand gently, so as not to startle her and cause another scene like the one in the hospital. "Mother, how are you this morning? Do you like your new room? I've brought some pictures from home and some of your favorite books. Oh, and I brought your journal, I thought you might enjoy having it near you while you're resting." Charlie began arranging the pictures and the books across the bed, hoping to attract her mother's attention with flashes of familiarity. "Princess Leia is missing you like crazy. I'm living at the house right now, I hope you don't mind, but PL needs to have someone near her that reminds her of you. And Bernie has been stuffing me full of carbs. She's going to come along with me to visit you soon. You really look quite beautiful this morning."

Before Charlie had a chance to plunge into the real reason for her visit, Celeste tapped on the door and walked in smiling like someone who woke up chirping with the birds. "Good morning, Miss Mondary, you're out early. Your mother's had a pretty good night. She woke up around five-ish, so I went ahead and got her all cleaned up and ready for her first full day at Still Waters. I'll be bringing breakfast in to her soon, so maybe the two of you would like to eat together."

"Oh, thanks but no thanks," Charlie answered. "I'm not much of a break-fast eater. Besides, I have a lot to do today, so I just wanted to check on Mother before I dive into my list." Knowing her *to do* list was as empty as her mother's mind, Charlie quickly turned her face away from Celeste fearing her eyes might expose the truth of her employment, which was non-existent thanks to Mr. Campbell.

"Alright then, I'll leave you two alone, but if you need anything, just press the call button; it's pretty quiet around here so you won't be disturbing me at all." Celeste smiled and shut the door leaving Charlie feeling pressed to get to the point of why she came to Still Waters at the waking of the sun.

"Okay Mother, here it is. I need you to listen carefully to me and I *need* you to answer me. I picked up one of Grampa's devotionals from your basket by your chair last night and I found my name written across a very peculiar date. It was November 16th, 1999. Do you remember that day, Mother?" Charlie moved in close to her mother's face and mouthed her words slowly hoping that by some chance of the miraculous Ellie Mae might just wake up and answer her question. "Did you hear me Mother? November 16th. 19-

99. I need to know why you did that. Why did you write my name on that particular day?" She hated sounding like a prosecuting attorney, but she was desperate. "You knew didn't you, Mother? Why didn't you say something? Why didn't you confront me?" She felt her voice rising with her emotions. "Mother, if you can hear me, please tell me what you knew and why you never said a word about it to me."

Charlie felt her mother's hand curling around her fingers as her face turned toward her daughter. "Good morning Charlie. It's going to be a very good day today. Now you go and get your books or you'll be late for the bus."

It wasn't the response she had hoped for, nevertheless it was surprisingly coherent. As if the building had suddenly caught fire, Charlie pressed her thumb against the call button several times. Celeste came quickly to her room, looking unruffled but efficiently concerned. "It's Mother," Charlie said. "She's talking! I asked her a question and she answered me. She's not making any sense but it's something isn't it? Does this mean she's getting better?"

"It means that your mother is trying to communicate what she's seeing with who she thinks she's talking to. Actually, when she woke up this morning she called *me* Charlie. And that's a good sign because it means you're very much on her mind. I've written it down in her chart. Doctor Burton will be in this morning to finish his assessment of her condition. This is a significant event, Charlie, because it helps us to find a baseline that we can use to measure her progress." Celeste turned to leave then spun around with an afterthought. "Oh, just one more thing; I wanted to be sure to let you know that this afternoon we're planning to sit your mother by the window overlooking the lake. I understand she lives on the shore at Bowers Beach. I love that place, especially on hot summer days. So maybe between the pictures and the books you brought her today, along with the view of the water, she might find a few memories to grab hold of that will help her snap back into the present. I know people tend to think that Alzheimer's patients have lost touch with reality, but I think there's more going on in their minds than any of us can see or understand."

Charlie did her best to take in what Celeste was saying while her mind conjured up thoughts of a different kind. She needed answers and from the looks of things, she wouldn't be finding them today. "Thank you, Celeste. This is all pretty new to me so I don't quite know what to think or even what to hope for. I just want Mother to find her way back to us. I'll check in on her later this afternoon." Charlie began collecting the assortment of memorabilia off the bed and put them back into the tote bag she carried them in. She got up from her chair and handed the bag to Celeste. "I know Jodie isn't in yet, but would you make sure she gets these? I was tempted to stuff Princess Leia in there also but I was pretty sure you have enough to clean up after, so I left her at home. But there's a picture of her sitting with mother on the porch. I guess that will have to do for now."

Celeste flashed a questioning grin. "Thanks Charlie, I'll put these in Jodie's office."

Note to self; reserve your humor for nurses who have a sense of it.

Charlie hung her purse over her shoulder then planted a gentle kiss on Ellie's forehead. "Goodbye Mommy. I'll be back soon. Enjoy the pictures and the books and the water today. You've got a lifetime of rememberings all waiting for you to sort through." As she stepped out into the chilly autumn air she couldn't help but feel her parting words were as much for her as they were for her mother. So, Charlie girl, it looks like you might need to sort through a few things yourself; beginning with who you are, where you belong, and what you're going to do with the rest of your life. Yeah, that's going to keep me busy for a day or two.

How do you know what your life will be like tomorrow?
Your life is like the morning fog
—it's here a little while, then it's gone. James 4:14 NLB

Chapter Ten

Charlie felt a twinge of life returning to her as she drove through the streets of Dover. She needed to see and smell and taste the things she loved, the things that reminded her of who she was before Kent General Hospital, Still Waters, and the events that sent her back to Bowers Beach. As if on automatic pilot her car headed for The Green to King's Highway where the old Governor's mansion had been turned into a café that drew its customer's right into the pages of Dover's history. Charming on the outside and warm on the inside, it was her go-to place when she needed to kick back with something decadent.

She loved this café, not just for the coffee and fresh pastries, but for the ambience that settled her spirit and made her feel at home in the city where life was busy, but not too busy, collegiate but not stuffy, and warm but not *farmy folksy*, whatever that meant. Charlie loved the diverse blend of life-styles that ranged from the intellectuals who held snobbishly to the finest of imported beans, to the earthy eclectics who were ever faithful to organic teas with eccentric names. And then there were people like herself who randomly chose whatever the mood of the day inspired. Today was definitely a Macchiato kind of day. She inhaled a deep and cleansing breath then walked in with the reverence of a nun entering a convent. She laid her coat over her favorite chair and headed straight for the counter to place her order.

Soon the drizzle of chocolate and caramel, crisscrossing over the mountain of whipped cream rising majestically over the rim of her cup, was snuggled firmly in her hands. The aroma of sugar and coffee gave her senses permission to absorb the luxury of entering a worry free zone for however long she could make it last. And it wouldn't last long. By the third sip Charlie succumbed to the reality of knowing it would take more than caffeine and a flakey pastry liberally doused with powdered sugar to release her from her fears of becoming a homeless, jobless, motherless, mess of a woman. By the time she'd taken her last sip of the fat and calories, that would take a week of exercise to exorcise from her body, she knew what she needed to do. Okay Charlie, when the going gets tough the tough make lists.

Pulling out her iPad, she pressed the Reminders icon and typed - Things To Do to Get Your Life Back on Track. With the blank space staring at her she proceeded to transfer everything that filled the left side of her brain into the iOS living inside the slim packaging of modern technology. Fifteen minutes later, Charlie stared at the list in front of her and felt a surge of power moving in to fill the place where fear resided. And there we go! A plan fit for a diva! I'll just start with number one and move through the rest like a bat out of H-E-double-toothpick. And when I'm finished I'll buy myself something fabulous, and every time I wear it I'll remember how not to let life consume me!

Anxious to get started, Charlie dug through her purse looking for her cell phone and scolding herself for not putting it in the narrow pocket specifically designed to keep it handy. She blew a sigh of relief when her fingers felt the bumpiness of the rhinestone casing. She hit speed dial and waited for the sound of the beep.

After five rings the line switched to the chorus of *Wild Thing*, followed by Tia's greeting, "So wild thing, leave me a message at the sound of the beep." Charlie jumped right in. "Hey Tia, its Charlie. Listen Hon, I know how much you love my apartment and how you've been wanting to get a place of your own now that you're done with grad school, so I'm wondering if you'd like to sublet my place for about a year. I won't need cash down, it's already furnished, and my rent is fixed for the next three years. This will give you time to get settled into your new job and by the time I'm ready to move back in you'll be ready to move out. Give me a call back and let me know what you think. But I think it's a perfect plan for both of us. Later Gator."

Feeling more than confident Tia would be all over Charlie's proposal, she checked off number one on her list and scanned through the rest. #2.

Pack up your personal things from your apartment and move back to Bowers Beach. #3. Call the Cleaning Queens and set up a day for them to clean your apartment before Tia moves in. #4. Land a new decorating contract. #5. Get your hair done, your toes painted, and new porcelains for your fingers. #6. Go back to the gym and work off the macchiato and Danish that are adding to the pounds already gained after too many plates of hospital food. #7. Meet with Dr. Burton and set up a plan for mother's full recovery. #8. Go through Mother's desk, organize her paperwork, and make sure all her bills are being paid. #9. Meet with Mother's lawyer (thank God it's not Jeffery) and her financial planner to go over her will, her property management needs, her health insurance needs, and her long term financial needs.

"And Number Ten", she said out loud, "Take Mac MacKenzie up on his invitation to dinner." She closed her iPad, slid it into its sleeve, slipped it into her purse, and sprang up from her chair, feeling like a woman with a new lease on life. I can do this. I'm able. I'm stable. And I'm really good at lying to myself. No matter. I have a plan and sometimes that's all a girl needs to make it through the day.

A strange feeling swept over her as she inserted her key into the door of her apartment above the Bayard Pharmacy. Why do I feel like I'm walking through my own obituary? She stopped at the threshold of the main living area, letting her armload of empty boxes tumble to the floor while the ker-plunking of cardboard against hardwood shot through her senses like bullets to her soul.

She kicked off her shoes and sank into the sofa as if it were a second skin. Stretching out her long legs and propping her feet on the red leather bench in front of her, she scanned the room with satisfied appreciation. She'd worked hard to make sure the color palette complimented her surroundings without carrying the theme of historic charm to extremes. This was her home, these were her colors, this was her furniture, her walls, her doorknobs, her place to lose herself, and her place to find herself.

She loved looking out the windows in the spring and summer and watching tourists wandering around The Green, snapping pictures of the red brick buildings that housed the history of this small but mighty state founded by William Penn, the first state in the Union to be ratified, and the place where the Legislative Council gathered at the Golden Fleece Tavern to sign their names to the Bill of Rights. Countless stories were buried here within the bricks and mortar, stories of heroism, patriotism, love, laughter, and even murder. But when fall and winter came it was all about the locals, grabbing coffee and a paper at the Dover Newsstand Cafe, picking up gifts at Delaware Made, meeting for lunch at 33 West, and listening to the clapping of horse and buggy announcing the periodic visits of the Amish. Having grown up in Bowers Beach where a small sprinkling of homes dotted the shore along the bay, the quaintness of The Green filled her with a sense of belonging to a place where she could interact with her community without feeling strangled by it.

Charlie reached for the soft afghan from the arm of the sofa, and buried her nose in the sweet scent of cashmere. You don't get to cry over this Charlie girl. Now get hold of yourself, get up, and get moving! She had made it a habit, months after her father's death, to give herself a soft kick in the rear whenever she felt the urge to curl up in a ball and stay there until there were no mornings left to wake up to. By late afternoon the boxes were overflowing with her personal belongings, leaving just the dishes, glassware, silverware, cooking utensils, and cleaning supplies for Tia. Knowing her work was finished she stood by the door, biting on her bottom lip, as she mentally checked off one more thing on her list before moving on to the next. She placed a quick call to the Cleaning Queens and headed to the parking lot where her car was packed to the roofline with the jot and tittles of the life she loved - perhaps too much.

A half hour later Charlie was hauling boxes up the stairs of her mother's home. Each step felt like a trip to the gallows. The scuffs on the wood stairs brought back pictures of the days when she and Basil Junior would run up to her room to hide from the sounds of thunder crashing over the water on the great Atlantic. The old wallpaper, yellowed and torn, sickened her from the inside out. Her memories were both bitter and sweet. And they were all she had to look forward to while she fulfilled her daughterly duties by keeping the fires burning until her mother was well enough to come back home again. Tomorrow she would find out from Dr. Burton just how long it would take to make that happen. Till then it would be a night of unpacking her stuff and speaking cat with Princess Leia.

Charlie's appointment with Dr. Burton was set for 11:45, giving her just enough time to sleep in, clean up, make coffee, feed the little princess, clean her litter box, and then hit the road to Still Waters. She used her travel time to check off a few more things on her list. She called Pizazz to make an appointment for her nails, then Essentials Design for her hair. By the time I'm finished wading through medicalese from whoever this Dr. Burton is, and visiting with mother, I'll be ready for some *me time*. Maybe I'll even join the girls tonight at Frazier's.

Megan chirped a happy greeting as Charlie walked through the door at precisely 11:44. "Wow, you're like exactly on time. Doctor Burton is on his way back to his office. So follow me and I'll take to you to him. You want some coffee to bring with you? I just made it. It's a new blend of Kenyan breakfast roast. And it's delicious."

"Um, maybe later," Charlie said, not wanting to waste a moment on anything but getting in and getting out of Still Waters. Megan opened the door to Dr. Burton's office and stepped in. "Doctor Burton, Charlie Mondary is here to see you. She's right on time! Shall I have her come in?"

His voice sounded like a deep bellowing wind rising up from the tuba section in an orchestra pit. "Thank you, Megan. Yes, send her in." Charlie stopped at the threshold noticing how the carpet changed from a solid burgundy to a geometric pattern with just the right balance of camel, gold, and burnished red. Masculine but not too severe. Professional but not pretentious. I like that. Fearing he would sense her insecurity, Charlie covered herself in a veil of false confidence and held out her hand to the doctor. Never let them see you sweat.

"Good Morning Ms. Mondary, I'm Doctor Burton. It's good to meet you. Please have a seat." Charmed by his good manners and the white mustache that met his goatee just below his smile, stirred her to wondering if this is what her father might have looked like if he had lived long enough to become an older man. She looked down at her shoes hoping her thoughts weren't transmitting how vulnerable she was to mature men who bore the affectionate persona of fatherhood. The chair facing the massive mahogany desk was waiting for her, so she dropped her purse on the floor next to her feet, rested her hands over the studded arms covered in rich brown leather and prepared herself to hear some good news.

"Thank you for seeing me, Doctor Burton. I'm sure we have a lot to go over regarding my mother's condition. When all this first happened with Mother, I just wasn't able to absorb much of what the doctors at the hospital were saying to me, so I'm afraid I'm still in the dark as to why she is where she is and how long it will take before she gets better." Knowing she was beginning to ramble, Charlie looked into the patient face of the man sitting across from her. "Does that make sense?"

"It makes perfect sense, Ms. Mondary," Dr. Burton answered. "Though I hope it will be alright with you if I call you Charlie. That's a great name by the way. How did you happen to come by it?"

She liked him. "I was named after my grandfather, Charles Wesley St. Clare. You might have heard of him. He was an architect and an author here in Dover. I always loved being his namesake. It kind of gave me a sense of being able to stand up for myself whenever the boys at school felt like flexing their muscles during recess."

"Good for you Charlie, I've always told my daughters, when it comes to men they need to stand tall, stand strong, and take no prisoners. But then when they find the right man they need to lay those weapons down and hold them softly because we men are pretty breakable you know." Dr. Burton's grey eyes crinkled with kindness. "So, I think the best place for us to start is for you to ask me whatever questions you might have about Ellie Mae's condition."

"Great." Charlie leaned forward and began right where her questions did. "Well, to start, I guess I need to know what your plan is for Mother's full recovery and when I might expect to be able to bring her home."

An uncomfortable pause filled the room as Dr. Burton stared into Charlie's eyes with a look that she was sure was about to crush all her hopes for her mother's happily ever after.

"Charlie, I'm afraid you've just asked the one question that no one has an answer for - at least not the answer I think you want to hear. Your mother is in a state of early onset Alzheimer's, a disease for which there is no cure. At this present time her symptoms are quite severe. So my plan is to find a treatment that will help to alleviate some of her existing issues so we can better address the progression of her disease. We've already started her on a low cholesterol diet which is also compatible with her resistance to insulin. And we're working to adjust the medications to bring her diabetes under control and help us combat the mini-strokes that contributed to her collapse. I'm cautiously confident that once her body becomes more stable, we'll be better able to explore the various new treatments available to us for dealing with her Alzheimer's. This is a process Charlie. And processes take time. I hope we will begin to see Ellie Mae develop small moments of clarity over the next few weeks. Anything beyond that will be impossible for me to predict. Now, before we continue, Charlie, I need to know how you're feeling about what I've just explained to you."

Charlie willed the coffee she had for breakfast to return to her stomach. "I, I don't know what to say. This just can't be. My mother is *not* going to be like this forever. She can't. She just can't. It's not acceptable, Doctor. I won't accept that! Not now, not ever. My mother has to get better! She has to come back. You have to help her come back. That's why I brought her here. If you can't manage her condition I'm just going to have to find a doctor who can."

"I'm sorry for how hard this is on you, Charlie. And I can understand your need for better answers than I'm able to give you right now. You are, of course, free to call in as many experts as you choose. In fact I would be happy to help you find them. Sadly, I'm afraid the results will only lead to the same conclusions. So, if I may, I'd like to take you through her case step by step.

When we're done you may feel differently. Are you up to that?"

Afraid to say another word, Charlie chose to listen while Dr. Burton explained the workings of the human brain and its failure to behave the way we want it to. By the time they said goodbye, her mind was reeling with terms like brain lesions, plaques and tangles, beta amyloids, and insulin resistance. She stuffed the colorful pamphlets with pictures of adoring daughters holding the hands of their wrinkled parents into her purse and ran for her car without stopping to see her mother. She couldn't. And for now, she wasn't sure if she ever could.

Charlie's hands shook uncontrollably as she tried to fit her key into the ignition. Exasperated and exhausted, she grabbed hold of the steering wheel with both hands and pressed her forehead against it as hot tears splashed across her knees. Her meltdown was interrupted by the sound of a bell chiming from her purse signaling a text message. She grabbed for her phone, touched the green icon, and saw three messages waiting to be retrieved. The first was from Tia; *'So sweet of you 2 think of me but I'm just not ready 2 move out yet. Maybe in a month or 2. Call me. B.F.F., Tia.'* The second was from Pizazz Nail Salon; *'Salina became ill this morning and had to go home. Would you like to reschedule?'* And the third was a sales alert from a company she'd never heard of before. So all she had left on her schedule for today was a hair appointment, which she no longer cared to keep.

Bernie pulled her red porcelain tray from the top shelf in her pantry and put a round paper doily in the center of the tray. When the toasted cheese sandwiches had reached the perfect stage of buttery brownness, she cut them into quarters and arranged them on the plates like butterflies *'waitin' to be caught by hungry little girls.'* Then she took the pan of steaming hot chocolate from the stove and poured it into two large mugs, while finishing them off with a couple generous sprinkles of freshly ground cinnamon and a big fat marshmallow. "Now here you go, Honey Girl. I don't know what's caused those rivers of mascara to make tracks down your cheeks, but I've got all afternoon to listen. So you just eat up and then we can start talkin'."

"Have you ever looked at your life Bernie," Charlie began, "and felt like you were watching the most depressing movie you've ever seen? Ever since I found Mother sitting on her porch, lost inside her own head, my life has been spinning out of control. I've tried, Bernie, I've really tried to make it stop, but it just keeps getting worse and all I want to do is make it stop. But I can't!"

Bernie reached across the table and took hold of Charlie's hand. "Oh child, I know. Believe me when I tell you, I know. That mornin' when I walked into little Elijah Levi's room and found my sweet baby laying there without so much as a breath of air left in him, all I wanted to do was curl up with him and die. He wasn't but three weeks old; healthy, happy, and ready for life. Then like a drop of rain against hot sand, he was gone. There isn't a day gone by that my heart hasn't ached for my sweet boy. And the good Lord never saw fit to put another baby in my womb. Mr. Mason and I tried and tried until we both got tired of tryin', then we just sat out there one cold March mornin', lifted our hands up to heaven, and gave it all to Jesus. All the pain, all the rage, all the dreams that were never to be fulfilled. We cried and then we sang,

> *"If you get there before I do*
> *Coming for to carry me home*
> *Tell my sweet Elijah his Mamma's coming too*
> *Coming for to carry me home*
> *Swing low, sweet chariot*
> *Coming for to carry me home."*

The sound of Bernie's deep vibrato painted pictures of black women draped in white with swatches of red fabric wrapped around their heads and singing songs of freedom in fields of cotton. This woman who had taught Black History at Delaware University sang like one who lived it. "Now, my darlin' Charlie," Bernie continued, "why are you tryin' so hard to do what you can't do."

Charlie thought for a moment, surprised that she couldn't seem to find a single answer to Bernie's simple question. "I guess I don't know *what* I'm trying to do." And with her simple confession of helplessness, the rest followed in a steady stream of words. "Maybe I just want to get my life back under control. I want things to go back to where they were before I found Mother on that porch. I want to be a better daughter. I know I need to be a better person. I thought I was a better person until all this - this stuff happened. I wrote a list of things I needed to do to get my life back, and before I made it to number four, one, two, and three fell apart. Now I'm right back where I started. And the doctor who's overseeing Mother's case at Still Waters was no help at all. He made it all quite clear that Mother won't be getting better any time soon. And I can't bear that, Bernie, I just can't accept it. And I know this is completely stupid and selfish, but I hate that house. It's old, and dusty, and depressing. And this is going to be my life, Bernie! I'm going to live in that museum of a house, with a crazy cat, and no career, no ring on my finger, and no children to carry on the family name. And when I die, everything my mother, my father, my grandfather, and all the rest who went before him, will just die with me. Why? What kind of a cruel joke is God playing on me? What did I do to …" Before she could finish her tirade she burst into tears.

Bernie listened as if there were no time to pay attention to. "There, there, Honey Girl, you just let it all pour out. It sounds to me like you've been tryin' to try, but your tryin' isn't helpin'. I know how that feels. Lordy, I sure do know how that feels. It's like tryin' to beat those waves out there back with a hammer. Useless. That's what it is – just useless."

Charlie waited for the sermon that always followed Bernie's metaphors, but the picture she painted for Charlie was enough to cause her to wonder and sometimes wonder is better than words. "Bernie, what if the best place to be is where my mother is right now; no stress, no responsibility, no memories, no regrets, no ambitions driving you to reach for things you can't describe. What if it's better to go to where she is rather than have her come back to where we are?"

A cloud of quiet hovered over them as their toasted cheese sandwiches sat on their plates as unfinished as their thoughts. Then Bernie leaned across the table and with her eyes dancing with a fresh batch of wisdom said, "Oh but Honey Girl, what if your Mama is seein' more than what anyone can see? More than anyone could know? What if God is opening the windows of heaven to her right now and is showin' her what's comin'? Now wouldn't that be somethin'?"

I am the vine; you are the branches...If you remain in Me and my words
remain in you, ask whatever you wish, and it will be given you. This is to My
Father's glory, that you bear much fruit, showing yourselves to be My disciples.
John 15:5, 7-8 NIV

Chapter Eleven

Audrey walked along the river arm in arm with her Savior, breathing in the joy of His presence. She had become as accustomed to Heaven as one becomes accustomed to the sound of the birds chirping in the trees, or the taste of a summer breeze; the kind of familiarity that comforts the soul but still puts goose bumps on your skin. "You know, Jesus, this has been an incredible journey through my daughter's life. I've filled her books with thousands of words. I've watched her grow and change from a funny little girl, who dressed poor Basil up in tutu's and pirate costumes, to a young woman who could pull notes out of the air and turn them into masterpieces the moment her fingers touched the keys of her piano. I've watched her become a beautiful friend, a sweet daughter, a devoted wife, and an exceptionally wise mother. The tragic beginning for my dear Anne has turned into the most amazing story of love, and hope, and courage."

Jesus' whole being seemed enveloped in understanding as He walked with Audrey to the bench where they often sat to talk about life, and death, and all things in between. "I can see that inquisitive mind of your spinning with thoughts and questions."

"I can never fool You can I?"

"Would you ever want to?"

"Never," she said. "There's beauty in being fully known and rightly understood. Being known by You has satisfied me in ways I never thought possible when I was living in mortal flesh. I see without fear. I reason without fault. And I question without questioning truth, or purpose, or the kind of fairness that earthly beings never seem to feel they get enough of. No, Jesus, I never want to fool You. Though there are times when I think I'd like to surprise You and sometimes I think that sometime I will."

As Audrey gazed into the eyes of Omniscience she understood what she had struggled to understand before her arrival to Forever - that prayer was quite simply the harmonizing of two voices sharing the same heart. And this time of intimate conversation surely felt like prayer to her as Jesus peered into the depth of her eyes and captured her thoughts before she had words to express them. "You wonder if your daughter will never complete her earthly mission because she's imprisoned in her own mind. And yet, Audrey, you have already seen, in part, how the destiny of all creation flows into the pages of My Father's perfect will."

Audrey took a few moments to digest His words before she responded with what her heart had been pondering since the day Anne, known on earth as Ellie Mae, took her first step into the abyss of Alzheimer's. "You know Jesus, our beautiful daughter is such a courageous prayer warrior. It's amazing how quiet and shy she can be until she opens her mouth in prayer - then her spirit speaks with the boldness of a lion guarding her pride. It is her greatest gift and she uses it well. Like, on that day when she sensed her daughter was in danger. She asked You to protect and rescue Charlie and to bring her back to You. At the very moment her cries reached Abba's ears, her daughter's life was spared. Charlie would have died on that table along with her unborn child, if the bleeding hadn't miraculously stopped. The look of fear on the abortionist's face, when his scalpel punctured her uterine wall, nearly took my breath away. But Anne went to her knees and Abba touched Charlie's wound and saved her life. Anne never knew where Charlie was or what she was doing on that awful day. She just felt the pangs of knowing her daughter was in trouble. I'm so very proud of her. You must be too. But I know how much her heart aches for Charlie to love You back for all the love You've given her."

"I'm eternally proud of Anne. Long before she was placed within your womb, Abba gifted her with a merciful heart and a discerning spirit and she has been faithful to use those gifts for My glory. She's a woman who has endured many losses, yet she's never ceased to run to Me for help. She's been overwhelmed, but never overtaken. Hurt deeply but never bitter. Lonely but never lost. She's clung to My Words with childlike trust and courage. She is a strong woman living within the walls of humility. And she's a constant source of frustration to the Enemy of her soul. So as you continue to write your daughter's story, remember these things. Nothing about her life be lost simply because her mind has gone on an extended vacation."

Audrey breathed a sigh of relief as Jesus touched the place where her deepest thoughts resided. She cherished knowing she could ask Him whatever questions she needed to ask without fear of sounding faithless. "So Jesus, where is my daughter now? Behind her blank stare, I mean."

"Look at those trees, Audrey." Audrey followed Jesus through the sunlit path until He stopped to touch one particular tree whose bark was gnarled with age, and whose limbs twisted around each other as if they had danced together for a thousand years. The leaves were large and green, and as shiny as the dew sparkling against the wet grass. Then he turned to Audrey and said, "When do you think these leaves sprouted from their limbs?"

"I don't know. They look like they just uncurled from their buds today."

"Exactly! That's because unlike Earth, the leaves on Heaven's trees never wither or fade. And so it is with prayer, Audrey. Nothing Anne has brought to the Throne has been lost, or forgotten, or left uncared for. All that has ever concerned her remains as fresh whispers in Abba's ears. Like the leaves on these trees they live to display the endurance of My Father's love."

Audrey swept her fingers across the leaves as if they were celestial strings. "Oh Jesus, I will never see a tree the same way again. It's like Heaven is a forest filled with living prayers." As she tried to count the abundance of leaves hanging from the trees she turned to Jesus with the one question still unanswered. "But, Anne can no longer pray. She's sitting alone in a world she can't understand. She's living in a place where nothing is tangible, or even identifiable."

"Her mind may be locked in nothingness, Audrey, but believe Me when I tell you, her spirit is as alive as it has been since the moment life was breathed into her. The world can only measure life by the beating of the human heart and the waves of the brain's activity. But life, true life, is measured by the life of the spirit that never dies. The spirit of Abba's children and the Spirit of Abba are inseparable. One belongs to the other the way a leaf belongs to a tree."

Her heart was drenched with the joy of new understanding. "Oh someday she will see it all won't she. Anne will read her story and know the worth of her soul."

Audrey pressed open the pages of a new book as she peered through the Portal anxious to record the next chapter of her daughter's life.

The chill of winter has come to announce the changing of the seasons, but for you, my darling daughter, life is today just as it was yesterday; a monotony of changelessness. The smile that once graced your beautiful face has gone missing along with the hope that sparkled in your dark brown eyes. And yet there is a beauty within you that remains untouched by disease. Perhaps that's why you've become such a beloved guest at Still Waters. I believe they know when they're near to you, they're near to the God who loves you, for His presence surrounds you.

Audrey continued to write every little detail of her daughter's day; details that would seem dull and uninspired to mortal minds. She watched and listened with fascination as Celeste gently lifted Anne into the wheel chair sitting close to her bed. "So Miss Ellie Mae," Celeste said, as she turned the chair toward the door, "are you ready for another day by the window? The lake is especially beautiful today."

The music playing quietly through the sound system accompanied them as Celeste escorted her patient down the hallway, and though her eyes were fixated on the frilly edge of the sleeve on her gown, Ellie's foot seemed to be tapping softly to the sound of her favorite hymn, "Great is Thy Faithfulness."

Dear Anne, I can't wait to share this with you when you arrive. What a treasure you are. One day you will read these words and you'll see your life from a whole new perspective and you'll know the depth of beauty in God's sovereign plan. It must all seem so strange to you right now, but hold on my dear daughter, your story isn't over yet. Oh no, I have a feeling there's much for you to discover behind your window.

For there is a root of sinful self-interest in us that is at odds with a free spirit, just as the free spirit is incompatible with selfishness. These two ways of life are antithetical, so that you cannot live at times one way and at times another way according to how you feel on any given day.
Galatians 5:17-18 The Message

Chapter Twelve

Ignoring the rumblings in her stomach, Charlie burrowed deeper into the downy covers while hiding her head underneath the mound of pillows scattered around her. She hadn't changed out of her pajamas in three days. And if it weren't for Princess Leia, who insisted on fresh food and water every morning, and refused to step her prissy little paws into her litter box unless it was clean, she might not have gotten out of bed at all.

There was no mistaking from the smell of the sheets that a cloud of depression had moved in and taken over. And though she knew the worst place to be when she felt overwhelmed by life was where she was, it didn't matter. Nothing mattered. So she exhaled softly, wiped the drool off her cheek, patted PL on the head and groaned, "Go back to sleep kitty witty; it's not like we're going to miss anything between now and noon."

But before she was able sink back into sleep the phone rang. She fumbled her fingers across the bed to the nightstand and lifted the receiver. "Hello?"

"Charlie, this is Jodie. I have some good news for you. Your mother seems to be experiencing a surprising moment of lucidity. I was sure you'd want to know right away. We never know how long these fragments of time will last. Is there any way you could come right over?"

"Um, sure, I just need to take care of a few things around here and I'll be there as soon as I can. I'll see you in say about an hour and a half?"

Not feeling close enough to her new friend to question her lack of enthusiasm, Jodie did her best to sound professional without being condescending, "I hope that will work, Charlie. Doctor Monroe has instructed Celeste to stay with her and to interact with her as long as she can. But since this is the first time Ellie has shown any sign of comprehending her surroundings it's impossible for us to gauge how long it will be before she slips back into her own little world again."

"I see. I'll get there as soon as I can." Her face flushed with embarrassment as she set the phone back into its cradle. *So Lord, are You sending the depression police over to shake me out of my funk? That's not fair, You know. It's been a long time since I've taken a nice long vacation with self-pity. Another day or two would have been just fine with me, but n-o-o-o! You just had to call me back to life before I was ready. Thanks a lot!*

After a much needed shower, Charlie twisted her wet hair into a tight knot at the back of her head and pinned it into place. With her toothbrush stuck inside her cheek she grabbed the nearest pair of jeans from the floor by her bed, a sweater from the pile of clothes on the window seat, slid her feet into her favorite flats behind the door, and dashed downstairs for her coat, purse, and keys. Her heart was pumping overtime as she jumped into her car and sped off for Still Waters, brushing her teeth along the way.

The lobby was quiet when she walked in. *Little Miss Megan must be stirring up some new blend of coffee. Glad I missed it.* Charlie turned in the direction of Jodi's office and seeing her door was closed she spun around and headed down the hall leading to her mother's room.

The room was empty. Charlie held her breath as she began wandering through the halls trying to remember how to get to the sitting area with the large window overlooking the lake. As she peeked into each room along the way she felt as if she were walking along a cliff at midnight without a flashlight. *One day you're planning your next vacation and the next you're strapped to a bed not even knowing you're strapped to a bed. I hate this place.*

"Hey Charlie, I'm so glad you're here." Charlie turned to find Jodie's arms ready to engulf her in a hug she wasn't sure she wanted to receive. "Your hair looks great like that. I wish I could find something else to do with mine, but it's just too thin to work with. So, let me take you to your mom."

As they made their way to the sitting area Jodie rambled on about hair, and clothes, and how she hated to go shopping alone because she could never seem to spend money without the encouragement of a friend who would say, "Buy it - it's you." The mindless girl talk put Charlie at ease as they headed toward the window where her mother sat smiling and holding Celeste's hand. An unexplainable wave of envy washed over her as she watched the bond of affection joining the two of them together like two peas in a pod. She hated peas.

"Mother?"

"Oh Charlie, come and meet my new friend." Ellie Mae's voice sounded surprisingly normal and younger than it had in what seemed like forever. The light of morning highlighted the strands of her mother's hair and blushed a warm glow of color over her pale cheeks. Charlie couldn't help but feel she had miraculously turned the corner from death to life as it was before the "A" word changed everything.

She hurried over to her mother's side, purposefully lifting her hand from Celeste's. "Thank you for sitting with Mother, Celeste, but I'm here now and I'm sure you have other patients who need your attention." The hint to leave couldn't have been clearer if it had been posted on a billboard along the SR 1.

"You look so pretty today, Mother. Lavender is a great color on you." Ignoring the pangs of her pettiness, Charlie quickly took the place where Celeste had been. "I'm sorry I haven't been able to visit you for the past few days, I've just been buried with stuff." She wasn't lying. Not really. She was just doing what she always did when she felt the heat of her mother's brown eyes drilling for truth in her half-truths.

Ellie Mae squeezed her daughter's hand. "Oh Charlie, you were just here yesterday. Remember? We sat right here and watched the little girl playing with her puppy outside. I swear, Charlie, sometimes I think you get so busy that you forget what shoes you're wearing."

Charlie decided to play out the conversation with as much logic as she thought her mother could absorb. "What little girl, Mother? You know it's been pretty windy all week; too cold for playing outside. Maybe you're remembering another day."

"Oh no, she comes here every day. She loves to dance. And she always waves to me before she goes away. But that puppy is growing so fast she can barely carry it anymore. Pretty soon it's going to have to carry her. She reminds me of you when you were little - so happy and full of vinegar and sugar."

"What's her name, Mother? Does she live near here?"

"She doesn't talk. She dances. That's enough for now. Another day I'll know her name." With her gaze fixed on the window Ellie Mae began to slip back into the sea of oblivion. "I want to dance."

"What...?"

"Too afraid to dance."

Frustrated and confused, Charlie turned to Jodie for help. "Is that it? Will she come back?"

"I think she will. Her blood sugar has stabilized and her heart has been responding well to the meds Doctor Monroe prescribed for her. We're hoping her improving health plus time will provide a good physical atmosphere for more frequent times of lucidity."

"Lucidity? Really? She's watching a child who doesn't exist dancing in the wind and playing with a dog who isn't there. Somehow that doesn't smack of lucidity to me."

"I know Charlie, but sometimes we just have to measure improvement against the backdrop of where our guests have been the day before. Small steps are huge leaps here. I guess that's the fun of our job. We get to live in the adventure of their journeys through their ever-changing realities."

"Well in my reality I have a full day waiting for me, so I think I'll head on out and check in again tomorrow." Charlie gave her mother a peck on the cheek, said a quick goodbye and turned in the direction of where she thought the lobby might be. "Okay, I give up. I have no idea where I'm going."

"Yeah, this place is a maze, but it will make perfect sense the more you get to know it." Jodie wrapped her arm over the back of Charlie's shoulders and walked with her to the front door. "Charlie, I'd love to get to know you better. Do you think we could go out some night for pizza, or tacos, or just find a place where we can hang out and have a little bit of fun? I don't know about you, but fun hasn't been on my agenda for a really long time."

Jodie's ability to turn vulnerable on a dime nearly threw Charlie off her game. "That would be great, but I dashed out the door so fast I forgot to grab my phone. Why don't you text me later and I'll see if I have a free night in the next week or three." Charlie pressed her hand on the front door, praying her phone wouldn't ring and prove her a liar.

The clouds hung low in the sky, nothing new for east coast weather, but today she needed more from the local forecast. She needed sunny with a chance of hope. Charlie left Still Waters and headed for the nearest highway that would take her as far away from home as she could go in a day. Long drives had a way of clearing her head and keeping her from the destructive impulses hissing at her from her dark side and causing her to feel things she hadn't felt since her last days in college. She wanted to eat a table full of food so she could run to the restroom, shove her finger down her throat, and regurgitate it all away. She wanted to find something sharp that would slice through her skin and let the pain flow freely from her body. But for today, she would settle for driving mindlessly through the grey skies until the moon rose up and the stars guided her back home. And it all seemed to be working until she stopped for gas and heard her phone ringing in her purse. She prayed it wasn't Jodie. The familiar charm of the man's voice sent an unholy chill of delight down her spine, causing her to purr with a coyness that made her tremble with both disgust and pleasure. "Well Jeffery, what terrible reason do you have for calling me at this boring hour of the day."

"Oh, I'm just sitting here in my loft remembering life when all I had to think about was finals, football, and you wearing my letterman's jacket. I've got a bottle of Chardonnay in a bucket of ice, and two glasses. Why don't you come over and sit with me by the window and we can watch the day fade away together, like we used to before we started using each other as dart boards. So, what do you say - a glass of wine between friends?"

Charlie heard the beeping of another call coming in, but she chose to ignore it. "Aha, you've been dumped. Was she blonde, brunette, or redhead? No, couldn't have been a redhead or you wouldn't be calling me, because when we broke up you told me you would never be able to date another redhead without calling her Charlie. Is that what happened Jeffery? Did you call her Charlie?"

"She was blonde, or at least she was as blonde as she paid to be. Come on, Charlie, haven't we grown up enough to spend some time together without trying to top each other's insults?"

"Hm, I thought that was all part of the game. But I'm up for a little mystery. I'll be there in about an hour."

As she slid the red button to the left she tapped the icon for missed calls. Dr. Mac MacKenzie. Sorry, Doctor, but I'm just not in the mood for the smell of white and all things that reek of Alzheimer's. Maybe another day, like when I'm more depressed than I am right now.

With a nice full tank of gas, Charlie climbed back into her car, cranked up the music and headed back to Dover, wishing she were as strong a woman as she pretended to be. Jeffery's right, what's the harm of ex-lovers learning how to be in the same room together without killing each other? Besides, it's not like I have anything better to do.

Charlie hummed mindlessly while waiting for the elevator to deliver her straight into enemy territory. But it didn't matter. Nothing seemed to matter; besides, a little jousting with the demon without seemed easier than battling the demons within. So she pulled a few curls over her ears, ran a tube of light pink gel over her lips, pinched her cheeks, and rang the bell.

Jeffery was as handsome as ever. Without even saying hello he wrapped her in his arms, kissing her neck, and causing her to melt into him with unrestrained passion. She felt the weight of her hair falling across her shoulders as his hands reached behind her head, pulling the pins that held it all in place. "I've missed you," he said in a raspy voice. "Come on in, the wine's chilled and I'm not; can't think of a better way to spend my day off."

They walked hand in hand to the plush chairs facing the gas fireplace. The coffee table was set with an ice bucket, two long stemmed wine glasses, and a plate beautifully arranged with rounds of toasted baguette, plump purple grapes, and baked brie. "Well, I see your palate has come a long way since the days of pizza and beer." Charlie sat down, her heart pounding and her hands sweating.

They spent the first two hours reminiscing over old stories - the kind that always improve with age. After Jeffery had his fill of feigning interest in Charlie's life he took over the conversation, weaving together tall tales of his successes in law and love until her head began to spin with all the reasons why their relationship was so toxic, so self-indulgent, and so not what she wanted. He poured a third glass of wine and suggested they move to the couch. Charlie knew where this was heading. "Thanks, Jeffery, but I need to go home so I can feed PL and catch up on a few phone calls that can't wait until morning."

"Oh come on, baby, don't go yet. It's early. We can order in some Chinese food and listen to some music and then just see where the night takes us."

"First of all, I'm not your baby. You know I've always hated when you call me that. And second, the night isn't going to take us anywhere but to our own beds. I'm sorry if I've given you the wrong impression, Jeffery, but I'm not looking for a one night stand to help me feel better about my life. I don't know what I'm looking for. If I did I wouldn't have come here in the first place. Now, I think it's time for me to leave before we end up adding another reason to our long list of why we're bad for each other."

The room began to spin as Charlie stood up to leave. Just as she was about to sink back into her chair Jeffery caught her in his arms. The pressure of his hands squeezing the life out of her shoulders snapped her back to her senses.

"I know you, Charlie. I know you better than anyone else. And I know what you want."

"If you knew what I wanted you would walk me to the door like a gentleman. But you're not a gentleman Jeffery, you're just the same belligerent brat you've always been. Now let go of me. I don't want to do this. I just want to go home. So for once in your pathetic life you'll just have to take *no* for answer."

"You're not going anywhere. Look at you, you can barely walk let alone drive a car. Face it, Charlie, you want me and you know it."

The next few moments seemed to move in slow motion as Jeffery grabbed hold of her hair with one hand and began pushing her to the couch with the other. Charlie's arms rose up in violent protest knocking him backwards. Struggling to regain his footing he lunged forward with his teeth clenched and his eyes blazing with anger. A triple shot of adrenaline triggered Charlie's survival instincts. Without even thinking she curled her hand into a tight ball and swung with every ounce of strength she had and then some. Pain blasted through her arm as her fist connected with his jaw. She heard a crack and then watched as Jeffery's head bounced against the coffee table before he hit the floor.

He didn't move. Charlie bent over him. "Jeffery! Open your eyes! Don't you dare do this to me. I mean it, Jeffery - wake up!" But he just lay there like a corpse. Fear rushed through her body as pictures of handcuffs and mug shots flashed through her brain. She didn't know what to do or who to call. Then she did the one thing she could never have imagined doing. She grabbed for her phone and hit reply to the call she missed while driving to Jeffery's loft.

Though I walk in the midst of trouble,
You preserve my life;
Psalm 138:7a NIV

Chapter Thirteen

Mac stared at his phone as if he could will it to ring. How long has it been since I left her that message? Maybe she doesn't want to talk to me. Maybe she thinks I'm an idiot. I should just go home. Fifteen more minutes and then I'll go home. He didn't know if he was more afraid of her rejection, or if he was more terrified of her acceptance. Either way, she was a scary kind of pleasure to his fragile ego.

Ten minutes later the phone buzzed in his hand. "And there she is." Charlie's name beamed at him through the screen as he counted the number of rings. Answer it too soon and you'll look desperate. Too late and you'll look arrogant. But then, you're the one who called her. She's just the one who's answering. It's not hard, Mac. You're a man. She's a woman. Jeez, answer the phone. "Hello, this is Doctor MacKenzie." The formality of his answer left him feeling stupid and wishing he could hang up and try it again.

"Mac, this is Charlie. I think I just killed Jeffery. He fell backwards and hit his head on the coffee table and he isn't waking up. I don't know what to do. I didn't know who to call so I called you. Please help me."

Okay. So this isn't going like I thought it would. Swallowing the questions that were nipping at the tip of his tongue he did a quick character exchange from enamored school boy to brilliant doctor. "Okay, Charlie, I need you to stay calm and listen to me very carefully. Can you do that?"

"I think so. But my hands are shaking and I feel like I'm about to throw up or have a heart attack."

"That's all pretty normal. Now, first I want you to wet your finger and hold it under, whoever this Jeffery is, his nose so you can feel whether or not he's breathing." Mac tapped his fingers on his desk waiting for a response. "Is he breathing, Charlie? Do you feel breath on your finger?"

"Yes. He's definitely breathing. But he's out cold."

"Alright. You're doing great. Now, I want you to press your thumbs gently over his eyelids, lift them up and tell me what his pupils look like. I need to know if they're big or small."

By the sound of her breathing he knew she was still holding the phone next to her ear. "Charlie, you'll need to put the phone down first. It's okay, I'm not going anywhere."

"Oh, right." The phone went silent.

For the first time in what felt like forever, Mac had actually met a woman who made him feel like more than a doctor and now here he was helping her know if she had just killed someone. *What was I thinking? I hardly know her.*

"Are you still there?"

"Yes, Charlie, I'm still here."

"Okay, his pupils are kind of small, but not tiny. Tell me that's a good thing and that he's not dying."

"If I thought he was dying I would have told you to call 911." Mac bit hard on his upper lip. "Sorry. I didn't mean to snap at you. So, no - it doesn't sound like he's dying, but he could have a concussion or in the worst case, a skull fracture. Is there any blood coming from his head, nose, mouth, or ears?"

"No blood."

"Good. That's really good. Now one last thing, do you know how to take someone's pulse?"

"I think so. Maybe. Actually no, I don't."

"No problem, I'll just walk you through it. But you'll have to hold your phone with one hand while you take his pulse with the other. Are you ready?"

"Ready as I'll ever be." Charlie blew a comforting breath over her inflaming knuckles. *What made me think watching the sun go down with a man I loathe could ever have ended well. I hate this day. I hate my life. I hate Jeffery Allen Luckeroth.*

"Alright, here we go. Now pick up his left hand and put your thumb underneath the inside of his wrist and let your fingers rest lightly in the space between the two bones just below the fatty part of his thumb and then listen for what you feel. Is it going *thump...thump...thump?* Or is going *thump, thump, thump?*

The phone went quiet. From the sound of the names she was mumbling under her breath Mac could only assume that this Jeffery was not on her good side. A few seconds later the phone was back in her hand.

"I think it's going *thump...thump...thump;* kind of even, but kind of slow. Is that good or bad?" Before he could answer her question she yelled into his ear. "Oh wait, I think he's starting to wake up. What should I do now?"

"That's good. That's a good sign. Just what we need to have happen. Now stay with him and either call 911 or tell me where you are and I'll get there as soon as I can. If he shows any sign of convulsing, or drifting into oblivion, or bleeding, don't wait for me, just call 911 immediately. One way or another he needs to get to a hospital just to make sure he's okay."

"I'd rather you came here first - I'll explain it all when you get here. We're just a few blocks away from your office. I'm so sorry. I know this must all seem crazy to you. Please hurry."

Yes, it was all crazy. Every little bit of it was nuts. Nevertheless, he scratched the address down on a post-it-note before grabbing for his coat and keys. Well, you've done it now Mac. You've gotten yourself into something complicated just when you were hoping for an uncomplicated walk back into life.

Fifteen minutes later and Mac MacKenzie was standing at the door to Jeffery's loft. He rang the bell and waited for a response. What he heard instead was Charlie's voice shouting from inside. "It's your fault, Jeffery. You're a creep and you've always been a creep. So just sit there and don't move until I say so."

Yep, this is just what you've been looking for – a woman with hutzpah.

Charlie opened the door hiding her right hand under her sweater while inviting him in with her left. Hm, what's up with that? A bleary-eyed man whom Mac could only assume was Jeffery was sprawled on the couch with a towel pressed across his forehead. Without waiting for introductions, he walked directly over to the coffee table, opened up his medical bag and quickly grabbed for his stethoscope. But before he could reach for Jeffery's arm, Jeffery pushed him away growling a host of obscenities.

"Listen, buddy," Mac bristled, "I don't know who you are or how you ended up on the floor with your lights out, but it looks to me like you got what was coming to you. Now, you can risk dying in your sleep tonight, or you can let me take a look at you; it's your choice."

"Yeah? Well I'm not your buddy. And the only thing wrong with me is my attraction to scheming little manipulators. So pack up your toys and take your crazy friend with you."

Just as his temper was about to head straight into the red zone, Charlie stepped in front of him, wincing as she pressed her hands against his chest. "Mac, don't waste your time on him. He's not worth it. Let's just go."

He couldn't help but notice the purplish bruise across the knuckles of her right hand. "What happened to your hand, Charlie? Did he hurt you?"

She batted her eyes at him like a damsel not really in distress, "He tried to but I slugged him. He went down like a girl."

"Wow. I'm impressed. And a little scared." He slipped the palm of his hand gently under hers. Her hand was soft and delicate and definitely not built for boxing. "It doesn't look like anything's broken, but there's a nasty mess of bruising going on and I'm afraid it's going to be pretty sore for a couple of days." Taking a quick look around the room his eyes landed on the ice bucket. "I'm gonna grab some of that ice and wrap it in a napkin; that'll keep the swelling down until we can find a decent cold pack."

He looked into her emerald eyes as he held the cold compress against her bruises. It was all he could do to resist the urge to draw her into himself and keep her there. "I know you must be anxious to get out of here, but I'm afraid we're going to have to call the paramedics and babysit Mr. Glass Jaw over there until they arrive. If he still refuses help we'll at least know we did our best to make sure he's okay. Then I think it might be a good idea to head over to the Country Eaterie. I'm hungry and you look like a girl who could use some comfort food before I take you home."

"What about my car?"

"No problem. Tomorrow's my day off, so I'll pick you up in the morning and drive you back into town."

"Really Doctor Mac, I'm going to be fine. You don't need to hover over me."

"Actually I do, for more reasons than I care to admit."

"I'm so sorry for putting you in such a terrible position. It was awful of me to call you. I just didn't know what to do. And since you were the last person who called me I just panicked and hit reply."

"Yeah, pretty girls say that to me all the time."

"Oh, I'm sorry Mac. That's not what I meant. Actually I don't even know what I meant. I'm babbling aren't I? I do that when I'm nervous. I'm a babbler." Charlie sat back in her chair and stared at the handsome man seated across from her. His face was gently weathered, like a tree that had learned to bend with the wind. And for the first time since she called him to come to her rescue she succumbed to that quiet voice inside her head telling her to stop talking. Though the silence felt deafening.

The waitress, with glasses that looked like something out of an old television sitcom, delivered their food. Slices of turkey lay over a bed of mashed potatoes drowning under a sea of milky gravy with a side scoop of cranberry sauce - jellied of course. "Thank you for ordering for me. Looks great. A whole plate full of carbs. This must be what all boxers eat after a fight." She stuffed a forkful of meat into her mouth just to help her quit talking while Mac stared at her through china blue eyes. She would have given anything for a do over. *He must think I'm a hot mess of a woman.*

"So tell me about Jeffery. Have you been dating him for a long time?"

Speaking of hot messes! Charlie turned her head to the window. The ducks were waddling along the grass near the water. She wished she could waddle away with them. *He deserves as honest an answer as I can give him.* Pressing her fist against her lips to buy her a few seconds to collect her thoughts, she looked into Mac's eyes and gave him the Readers Digest version of how she ended up with bruises on her knuckles and egg on her face. "I've known him since college and no, we're not dating. I was just having a bit of a meltdown when he called me and asked me to come over to 'watch the sun go down.' Sorry, air quotes are so last century." She blew out a huge breath as she pulled her hair back and held it in a ponytail behind her head. "I know. It was stupid. I knew it was stupid and it was like I just didn't care."

"So, I'm confused. You've known him since college. You're not dating. But he called you and you went over because you were having a bad day. What does that mean, Charlie?"

She released her hair. "Hm. It means I'm a pathetic woman. He was my big crush in college. I thought he was the love of my life but as things turned out, he wasn't. I've barely dated since then and sometimes … well sometimes I just get weak and I fall for the same old same old. It's that dog returning to its vomit thing." Her face twisted with regret. "Sorry. Not a good picture to paint while we're eating."

"I was done anyway."

"Me too. I'm really not at all hungry. And I'm fine now, so if you want to just take me to my car, I'm good to drive home by myself. Really. I'm done with stupid for the night and …" But before she was able to finish her thoughts Mac touched her hand so softly that she lost track of what she wanted to say.

"No, I'm taking you home. It's dark and drizzly and I have every intention of keeping my word to you. No strings attached. And no arguments. And I think you've said enough 'I'm sorrys' to fill a book, so let's just have a nice quiet ride to – Bowers Beach, okay?"

"Okay."

The ride to Bowers Beach was purposefully unexciting as Mac and Charlie engaged in simple conversation, chatting over things that had little to no relevance to the events of the past two hours. And while she knew he was trying to steer her thoughts away from all things depressing, she couldn't seem to free herself from the sickening flashbacks of feeling Jeffery's lips slurping across her neck, or forget the force of his passion demanding to take from her what she had no intention of giving. She put herself in a dangerous position and she hated herself for it. Nevertheless, for the first time in days she felt as if her life might just be on the verge of getting better.

"Turn left at the stop sign, and Mother's house is just down the road."

"Why do you call it 'Mother's house'?" Mac asked. "Isn't it your home also? I mean you did grow up there, didn't you?"

"Of course I did. We all did. It's been the family home since my grand-father built it way back in the fifties." Interrupting herself she announced, "And we're here. Thank you so much for driving me home. I guess I didn't realize how shaken I was by everything. Would you like to come in?"

Mac curled his finger under her chin and turned her face toward him until her eyes were even with his, "I would love nothing more than to spend time with you, Charlie, and for that reason, I think it's better to say good-night right here while I still have my wits about me."

"And there you go again," she quipped, "what is a wit anyway? And how do you keep them about you? Honestly Doctor, where do you dig up these outdated phrases? It's like part of you is living inside a black and white screen somewhere in Mayberry."

Mac clutched his heart with both hands as if a dagger had been plunged into him, "I'm cut to the quick. But I guess I should thank you because your attacks on my dignity are making it easier for me to say goodnight." His face turned serious as he added, "So, I'm saying goodnight to you for now. But remember, you promised to have dinner with me sometime, and I hope that sometime will be soon."

Mesmerized by the kindness in his eyes and his slightly crooked smile, Charlie could hardly find a comeback to come back from. "Um, yeah, I'd like that. Now, about tomorrow -what time should I be ready?"

"I'll be here by nine. With donuts. Don't be late."

As she watched his car pulling away from her she noticed the lights were still on at Bernie's. She dropped her keys back in her purse, and stepped briskly over sand and dried grass for some much needed mothering.

Bernie's frame filled the doorway as she embraced her shivering "almost daughter". "Now where have you been Honey Girl? I've been worried something sick over you for days. You come right in here and sit yourself down. Lord have mercy, you look like you haven't eaten since Moses crossed the Red Sea." The warmth of Bernie's hug seemed to knit all the scattered pieces of her heart back together.

"I know. I've had a tough few days. It's like something beasty in me rose up and took over. I don't know what's wrong with me, Bernie." The floodgates broke loose as Charlie buried her face in Bernie's shoulder and let the pain flow free.

"There, now that's better, isn't it? Sometimes we girls just need to have a weepin' time. Now you sit down and you can tell me what those tears are all about. I've got a nice Brown Betty in the oven and by the time we're done talkin' it'll be just about right for the plates."

She sat across the table from Bernie catching her up on what was becoming a bad soap opera, ending with a right hook to Jeffery's jaw.

Bernie patted Charlie's hand, "Girl, from the looks of that hand, I'd say his face ain't feelin' any better than your knuckles. But I'm glad you gave him what he had comin'. I never liked that young man. He's got steely eyes, the kind that smile while the knife cuts right through your heart. Now I'm going to get you some ice and while you let the cold take that swelling down, I'll fix us up some dessert."

"Yum!" Charlie quickly opened her mouth to let the steam of the hot Betty meet with the cool air. She set her fork down while swallowing her dessert. "Bernie, why am I such a mess? Everything I touch turns to chaos. I used to know who I am and where I'm heading. Then Mother's life crashed and now mine is crashing with her. I mean, I love my mother, I really do."

Bernie leaned in close, "Oh child, now I know you know this, so I'm only sayin' it to remind you of what you already know. This is life, Honey Girl. God knows it's full of peaceful skies, and it's full of angry skies. So, you have two choices as I see it. When the storms of trouble start stirrin' up the waters of your soul, you can either come crashing against the shore like an angry wave, or you can roll gently over the sand and accept your destiny. It's up to you."

"But what if I don't know how to do that, Bernie?"

"Well then, you just tell the Good Lord you don't know how to do that and He'll show you where to start. Then you just walk it through with Him; one step at a time."

The Lord your God is with you, He is mighty to save
He will take great delight in you
He will quiet you with His love
He will rejoice over you with singing
Zechariah 3:17 NIV

Chapter Fourteen

Feeling completely exhausted by the events of a very bad day, Charlie wiped the crumbs off her chin with her napkin, said goodnight to Bernie, and made her way back home, *one step at a time.*

The house was dark and cold - a grim reflection of her life. After turning on the lights and cranking up the heat, she headed for the cupboards to grab her favorite zebra printed mug. She dug through the massive varieties of tea in the glass canister on the counter until she found the chamomile with ginger. My favorite. This is a two bag night. With the mug filled to the brim with water she stuck it in the microwave, closed the door, and pressed *Beverage* twice. The Queen would have my head over what I do to tea.

Holding the warm cup between the palms of her hands she walked quietly up the stairs craving the comfort of her fleece pajamas, fuzzy throw, and a good book from her mother's room. But as she reached the second floor of the old beach house, a chemtrail of nostril-stinging odor seemed to be emanating from the place where she spent the last three days living like a slug under the covers of depression. Okay, so I guess I won't be sleeping in my bed tonight. With her nose pinched she dug through her drawers looking for a clean pair of pajamas and a fresh pillow case before heading back downstairs to spend the night in the overstuffed chair.

A puny little whine greeted her from somewhere beneath the comforter on her bed. Soon the round bundle of matted fur rose up and stretched her legs while her jaws opened wide in a long and lazy yawn. Princess Leia then padded across the mess of covers and stared at Charlie with that *why do you always leave me* look. "Oh, poor little Miss Prissy. Feeling all sorry for yourself, aren't you." She tickled her fingers through the soft under-fur of the kitty's chin. "Have you been in this bed all day? Look at you - you're all sweaty and sleepy. You're quite pathetic you know. But so am I. So how about the two of us commiserate in our pathetic-ness together downstairs?"

Soon Charlie was balancing her tea, blankee, pillow, and an armful of her mother's journals, as she headed downstairs with Princess Leia following close on her heels. She hadn't planned on stealing her mother's innermost thoughts, but when she saw the stack of journals next to her mother's bed, she felt overpowered by an unexplainable urge to pry open the past and see life through the eyes of the woman who had become such a mystery to her. So pushing all thoughts of betrayal aside she turned on the lamp next to the chair and prayed that sleep and sweet dreams might find her.

Though her body groaned with fatigue her mind was anything but tired. Nestled into the curvature of the chair, with Princess Leia's purring vibrating against her side, Charlie sipped her tea and reached for the first book on the stack of her mother's journals. She held it up to her nose and inhaled the aroma of aging paper and the scent of lavender that always accompanied her mother's things. The old leather cracked as she opened the book and entered into the private world of Ellie Mae St. Clare. The title page had three lines written in the familiar slant of her mother's script;

Just Thinking
From the thoughts of Ellie Mae St. Clare soon to be Mondary

The clock on the wall chimed twelve times. Midnight. She slipped her finger carefully under the page while the sound of her mother's voice echoed through fading ink.

January 1, 1978

"*I can't believe that in three months I will be married to the most wonderful man I've ever met. To think that Officer John Lawrence Mondary would fall in love with mousey little Ellie Mae St. Clare is beyond my comprehension. But he said he loves me and it would be just silly not to take him at his word. Sometimes I think he just loves the idea of me and my family tree. I know he loves my father. Who wouldn't? Daddy is brilliant and talented; he dreams of buildings and then makes them happen, and he takes words and puts them together in ways that are life changing for everyone who reads them. And, of course John loves Grandma Esther just as much as I do. There's nothing Gramma can't do, from cooking to painting, to entertaining, GE is the kind of woman every other woman wants to be. And from all I've been told, my mother was beautiful, quick witted, and great with words. And then there's me. Plain. Simple. And barely adequate in anything worth noting. I'm miserably shy. The only gift I have is my piano, but the thought of playing in front of others terrifies me. No, the keyboard is just between me and heaven. It's prayer to me. And private. Oh so private. I love to rest my fingers on the keys and just let songs without words write themselves through my spirit. But then, of course, I hide them. Truly, I am a cowardly soul. But he loves me. John Lawrence Mondary loves me!*"

The clock on the wall chimed twice. Two hours passed as Charlie finished the last page of her mother's journal for 1978. But there were more. Each one dated for the beginning of another new year. She breathed out long and slow. Who are you Mother? How did I not know how insecure you are? How could you not have known how beautiful you are? I can't think of a single person who didn't love you the moment they met you. I guess I was so used to hearing you praise me, encourage me, laugh with me, cry with me, that I never gave a thought to how you saw yourself as a woman. I hate that you've spent your whole life thinking you were dull and simple and unattractive.

A tear fell off Charlie's cheek bleeding through the ink on the last page of her mother's words; *"I'm so blessed to be so happy. I have the best husband a woman could hope for – all that's missing is a baby. Soon, Lord Jesus, let it be soon."*

Stabs of guilt pricked her conscience as Charlie's eyes scanned the room in search of hidden spies poised to catch her in the act of invading her mother's privacy. But the discovery of her mother's inner self energized her to the point of obsession. *I need to know you, Mother. I need to know the you I never knew. Great, I'm turning all poetic.* Then a brilliant thought sparked her imagination as she pointed her finger in the air. *Music! She said she wrote music and stored it away! But where? Where would she hide her masterpieces? And what if I can find them, record them, and bring them to her? Maybe the songs of her soul will bring her back to me? Oh God, please let it be so.*

Charlie gently lifted Princess Leia off her lap and laid her back down on the warm chair. She raced upstairs and stood at the threshold of her mother's room wondering where to begin. After looking under the bed, through every nook and cranny of the closet, and all her dresser drawers, she curled her index finger across her upper lip as her mind slid into overdrive. *The armoire! Of course!* She hurried over to the alcove where the old structure stood tall and stately. Charlie placed her hands on the handles of the doors and opened them slowly releasing the smell of lavender sachet. After rummaging through the old shoes underneath the winter clothes hanging from the rod, and taking a moment to run her hands over the fur coat that had been in her family since the Mayflower, she looked up and saw something red peeking out from the back of the upper shelf.

Her heart began to race as she pictured her mother sitting on her bed holding the red satin box in her lap and looking surprised when Charlie came bouncing into her room with a burst of bubble gum stuck to her face. *That's it. That must be it!* She stood on her tip-toes and lifted the box from the shelf. *I'll never complain about being too tall again.*

Charlie sat on the edge of the bed with the red satin covered box noting how delicate the fabric felt against her fingertips. Slowly lifting the lid she peeked in as if the music of her mother's heart would begin wafting up from inside. There they all were. A stack of loose music sheets dotted with hand written notes and accent marks. As she began searching through them she noticed that each song was named and dated. It's like a musical of your life.

Surprised by Love (To John) 3/29/1978
Remembering Basil 6/12/1961
Thank You for Spring 4/24/1970
Because God Loves Me 9/4/1965
For Mother on My Birthday June/26/1976
Kiss Mommy for Me (To Daddy on the day of his departure) 5/16/1986
Goodbye my Love (for Lawrence who waits for me beyond the horizon)
8/12/1992

Her hands trembled as if she were holding Holy Grail. How could you think you had no talent, Mother. Of course I haven't played them yet, but you're the one who taught me how to play, so you must have been brilliant when you were alone at the keyboard. Do I dare play them? There must be over thirty pieces here. How did you manage to do all this and keep it a secret from everyone?

Having thumbed through all the various pieces she spied what appeared to be about three sheets of folded paper resting on the bottom of the box and tied with a red satin ribbon. She picked them up, untied the ribbon, and pressed the pages open against the chenille spread. A surge of fear drained the blood from her hands as the title slashed across her heart:

Coming Home. For my Charlie. 11/16/1999.

There it is again! The worst day of my life; the day I've kept hidden from everyone but Jeffery and Cheri. How is this possible, Mother? What did you know? How did you know? None of this makes any sense.

She put the mysterious piece of music on the top of the stack before replacing the lid. Questions stalked her steps as she made her way back downstairs and over to the baby grand that sat like a memorial to happier days when she and her mother hovered over the keys, one teaching, one learning, both loving the music that knit their hearts together.

The clock chimed once for the half hour. It was two-thirty in the morning. In a few short hours Mac MacKenzie would be coming over to pick her up and she would have gone the entire night without sleep. But it didn't matter. She needed to play the music that bore her name.

She pulled the chain on the weathered brass piano lamp and blew off the veil of dust covering the fallboard that protected the keys. After carefully lifting the lid, she traveled backward in time while visions of her mother pointing to each and every part within the belly of the frame tested her youthful patience. "Mommy, why do I have to learn all this? Why can't we just start playing the songs in my book?" A gentle voice whispered back at her, "Because dear, the more you learn about how music is made, the more you will understand what really happens when your fingers touch the keys. Learning the language of the piano will forever tie you to the history and the traditions of the musicians who made this all possible. Now tell me what these are called."

Her voice turned seven as she pointed her finger inside the piano and whispered, "Those are the piano wires, and these are the hammers that tap the wires when we tap the keys. And these are the dampers that control the vibration on the wires that make the music. I think." Her lips curled in a satisfied grin, the kind she always had when she got the answer right. She pulled out the bench, sat down, and placed the music against the stand. After studying the notes as if she were interpreting a foreign language, she placed her hands in position and began to play. Slowly.

Her first time through the entire piece was purely practical as she studied the timing, and tried to get a feel for the sentiment. But by the third time through, Charlie's heart began to swell with emotion as the plaintive sounds of her mother's heart filled the room. This wasn't just a song, it was a story - her story joined into her mother's story, vividly painted through sounds without words.

The clock chimed four times. Charlie had been playing her song for so long her hand throbbed with searing pain. She needed sleep. She reached up and turned off the light on the piano and headed for the chair where Princess Leia was sleeping soundly under the blanket. Lifting up the corner she slipped in next to her, pulled the blanket up to her chin, tucked her hands under her cheek, and closed her eyes, while the music played on in her mind like a familiar lullaby stuck on repeat.

The light of early dawn began to shine through the curtains in the living room, while Charlie, lost inside the world of half asleep, began to sing;

Coming home, I'm coming home
I've been gone for so long.
Coming home, I'm coming home
I've been gone for so long.

As her eyes opened she felt the icy chill of tears on her face and for the first time in what seemed like forever, she felt as if the hand of hope was waking her up to the dawning of a new day. The words that caressed her thoughts while she slept greeted her with an unexplainable sense of purpose. She quickly jumped up from the chair, much to the displeasure of Princess Leia, and fumbled through the desk for a tablet and a pen, then returned to the piano to see if the words matched the music her mother had written. They did. But what did they mean?

And He who was seated on the throne said,
"Behold, I am making all things new."
Revelation 21:5 ESV

Chapter Fifteen

Bent at the waist with her wet hair dripping the remains of her shower over her toes, Charlie wrapped the extra-thirsty towel around her head, gave it a good turban-like twist, then wrapped a second towel snugly around her shivering frame. She leaned into the bathroom mirror in search of her face. Her hand squeaked across the glass as she wiped away the haze of steam hiding the smile of the woman looking back at her. "Good morning, Charlie! You're looking rather perky for someone who's had almost no sleep at all."

She slid quickly into her skinny jeans with studded pockets in the back, and a soft pink sweater that made her feel like a fresh batch of cotton candy. Her feet were still wet as she shopped through the growing assortment of shoes scattered near the closet door looking for her new navy leather flats, the ones with tiny rhinestones that arched symmetrically around the heels. With as frosty as the fall air had become, boots would have been more appropriate, but she was feeling more like Sally looking for her Harry, than Annie Oakley looking for her horse. Mac would be here soon. The shoes were perfect.

As always, she wasn't sure what to do with her hair; let it fall in unrestrained curls, pull it back in a casual messy knot, or flat iron it until it fell into submission over her shoulders. She decided the work was worth the effort, so she grabbed the iron. The doorbell rang just as she finished the last section of hair. Pleased with the results, Charlie ruffled her fingers through her mane, and winked in satisfaction. She bounced down the stairs happy to be feeling like a girl again. A girl who wasn't overwhelmed by life. A girl who was on the brink of falling in love with a boy. And a girl who might just have a future after all.

The smell of freshly baked donuts greeted her as she opened the door. "Oh yum, you really did it. You brought us donuts!" She took the box from Mac's hands and set it on the table. "Sit down and I'll make us some coffee."

"Oh no, you just sit yourself down. I have lattes waiting in the car. I didn't want them to spill so I left them on the seat next to me. Between the smell of sugar and the aroma of caffeine, I'm now officially starving." Mac turned toward the door then spun around with his finger pointing in Charlie's direction, "Don't you dare touch that box till I return."

"Yes sir, Captain America! I'll just get us some plates and a roll of paper towels so you can mop up your drool."

"Really? Am I drooling?"

Charlie rolled her eyes, "Oh for heaven's sakes, Mac, I'm just pulling your leg. And please don't look down to see if it's longer, just go get the coffee and I'll take care of the rest."

Soon Mac and Charlie were sitting across from each other like two people who had never not been friends. "You know I'm quite the connoisseur of fine donuts, Charlie," Mac said as he bit into his Crueler. "It's a passion with me. I'm not kidding. I eat donuts in my sleep. One day I hope to write a book about them. I'm going to call it *The Donut Hunter*. But since we have a Dunkin on every corner, I'm afraid I won't be able to begin writing until I have time to travel the donut globe.

Did you know that every country has its own kind of donut?" Charlie looked at him as if there were a hole right through the center of his chocolate glazed head. Nevertheless he continued on. "Yes they do; Italy has their struffolis, Spain has their churros, Germany has their Bismarck's, and Hawaii, which although it's a state feels more like another country, has their Malasadas. And someday, when I've made enough *dough*, I'm going to head out of Dodge and taste every single one of them."

She shook her head and smirked, "Did you really just say that?"

For the next hour conversation over their favorite things flowed freely as they sipped their lattes and licked powdered sugar, raspberry filling, and chocolate frosting off their fingers. Charlie couldn't remember the last time she found idle chit-chat to be so deliciously satisfying. She had completely forgotten her car was waiting for her in the parking garage under Jeffery's loft and though the bruises on her knuckles still remained, she no longer felt the embarrassment of having to call Mac to come to her rescue. Jeffery was now old news and, for the first time in forever, all she wanted to do was to curl up in conversation with the quirky doctor whose eyes looked like the ocean had filled them with a thousand shades of blue.

"So tell me about this home."

"What do you mean? What's there to tell? My grandfather built it for my grandmother, Audrey, who died after giving birth to my mother. And my mother's lived in it her whole life. When she married my father, they decided to live here with Grampa and my great-grandmother Esther. Grandma Esther died before I was born and then Grampa died when I was ten years old. Then my father died. In fact his plane, he was a pilot at Dover Air Force Base, went down somewhere out there." Charlie pointed out toward the sea. "So it's a big old home, that feels and smells like death. And there you have it; the end of my sad, sad, story."

"But *you're* still here, right?"

"Temporarily, yes. But I have an apartment in town that I can't wait to get back into."

"But you're an interior designer, right?"

Charlie looked at Mac suspiciously. "Right. But what does that have to do with anything? I mean, it's not my home. It's my mother's home. I'm just staying here to take care of her cat and to try to make sense of where it all goes from here. Mother hasn't changed anything in this monstrosity of a house since long before Daddy died. I wouldn't dare change the only thing she has to come back to."

By the look on Mac's face Charlie braced herself for another doctor-patient consultation where all her hopes are dashed to the ground by science. "Charlie, in all likelihood, your mother isn't coming back here. Her condition may improve somewhat, but from all we've learned from her tests and her family history, her heart issues, along with her diabetes, are genetic. I'm not sure where the Alzheimer's came from, but I strongly suspect it was triggered by her pre-existing conditions, conditions she either ignored or had no knowledge of. I know this is hard for you to wrap your beautiful head around, but Charlie, your mother is in the best place she can be. Still Waters is now home to her. Alzheimer's has become her new normal. And this place, this big old amazing home, is now yours. Now what are you going to do to put your mark on it and bring it back to life again?"

The words that woke her up, after her long night of playing and replaying the song her mother wrote just for her, came singing back to her. *"Coming home, I'm coming home. I've been gone for so long."* Suddenly the simplicity of the verse took on a significance she could never have predicted. But it would take more than a song to convince her that this old home was an early deposit on her inheritance.

"So what you're saying is that because my mother's no longer capable of saying *no* to me I should just waltz in and take over her home as if it'd never belonged to her."

"No, Charlie. I'm saying you should continue your family's legacy by caring for what they've built. I'm saying you should use your gifts and talents to honor their memory. You must have thought about it. So, let me ask you a question. If this *were* your home what would you do with it? I mean, while I'm dreaming about travelling the world in search of donuts, what are you dreaming of?"

Charlie's mind began to whirl with all the ideas that had been stored up in her since the first day she walked into her first design class at Boston University. Every project, every paper, every study in interior design, was measured against the possibilities of how her home could look if only someone would hire her to do it. It never occurred to her the day would come when she could hire herself, and that maybe, just maybe, everything she'd ever studied was for this very moment - to remake beautiful.

She hesitated for a moment as if she were afraid to open the door to the desires that had been itching for release. "If, and I'm only saying *if* I were to do what you're saying, I would begin right here, in this kitchen. I would remove the wall that separates the kitchen from the parlor and make it one great open space. I would take out all this warped bead board and tear off all the wall paper and put up fresh plaster board throughout the whole house. Then I would paint the walls in complimenting colors that reflect the colors you see through the windows along the back wall of the parlor.

And I would have an island built right here where we're sitting that has a sink and a stove top built into it with bar seating around three sides. I would put a dining table off to the side of the parlor so you can have dinner with a view of the bay. And I would divide up the mud room and turn half of it into a breakfast nook."

Charlie rose up from her chair and moved into the parlor. "And I would stop calling this a parlor! That's like a hundred years ago. I would fill this room with soft furniture you can snuggle into with a good book and a large cup of cocoa. I would keep the charm of the beachy-ness but I would update it. I mean, no stereo-typical touristy stuff like lighthouses and sailboats, and those goofy signs on driftwood that say, *Life's a Beach!* I would keep everything simple and clean and shore-like. And I would take out all these wooden shutters and replace them with storm proofed doors. No curtains, just glass. And I would take my Gramma Esther's watercolors and reframe them with wide borders and brushed steel frames and let their palettes set the mood for the entire house.

"And then there's the upstairs! We're talking an entire redo. The bathrooms are atrocious. The bedrooms are a mildewy mess. We'll need all new hardwood floors. And then the porch needs to be completely replaced, maybe with that new composite material that lasts a lifetime. And I would extend it farther out into the sand so there would be more room for outdoor seating and an outdoor kitchen, with pergolas for shade. Of course that means more pilings since everything here has to be above sand level."

Charlie felt Mac's arms circling around her waist as he turned her around until his nose was near enough to her face to feel the warmth of his breath. "Now, there's the girl I've been longing to meet. You're an amazing woman Charlie St. Clare-Mondary. Full of life and brilliant ideas. And I would be honored if you would be so kind as to let me kiss you."

No answer was needed. Charlie and Mac melted into each other. His lips were soft and his embrace was tender and sweet. She had never felt this way before and she liked it. So this is what love is. Mother was right - God gives His best to those who leave the choice to Him.

"Why don't you grab a coat and let's go make a day of it. I'd like to visit your mother, and then maybe we could just go for a drive, find a good place for fish and chips, and then I'll take you to your car. This is not a date, though; it's just the beginning of a great friendship."

"Do you kiss all your friends?"

"Only the ones I hope to kiss again, at the door, after we've dined over candlelight with our bibs dripping in lobster sauce."

Can anyone hide in secret places so that I cannot see him?" Declares the Lord.
"Do not I fill heaven and earth?" Declares the Lord.
Jeremiah 23:24

Chapter Sixteen

Charlie climbed into Mac's car feeling like a first grader who had just been handed a mega-force espresso and a puppy. Her mind was a jumbled mixture of doubts and possibilities. Who did she think she was to even attempt remodeling the home her grandfather built? What were her motives? Where would she begin? How was she going to manage a job like this all on her own? She would need help from someone whose design skills were compatible with hers. She needed Cheri. But Cheri didn't need her. She had been doing more than fine all on her own on the other side of the map.

As she pulled the seat belt across her lap she scanned her surroundings and scrunched her eyebrows together as if she had just reentered earth's atmosphere. "Is this the same car you took me home in last night?"

"The very same. Obviously you weren't in a frame of mind to remember what kind of vehicle came to your rescue after Jeffery's near death experience. And just for the record, Charlie, it's not a *car*, it's a 2008 Jeep Unlimited Sahara." Mac gently patted the dashboard. "She's beautiful isn't she. This baby has a 205 horse-powered engine with a six speed stick on the floor. She can climb mountains, crush rocks under her Goodyears, and slug through mud and sand with gusto. Gotta love her."

"And yet you call it a she. Is that how you like your women; rugged and earthy?" Charlie looked down at her shoes and wondered if she should have gone for the boots after all.

"I, I don't have women. I just have this humble Jeep. She's all mine and she's all paid for. And she's always there for me. It's a guy thing. Guys like cars, Charlie. We're kind of defined by them. Some guys, and I suspect Jeffery fits this category to a tee, like their cars to be sleek and sporty so they can parade their success around like billionaire wanna-be's, while others go for big trucks so they can put on their flannel shirts and haul things. And then there's me - I'm just a simple guy who loves his Jeep."

"You're a very funny man, Mac." Shoving all her plans for the beach house into the back of her mental closet, while savoring the kiss that still lingered on her lips, she headed straight for the question that had been occupying her thoughts since Mac first announced his plans for their day. "So tell me, why do you want to see my mother? I mean, she's not your patient anymore."

The look on Mac's face as he tilted his head toward her caused Charlie's cheeks to blush with the color of her sweater. "Charlie, ever since that day when you sat in my office, blasting me with questions, and littering the carpet with soggy tissues, I haven't been able to forget you. No matter where I am, or what I'm doing, you're always on my mind. I want to know where that fire came from and all I want to do is spend time with you, look into your eyes, and read your story. You fascinate me Ms. Mondary. And I can't help but believe one of the pathways to knowing you is somehow linked to your mother."

Mac's words were so perfectly chosen that she found herself wondering if they were stolen from an old movie written when love stories were sweet, and innocent, and free of perverse intentions.

"I guess that's how it is with all of us, right? We're pictures of our family. No matter how hard we try to break free, they're embedded in our DNA?"

"Yeah, I couldn't agree more. I look like my dad but I tend to think like my mom, except for my humor. That's my dad big time. And of course my flair for fashion is purely a knock off from my sisters and my taste in cars is an inspiration to my brother who has this inner need to top me whenever possible. His Jeep is newer than mine. But enough about me. So tell me, what was your mom like before she ended up at Kent General?"

There was so much she could have said but little that she wanted to. "That should be an easy question, right? But I'm not sure I know the answer. I thought I had my mother all dissected and evaluated until last night. But I discovered some things about her last night that made me realize I never really knew her at all and worse than that, everything I thought I knew about her was wrong. And now it's too late." She felt a rush of tears rising to the surface. "I truly am the worst daughter on the planet."

"From where I sit, I think you're being pretty hard on yourself, Charlie. It's completely normal to feel overwhelmed with guilt after a loved one slips away in the blink of an eye. I see it happen all the time."

Charlie nibbled on the inside of her lip as she looked for a way to end this conversation. But the door was already open. There was no way out but through. "Thanks for your optimism, but you really don't know me, and if you did you'd know that I really am a terrible daughter. I'm selfish and self-centered, and completely spoiled. I've spent much of my adult life resenting my mother for what I thought was her choice to be unremarkable. It was like when I left home to go to college Mother suddenly became needy and helpless. I didn't know what to make of it so I just shut her out of my life."

Mac quietly absorbed Charlie's words before responding. "Hm, that's strange. That's not the picture I got from you while she was at Kent. What I saw was a daughter who fought for her mother, who rarely left her mother's side, and who wasn't going to settle for anything less than the best place for her to live after she was released. And what I see now is a daughter who still, against all odds, is holding out hope for her mother's full recovery. Forgive me for being dense Charlie, but I'm having a hard time finding anything awful in that. So, how about we table the awful daughter story and focus on something else – you know, like what was she like when she was just walking through a normal day being a mom. My brother's a psychologist. I learn all this stuff from him."

The challenge took her by surprise. Charlie never thought of the daily humdrum of her mother's life to be particularly interesting, but taking the focus off of herself was almost as therapeutic as Bernie's Brown Betty. And as her mind began to drift backwards in time she found she had more to talk about than she thought she did. Small things long forgotten bobbed across the surface of her memories. She recounted the way her mother never failed to tuck her in at night with a song and a prayer, the paper bag lunches with funny little stick figures drawn in crayon on the front, and after school visits at the piano bench with a plate of snicker doodles waiting patiently to celebrate her progress. All those *unremarkable* things that helped to shape and mold her suddenly became stories worth remembering.

A pleasant sense of peace filled the air as Mac parked the Jeep and flashed a quick *we're here* smile. "Thank you, Mac. For some unexplainable reason, I'm as anxious as you are to get to know my mother. And you're right, it's like the key to knowing me is hidden somewhere in her. I just hope it's not too late to find what I'm looking for."

Charlie fought back tears as Mac wrapped his arm around her shoulders while walking into Still Waters. All the years of wondering what it would feel like to bring the love of her life home to meet her parents began to crash over her in unexpected waves of grief.

The morning filled with the sweetness of laughter and donuts and conversation that turned the tide of her memories was suddenly being ripped away from her by the remembrance of losses that were quickly doubling and tripling in size. Her grandfather was gone. Her father was gone. And now her mother's mind was slipping away, leaving Charlie on the threshold of being an orphan. A flashback of the last words Charlie wrote in her diary, the day after her father's funeral, pulled her back into the past. She could see every word on the page as if they had just been written.

"Dear Diary, I hate that God buried my Daddy in the sea and left me without a father to walk me down the aisle when I get married. And I hate that Mother and I will live in this big old house all by ourselves. I hate that all I have left is you to remind me of how mad I am at everyone. And that's why I will never write to you again. So goodbye Dear Diary, you've been a terrible, terrible friend."

Charlie held her breath as she and Mac turned the corner leading to the sitting room where Ellie Mae spent her days staring at the water. "There she is, in front of the window." She slipped out from under Mac's arm, walked to her mother's side, and placed her hand gently on her arm. "Mother, it's me, Charlie. How are you feeling today? I've brought someone with me who wants to meet you."

Ellie turned to her daughter and smiled, "Oh, Charlie. I'm so glad you're here. I want you to meet my new friend. Her name is Anne."

Charlie looked up at Mac fearful that her motives for needing her mother to snap back into reality were shining in neon letters across her forehead. Until this very moment Charlie hadn't really thought about what life was like behind the walls of Alzheimer's, she simply needed her mother to recover so she could feel better about herself as a daughter, and so she could put whatever Ellie Mae knew about that awful day on November 16th, 1999 to rest. And as these two truths battled against her soul Charlie fell to her knees and laid her head in her mother's hands. As she wept her mother began patting her head and stroking her fingers gently through her hair.

Charlie lifted her eyes to meet her mother's smile and felt the warmth of her heart hovering over her. "I've forgotten all this, Mother. I forgot how kind and unselfish you are. Even now, when your mind is locked in who knows where, you're still my mom, and I miss you. I really do miss you. I've been so unfair to you. I'm so sorry." And in that teaspoon-ful of time Charlie knew she was standing on the brink of decision - continue her downward spiral into the cyclone of resentment and confusion, or yield her heart to the unknown and the uncontrollable future that would come whether or not she chose to accept it. In her heart she knew the answer.

"Mother, tell me about Anne."

Ellie Mae smiled sweetly as her eyes remained fixed on the window. Then her hands began to wave through the air as if an ensemble of flutes were waiting for her permission to play, "She's free! Free, free, free. She's free. Anne is free."

The drive from Still Waters was quiet and comfortable, like two old coats that had been sharing the same space in the closet for years. They talked about nothing in particular, which Charlie found to be not only charming but even a wee bit sexy. "So, where are you taking me for lunch, because all those donuts we dove into this morning are pushing me off the cliff into a hypoglycemic tantrum."

"It's a surprise," Mac said.

"And would this surprise include food that's made without sugar?"

"Oh, Charlie, just think of me as a guy in a Jeep sent to you from above to help you with your trust issues."

The turn signal started clicking as Mac applied his foot to the brake, reducing their speed and turning off the Highway to Bay Road. "Woohoo! Medings! I would sell my shoes right now for a nice bowl of creamy crab chowder and some fried fish drenched in malt vinegar. You're amazing, Doctor MacKenzie!"

"Yes I am, Charlie. And you'll need to remember that as you get to know me. But before we go in just remember, this isn't *the* date. It's just lunch. *The Date* will come later.

Cleaning up the last little pieces of deep fried batter from her plate, Charlie looked across the table from Mac and wondered what she did to deserve a man like him. They talked about all sorts of things, like where they went to school, who their worst teacher was, and when they knew they were getting too big to hold their mother's hand while crossing the street. "So, tell me Mac, if you weren't a doctor what would you rather be doing with your time?"

"Hm, that's a great question." Mac took a long drink of Pepsi letting the cold carbonated liquid clear his throat. "If my life wasn't filled with a steady stream of sick people needing to get well, I think I would just want to spend all my time on grassy fields coaching eight-year-olds in soccer and baseball."

Charlie's eyebrows rose into her forehead. "Really? Wow, that's so not what I thought you'd say. I kind of pictured you driving your jeep over the plains of Africa in search of elephants and crocodiles, or bungee jumping over rocks and rivers in New Zealand. But soccer and baseball with eight year olds. That sounds, how can I say it - tame! Really, really, tame. So why in the world would you want to watch a bunch of sweaty boys running around pretending they're David Beckham?"

Mac fidgeted with his straw, bobbing it up and down in his glass, as he fumbled for a way to reveal to Charlie a side of his life he rarely shared with anyone. "Because Charlie, one of those *sweaty* boys is mine, and I would love nothing more than to spend a lifetime with him doing whatever makes him laugh out loud."

The restaurant went suddenly quiet while Charlie's world spun in slow motion. "You, you have a son? You're a father. So, what does that mean, Mac? Are you a single father?"

"Not really. No."

"Then you're divorced."

"No," Mac took a deep breath before finishing his answer. "I'm not divorced."

This was a game Charlie didn't want to play, so she dug deeper hoping to find a light at the other end of the conversation. "Then, did your wife pass away?"

"No, Charlie, my wife isn't dead. At least I don't think so."

Feeling like she might just heave her lunch into her empty plate, she pressed her hand against her stomach and tiptoed her way to what seemed to be the last and worst conclusion. "So-o-o-o, you're not a single dad. You're not a widower. That means you're what? Married? Are you married, Mac?"

Mac closed his eyes searching for a brilliant way to answer her question. Finding nothing to cushion the blow he suspected would change the way she was looking at him, he blew out a guilty breath and let the truth take its place at the table. "Yes, I am. I'm married. It's complicated, Charlie."

Disillusioned, disappointed, dismayed, deceived, decapitated, and every other D-word she could think of ricocheted off the walls where her head was pounding for relief. "Thank you for lunch, Mac. I'd like to go and get my car now. So if you wouldn't mind paying the bill, I need to use the restroom."

The drive to the parking garage was painfully silent. Why doesn't he say *something?* Maybe it's because he has nothing to say. He's married. And he has a son. What kind of a man does that?

"You can just let me off by the curb. My car is just a couple of spaces from the entrance." Charlie picked up her purse and pressed her hand down on the door handle of Mac's Jeep. Before her foot stepped down to the sidewalk she looked at Mac one last time. "You kissed me, Mac. You wrapped your arms around my waist, turned me around and laid your lips over mine and you kissed me. And yet you're married. Why? Was I just another notch on your stethoscope? An easy mark? Jeffery's left overs?"

She wanted to say more but there was nothing more to say. He hadn't looked at her once since they left the restaurant. Just as she was about to fill the silence with one more attack on his character, Mac lifted up his head and faced her. His eyes were brimming with tears. She had never seen a grown man cry before. And though she wanted to slap him, something inside her wanted to rescue him the way he rescued her. "You're none of those things, Charlie. You're..." He released a slow and quivering breath. "I'm sorry. I'm so very sorry."

Now we see things imperfectly as in a cloudy mirror,
but then we will see everything with perfect clarity.
1 Corinthians 13:12 NLB

Chapter Seventeen

One of the thousand things Audrey had come to love about the Portals of Heaven was the immensity of it all. And the Assembly of Witnesses was without number, all watching, praying, praising, pointing, and conferring in clusters, as they observed the journeys of mortal saints making their way through the various seasons of their lives on Earth.

Inservio was right, he was always right - Audrey had become quite accustomed to the timelessness of Eternity while writing her daughter's story into the books of Abba's family tree. She no longer found herself measuring earthly time by heavenly time or wondering where the two connected. She simply watched and wrote, often sharing her words and insights with Charles, Esther, Rose and Grandmammy, and Lawrence, as they traced the events of Anne's story unfolding through the Portals.

"Charles, you raised her well. Anne is a tender soul, so full of humility and grace. We've had such a talented family, so full of vision and ambition. And yet, there's Anne, wanting only to play her music for an audience of One. She's quite remarkable, isn't she?"

Charles rubbed his chin in thoughtful reflection, a habit Audrey had grown to love during the days when they were husband and wife. "Perhaps it was God's way of preparing her for Charlie. I'm afraid our granddaughter is like a wild horse bent on independence and with a nose for defiance. Clearly, she has no idea how her mother's prayers have kept her safe through all her self-imposed calamities. She's me, you know, only without the beautiful beard."

"Oh she *is* you, Charles," Audrey laughed, "strong, and opinionated, and yet tender to the touch. But, I think we're seeing Charlie arriving at the crossroads of change, don't you? We all need our carpet times, Charles. Mine came just before I closed my eyes and heard Abba asking me if *I loved the Lamb*. And, of course, yours came while stumbling around that dark room, terrified by the images in your dream, and broken by the grief hanging over you since you left the hospital with a death certificate in one hand and a diaper bag in the other."

"Hm, *Carpet times*. You've always had such a way with words, Audrey. I only wish I would have known the name you chose for our daughter before I literally threw the decision over to my poor mother."

Audrey laid her hand over Charles'. "It was a logical choice though, wasn't it? Esther knew how much I loved my Grandmammy. You could never have guessed that I would have named our daughter after my favorite character in all of literature. I was quite the conundrum wasn't I?"

"Yes, you were. And yes, you are. But it didn't matter. She was our little Ellie Mae, the red headed girl with her winning ways. She's never had to hit the carpet to live a fully surrendered life."

"I think that's because her life began with loss and throughout the years those losses have only increased. But unlike the rest of us, who fight first and pray later, Anne just seemed to know that her true home was not on Bowers Beach. Charlie thinks her mother watches the sea because she's living in the past. But I have a feeling that Anne watches the sea because she sees the future waiting for her on the horizon line of her story."

Charles and Audrey leaned over the Portal and whispered a blessing over their daughter. "You're not alone Ellieanne. You're not alone. We're all here - watching you. The window is clear on both sides."

The girl pressed her fingers against the window and stared at Ellie through the glass. She was tired of playing alone. Her dog nuzzled up next to her with his cold wet nose and laid his big soft head in her lap. Ellie Mae was tired too. She fell asleep humming something that made her feel very much like she was near to home.

Dear brothers and sisters, When troubles come your way, consider it an opportunity for great joy. For you know that when your faith is tested, your endurance has a chance to grow. James 1:2-4 NLB

Chapter Eighteen

"He's married, Bernie. He's married and he has an eight-year-old son." Charlie wiped her eyes with the towel she grabbed off the handle on the silverware drawer in her mother's kitchen. "How could I have been so stupid? Why didn't I know he was just too good to be true?" Then she threw the towel into the sink and pointed to the ceiling with her finger, "I swear Bernie, I'm done with men! I'm sick of them. I don't need them. I'm happier without them. They're all alike! Oh sure, they come in different colors, shapes, and sizes, they drive different cars, some eat baked brie and others eat donuts, but behind all their egotistical cover-ups, they're all the same; cheating, lying, self-infatuated pigs."

"Oh Lordy, Lordy." Bernie clicked her tongue off the back of her teeth. "Darlin', I can't remember when I've seen you in a worse state than you're in right now. Now you just come over here and tell me what happened."

Charlie sat down and tried as best she could to speak rationally. "He came by to pick me up this morning looking all casual and adorable with a box of donuts and a day planned for the two of us to visit Mother, have lunch, then pick up my car from where I left it last night." Her face flushed with color as Bernie's eyes preached a wordless sermon in a glance. "I know. In the space of twenty-four hours I've managed to knock one man to the floor and another one to the door. What can I say? When it comes to men I just get stuck on stupid."

"No, Honey Girl," Bernie smiled, "you just have a wayward spirit that keeps lookin' for peace in all the wrong places. Now you tell me about this Mac and what it is about him that has your heart all a twitter."

"Oh, you couldn't be more wrong, Bernie. *That man* does not have me all a twitter. He's not worth a twitter." Charlie began recounting the events of her day leading up to the moment when it all went south. "He just looked at me, Bernie, with those crystal blue eyes, and said as calmly as if he were telling me the time of day, 'Yes Charlie, I'm married.'"

"And what did you do?"

She stuck her nose in the air with shameless conceit. "I told him that lunch was definitely over and ordered him to take me to my car. I hardly said a word to him after that." Even as the words were rolling off her tongue the look of guilt on Mac's face when she left, threatened to knock her off her throne. "When he pulled up to the parking garage I told him what I thought about him and left him there with nothing but his lies to keep him company. I'm done with men, Bernie. The good ones die and the rest just prowl around looking for another trophy to add to their collection."

Right on cue, Bernie quickly gathered her thoughts like a woman poised to preach. "Now, Miss Charlie Girl, I'm gonna give you the same assignment I gave my Black History students every year for all my thirty years of teaching. I'm going to tell you two stories with just one question at the end. So you just sit back and listen and think long and hard before you answer."

Retreat wasn't an option. So Charlie prepared herself for a long dissertation held together by run on sentences and peppered with profound truisms, while Bernie's eyes gloried in the anticipation of a good story ready to be told.

"Now, way back in the early 1800's there was a white woman who lived on the Delmarva Peninsula named Patty Cannon. Her home was perched along the lines where the slaves were runnin' up North to escape their masters. Now Patty, and her gang, knowin' how scared and hungry those slaves were feelin', would kidnap them and hold on to them just long enough to sell them back to their masters or whoever had money enough to take them off their hands. Then all the leftovers were tortured and buried around her home in Johnson's Corner. That woman was as evil as the night is dark and just before justice could be served against her, she drank herself some poison and died in prison. I heard a while back that someone actually delivered her head, in a red hat box, to the library in Dover. Now isn't that somethin'?

And then there was a white man named Levi Coffin. Now there was a man who walked his talk. Folks called him the President of the Underground Railroad because of the thousands of slaves that passed through his care while tryin' to escape their masters. Levi Coffin never saw a black face he didn't love or care for with severe kindness and long suffering mercy. My own Mr. Levi Mason was named after that same Levi Coffin and I dare say he bore that name with great pride.

So, my question for you is this - based on these two stories, how would you describe to me what white people are like?"

The effects of her sleepless night and the disappointments of her day left her feeling more full of questions than answers. "So, what you're saying Bernie, is that I need to let Mac prove what kind of a man he really is! But what if I already know what kind of a man he really is. What if he really is just like Jeffery, only better at hiding his lying ways? What if God is just setting me up for another round of heartbreak and humiliation?"

Bernie finished her point with the skill of a surgeon and the creativity of an artist. "Charlie, my mamma had the biggest eyes the Good Lord ever carved into a human skull. I mean to tell you, those eyes bugged out like a frog in search of spring. And when she got angered there was fire in those eyes …but there was never more fire in those eyes than there was grace. My Mama always gave us children one chance to defend ourselves. And if our explanations met with her approval she would wrap her big ole arms around us and squeeze the fear clean out of our bones. And if we couldn't convince her that we were nothin' but innocent, she would grab a switch from the hickory tree alongside our house and whoop the bad right out of us. Do you understand what I'm sayin' to you, Honey Girl?"

"I'm trying to, Bernie, I really am." Charlie rubbed her temples with the tips of her fingers as if trying to herd all her rambling thoughts into one corner of her brain. "I'm not very good with men. I don't get them. But I guess I'm not very good with grace either."

Bernie rose up out of her chair and took hold of Charlie's hand. "Right now, Miss Charlie, you're not fit for anything but a good night's sleep. Now why don't you march upstairs and I'll bring you a nice cup of tea and some Tylenol."

"My bed's a smelly mess, Bernie. I'll just sleep down here again tonight."

"No you won't. You just come along with me and we'll clean it up together. Some nice fresh sheets and a crack in the window, and you'll be waking up feeling much better about life in the morning. Then I'll make you a nice warm breakfast and we can think this all through together."

Charlie stuffed a forkful of the cheesy omelet into her mouth while Princess Leia watched from the corner of the table. "PL, unless you can eat with the proper utensils you need to get down from this table." But the cat just sat there staring at her with her eyes fixed on Charlie's plate.

"You heard her, Miss Kitty, now you get your furry paws off this clean table. I swear your Mama let this cat run this house as if she were the one who built and paid for it. Now Charlie, how are you feelin' this mornin'?"

"I wish I knew. But I was out before my head even hit the pillow and I don't think I moved an inch all night long. Sleep is a wonderful thing. Speaking of sleep, did you even go home last night?"

Bernie poured Charlie another glass of orange juice and then scraped the last of the hash browns onto her plate. "I slept in the guest room. I don't think a living soul has entered that room since your Gramma Esther passed. I didn't want to leave you alone just in case you woke up in a fit. So, I just took my shoes off and climbed under the covers. As it turned out, I don't think either one of us opened our eyes until that crazy clock clucked about seven times."

"And speaking of Gramma Esther's room and Mother's clock, something good did happen yesterday. I think it was good, but I'm just not sure if it's right." Charlie drew circles through the hot sauce that dripped over her hash browns. "While Mac and I were devouring our donuts, he had the craziest idea. He thought I should quit looking for another design contract and hire myself to redo Mother's house. In fact, he told me I should stop thinking of this place as Mother's house and start living in it as if it were mine." Then

Charlie's eyes narrowed as she searched Bernie's face for a sign of approval. "So, what do you think, Bernie? You know this place is in deep need of help. I mean, I want to. But should I? Really?"

Bernie clapped her hands together and let out a loud *thank You, Lord Jesus!* "Now there's the first sensible thing I've heard you say since you swore off men last night. So, Honey Girl, how bad could that man be when he makes suggestions like that? You know this house is gonna sink into the sand if somebody doesn't do somethin' with it real soon. And I've been wonderin' just when that someone was gonna wake up and do what she was born to do." Then Bernie leaned in to Charlie's face and cupped her chin in the palm of her hand. "Charlie, your Mama would love nothing more than to know her baby has moved in and taken over. It's been too much for her. Now she's told me for years that she's just been waitin' for her daughter to have the time to come and pour some love into this place. So what's it gonna to take to get started?"

A smile curled across Charlie's lips. It felt good to smile again. "I think I just need a plan. And I need someone to work it out with me. I need Cheri."

Getting up from the table, Bernie headed for the counter and then returned with a cup of coffee in one hand and Charlie's purse in the other. "I'm sure your phone is in here somewhere. Why don't you find it and give her a call while I put these dishes in the dishwasher. Where's that girl livin' now anyway?"

"She's in some little town near Portland."

"Maine? You mean she's been this close and the two of you have been livin' like strangers?"

"Not that Portland, Bernie. Portland, Oregon. And it would take a lot of convincing to get her to come back to the east coast. With her parents both gone now, she's found a place to settle into with a home, career, friends - everything she's worked for. I doubt this is going to work."

"Doubtin' never done nothin' worth countin'. Now you give that girl a call - worst she can say is 'no.'"

"Right. She could say no. But then again she could say yes." Charlie scrolled through the names in her phone. There it was - Cheri's name with her picture above it, smiling that sweet smile of hers. How can I do this? It's crazy to think that after all this time Cheri is going to just hop on a plane and appear at my doorstep with her sketch pad and fabric swatches. It's not like I've been a good friend to her over the years. I've been a terrible friend. I've been the kind of friend who only calls when she needs something. And here I go again. Her heart thumped a few beats as she counted the rings before the recorded voice broke with its monotone greeting, "Hello. You've reached the number for Cheri Collins. Please leave your name and number with a..."

"Charlie!" Cheri interrupted her message. "I was just thinking about you this morning! I can't believe you called! Is everything okay?"

"Yes, everything's fine. Well sort of fine. I mean there's been a lot of stuff that would take forever to catch you up on. But I'm sitting here with Bernie. You remember Bernie don't you?"

"No one ever forgets Bernie, Charlie. I can quote all her little sayings in my sleep. How is that woman? She must be like a hundred by now."

Charlie watched her old friend wiping up the counters and putting food in the fridge. "No she's not a hundred ...yet. But I think she's getting close!"

Bernie spun around and put her hands on her hips. "You tell that girl I can send her a slap right through that phone! Or a hug. It's all up to her!"

"Bernie sends her love. Cheri, I need to ask you something. Something huge. And I know it's too huge for you to even be able to sort out on the phone, so I'm just going to toss it out there for you and give you some time to think about it." Charlie took a deep breath and blew it out slowly. "Okay, here it goes. I need you. I'm thinking of doing a complete makeover on my mother's home and I can't do it all myself. I want to hire you to come here and help me get it all done. We make a great team, Cheri. I know it's a come down from all you've been doing. I know you're probably swamped with offers. I'm sure..."

"Charlie!" Cheri cut in. "Stop! Slow down! Give me some space to absorb what you're saying. So do you want me to come for a visit? Or do you want me to like relocate? How long are you thinking? What are you thinking?"

Soon the two were laughing, and interrupting each other just like old times while Bernie just shook her head in fascinated wonder. With the phone pressed to her ear, Charlie's eyes followed Bernie who was loading the dishes into the dishwasher and mouthed a quick *I'm sorry* as she handed over her empty orange juice glass. But before the glass reached Bernie's hand Charlie gasped in shock and awe, "Really? Are you serious? I can't believe it. How soon can you come?"

"Why not? Life hasn't been the same since Daddy passed. I'm all alone here. I've just finished a huge business complex in The Pearl – that's one of the ritzier sides of Portland. I am so ready for a break. But working together would be a better kind of break than sitting around eating bonbons and watching *General Hospital*. It wouldn't take much to close up shop here. The lease on my office is almost up and I was thinking of moving it somewhere else anyway. So all I would need to do is pack it up and store it all in my garage. That should take me about two weeks, and I can be on my way. And that would give you enough time to convince the weather man to send some decent weather your way before Christmas!"

Charlie's head was spinning with excitement. "Wow! I can't even believe this, Cheri. I have a two bedroom apartment by The Green in downtown Dover. You'll love it. After Mother had her episode – I'll explain all that when you get here, I moved into the beach house. So you can either move into my place, or in here with me. Or we can both live there and then we wouldn't have to trip over all the mess that comes with remodeling. Whatever." After the basic plans were made, Charlie choked back tears and said goodbye to the friend who she loved more than a sister. "I love you, Cheri. I can't wait to see you."

"Miss you like crazy, Charlie. See you soon."

She set her phone on the table and moved over to the sink to be closer to Bernie. "Oh Bernie, you were right. It's like Cheri was just sitting by the phone waiting for me to call." Then Charlie wrapped her arms around Bernie's neck and kissed her on the cheek. "See, why would a girl who has friends like you and Cheri ever need a man to come in and complicate everything?"

"Hm. Well I was waitin' to give you these after you had some time to get yourself all woke up and ready. I guess now might be that time." Bernie walked into the mud room and came back out with a large bouquet of roses. "There's a note attached. You might want to read it before you send them flying off the back porch."

Charlie did her best to keep from smiling as she took the bouquet from Bernie and sat it down on the table. She lifted the envelope from the plastic holder, opened it up, and read the card. It was written by hand in what looked like Mac's writing.

Charlie. I'm sorry for how our day ended. I'm not very good at knowing how to handle conflict. For the sake of my son I have to be very careful about the details of my marital status. The most I can hope for at this point is for the chance to explain everything before you give up on our friendship. I'll call you tonight. Like these roses, Charlie, some things are just too beautiful to walk away from. Love, Mac.

Charlie handed the card to Bernie. "What am I supposed to do with this?"

Bernie handed the card back to Charlie. "I would say you wait for that call and if you don't like what you hear you find an old hickory tree and break yourself off a nice long switch."

Do not withhold your mercy from me, O Lord;
May your love and your truth always protect me.
Psalm 40:11 NIV

Chapter Nineteen

Charlie spent most of her morning carefully pouring over the aging blueprints of the Beach House built by her grandfather long before she was born. Theirs was one of the first homes to dot the bay straddling Bowers Beach. Over the years a small and tightly knit community rose up from the sand one place at a time, including the house next door where Bernie and Levi Josiah Mason moved in and became family with Ellie Mae and Lawrence John Mondary.

The history of her family lived inside these massive blue sheets of paper filled with white lines, and boxes, and symbols that only a seasoned architect could understand. And yet the artistry shared between her and her grandfather created an eternal bond between them. His hands skillfully planned every door, every window, every floorboard, and every room with the intention of providing a place for his family to live and grow and carry on the St. Clare name. *How can I do you justice, Grampa? How can I add to what you've given us? I need you to help me see what was in your heart when you first stood along this shore and let your imagination construct a home that you intended to last through all our generations. Surely you knew the day would come when someone would need to build upon what you began. And there's no one left to do that but me. So, please help me.*

Drawn by an irresistible force, Charlie slipped into her grandfather's old pea coat still hanging in the hall closet, and walked outside along the water facing the back of her mother's home. *When am I going to be able to call this 'my home', Mother? It doesn't look like me at all. It looks like you, mute and still and stuck in a warp of time that I can't bear to hold on to. How* can I bring this place up to date without sacrificing the past for the present?

She picked up a shell half buried in the sand and felt a strange kind of kinship with the jagged remains of what once housed a living creature. As she examined the broken edges she found herself reflecting over her own life and wondering where the pieces that fit in the missing places had gone. With one finger, she began to inspect the tiny grains of sand clinging to the shell while the sound of her grandfather's words whispered to her through the passages of time. "Sand is a metaphor for life, Charlie. Never take it for granted. Each little piece was individually sculpted by adversity and added to the whole. Together they make up the shore on which we stand, with all their stories fitting together into one great theme - redemption. Think of it! The foundation of where we live was built upon the wreckage of creatures just like these. This is our legacy, Charlie. This is who we are. Never forget that."

"I have forgotten, Grampy! I've forgotten almost everything. I'm so sorry."

Charlie slipped the shell into the pocket of her grandfather's coat and wrapped her arms around herself as if to feel the warmth of his presence holding her together. Seized by the timelessness of the moment a voice within her spirit began to sing the verses that came to her when she discovered her name written on a piece of her mother's music hidden in the red satin box.

Coming home, I'm coming home.
I've been gone for so long.
Coming home, I'm coming home.
I've been gone for so long.

As the rhythm of the waves rolled gently near her feet, new verses began to flow effortlessly into the existing chorus:

Lost inside my foolish pride
Said I couldn't stay.
You stood there with open arms
But I turned and walked away.
Free to run, free to fall

Love let me go
And love brought me home
With each step, I hear Your voice
Whispering my name.
Whispering my name.

There it is again. The song. Running into the house, Charlie grabbed the tablet where she'd scribbled the first few verses of her mother's music and began writing as fast as her fingers could catch the words from the netherworld of inspiration. Not one was lost! *Love let me go! Love brought me home!* Really God? Oh God, what is this strange thing happening in me?

Her fingers rippled across the keys of her piano as she placed the new verses inside the notes while images of her family hovered over her. It's my heritage, Mother, isn't it? Great Grandma Esther, Great Grandpa Wesley, Grandmammy Eleanor, Gramma Audrey, Grampa Charles, you, Daddy, and me. They're all here. Not in this house, but here in me. 'Love brought me home!' My home, Mother. My home! I'm home! Thank you, God. Now show me what to do with all this.

Charlie felt her cell phone vibrating in the pocket of her jeans as she walked back to the table where the blueprints were waiting for further inspection. She pulled it out with her thumb and index finger. "Hello, this is Charlie."

"Charlie, it's Mac."

An uncomfortable pause stilled the air between them. Fear mixed with hope niggled at her nerves. "I promised I'd call you today. I know I owe you an explanation. I guess I'm hoping you'll give me time to explain. I'm sorry I didn't do that yesterday. I – I…well, I'm a dork. When I get nervous I just clam up. I shouldn't have. I just didn't know what to say. No, I actually I did know what to say. I just didn't know how to say it. So, I…"

"Shut up Mac." Charlie did her best not to laugh into the phone and shatter whatever confidence it took for him to call her. "Why don't you just be quiet and let me help you get past this awkward moment?"

"Yeah, being quiet would be a good thing for me right now."

"Okay. First of all, thank you for the roses. Nice touch. They're beautiful.

Bernie spent the night here last night because she was worried about my sleep deprivation and thought I needed to wake up to a good breakfast. When I was finished eating she brought out the bouquet and handed it to me. Fortunately, for you, she had all last night and this morning to help me sort things out. So, here's the deal - I'm going to give you one chance to tell me about your marriage, and if I don't like what I hear I will never speak to you again. Is that clear? One chance. Just one."

Mac released a long breath of controlled tension. "I hear you, Charlie. Thank you. I have nothing to tell you but the truth and if that doesn't satisfy your need to know who I am and what I'm like, then I'll back off and delete your name from speed dial. But I'm praying it won't come to that. So, I made a reservation at The Cultured Pearl in Rehoboth for 7:30 tonight. I know I promised you Shucker's but maybe we can do that another time. I can pick you up at 6:15, if that works for you."

"Well, you move fast, I'll give you that. Okay, I'll be ready. Don't be late. Now am I to assume that this is *our date?*"

"Since this might be my last opportunity to see you then - yes, this is *our date*. I'll be there at 6:15. And Charlie...thank you."

Charlie heard a timid knocking on the door. She checked the time on her phone. Exactly 6:15! Good job, Doctor Mac. Taking one last look in the mirror she felt satisfied the little black dress with a simple gold necklace and black patent leather pumps were more than appropriate for a night that was destined to end either with a kiss or a crash. The future of their relationship depended on one thing; Mac's explanation of why he failed to tell her from the get go that he just happened to be *MARRIED!*

After yelling an undignified "come in," she reached for her purse on the bed and whispered into a sleeping Princess Leia's knobby ear. "Hey, Miss Prissy, I'll be gone for a while, try not to miss me too much." She never flinched. In fact, she seemed unusually still. A sting of dread coiled through

Charlie's veins. "PL? Did you hear me?" Nothing. her heart skipped a couple thousand beats as she poked her index finger on the kitty's side. Still nothing.

"Ma-a-a-c! Get up here! Hurry!"

It took him about two seconds to make it to the top of the stairs. She heard him stumbling down the narrow hallway until he found her crumpled on the bed and crying. She turned to him pleading for help. "Something's wrong with Princess Leia. You're a doctor! Do something."

He moved quickly to her side speaking as gently as he could, "Honey, why don't you move away and let me take a look at her." Barely noticing his words of endearment Charlie moved out of Mac's way, mumbling something that sounded like prayers for help. Mac could use a few of those prayers right now, knowing nothing he'd learned at med school had prepared him to be a veterinarian. He lifted PL's head and placed two fingers along her neck while checking for a pulse. He laid her head back down on the pillow and turned to Charlie. "I'm so sorry Charlie. I'm afraid she's gone. It looks like she just passed peacefully in her sleep."

"Are you sure? How can that be? She was fine this morning. She ate her food and even finished off the hash browns on my plate. Maybe she's just sleeping - really hard! Check her again!"

"How old is she, Charlie?"

Charlie waved across the air with her hand. "I don't know. Mother found her under a patch of beach grass when I was in high school." She tried counting on her fingers then gave up in exasperation, "Fifteen, maybe seventeen, maybe …I don't know! She's old!"

"Old cats die, Charlie. I'm so sorry."

Her heels clicked across the old wood floors while she paced between pain and practicality. "Poor kitty. Poor little Princess. She was all alone. I hope she wasn't scared or in pain." She stopped in her tracks and asked the obvious. "What are we going to do with her? We can't just leave her here!"

Mac ran his hands through his sandy blonde hair. "I don't know. I guess we could bury her outside somewhere."

"Mac, I live on the beach. It's full of sand. If we bury her here she's just going to," then she paused as the words stuck in her throat, "come back up!"

Charlie was numb to the brain and needing Mac to be the one with all the answers so she just stood still and waited for him to take charge. "Well," he said, "let's think this through. I'm sure all the pet hospitals are closed by now, but the Humane Society probably has an all-night drop off." Pulling the sheet over Princess Leia he looked around the room and asked, "Do you have a box we can lay her in?"

"No," she said. "And I can't just drop her off like a…I don't know what! Let me think." Pressing her fist against her forehead she resumed pacing. "We have to take her to Doctor Sorenson. He's a family friend and he's been taking care of all our pets for as long as I can remember. I'm sure it's what Mother would want."

"Okay. That's good. But his office is probably closed by now so we need to figure out a place to keep her until morning." A light bulb moment surfaced before he had a chance to run it through the grid of reason. "Do you have a freezer? If you do we could keep her there until morning. Then we can take her to the vet and they'll know how to - dispose of her in a compassionate way."

Charlie rubbed her arms as if they'd been attacked by a swarm of microscopic gnats, "Ewww! Seriously? That's really disgusting, Mac!" Nevertheless she headed for her closet and began rummaging through her shoes in search of a box. She could at least meet the crazy doctor part way in his attempt at being helpful. "Here, this should work!" She emerged holding up a black boot box with *Fancy Feet* splashed across the lid in shiny copper letters. After shoving the box in Mac's hands she opened one of her drawers and pulled out a black wool scarf. "Here, we can put her in here and wrap her in this. And by we I mean you. I don't think I can handle watching you lift her up from the bed, so I'm going to wait for you downstairs."

With her quick and decisive exit Mac was left alone in a woman's bedroom, with a dead cat. A few minutes later he met Charlie in the kitchen, holding the boot box that had become Princess Leia's temporary resting place. "I'm thinking we can either put her under the house for the night, or in the freezer. Which do you prefer?"

"Neither, but the freezer probably makes the most sense. The moisture in the air outside will just make everything yucky by morning." Charlie led

Mac to the mud room, opened the lid to the freezer and waved her hand across the contents. "Pick a spot. I don't think I want to be here for the closing of the lid."

After the deed was done, Mac walked back into the kitchen and sat down next to Charlie at the table just in time to hear her dredging up all the guilt that was bubbling under the surface. "How do I tell Mother? I moved in here to take care of her house and her cat and I haven't done a very good job with either. Now the cat is dead and I'm making plans to change all that remains of what she remembers about the only place she's ever called home."

"I'm sorry, Charlie. For everything. This has been a tough night and it's barely even gotten started." He reached for her hand. "Listen, if you would rather not go out to dinner right now I understand. Why don't I just cancel the reservations, or maybe I can make us something to eat right here. How does that sound? Scrambled eggs? Pancakes? PB&J? Really, I'm a whiz in the kitchen."

She took her hand back and pressed it against her forehead. "I'm sorry, I forgot about dinner. Thanks, but you've gone above and beyond the call of duty – again! Once I found Princess Leia everything else just didn't matter. But it's not like I can do anything about it, right? Besides, I promised I'd hear you out, and I need to *hear you out* somewhere other than here. So, if it's not too late I think we should go ahead and leave for the restaurant." She stood up and smoothed her hands over her dress, then pushed her hair behind her ears with her fingers. "Yeah. Let's go to dinner. But first I think I need to go upstairs and freshen up."

Before leaving the kitchen she looked back at her date who was smiling kindly through his words. "Okay, then you go do what you need to do and I'll call the restaurant and see if we can push the reservation ahead by half an hour. I'll just wash up here in the kitchen. By the way, you look beautiful, as always."

He's a charmer. But is he a keeper. I guess I'll know the answer to that question soon.

Charlie's face reflected the warm glow of candlelight as he searched for a way to explain the undeniable fact that he was married. "Are you alright?"

"I'm trying," she answered while spearing a shrimp with her fork, "but I haven't been *doing alright* in so long that I can't seem to remember what alright feels like anymore."

He wanted to reach out and touch her hand. He wanted to tell her that she was the most exciting and beautiful woman he has ever met. He wanted to let her know he was falling hopelessly in love with her. He wanted to pull a tiny box out of his pocket, get down on one knee in front of the whole restaurant full of people, and ask her to marry him. But most of all he wanted not to hurt her. And he knew the only way to protect her from pain was to tell her the truth about his life, his son, and his marriage. So he drew in a chest full of air, cleared his throat, and prayed a desperate prayer for help.

"Charlie, this isn't the way I imagined our first date. But I promised you the truth, and though it may seem hard to believe, the truth is something I've tried to live by since I first went to college."

Her face was like a blank screen waiting for the right words to fill it. "Why not before college, Mac? I mean that sounds like you had to make a conscious decision to live differently than you were living before."

"Wow, smart and beautiful. Yeah, I went off the deep end for a while and I did a lot of things I'm not proud of - things that broke my parents' hearts."

"What kinds of things, Mac? I'm sorry for sounding like a private investigator, but if I'm going to understand you, I think this would be a very good place to begin, don't you?"

Wow again. She knows how to get right down to it, doesn't she? But this is why you're here Mac, so man up and face the firing squad. He put his fork down and took the witness stand with as much courage as he could muster. "You're right. Tonight is our night for full disclosure. I'll just give you the Reader's Digest condensed version."

Mac rested his elbows on the table. "It started during the summer between my junior and senior year in high school. I wanted to be," he broke for air quotes, "'*in with the cool guys.*' You know - do what they do and hope they'll let you into their little club." She laughed. Unloading his boatload of truth was feeling better than he thought it would. He kept on going as if there were no stop signs to interrupt his trip to transparency. "So I started off with beer, tequila, and whiskey, and graduated to pot, and from pot to speed. The rest is a blur of wild parties on the beach, girls in wet tee shirts, and the rush of feeling my car shaking when the speedometer hit a hundred and five. And then it all came to an end the night my best buddy since first grade swallowed up a handful of speed and washed it down with a bottle a of bourbon. He never woke up from his coma. I remember standing over his casket and begging him to wake up. And I swear to you, Charlie, his voice rose up from the dead and spoke to me as clearly as I'm speaking to you now, 'no, you idiot – you wake up!' So I did. I confessed everything to my mom and dad and I went to my youth group leader at church and confessed everything to him. Tad mentored me that whole next year through to graduation. It took me a long time to put away all the guilt and accept God's forgiveness for all the awful things I did. But there isn't a day goes by when I don't think of Brad and wonder where he is and what he would have been, if only."

"Yeah, I get the *if only's*. I have a litter box filled with them. So you got religion and now you're all better."

"No. I got real with Jesus and now I know I'm *not* all better. I'm just a sinful man in deep need of a Savior."

The look on her face told him he was dealing with more than a woman who felt lied to – like maybe his confessions were unlocking a few secrets of her own. She took a drink of water before resuming her interrogation. "So you got married. You had a son. And then you decided you'd like to add a girlfriend to the mix and you chose me. Right?"

The pain of her cruelty surprised him. "No, you're not right at all, Charlie. In fact you couldn't be more wrong. But it's not your fault. It's mine. I should have explained things from the beginning, before I called you that night and asked you if you wanted to go out with me. Before I took you home from Jeffery's. And before I brought you donuts and a latte. I'm so sorry. Please forgive me for not being straight with you."

"I'll forgive you Mac, when you get to the point. Maybe."

Ouch. "Okay, that's more than fair. So here it is." Mac laid his hands, palm sides down, on the table and leaned his back against his chair. "I met her in college. Her name was Irene. She was charming and brilliant and she liked me. I know, it's pathetic, but I was scared of girls so anytime a girl showed interest in me I was like putty in her hands. Anyway, we started dating. She knew I was a Christian and she said all the right things that led me to believe we were both on the same page. We were married the year before I started med school."

Though this wasn't the whole story, it was accurate enough for tonight. I'll tell her the rest later. If we have a later. "But during my first year of residency she got pregnant with Zak. Zak's my son.

I should have known something was wrong from the second we brought him home from the hospital because while everyone was making a fuss over our new baby, Irene just seemed…detached. I attributed her moods to post-partum depression. I tried to encourage her to see a doctor, but she refused. She wouldn't let me touch her, or help her, or do anything to comfort her. And then one day I came home from the hospital and before I could get my key in the lock I heard Zak crying through the door. There was something about the sound of his cries that made my blood run cold. I hurried into our apartment and called out to Irene but there was no answer. I can still feel my heart beating every time my mind goes back there." As if he were reliving every moment, he paused to let his emotions catch up with his words. "I was so panic-stricken as I ran to the nursery that I had to tell myself to breathe. The smell of urine hit me before I even got to the door. I rushed in and found my son alone in his crib, wet and hungry. And scared. He was only three-months-old, Charlie. Three months!"

Mac wiped the tears from his eyes with his napkin while Charlie sat with her mouth hanging open in disbelief. After he regained his composure he began where he left off. "I picked him up and held him against my chest. His little body was cold and shivering. So I changed his clothes and wrapped him in a blanket and then I started running all over our small apartment looking for Irene. It was a *small* apartment, Charlie - it's not like anything bigger than a cockroach could have gotten lost in there. But she was gone. Her clothes had been cleaned out of our closet. Her makeup was gone. Her books and her computer. I mean everything that had her fingerprints on it was GONE! Zak was screaming. I was screaming with him. And then I saw a large yellow sticky note stuck on the front of the fridge. It was from her.

I'll never forget standing there, holding our baby, and reading those words written with a red felt tip pen: "*I can't do this anymore!*"

Mac looked up at Charlie. There were tears in her eyes. Then she reached out her hands and placed them over his. She cared. Thank, you God.

"Where did she go, Mac? What happened to her?"

Mac just shook his head as if the wonder of it all was still new to him. "I don't know. She just disappeared into thin air. I haven't heard from her since. No phone calls, no letters, no forwarding address, no '*Hey, how's our son doing without his mommy?*' Nothing! So, yes Charlie, I'm married. I have an eight-year-old son. And this is my life. And I'm hoping that in spite of everything I've just told you, you won't be too afraid to come along and share it with me. Will you come along and share it with me, Charlie?"

The floodgates were open. There were no words left to be said. Just the tears shared between two broken people who needed time to see where their lives were heading as unseen witnesses cheered them on with holy joy.

It had been eight years since Mac felt free to love again. Maybe for the first time. But somehow now that the truth was on the table he looked at the beautiful woman sitting across from him and sensed there was more of their story waiting to be told.

And the one sitting on the throne said,
"Look, I am making everything new!"
And then he said to me, "Write this down, for what I tell you
is trustworthy and true."
Revelation 21:5 NLB

Chapter Twenty

It would be another sleepless night. But not like the others, where the night crazies danced around her bed mocking her with accusations and questions for which there were no answers. No. On this night broken trust was mended with a forgiving kiss at the door. As she sent Mac off to his Jeep feeling accepted and understood, Charlie climbed the stairs to her room feeling like hope was waiting in the wings to embrace her with new life.

She propped her pillows against the headboard and climbed under the covers wearing her fleecy pajamas and fuzzy blue socks, then picked up her cup of chamomile ginger tea from her night stand along with the mysterious pink envelope Mac put in her hands before he said goodnight. She wanted everything to be perfect before she opened it. This had to be something he did *before* he came by to pick her up for their date. Was he just being cocky with confidence or was this another example of his boyish trust? It didn't matter. Her curiosity had been pleasantly piqued.

She took another sip of tea and without thinking her hand instinctively patted the space where Princess Leia should have been. The freezer! Oh PL, I'm so sorry. We couldn't think of anything else to do! You poor baby. Please forgive me. How can I lie here feeling all happy and romantic when you're where you are right now? But it's not like I can just wave a magic wand over you and bring you back. So, I'm going to pretend you're all warm and toasty in the chair downstairs. I promise I'll do right by you tomorrow. Tomorrow is another day. Goodnight, Kitty.

As she held the envelope in her hands she closed her eyes and let the lingering warmth of Mac's lips on her cheek set the mood. Then she slid her index finger under the flap and lifted it ever so gently. Doing her best to savor the moment, she slowly lifted the card out of the envelope and smiled at the scene emerging. A sepia toned picture of an old man and woman looking out on the horizon where the ocean meets the sky, were holding hands as if they had been counting those sunsets all their lives. Beautiful. Touching. Mac truly is an old soul.

She opened the card. No cheesy tag line waiting to wow her - just a blank page with his thoughts hand scripted in his best writing.

> *Dear Charlie,*
>
> *Thank you for giving me this one chance to explain my complicated life. I wish I had more to offer you than a question mark. But what I can give you, should you desire to continue dating a man like me, is my solemn promise to respect the woman you are and preserve your purity.*
>
> *I'm desperately praying for God to find Irene and bring closure for Zak and me, so the three of us can see where this road is leading. I have an appointment with a lawyer to finally end this marriage that isn't a marriage. It's something I should have done a long time ago. Charlie, I want to invite you to take a leap of faith with me into the future that's waiting to be discovered. So as you fall asleep tonight I pray these words will encourage you to say yes to wherever God is leading.*
>
> *'Grow old along with me!*
> *The best is yet to be,'*
> *Love, Mac*

Silly man; there would be no sleep tonight.

The sun sent shimmering beams across Charlie's face. Her eyes squinted as she looked around her room, surprised that sleep came in spite of her hyperactive imagination that ran wild for what seemed like hours, remodeling *her* home, preparing for Cheri's arrival, telling her mother about Princess Leia, and planning a wedding. A wedding? What was I thinking? We haven't even had a second date yet. And still, if I can ever get this house started and then finished, it would be a great place for a reception. Stop it, Charlie. Stop it. Stop it. Stop it. Besides, once he hears the sordid details of your life he'll run back to his Jeep and head for the hills.

Her stomach churned as she reached for the coffee in the canister on the kitchen counter. Looking in the direction of the mud room she gathered up her courage and went in. There's no reason for Mac to drive all the way out here again this morning just to deliver PL to the vet. I can do this by myself. She rubbed her hands together before lifting the lid of the freezer where Princess Leia spent the night. Okay, baby, it's you and me. I'll just pick you up and set you outside by the door so you can thaw out. Just the thought of holding the cold box in her hands sent shivers down her cowardly spine. So she quickly slammed the lid shut and went back into the kitchen. Coffee. I need coffee.

Charlie's phone began to dance across the kitchen table. Thankful for the interruption she quickly ran to pick it up hoping it was Mac so she could let him know she was fully capable of handling the kitty crisis on her own. He'll be so proud of me. Smiling at the thought of hearing Mac's voice she cooed into the phone. "Hello-o-o-o, this is Charlie."

"Hey, Charlie, guess what? I've got a date. I was so excited after we talked yesterday that I just started packing my office like a crazy woman. I'm almost finished, so there's no reason I can't be ready to fly to Dover by next Thursday. I hope you still want me because minus the plane ticket, I'm almost there."

Charlie nearly choked before she could spit out an answer. "Cheri! I wasn't expecting a call this soon! You move fast, girlfriend! Of course I still want you. More now than ever!"

"Why more now? Is everything alright? You sound so - happy. That must mean there's a knight in shining armor riding into your future. Please tell me I'm right because one of us needs to hit it big on the man front."

"Oh Cheri, you can't even begin to imagine what's all going on here. But I'm going to save it for next week. Trust me, it's the reason slumber parties were created. So I think you should stay with me for a couple of days before you move into the apartment. Besides, once the house starts getting destroyed by renovations I'll probably want to move over there with you."

"What about the little princess? What are we going to do with her? I guess we can move her to Dover with us. But she'll probably completely freak out."

Charlie pressed her lips together while trying to think of a good way to break the bad news. "Hm, well I'm afraid that freaking out is no longer an issue. The Princess is currently no longer current. I'll tell you all about it later." But before she could continue a beep interrupted their conversation. "Cheri, I need to take this – it might be my knight. So go ahead and book the flight, text me the info, and I'll reimburse you for the ticket when you get here. And don't argue about that with me. It's the least I can do. Later friend! Love you."

Charlie pressed her hand against her fluttering heart. "Hey, Mac, how's your morning going?"

"I didn't sleep at all last night so I began my morning thanking God I'm not a surgeon. How are you doing? Did you sleep? I don't have to be in the office until noon, so I thought I'd dash over and take care of the guest in your freezer."

"Actually, I was just about to take care of it myself, but as soon as my hands reached the boot box I just froze." Her face screwed in disgust before continuing. "Sorry, I just can't seem to deal with all this without saying stupid things. It's like I'm possessed with the spirit of bad puns. I'm not usually this cruel. I really am sad about PL's demise. But ..."

"It's overload, Charlie. It's perfectly normal. You've been through a lot and maybe this is just the release valve your emotions need to help you let off a little steam before your head blows up. And frankly, my friend, you have to admit - it is funny in a disturbing sort of way. So, I'll be there right after I drop Zak off at school and we can take her to your vet and let them handle it all from there."

There was something refreshing about hearing Mac talk so easily about his son, as if this faceless child had always been a part of their relationship. Mac, Zak, and me! She placed her hand on her belly and felt life where life had once been before it was ripped away. How am I ever going to tell him about what I've done? How do I tell him I may never be able to have children? Later, Charlie. Just go get dressed and think about it later.

With less than a moment to spare, Charlie quickly jumped into her jeans and sweater then made a hurried call to Bernie. After the third ring she left a message. "Bernie, I hope you don't have plans for later this morning, because I have so much to tell you and I thought I'd pick you up, take you with me to visit Mother, and then take you to lunch. Get ready to be amazed and astonished."

The sound of Mac's Jeep turned her into a bowl of Jello. Falling in love was new to her and knowing how to respond to the sound of his voice, the touch of his hand, and even the anticipation of seeing him at her door, set her nerves to tingling. But she liked it. She really liked it. Today was Day One of a new beginning. And oddly enough she found herself with an insatiable need to go out and buy a nice new pen and a journal. Good grief, I'm becoming my mother!

When she opened the back door she grinned from the inside out. He was more attractive than ever. That sandy hair, those eyes that smiled without words, and that swagger in his steps, stole her breath away.

She smiled as she watched him hop up the ten steps that led him straight to her door. He drew her into a friendly hug and whispered in her ear, "Forgive me for being presumptuous, Charlie, but I'm hoping you wouldn't mind too much if I kissed you good morning."

"Seriously, Mac, you are a dork." Charlie wrapped her arms around his neck and feeling lost in the scent of leather and soap she answered his question for him with a long and lingering meeting of their lips. "There, I think that's a perfect way to start our day." With that settled she led him to the mud room and pointed to the freezer, "Now let's get this over with before I chicken out."

The drive to the vet was nearly painless, with just a few stabs of guilt whenever Princess Leia's name came up. The last time Charlie remembered walking into Dr. Sorenson's office was when she and her mother brought Basil II in for his last check-up; the one where the decision was made to let him go. Her heart still felt the pain of that decision. Some day – Basil III.

Mac handed the box to the young woman in white while Charlie filled Dr. Sorenson in on the details. "She was fine when I left her yesterday. Then I went to kiss her goodbye before going to dinner with my friend and she was gone. I guess she just died in her sleep."

"Actually Charlie, I never believed she would live as long as she did. Your mother took extraordinarily good care of her. We'll cremate her this morning and if you like you can opt to have her remains placed in an urn, if that's what you prefer."

"No. I don't want to do that. I have a great picture of PL and Mother sitting together in their favorite chair. I think I'd rather just have that framed. No box. No urn. No grave with a headstone."

Dr. Sorenson placed his hand on Charlie's shoulder, "I understand. You know your mother was one of the first clients to walk through these doors when I first opened my practice here in Dover. She came in with Basil, who was just a puppy at the time. He had eaten a whole bag of raisins and it didn't sit well with him. Ellie has become a very dear friend. She's a lovely woman - too young to be where she is right now. Please give her my best the next time you see her. Now you just go ahead and leave and we'll take good care of the princess for you."

After a hug and a handshake, Charlie and Mac were on their way back to the beach house and, if mercy could be stretched that far, to a new season in both of their lives.

Are not five sparrows sold for two pennies?
And [yet] not one of them is forgotten or uncared for in the presence of God.
Luke 12:6 Amplified Bible

Chapter Twenty-one

Her eyes stared through the window overlooking the lake. Words and music and images beyond her comprehension melted together like the slush of rain mixed with snow. She longed to see the girl behind the glass, but the window was blank. Everything today felt blank as her fingers tapped rhythmically over the nap of her afghan.

Ellie Mae missed the mysterious friend who, in a short period of time, had changed from a curly red-headed child to a young woman whose eyes danced with life. She had come to love everything about her. The way she appeared out of nowhere, only to disappear into thin air. The way her shy smile matched her peaceful spirit. The way she took notice of little things like birds, and acorns, and the formation of clouds sculpting puffy pictures across the sky. And especially the way her fingers floated across the keys on the piano near the edge of the lake as if she had entered the worship of Heaven with her songs.

And so she stared intently at the lake hoping she would appear. Then in a blink of a moment she was there, sitting on a bench facing the window with nothing separating them from each other but the glass. Anne folded her hands into her lap and leaned forward as if she were inviting Ellie Mae into her very soul.

Her fingers tapped faster. If only she could reach out and touch this girl who seemed to have the power to break through her nothingness. Instead she just sat there lost in a blank stare while tears rose up from somewhere in the dark where time was meaningless and words sat in her brain like a scattering of puzzle pieces waiting to be assembled.

Celeste picked up the shawl that had fallen on the floor next to her chair and wrapped it around her patient. "I see you, Ellie Mae. I see you." During the weeks since she became a resident at Still Waters, Celeste had come to understand all those little behavioral patterns that helped her to know what Ellie Mae was feeling and what she needed. When her head shook back and forth, she was distressed. When she licked her lips repeatedly, she was thirsty. She hummed when she was tired. She wrinkled her nose when she didn't like her food; instinctive reactions that clung to her personality, refusing to be annihilated by the treachery of disease.

"Ellie? Can you hear me?" No response. "Ellie, I need to take your blood pressure and pulse. Just relax and breathe nice and deep for me. This will only take a minute."

It wasn't like she could object. Her body had become an offering of lesser things. The tightness of the band around her arm released its grip as Celeste spoke into the pager clipped to the collar of her brightly colored scrubs.

"Doctor Moran, I think you need to come and take a look at Mrs. Mondary. Her blood pressure is up and I don't like the way she's looking right now. I'm with her in the sitting room."

Celeste took her temperature and found it to be just slightly elevated. "So, dear lady, how are you feeling? You're looking a little puny. But it's okay, Doctor Moran will be here soon." Holding Ellie's hand gently in hers she continued talking to her as if she was grasping the meaning of every word. "The weather's beautiful today isn't it? Cold but sunny. I love days like this. Have you been watching the ducks in the water? I'm surprised they're all still here. Usually they fly south for the winter. I think they do. Actually I'm not an expert on the comings and goings of ducks."

Dr. Moran walked up to his patient from behind and pulled up a chair next her. "So, Mrs. Mondary, how are we feeling today?"

Moving to the opposite side of where Dr. Moran was sitting, Celeste began to fill him in on the sudden changes in Ellie Mae's condition. "When I came in the sitting room to check on her I noticed her head was leaning to the left and she was propping it up with her hand. Her face looked flushed and her eyes looked more listless than normal. This morning her temperature was right on point, but now it's up to ninety-nine point three."

"Good watching. Let's go ahead and bring her to The Wing so we can hook her up to a monitor and run a few tests. I suspect we're either looking at the beginning of a virus, or she could be in the throes of a TIA. How was her blood sugar this morning?"

"Really doctor, everything was normal. She didn't eat much, but that isn't unusual for her because she's not big on breakfast." Celeste unlocked the wheels of Ellie Mae's chair and pointed her in the direction of the corridor that led to the small but well equipped medical wing of Still Waters. "I'll meet you there and I'll page Jodie on the way so she can contact Mrs. Mondary's daughter."

"Honey Girl, haven't you just had the week that was! Mercy! And now look how it's all comin' together! You've hired yourself to do somethin' wonderful with that old house. You've got yourself a fine man with a son to boot. And, your Cheri is on her way. Now, I'd say God has been smilin' down on you! Hallelujah and praise You, Jesus!"

"I know. It's all more than I can absorb. Thank you for coming with me today to see Mother. I hate having to tell her about Princess Leia. It's like another loss for her. I know she probably won't grasp it all, but still."

Bernie wiped her face with her starched white handkerchief as she turned to Charlie. "Now why do you need to go and tell her that? Your momma doesn't need to know her little princess is gone. She just needs to know she's loved and she hasn't been tossed away like a used pair of shoes. Anything else is just a bunch of unnecessary words. You're a good daughter, Miss Charlie. So let's just go and love on her some."

Before Charlie could respond to Bernie's wisdom, her cell phone rang through the speaker in her car. "Hello, this is Charlie."

"Charlie. I'm so glad I reached you. This is Jodie. Now, there's nothing critical to worry about, but we've taken your mother to the medical wing to run some tests."

Charlie swallowed hard. "What? Is she alright? What happened? She was fine yesterday."

"Actually she was doing well this morning also. But then just a few minutes ago she began to show some signs of distress. Celeste paged Doctor Moran so he could come and check her out. Her blood pressure is elevated and she's running a slight fever. This isn't an emergency, Charlie, but I think it would be good if you could come as soon as you're able."

"I'm already on the road. We'll be there in about five minutes. I really don't remember how to get to the medical wing, so could you please meet us at the door? You know how I am with directions!"

"No problem, I'll be right there waiting for you. See you soon."

Charlie steered her car with one hand while chewing on her fingernail with the other. "Why does this keep happening, Bernie? I just think I've found a place to breathe and then *slam* - it all spins out of control again! This is why I don't get prayer. It's like God is up there playing games with us, tossing us a few bones and then pulling them out of our teeth when we catch them. Why? What's the point? What does He want?"

Bernie's eyes filled with tears, the kind of tears that fall when mercy has reached its full capacity. "Listen to me sweet baby. You know I'd take this all away from you if I could. Lord knows there's nothin' I wouldn't do to make you happy. I love you with every drop of love I have to give you and then some. So when you ask me questions like this I just want to reach up to the Father and grab hold of the answers and hand them over to you. But I can't. But let me tell you what I can tell you and that is, He's good Charlie. The world doesn't know Him but His sheep do. He's good. And with all that's bad in this life, well Darlin', we just need to rest ourselves in that. He's good. You just keep lookin' for it and don't let the bad overshadow it. He's good, Child. So let's just go in there and be the sheep and let the Shepherd be the Shepherd."

"You should have been a preacher, Bernie."

The sound of her friend's laughter filled the car. "Oh, Honey, you know I already am! I'd preach to a post if it would listen. And you know why?" She looked at Charlie straight in her face with her eyes as big as golf balls, "Because He's gooood."

"I love you, Bernie." Charlie parked the car close to the front door of Still Waters. "Okay, let's go see how Mother's doing."

Dr. Moran was just leaving the Medical Wing as Jodie led Charlie and Bernie to it. "Doctor Moran, I think you remember Charlie, Ellie Mae's daughter? And this is Bernie Mason a good friend of the family. How's our favorite patient doing?"

Dr. Moran removed his rubber gloves before shaking Charlie's hand. His fatherly kindness brought an immediate calm to Charlie's scrambled emotions. "She's stabilizing. That's a good thing. Thanks to Celeste, we were able to catch her in the midst of a TIA - transient ischemic attack. I feel pretty confident that she hasn't had an episode like this since she arrived so, in a way, it was good for us to be able to observe her while it was happening. And though we would certainly prefer that she not have them at all, it still helps us to track her symptoms and have a better handle on how to prevent them. She was given aspirin immediately followed by Aggrenox; a blood thinner. We'll be keeping her here for a few more days so we can monitor her more closely and make sure she doesn't stroke. But her blood pressure has gone down significantly, her blood sugars are nearly normal, and her temperature is on its way down to normal also. So, barring any other complications we should be able to bring her back to her room by the middle of the week."

Bernie stood straight and tall, letting her eyes capture Dr. Moran's full attention. She reached for his hand and shook it firmly. "Doctor, I have a few questions, if you don't mind."

"I don't mind at all. I'm always up for a few good questions," he answered.

"Thank you. Now I've only been able to visit my friend a few times since she moved in here. I'm not as young as I used to be so I only drive when the weather is clear and the traffic is low. But I'm concerned about how seldom Miss Ellie speaks, and she's always sitting in a wheel chair. She's a young woman, Doctor, and from all I've been reading about the relationship between TIA's, diabetes, and Alzheimer's, keeping her body moving is critical for maintaining her physical stability. So, my question is – is this woman getting any exercise at all?"

Charlie's face flushed with embarrassment. Nevertheless she was grateful for the way Bernie was able to ask the questions she only had the courage to wonder about. Not to mention how quickly she was able to leave her black preacher woman waiting for her in the car and step into professor mode with perfect English.

Dr. Moran's smile twisted to the side leaving a crease in his aging cheek. "Well, that's a very good question. And the answer is 'yes'. We encourage our guests to walk as often as they're able. And you're right, exercise is vitally important to Mrs. Monday's health. So we make sure she walks to and from the restroom, to and from the lunch room, and our nurses take her on regular strolls through the halls as often as possible. She receives physical therapy from her bed once a day. But because she is incognizant of her surroundings we're careful to make sure her mobility is limited to scheduled routines so we can insure her safety. That's why when you've been here to visit, she's either been in bed or in a wheel chair. I hope that clarifies some things for you."

Satisfied with his answer, Bernie responded with approval. "Thank you, Doctor, that answers all my questions for now. Ellie Mae is very important to us. Now about her verbal communication. What are you doing to help her?"

Charlie left Bernie to finish her interrogations while she followed Jodie into The Wing to see her mother. The sight of Ellie Mae, tucked under starched white sheets brought her right back to the uncertainty of those first few days after she found her mother suspended in time on the back porch. She stopped short of the bed to catch her breath. Jodie wrapped her arm around Charlie's shoulder. "I know this is terribly disappointing, Charlie. But don't let this minor setback throw you. Your mother is in very capable hands. I'm sure she'll be back to her room very soon."

"Thanks, Jodie. I just hate seeing her like this. She just looks so helpless. How can a grown woman look so little? I'm so sorry. I forgot about your mom. This must be so hard for you, Jodie. Why do you do this to yourself? I mean, surely there are easier places to put your skills to good use."

"Thanks. But really, I can't think of a better way to work through the grief of losing my mom than to stay near to people like you and your mother. I'm selfish I guess. But I find my best comfort comes through comforting others with the hope I was given when I needed it so desperately."

"But she died. How is that hopeful?"

Jodie turned to Charlie and spoke just above a whisper, "Yes, my mother died, but that wasn't the end of it. Her life taught me how to live and her death taught me how to die. And when she placed her feet on Holy ground I know that Jesus just held her in His arms and blessed her for a job well done. Think of it, Charlie, you're standing in the midst of greatness right now. Your mom is doing her best work right here, right now. Believe me, Charlie, you don't want to miss a thing of it. Cherish every moment and glean every lesson it has to teach you."

"Lordy! Now aren't you both a sight for joyful singin'?" Bernie joined Charlie and Jodie as they stood over Ellie Mae. "She's a beautiful woman isn't she? Always has been. My, my, my – didn't God just do a mighty fine job on her. Beautiful." Then Bernie sat in the chair next to her friend, and began to carry on a conversation as if they were sipping tea, chatting over the events of the day, and comparing notes on what it feels like to be a young woman in an old woman's body.

Drawn by Bernie's lively conversation with Ellie Mae, Jodie and Charlie moved two chairs over to her bedside. It didn't take long before the three of them began chirping, and laughing together until Celeste came in with her *party's over* look. "Sorry ladies, but its lunch time and after a very busy morning I'm sure your mother's hungry. So, unless you'd like to share her soup and yogurt, I'm afraid I'm going to have to ask you to leave."

"Hm, as you see, the director of Still Waters has almost no authority around here. But that's okay, I've been booted out of better places than this. Besides all this partying has left me starving."

"My car is right out front. Bernie and I were planning on having lunch anyway, so how about you join us. It's my treat! I owe you both a feast."

The comfort of the warm chicken and dumplings left Bernie and Charlie feeling well fed and contemplative during their drive back to Bowers Beach.

"It's just life isn't it, Bernie?" Charlie thought out loud. "It's life at its worst and life at its best. I wish I could say I understand it all, but I don't. But I want to. Maybe I just don't know how to step off this roller coaster that's become my norm."

"Charlie girl, you're a wise young woman. More like your Mama than you're ready to fess up to. But it's comin'. I'm glad we hauled Jodie off to lunch with us - somethin' tells me she's a package from heaven sent to help us walk through the days ahead." Then Bernie reached out her hand and patted Charlie's knee. "Now I don't want to bring you back down to the pit, Darlin', but somehow I feel like God is preparing us for a whole other season of life. I don't know when it's comin' and I don't know how it's comin'. But some of it is already here and the rest is on its way. And Charlie, when the rest comes I want you to be ready. God never lets His stories end worse than they started. I promise you; whatever He has up His sleeve is gonna' set your feet to dancin' and your heart to singin'. I just feel it in these old bones of mine. Yes I do." Then she burst out laughing, "It's either that or my bursitis. But my bursitis never has anything good to tell me. And Honey Girl, what these bones are tellin' me is good. You know why?"

Charlie turned her face to Bernie and forced her eyes to bug out as wide as they could go. Then they sang in sync with each other, "Because God is goooood!"

"My heart has heard you say, "Come and talk with me."
And my heart responds, "Lord, I am coming."
Psalm 27:8 NLB

Chapter Twenty-Two

After another night of crawling into bed with her phone in hand, and talking with Mac about a thousand little things until they could no longer stay awake, Charlie was startled out of sleep by the chorus of Sergeant Pepper's Lonely Hearts Club Band blaring from her night stand. She slammed her hand over the small programmable clock several times trying to find the off-switch. Instead it flew off the nightstand onto the floor taking her MP3 player with it. Note to self; change your wake up call to 'She Loves You, yeah, yeah, yeah.' Then the light dawned. Cheri would be stepping off the plane shortly before noon in The City of Brotherly Love.

By her third cup of coffee she managed to make a clean sweep of the house, choose the perfect shoes to go with her new jeans and sweater, and scrawl 'Cheri Collins' in bulging crayoned letters across a piece of poster board before heading out to buy a bunch of cheesy balloons on the way to the airport. The hour and a half drive gave her plenty of time to carry on mock conversations with the girl who, in less than a year at Boston University, became like the sister she never had.

Charlie felt giddy with anticipation as she walked through Philadelphia International with her balloons waving in the air above her head. When she finally made her way to Terminal B she found a large crowd waiting on the public side of the exit lanes, all laughing and chatting together as if they were having a party before their party arrived from wherever they were coming from. Soon a scruffy group of hunky boys wearing matching jackets rounded the corner, carrying pillows and backpacks and looking very much like a team who lost the big game. As soon as their feet hit the safe zone they were rushed by cheering family and friends with comforting hugs. Behind them lone travelers with cell phones pasted to their ears wove into the chaos joined by a group of tanned tourists sporting smug looks that said, "I went to Barbados and you didn't."

Once the excitement settled and the whole lot of them began to make their way to baggage, Charlie finally found a spot with a clear view of the next round of incoming travelers. It was all she could do to stand still and hold her little sign against her chest while the balloons bounced up and down like a bunch of crazed bobble heads. It was this kind of stupid humor she missed more than she allowed herself to remember. Finally, she spotted Cheri moving through the sea of people with the grace of a prima ballerina. Tears welled up in her eyes and as she raised her hand to wave Cheri's attention in her direction, the balloons took flight filling the space like a flock of helium-filled birds studding the air with bursts of shinning color. Several children broke through the security barrier trying to catch them, while their anxious parents chased after their children, and a throng of security officials with their hands pressed firmly against their holsters chased after the parents. It was a moment they would remember for years to come.

Once the chaos settled down, Cheri and Charlie folded into each other's arms laughing and crying. After several minutes of yakking about the flight and the odd little man who sat next to Cheri on the plane, they headed off arm in arm to retrieve the bags that were filled to the brim with enough clothes, trinkets, and toiletries, to last through all four seasons of Delaware's ever-changing weather.

The click of seatbelts marked the beginning of their trip back into a friendship that had been put on hold for far too long. "So, I figured we'd spend a couple of nights together at the beach house and then you can decide from there whether or not you'll want to move into my apartment near The Green. This is going to be such a blast, Cheri. You and I working together just like we always planned to do before you got sick and had to move back home." Charlie reached over and squeezed Cheri's hand, "I've missed you like crazy, Cheri. You're like the most comfortable pair of shoes ever made."

"Gee thanks, being a pair of your shoes raises me to a level that up until now I could only have aspired to. Now tell me about your mom. I felt so horrible when I got your email about her. I've been praying for her nonstop."

Charlie filled her in on all the details of Ellie Mae's descent into Alzheimer's. "It's like she's here but she's not here, Cheri. And I'm scared to death that I'm going to forget that she's the mother and I'm the daughter. I mean, here I am taking over her house, which is now *my* house, making major decisions about her health, paying her bills, sorting through her finances and deciding how to dispose of her dead kitty. And she's too young for all this. It's so not fair. Not for her. Not for me. Not for anyone. No one should have to go through this, Cheri. No one! Well maybe Jeffery, but no one else!"

Cheri groaned at the sound of his name. "Ugh. I wondered how long it would take for his name to slither into the conversation. But I know how you feel, Charlie, I really do. I had a great mom and a great dad, who worked hard to give me every possible opportunity for success. And now look at me. I'm a successful orphan. Both my parents are gone, and there's no one here to look at me and say, "Congratulations Cheri, you did what you set out to do. We're so proud of you!"

Charlie nodded, "I get that. But maybe that's why you're here. So we can fill in those missing gaps for each other."

"Yeah, I think you're right. You know when I went back to Wisconsin, and everything felt just so foreign to me, all I could think about was all those times together in our dorm, sharing everything from our hearts to our clothes, to our dreams for our futures."

"Until you woke up crying in pain and had to be rushed to emergency."

"Yeah, until that."

"I'll never forget sitting in the waiting room for hours wondering if I would ever see you again. How did we ever let ourselves lose each other, Cheri? When you moved back home we spent hours on the phone together. Then our lives got busy, you got better, we both immersed ourselves in school, then career, and before we knew it we became distant friends separated by time and space."

Cheri patted her heart with her hand. "But, Charlie, I've always kept you right here. And now here we are picking right up from where we left off as if no time has passed at all. It's like a snapshot of heaven where time is no longer divided between minutes, and hours, and days, and years."

A subtle scowl exposed Charlie's on-going war with all things religious. "And there's yet another thing I just don't get about God. If He's this great Eternal Being who lives up there without the stress of a ticking clock hounding Him with time, how can He expect us to follow His example when all we have are endless days with endless stress and endless problems that have no answers? Honestly, Cheri, I'm trying to understand Him but the truth is, most of the time I just don't."

"I know. I know how hard it is to hold on when it feels like everything you love is slipping away. But, we live in a broken, fallen world, my friend, and I don't know about you, but I don't think I could make it through today if I didn't have tomorrow to look forward to. I think time is just a huge gift God has given to us to keep us from giving up. When I went home I was sick in heart and body and I was angry. But after a while I started noticing that the days were passing by and new days were coming in to take their place. And finally I realized how amazing a new day can be. And now here I am - living in a new day."

They drove the last few miles in thoughtful silence broken only by the bumping of the wheels on the broken pavement leading to home. "Here we are. And here it is; a job that's way too big for both of us. So, my optimistic partner in design, are you ready to walk into your new day?"

Cheri stared at the old beach house while Charlie looked over the jumble of luggage wedged into every available space in her car. "Wow, we've got our work cut out for us, don't we?"

"Yes, we do, Cheri. So let's just take the two red roller bags and the rest can stay right here until you need them." When they opened the door to the kitchen they were greeted by a table full of goodies. "It looks like Bernie's been here. She's on a mission to rid me of my love for skinny jeans!"

"Sheesh! How did she do all this?" Cheri laughed as she checked out the table stacked with plates and bowls and colorful foil bags filled with enough fat and calories to call for an intervention by Weight Watchers. "Look at all this. Popcorn. Chex Mix. Lay's Potato Chips. And are these homemade Snickerdoodles? French onion dip. Fruit. Nuts. It's a veritable feast!"

Charlie picked up the note propped against two large plastic bottles of Coke. After reading through the long verse about the blessings of friendship she read Bernie's hand scrawled message out loud, *"Now you two girls just climb into your sweats and have yourself a good time catching up on each other's lives. And don't you dare come up for air until every last bit of this is gone. Pizza will be delivered at six. And there's a pan full of cinnamon rolls in the fridge, just heat them up when you're ready for breakfast. Love, Bernie"*

After wheeling the bags up the stairs and depositing them in the guest room, Charlie and Cheri obediently followed Bernie's orders. "I do love my sweats. And I'm starving – airplane food is pretty much non-existent these days. You're lucky to get a bag of peanuts. So I say let's head for the kitchen!"

With the coffee table filled with snacks they shoved the furniture around so they could sit as close to each other as possible. Balancing a plate of chips, dip, and cookies on her lap with a tall glass of Coke in hand, Cheri headed straight to the girl stuff. "So he's a doctor, he's a dad, he loves donuts, and he's sort of married, sort of not married. Sounds perfect."

"I know. Believe me, I know. But you're right - he *is* perfect. And that's the problem. He's too perfect. How that woman was able to walk out on him and leave a three-month-old baby behind is more that I can wrap my head around. And yet instead of hating her, Mac just absorbed all the blame and did whatever it took to protect his son. That's why he never divorced Irene. For the first couple of years he just kept expecting her to forgive *him* for whatever it was *he* did and come back to them. But that never happened. Then he was so busy being a father to Zak and taking care of sick people that he didn't have time to think about the state of his marriage. And now I'm falling in love with a man who's opened up his whole life to me and who thinks I've done the same with him. But I haven't and I don't know if I can."

Cheri's eyes closed the way they always did when she was searching for just the right thing to say. "Well, if this man is as perfect as you think he is, and if he's been able to move beyond the woman who walked out on her husband and her baby, why do you think he'd turn his back on you for something you did long before you knew him? We were all young once, Charlie. And we all have the scars to prove it."

"Yeah, I guess. Maybe I'm afraid to tell him because I can't forgive myself for what I did. You're the only one who knows, Cheri. You and Jeffery."

Her nostrils flared at the mention of his name. "I don't want to talk about Jeffery. Just the thought of him makes me want to throw up." She began brushing the crumbs of her cookie off her lips trying to compose the sudden surge of anger that threatened to take their conversation to a place where she had no intention of going. "Think about it. You just said Mac took on all the blame for what his wife did and yet you're doing pretty much the same thing. You're taking on all the blame for something that would never have happened if that disgusting creature hadn't done what he did. Right?"

"I don't know, Cheri. I agreed to it all."

"You were afraid not to."

"I don't know. It's not like he held a gun to my head. I was just so in love with him, or I thought I was in love with him, that I couldn't think straight. It's like my life is divided into two pieces of time; before Jeffery and after Jeffery. So, how do I tell the man I'm falling in love with, the man who has arranged everything in his life around the welfare of his son, that the woman he thinks I am killed her baby before it was born? How do I tell Mac that I may not be able to have another child? How can I do that to him, Cheri? The thought of hurting him is more than I can cope with."

"Charlie, if you didn't love him, it wouldn't matter. Don't you see? Your fear of hurting Mac only proves how perfect you are for him. Your past isn't your present. You're not the same girl who fell under the spell of Jeffery Allen Luckeroth. Mac has fallen in love with the woman you are today. God is doing a work in your life, Charlie; a work your mother's prayed for, I've prayed for, and your dear sweet Bernie has prayed for. So, my friend, when are you going to give up the fight, fall into Jesus' arms, and be an answer to all our prayers?"

"Mother knew, Cheri. I don't know how or what she knew, all I know is that on *November 16ᵗʰ, 1999,* my mother understood that something terrible was happening to her daughter."

Cheri's thoughts were spinning with questions. "How's that possible?

The only people who knew were me and Jeffery. And I can't imagine Jeffery having the guts to tell your mother what he did to you. So who told her? How did she find out?"

"No one told her, Cheri. I'm telling you, she just knew. I came home from the hospital one night and picked up one of Grampa's devotionals and while I was flipping through it I spotted my name written above one of the pages. So, I flipped back and there it was - *Charlie, November 16th, 1999* written across the top of the page of that day's reading. I never slept that whole night. The next morning I rushed to the hospital and started pressing my Mother with all kinds of questions - questions she was in no condition to answer. Days later I found this beautiful red satin box in Mother's armoire. It was filled with hand written pieces of music with every piece named and dated. It was like finding a musical journal charting all kinds of special days in Mother's life, like the day she married my father, the day Basil died, and the day Grampa went to heaven. I had no idea she was so brilliantly gifted. Seriously Cheri, each piece is like a work of art. Anyway, when I got to the bottom of the box I found a piece called *Coming Home,* and under the title she wrote, *For my Charlie, November 16th, 1999.* Cheri, she wrote that song on the very same day I had the abortion."

Cheri raised her hand to her lips. "Oh, Charlie, I can't even believe this. I'm speechless. You mean all this time she never said anything? Astounding. So did you play the song? What's it like? I'd love to hear it."

"Yes! I played it. And, yes it's beautiful. And no, I'm not ready to play it for you yet because the strangest thing happened after I found it. Once I started playing it I couldn't stop. I just played it over and over again for what felt like hours. And when I finally went to sleep my brain was like a tape recorder stuck on repeat. I couldn't have been asleep for very long before I woke up with lyrics flowing through the notes. I grabbed a tablet and wrote them down as fast as they were coming to me. I ran to the piano to see how they fit with the notes Mother wrote. They were perfect! I mean absolutely perfect. But the verses only come in little clusters at a time. I know it must sound ridiculous but I'm afraid I'll break the spell of it all if I share it with anyone before it's finished. It just feels so private; like someone's whispering the message in little doses at a time. Weird isn't it? Am I going crazy, Cheri?"

"Oh no, my friend," Cheri said. "You're not going crazy. You're just coming home."

After the pizza was delivered Charlie and Cheri grabbed their sketch books and got to work, examining every room of the old beach house, moving walls, choosing colors, changing out windows, and adding space to the already spacious home her grandfather built. There was such a sense of reverence in their work that Charlie felt as if all her fears of moving in on her mother's territory were being put to rest.

Hours passed before they emptied all their ideas onto the blank pages of their sketch books. Too exhausted to climb the stairs they simply fell back into their chairs in the living room and fell asleep in the middle of a conversation which neither of them would remember by morning.

Somewhere between sleep and stirring the song began to play through the quietness of Charlie's subconscious space. Trying not to disturb Cheri, who was purring contentedly in her chair, she tiptoed over to the piano, lifted the lid of the bench, and pulled out the tablet where the words to her song were waiting to be finished. The beam of the rising sun was just beginning to flicker through the window offering her enough light to see her words scrawled across the page.

As she hummed through the last phrase of what had already been written, a rush of verses pressed into her soul like guests scrambling for their place at the table.

So afraid to call Your Name
Seems I'd gone too far
Your love forgives the distance
And builds a bridge to where You are
Free to run, Free to fall
Love let me go

Ellie's Window: Surrender
And Love calls me home
With each step
I hear Your voice
Whispering my name.
Coming Home
I'm coming home.

Tears warmed her cheeks as she held the finished song close to her chest. The assembly of verses had become a portrait of surrender. Oh God. It's true isn't it? This is my song. This is my story. This is the answer to my mother's prayers. That's what this has all been about . You've been calling me to come home. My answer is 'yes.' Yes to You. Yes to coming home.

In the same way,
There is more joy in heaven over one lost sinner
who repents and returns to God
Than over ninety-nine others who are righteous and haven't strayed away!
Luke 15:7 NLB

Chapter Twenty-Three

Audrey had heard the applause of heaven countless times before. Thunderous peals of joy rising up in songs of praise for the prodigals who had turned the corner that leads to home. These were among Eternity's highest moments of celebration marking another victory won by Love. And this time the celebration was for Charlie.

Her thoughts went back to her stroll through the trees with Jesus as He explained to her the undying work of prayer.

"Audrey, when do you think these leaves sprouted from their limbs?"

"Oh, how could I ever know? They look so fresh and new, like they just uncurled from their buds today."

"Exactly, My wise daughter, for the leaves on Heaven's trees never wither or fade. And so it is with prayer, Audrey."

She ran to the portals where her books were waiting. Audrey leaned over and blew a kiss through the space that connected her to her daughter. You're just as beautiful as always. She picked up her pen and began to write as quickly as her fingers would allow.

Oh, my dear Anne, I wish with all my heart you could see what I see; your precious Charlie has just become an answer to your devoted, tearful, insightful, prayers. You are not a stone. Your life is not over. Your prayers are producing a harvest of righteousness right before Heaven's eyes. And soon you will know what the saints who have gone before you know. Our God is faithful. He has heard the cries of your heart and He has done it!

"Charlie? Charlie, are you alright?" Cheri kneeled down and tapped Charlie's shoulder as she lay on the braided rug near the window. Charlie yawned deep and loud as she curled her back and stretched her long arms as if she had been inhabited by the return of Princess Leia.

"Wow, I can't remember the last time I've slept so hard." Charlie looked up at the alarm in Cheri's face. "I'll bet you think I've been sleep walking."

"Well it does sort of look that way. The last thing I remember was the two of us snuggled into our chairs and drifting off to sleep in the middle of a brilliant conversation. I woke up expecting you to be in the kitchen making coffee, but instead here you are on the floor with your afghan. So yeah, it looks like a case of sleep-walking to me. Unless, of course, you've developed a yen for hardwood."

"Cheri, it happened again. The song. It came to me while I was sleeping. So I got up and grabbed my tablet, then I moved over here to the window so I could see what I was writing down. I didn't want to disturb you while you were - *purring*. After I wrote the last word I felt like everything in my life just fell into place. He was here, Cheri. I couldn't see Him but I knew He was right here with me. He loves me. Jesus loves me."

Cheri sat on the floor locking eyes with her friend. "Yes, He does, Charlie." She picked up the tablet. "So is this it? Can I read it? Don't bother saying *no* because I'm going to anyway."

Wrapping the afghan around her shoulders Charlie watched Cheri's face break into an approving smile. "So, what do you think?"

"I think it's beautiful, Charlie. It's like the story of your life has been written into song. Come on. Get up. You need to play it on the piano so I can hear how the words fit into the melody."

They got up from the floor and moved over to the piano bench. Charlie lifted the lid and leaned the tablet against the wooden stand above the keys. "Where's the music?"

"It's all right here and right here." Charlie pointed her index finger to her head and then to her heart. Her fingers ran across the keys in free and flowing rhythms. "Mother would never let me play anything without running through at least one scale first. I hated playing scales, but now I just love them, don't you? I mean, listen to them, they're beautiful. So melodic and so, I don't know, but the word *purposeful* comes to mind."

"Cruel is what's coming to mind. You're very cruel, Charlie Mondary. Now quit stalling and play."

"Okay, but you know I can't sing, so you're going to have to sing along with me or this song is going to lose its beauty before I get through the first verse."

The two voices blended together in almost perfect harmony as the words filled the living room with a concert of unrehearsed worship.

"It's wonderful, Charlie. It's like a musical journey of transformation from dark to light, from pride to humility, from lost to found, written before you knew where the words were taking you."

Cheri picked up the tablet and held it close to her heart. "This is such an amazing answer to prayer, Charlie."

"My mother's prayers?"

"Oh, absolutely, your mother is a tenacious prayer warrior. But Charlie, I've been praying, too." Cheri took Charlie's hands in hers as if their hearts were at last meeting in the place where their friendship first began. "I never wanted us to grow so far apart, but after I left college I was just so sick and my life was such a mess that all I wanted to do was crawl into a hole and die. I begged God to either show Himself to me or just kill me in my bed. Then one day I felt His presence breathing mercy over me like a fresh wind. His presence was so real, and I fell so in love with Him that all I wanted to do was to get to know Him more. Mononucleosis saved me, Charlie, it gave me lots of time to spend reading Psalms and the Gospels, and everything I could get my hands on that would reacquaint me with this God who rescued me from emotional death. But then the closer I got to Him the further you drifted away from me. Does that make sense, Charlie? Did you feel it too?"

"It makes perfect sense. I felt it too. Every time we talked on the phone you became more and more of a stranger to me. And I hated it. I felt like you were so busy becoming this perfect little Mother Theresa, while I was be-coming Madonna. But I was running, Cheri, from God, and from anything that even slightly smacked of being *religious!* I told myself it was because I'd evolved above the Sunday School, Bible verse memorizer, off to become a missionary in Africa, little darling my mother raised me to be. But I was just so filled with grief and guilt that it was all I could do to outrun the voice haunting me in the night when there was nothing to do but listen. But I'm tired of running, Cheri. I just want to sit and be found. I just want to come home to the God I knew before I put on my running shoes." After a few moments of letting her words settle into the quiet space in their conversa-tion, Charlie gasped. "Cheri, what if all this Jesus stuff causes Mac to think I've gone and jumped off the edge of my psychological pier?"

"You mean you and he haven't talked about your religious backgrounds?"

Charlie snorted through her laughter, "Obviously you don't date much. Trust me, Cheri, nothing can kill a love life quicker than a religious fanatic in search of the *perfect match.*"

"You're right. I don't date much. In fact, I don't date at all. Men scare me. Anyway, I'm not looking for a *religious* man, but I wouldn't mind it too much if God sent me a good man, who loves Jesus, and lives like he loves Jesus. But so far that hasn't happened. And I'm good with that. I like my life right now, and I like that you're back in it." Rising up from the piano bench, Cheri pat-ted her friend on her head, stretched out her arms and yawned, before resting her hand on her stomach. "I know this is crazy after all the stuff we consumed last night, but I'm starving! I'd hate to insult dear Bernie by not devouring that plate of cinnamon rolls. So, let's zap 'em in the micro and when we've finished our food frenzy we can go see your mom before you take me over to meet the man who has your heart all a flutter. And tonight we can map out our plan for how we're going to turn this old place into a magazine cover."

Charlie hung her arm over Cheri's shoulder giving her a sweet squeeze as they marched their way to the kitchen, "Always the perfect planner! Get ready world, the dynamic duo is back in town and we're open for business!"

"Yes, we are! And we're better, and stronger, and able to leap over slow moving turtles in a single bound!"

"Lord, I've missed you!"

Jesus said to the people who believed in him, "You are truly my disciples if you remain faithful to my teachings. And you will know the truth, and the truth will set you free."
John 8:31-32

Chapter Twenty-Four

Lush green trees peeking through the overhanging clouds provided the backdrop for their drive to Still Waters. The scenes along the way felt familiar to her. The brick houses, seafood restaurants, a Dunkin Donuts on every corner, and the road signs that oozed with the history of America's beginnings with names like Middleton, Wilmington, Rehoboth, and New Castle. She loved it here. And yet she feared it. She feared the memories of the event that sent her away from what had been her favorite place to live. But now wasn't the time to regurgitate the past, so she shifted her attention to her friend who seemed to be sorting through some fears of her own. "What's it like for you, Charlie? You make this drive almost every day to see your mother and every day you start out hoping things will be better and every day you leave knowing nothing has changed."

"It's just exactly like that, Cheri. I swear I could write a book about dashed hope. But this morning feels different somehow. I feel like I've been missing something that's been right under my nose all along, only I don't know what that something is. I'm sounding crazy aren't I?" Charlie paused in mid paragraph giving her thoughts time to catch up with her feelings. Then it hit her. She saw it all with perfect clarity. "I know what it is. I'm falling in love with my mother all over again. I feel like I did when I was little. I had this little girl love for *'my mommy'*. She was everything I wanted to be and more. Beautiful. Gifted. Sweet. And I knew I was her whole world and I loved her for that. Then everything changed. I grew up."

"And you met Jeffery!"

Cheri's words added a new layer to Charlie's unfolding revelation. "You're right, Cheri, it all changed after Jeffery. It's like I began to see my mother through different eyes. She became, I don't know how to describe it. She became pitiful and hopelessly needy. And the more I saw her that way the more I felt guilty for not liking her, and the guiltier I felt the more I blamed her for every painful thing that's ever happened to me. Life was all about *me* and spending time with my mother was something to check off my *To Do* list. I became dutiful, but not devoted. I can't imagine how that must have made her feel. Oh, Cheri, I have so much to make up for. And all I want to do is grab hold of her and tell her how sorry I am, but she isn't there. I come here every day hoping to find her. And she isn't there." Charlie raised her fist to her cheeks to stop the flow of tears that refused to stay put. "I'm sorry. There's something about being around you that makes me want to spill my guts all over the place."

"It's called friendship." Just speaking those words confirmed to Cheri that she was exactly where she needed to be. As scary as it was. "Now let's go see that beautiful lady. She's in there somewhere, Charlie. Let's go try to find her."

Megan was her usual chirpy self as Charlie and Cheri walked through the doors of Still Waters. "So what's on tap for today, Megan? Whatever it is I hope it's good and strong because my friend and I had a bit of a slumber party last night and we could really use a few double shots of caffeine right about now."

"We've gone Kenyan again," Megan answered like a barista who just consumed more of her product than her customers. "It's dark and rich and oh so good. So is this your sister, or your cousin? The two of you look totally related."

Charlie and Cheri burst out laughing while sizing up their obvious differences. "What gave it away - her blonde hair and blue eyes, or green eyes and red hair? No, Megan we're not related. This is Cheri. She's been my best friend since college and she's moving here for a while to help me do a complete makeover of my mother's home."

"Wow. So you're both like *real* designers, right? Like on HGTV."

Jodie arrived just in time to rescue Charlie and Cheri from Megan's enthusiasm. "Hey, Charlie, I'm so glad you're here. Good news. We've just moved your mother back to her room. She's doing so much better. Everything in her system is stable and she's even showing some significant signs of recognition."

After another round of introductions, Jodie led Charlie and Cheri to Ellie Mae's room. She was right. Ellie Mae was sitting up in bed and looking more alert than Charlie had seen her in weeks. "Oh, Charlie, you're here. Come and sit down and tell me all about your day. And who's this pretty girl with you?"

"Mother, do you remember Cheri? She was my roommate at Boston University."

"No, I've never seen her before. But I'm glad she's here. I'm bored without my window."

Charlie moved a chair close to her mother and motioned for Cheri to sit down while she sat on the edge of Ellie Mae's bed. She took hold of her mother's hand. "Would you rather be sitting by your window today, Mother?"

"No, no window today. Anne is busy. Anne can't come today, maybe tomorrow. Tomorrow is another day, you know."

"Yes, tomorrow is another day. Remember how we used to sing all the songs from Annie? 'Tomorrow', was our favorite." Charlie began singing while Cheri joined in and soon it became a quartet of Cheri, Charlie, Jodie, and even Ellie Mae, though the lyrics were a bit scrambled and the harmony wasn't all that harmonious. From there the conversation bounced from Anne to applesauce and how Ellie Mae's nightgown felt scratchy around her wrist. Nevertheless, it was a good day at Still Waters. Her mother seemed better and yet it all felt different in ways that Charlie had only begun to understand.

Two hours later Charlie parked her car in front of the Newsstand & Café on Lookerman Street before she and Cheri headed off to 33 West Ale House and Grill giggling like school girls along the way. As soon as they stepped through the door of the restaurant Charlie saw Mac waving at her from a table in the back. He was looking particularly handsome in his plaid shirt and jeans. She loved that he could pull off the casual doctor look without losing the dignity of his profession. Cheri leaned her head in close to Charlie's ear and whispered, "Oooh, he's not at all un-adorable is he?"

"I was able to snatch the last table so have a seat. I've got exactly one hour before I have to head back to the office. It's been a crazy day. Everyone has the flu but I'll spare you the details. Just trust me when I say Dover is about to experience a shortage of paper towels and bleach."

"Wow, that's way more information than we need to know right before we order lunch." Changing the subject as quickly as possible, Charlie turned her attention to Cheri. "Mac, this is my friend, Cheri Collins. Cheri, this is Mac MacKenzie. Cheri's been living in Portland for the last few years so we've had a lot to catch up on, and we've hardly had any sleep, and we've been eating nonstop since she arrived. And I have no idea why I felt a need to tell you all that."

Mac reached out his hand to Cheri as he pulled out a chair for her to sit down. "Portland, as in lobsters - Maine? Or Portland, as in Voodoo Donuts - Oregon?"

"You know about Voodoo Donuts? I'm impressed. I guess our *Keep Portland Weird* campaign is doing its job."

His left eyebrow rose up in protest. "I see nothing weird about donuts, Ms. Collins."

"Seriously Mac, could you please give her a few minutes before you scare her to death with your goofy humor?"

"Okay! You heard it. She's finally admitted that I'm funny! My work here is done. We can all go home!"

The time passed quickly as Cheri, Charlie, and Mac, traded stories of the foods they love, the movies they hated, and the places they wanted to see before they grew too old to see them. There was just enough seriousness to their conversation to give Cheri an eye for what kind of a man Dr.

MacKenzie was and just enough ribbing to tell her that he was perfect for Charlie. After the bill was paid and the goodbyes were said, Charlie and Cheri stepped into the wind and quickly climbed into her car. "So, what do you think about Mac?"

"I think I've just met the man you're going to marry."

"What? No way! We're not ready for the "M" word yet. We're still at the *maybe* stage. Oh, I guess that's an "M" word too, isn't it?" Charlie looked at Cheri while turning the key in the ignition. "But he isn't at all un-adorable is he." Remembering where they were, Charlie turned off the engine. "Wait a minute. What are we doing? My apartment's right down the block. Come on. Let me show you my home away from home."

After walking through all the rooms of Charlie's apartment they grabbed a couple of bottles of water from the fridge, flopped on the sofa, and put their feet up on the coffee table. "You've done a great job with this space, Charlie. It suits all our needs perfectly. The master bedroom is big enough for the two of us to share. Since I *purr* and you don't snore at all, the most we'll have to do is take out your queen sized bed and replace it with two twin beds and add an extra dresser. It'll be a little tight but it's manageable. And since we both love clothes and shoes, you can keep the closet and I'll hang my stuff in the closet in the office. I think we should move in here as soon as the design for the beach house is finished and the contractors are hired, that way we'll be closer to your mother, closer to the businesses we'll be needing to work with, and closer to the restaurants because we're so not going to have time to cook for ourselves and dear Bernie can't keep feeding us the way she has since yesterday or we're going to end up five sizes larger than we want to be. Is there a gym nearby?"

"Yes, my babbling friend. How you can run through a zillion topics in just a few sentences is purely amazing. I have a membership at Club Fitness over on Bay Road. Of course I haven't been there since Mother moved to

Still Waters, but I'm all paid up and I can get you in on a guest pass."

Quickly changing subjects Charlie continued. "So I guess the first thing we need to do, starting tomorrow, is to begin drawing up a solid plan for all the changes and upgrades and then we can start interviewing the contractors. You know I always want to jump ahead to choosing colors and shopping for furniture and accessories so it's going to be all I can do to stay focused on the daily grind of details, details, and more details. I hate project management."

"See, Charlie, that's why we're so good together. I love project management. It's a control thing. I love telling people what to do and I love cracking the whip if they don't. Who knows, this could be the start of the company we dreamed about when we were young design students in Boston. What did we call it? Blonde and Red - Heads in Design?"

"Yeah, but then that happened at two in the morning after too much beer and pizza. Then we got serious and I think we settled on C & C Partners in Design. I'm so glad we didn't waste our money on that one," Charlie yawned through her words, "that was a serious snoozer."

"Well," Cheri said, "remember we were trying to be dignified and respectable. But we're a long ways past graduation, and several years into experience, so we can afford to be unstuffy and think outside the box. You know if we're going to share this job together we're probably going to need a workable company name that reflects our glowing, albeit exhausted, personalities. So think about it, Charlie, once the beach house is finished and we publish the before and after photos in *Elle Décor* we'll need something that makes people say, *'now there's a couple of savvy gals that can take us from blah to - ah-h-h-h.'*"

"Ah Ha!" Charlie jumped right in, "I knew once you got here you wouldn't want to leave. We could, you know, go into business together. Why not? Two are better than one. So, first things first. We need a name." Tapping her finger against her chin, she got up and walked around the living room trying to pull ideas out of the air. "Okay, so let's say we draw off *create* because, of course, we're two highly creative women. Create Inc. 2Create. We Create. Nah! Don't like them."

"But it's a great start, Charlie. It reflects my heart for design. He's the

Creator, and I'm a re-creator. It's what I love about my job because I get to take what He's made and re-purpose it for people who don't know what to do with it."

"Okay, now you're on to something! So we need a name that expresses what it means to re-create. I like that." After a moment of concentrated silence an idea began to spark the right side of Charlie's brain. "I've got it. I think I've got it! Are you ready, because I think this might just be severely brilliant. Wait for it! It's coming!" As if a light bulb flashed in front of her she snapped her fingers and announced "Yes! And here it is - Design In-Creation. InCreation - as one word. Capital I – in and capital C – creation, joined together without a space in-between. InCreation. Design InCreation. Get it?" Charlie bowed in appreciation of Cheri's applause.

"That's it! You're right! It's brilliant! Our logo could have three swirls of color under the wording which would be classy without being over stated. No wait – too fluffy. How about copper swirls with gold letters set over a chocolate brown background. No, no, no - too masculine." Cheri paced across the room then turned back to Charlie and smiled with artistic victory, "How about three colors of metallic swirls, like copper, silver, and gold, set over a purple background with shiny black letters reading, *Design InCreation*. Embossed, of course."

"Love it! Big high five on Design InCreation with metallic swirls, black lettering, and purple card stock. We're awesome together, Cheri! Lord, I've missed you."

Just as they were about to celebrate the birth of their collaborative efforts, Charlie's phone rang from her purse. She quickly grabbed it and checked the caller I.D. "It's Mac."

"So answer it."

Charlie batted her eyes flirtatiously before sliding the green icon to the right. "Hello Mac."

"Hey Charlie, are you sitting down? Have you heard the news? If you're near a television you need to turn it on."

"You're watching television? Aren't you supposed to be making sick people well?"

"It popped up on my computer. This is serious, Charlie."

A jolt of fear wiped the smile off her face. "Why? What's happened?"

"Jeffery and his father have been arrested for insider trading along with a few other white collar crimes. They're being hauled off to jail as we speak. Looks like your old friend is finally getting what's coming to him."

Charlie felt her face flush red with fury. Wrapping her hand over her phone she mouthed to Cheri to turn on the television before returning to her conversation with Mac. "And you're finding pleasure in that – why? Is this a side of your character I should be concerned about?"

Silence filled the space between them. "I'm sorry, Charlie, but I'm having trouble understanding why you're so angry."

"I'm angry because you're sounding a little petty right now and I'm not sure I want to go down this road with you so unless you can explain yourself I think I'm going to be forced to hang up on you until you can behave like a grown-up."

Mac lowered his voice, "Okay Charlie, calm down. I'm sorry, I just…"

"And here's something else, Doctor MacKenzie, don't ever tell a woman to *calm down*, it will only make her more furious. Seriously, you're really a dork when it comes to understanding women." Her words cut deep into the flesh of Mac's heart.

"And I've got work to do so I'll just be saying goodbye now. I'll call you later." The click of the phone ended their conversation.

Charlie and Cheri sat on the sofa in stunned silence as images of Jeffery and his father, with their hands cuffed behind their backs, filled the television screen while the reporter announced the breaking news.

"At eleven-thirty this morning Attorneys Harold J. Luckeroth and his son Jeffery Allen Luckeroth were arrested in their offices on North State Street on charges of embezzlement, fraud, and insider trading. The sting operation spanned over two years of investigation by the FBI and the Department of Justice, following a series of tips by two former female employees who worked for Luckeroth and Luckeroth Attorneys at Law. Both father and son will be held without bail in the Dover City Jail until their arraignment on Friday. More on this breaking story at six o'clock here on WBOC TV – 16, Delmarva's News Leader. We will now return you to the Dr. Oz show still in progress."

Cheri's face went pale as she turned to Charlie, "Is this what you and

Mac were fighting about? Jeffery? Are you crying, Charlie, because Mac is mad at you or because Jeffery's been arrested?"

"I did love Jeffery at one time, Cheri. I can't help feeling sorry for him. He was in handcuffs for Pete's sake. What am I supposed to do? Laugh at him? Do a happy dance in front of his jail cell?"

After pacing the floor for a few minutes, Charlie turned around to explain her unexplainable emotions. "He's not all bad Cheri. It's not like he was Satan incarnate. We were both kids. We were trying to find who we were and where we were going. There were times when he was sweet and kind and full of hope for our future. I think he was just so confused about life and so afraid of disappointing his father. We were just..."

In mid-sentence, Cheri rushed to the bathroom covering her mouth with one hand while holding her stomach with the other. Charlie waited by the bathroom door having no idea what to do. "Cheri? Are you okay? Was it something you ate?" No answer. She went back to the living room and fell into the sofa feeling confused and helpless – worried about her friend and terrified that Mac might just have walked out of her life forever. I can't blame him. How can I expect him to understand me when I don't understand me? I called him a dork. I scolded him like he was twelve. What was I thinking? Now Cheri is sick. What if I lose her too? Oh, God, I don't know what to do.

She was still arguing with herself when Cheri came back to the living room wiping her face with a cold cloth. Pale and exhausted she looked at Charlie as if she were searching for the courage to explain her sudden exit from the conversation.

"I'm so sorry, Cheri. I didn't know you were sick. Are you okay? Do you need to go lay down?"

She turned to Charlie, biting the inside of her bottom lip. "Charlie, Jeffery is a lying, disgusting excuse for a human being. You can live in denial all you want to, but it won't change the things he's done to us, and to how many more women whose lives have been ruined because of his sociopathic ways."

Charlie's head reared back obviously confused by Cheri's outburst. "What? Where did that come from? I'm sorry, I don't understand. How did all this become about you? I mean, you and Jeffery hardly knew each other. I've always known you didn't like him, but what does that have to do with what you think he's done to *us*? Where did *us* come into this?"

The distance between them felt like a knife slicing through her heart. "Talk to me, Cheri. Because you're kind of scaring me right now."

She filled her lungs with as much air as they could hold then blew it out slowly before confessing the secret she had kept hidden since the day she left Boston U. "Alright, here it is, blunt and unabridged. He raped me, Charlie. A week before I collapsed in our room, Jeffery Luckeroth raped me.

"He came to our room one night while you were at the library. He told me he wanted to talk to me about you. So I let him in. His eyes were all glazed over like he'd been drinking. Then he just started yammering on about all kinds of stuff that didn't make sense. So, I told him I had a paper to write and that he needed to leave. That's when things got ugly. He grabbed hold of me and started kissing me. I tried to make him stop but he was too strong. Finally I just gave up. He put his hand over my mouth. From there everything just went dark.

"He stole my virginity and my dignity, Charlie, and when he was finished he just stood over me and laughed while I curled into a ball and cried. He told me no one, including you, would ever believe me. He said his father would annihilate me in court and make sure my future would be over before it even began. Then he patted me on the head and thanked me for being a good girl and keeping quiet about our little *'romp in the sheets.'*" Cheri stood up and pointed her finger at the television while she struggled to speak through her torrent of unstoppable tears. "That's your Jeffery, Charlie. That's the man you just defended. And that's the man who you're going to lose Mac over. And for what? Do you still love him? Are you still in love with that, that, thing that pretends to be a man?"

Feeling as if she had just been punched in the stomach, Charlie gasped for air. "No! No! Why?" She pressed her fists against her temples. "Oh, dear God. I didn't know. Oh Cheri, I had no idea. I'm so, so, so, sorry. How could he have done that to you?" The truth was invading her senses with such force that she felt as if she could hardly breathe. "It all makes sense now. Why you were so sick. Why you couldn't bear the sound of his name. And all the while I just kept calling you and giving you constant updates on how we were doing. And when I got pregnant. And the abortion. And all the while you were…How could I have been so stupid? What was I thinking? What's wrong with me? How can you ever forgive me for not seeing it?"

Cheri's heart broke with compassion. "Charlie, I should have told you. You didn't know because I never said a word about it. I couldn't. I was just so ashamed and confused. And scared. I spent two years thinking it was my fault."

"And you were sick, Cheri. You were so very sick. It wasn't your fault."

"You're right. It wasn't my fault. But it wasn't *your* fault either. It was Jeffery. We were innocent but he was guilty of lying, and cheating, and …rape. Who know how many victims have stories just like ours."

"But he didn't rape me."

"Really? Then answer me this - did you ever try to tell him 'no'? Did you ever tell him you didn't want to cross that line with him? Did you start out agreeing to have sex with him or did it all just come down to you giving him what he wanted?"

Like curtains being opened to the light, the truth of her relationship with Jeffery began to uncover all those nagging voices that hounded her in the night when he wasn't around to put his own spin on them. "I – I, did, Cheri. The first few times we *made love* or whatever it was we were doing, I did say no. At least I tried to say no, but he was so persuasive. I just remember feeling yucky afterwards. There were times when I would look in the mirror and wonder why I hated doing the things we were doing – and why I was pretending I didn't. But then as time went on I just figured that we were as good as married anyway."

"Because he told you, you were as good as married, right?"

"Yeah. He told me a lot of things, Cheri. And I believed every single one of them. I believed he would be faithful to me, but he wasn't. I believed he would love me after the abortion. But he didn't. And after we broke up I felt used and ruined. I think I felt tied to him because I never believed any man would love me if they knew what kind of woman I really am."

"Deceit is a dark path that leads to destruction. And he took you down that path, Charlie. Believe me I know. It took a long time for me to find my way back. Maybe that's why God sent me here. Maybe it's not about remodeling the Beach House. Maybe it was to help you find your way back. Just like your mother's song:

Ellie's Window: Surrender
'Free to run, free to fall,
Love let me go and Love calls me home.'

It's a new day, Charlie. It's time to let Jeffery pay the price for his sin. And it's time for both of us to put the past behind us and begin our new day."

Charlie wiped the tears off her face and brushed the hair away from her eyes. "I need to call Mac."

Beloved friends, let us love one another; because love is from God;
And everyone who loves has God as his Father and knows God.
1 John 4:7 Complete Jewish Bible

Chapter Twenty-Five

Charlie sent Cheri to the bedroom in her apartment for a much needed and well-deserved nap. Besides, she needed to be alone. She needed to sort through her emotions and come up with a plan for how she would apologize to Mac for the way she treated him. The pain of regret wrapped itself around her as she crumpled down on the sofa, hugging her knees to her chest and rocking back and forth. And for the second time in one day, Charlie turned her face to heaven and prayed. Earnestly. Simply. And with a humility of heart that felt new to her.

"Oh, God, where do I start? You know when it comes to prayer, I'm a hopeless babbler. So I'm just going to spew it all out and pray You can somehow make sense of it. Lord, I don't deserve a man like Mac. I don't want to lose him, but I don't know what to do. How do I tell him I'm sorry? I'm too afraid to even dial his number, but I can't bear knowing the pain he must be feeling right now. You know I haven't made a habit out of putting other people first and apologizing is like trying to speak in a foreign language. So here I am. Asking You for the one thing my heart needs most; help. Help me Lord. Help me. Please help me."

Charlie's phone rang before she had a chance to say 'amen.' It was Mac. Fear and excitement rushed through her trembling hands. All she needed to do was touch the key pad. Answer it you coward. Just press the button and say something. "Hello, Mac."

"Charlie, I'm so sorry. I shouldn't have thrown Jeffery's fiasco in your face like that. I don't know what I was thinking. I guess I just assumed, after the way he treated you…"

"Mac, stop! Please stop talking. I'm the one who's sorry – for so many things. I haven't been honest with you. Actually, I haven't been honest with myself either. I know I'm probably not making any sense right now, but Mac, we need to talk. Is there any way you can stop by my place? I'm at my apartment on Lookerman. Could you come by here after you leave your office?"

"If my patients weren't so sick I'd send them all home right now. As it is, it looks like I won't be able to leave here until around six or six-thirty. Will you still be there by then? If not I can come to the beach house. I'm sure my sister won't mind staying with Zak until I get home."

"No. Not the beach house. The extra driving time will just cut into your time with your son. I'll wait for you here. And Mac – you're not a dork when it comes to women. I'll text you the address. See you soon. Oh, and thank you."

By the time Cheri woke up from her nap the sun had already begun to fade into twilight. She walked into the living room and found Charlie lighting candles on the table off the kitchen. "So, are we having a ro-tic, as in romantic without the man evening, or is someone other than me going to be dining at this table with you very soon?"

"Mac's coming over. Soon. I know this is a terrible thing to ask of you, Cheri, but would you mind going somewhere so we can be alone? Like go out to dinner? All by yourself? Like an orphaned friend? I need to tell Mac about Jeffery, and my...well you know the rest."

"It's okay for you to say the word, Charlie. You had an abortion. I know this is scary for you but you're going to feel so much better once your secret is no longer a secret." Cheri reached out and hugged her as she whispered in her ear, "I'm so proud of you. And I would be honored to desert you so you can have some time alone with Mac. Remember, today is your new day, Charlie."

Stepping back she surveyed the table with aqua blue plates set on top of a cream colored cloth with matching napkins. Fresh white flowers with sprigs of shiny green leaves filled a glass bowl in the center of the table balanced by two crystal votive candles. "Wow, you did all this while I was sleeping?"

"All this and appetizers too. They're keeping warm in the oven. You've been sleeping for like a year, Cheri. I was just about to come in to see if you were still breathing." Charlie covered her stomach with both hands to calm the fluttering of butterflies inside. "I feel like a thirteen-year-old at a rock concert hoping Jon Bon Jovi will spot me in the crowd and ask me to marry him. I can't believe a man like Mac could really love me, Charlie Mae Mondary - the Queen of Insecurity and the Mistress of Screw Ups. Everything needs to be perfect. What if the good doctor doesn't do forgiveness? Think about it, Cheri, Irene *left* him. She walked out him. What if she left him because she couldn't live up to his expectations? What if I can't either?"

"And what if he doesn't forgive you?" Cheri said. "What will happen if the worst thing happens? What if he walks out that door and leaves you sitting at this table alone with nothing to hold on to but a broken heart?" Charlie's eyes blinked wide open as the fear of losing Mac nearly stopped her heart from beating.

"Charlie, will you really be alone? Because I'm standing here looking at a beautiful, talented, funny, strong woman, who has rediscovered the God who loves her. And I'm thinking He'll be enough to pick up the pieces and use every single one of them to make you better than you were before. Listen to me, my friend, if I've learned anything from all the worst things that have happened in my life it's this; you're safe when you're near to Him, because He is a God who will love you forever."

The chiming of a text message interrupted their conversation. "It's Mac. He's on his way. I hate to cut this Hallmark moment short, but you need to leave."

"Consider me out of here! I'll just go hit the mall, shop through a few stores and then find a place where I can have ice cream for dinner. So, just shoot me a text when it's safe to come home. I'm assuming we're going to spend the night here, right?"

"Yeah, but you'll have to pick up a couple of pairs of pajamas, and a box of Crunch 'n Munch. I'm pretty sure we're going to have a lot to talk about when you get back. You better make it two boxes. I don't share Crunch 'n Munch."

Charlie paced the floors fussing with the placement of her table settings while she waited for the fate of her future to come walking through her door.

And there it is. His, *I'm afraid to knock on her door so I'll just tap on it,* knock. She gave her hair a few fluffs with her fingers before she opened the door. The beauty of his smile and the vulnerability in his eyes stole the words right out of her head while Mac stared back at her like a boy who had just discovered the wonder of girls. Clearing his throat he handed her a gold box with a large silver ribbon. "They're truffles. Since my last peace offering was roses, I thought I'd change things up a bit. Plus, I figured they'd taste better than the foot I keep putting in my mouth."

She wanted to throw her arms around him and tell him what an adorable man he was and how she was falling completely and desperately in love with him, but the only words she could come up with was, "Thank you, Mac. Please come in." She took his coat and brought it into the bedroom.

"Wow, you've got a great place here. It's a lot bigger than it looks from the outside." Charlie walked over to the table hoping that he would run out of small talk. He didn't.

"I'd really love it if you would just come and sit down, Mac."

"Sure, I'd love that too." Mac pulled out the chair closest to him, "Is this okay? Or is this your chair? I can move to the other side."

"Mac, there're only two chairs to choose from. Seriously. You're making me more nervous than I already am." Mac pressed his lips together to keep himself from talking and sat down.

Charlie put the plate of warm crab and artichoke dip surrounded by peppered crackers on the table before pouring ice water into the goblets. After looking around to make sure she hadn't forgotten anything she sat down, unfolded her napkin and placed it across her lap. Mac followed her lead. She knew she would need to be the first one to break the silence. "Mac, I'm so sorry for the way I treated you on the phone." All her plans to step gingerly into her story changed the second she opened her mouth.

"There's so much about me and about my life you don't understand and there's no way you can understand until I come clean about my relationship with Jeffery. I'm afraid I'm not the virginal, innocent woman you think I am. That day when you told me you were married, I sat there acting all indignant because I thought you had deceived me. But, Mac, I'm the one who's been deceiving you. And I want you to know that if what I'm about to tell you leaves you wanting to run out that door, and forget you've ever met me, I'll completely understand. Because this isn't just about us, Mac, you have a little boy who needs his father to be wise about the women he allows into his life and I'm afraid I might not be that woman."

For the next hour Charlie recounted bits and pieces of her childhood and all those things that led up to her first encounter with Jeffery. Though he tried several times to get a word in edgewise she just kept going, determined to get to the point where her story turned tragic. The theft of her purity, the fear of losing the man she'd given her entire being to, and the day she walked into the clinic where her baby was severed from her body by the scrapings of a scalpel.

"I've learned a lot of things about Jeffery this afternoon. Things I wish I would have known a long time ago, but I was too naïve to accept them. The truth is, Mac, I don't think I ever really loved Jeffery. I feared him. And I think my fear of him kept me tied to him in ways that leave me feeling confused and ashamed. He's a terrible person and you were right to want him to get what's coming to him. That's why I needed to see you tonight. I needed to tell you that you were right and I was wrong, and I've been wrong for such a long time that I don't know how to make things right between us."

She looked into his eyes and tried to prepare herself for his quick and final exit. Instead Mac just sat there staring into her face as if he were trying to translate everything she'd just said into English. "So, is this it, Mac? Is this where you say good bye?"

He put his napkin back on the table. Her stomach knotted into a fist. He cleared his throat. She swallowed tears. At last the silence was broken. "No, Charlie, this is not where I say good bye. I'm just not very good with words when I'm angry."

"So you're mad at me."

"No. I'm not mad at you. How could I be mad at you for what that jerk did to you? When I think about how he talked about you that night at the loft, and how he gave me that sleaze ball grin when he looked at you!" His hands curled into white-knuckled fists. "He's lucky he's behind bars right now. If he weren't I just might be."

"I'm sorry," she said.

"I am, too. I'm sorry you felt like you had to hide all this from me. I'm sorry you thought I was this virginal guy who became the victim of a crazy wife. But I wasn't, Charlie. I've made a lot of mistakes. Irene was just one of them. My marriage to Irene was a nightmare from the beginning. Everyone but me saw through her. Everyone I knew told me not to marry her. My mother cried before, during, and after our wedding. My father couldn't look at me without growling. And my pastor refused to perform our ceremony. But the truth is, I married Irene because she was pregnant, Charlie. I got her pregnant. And to top that off, I never told anyone. I was so afraid of disappointing everyone that I just made up this pathetic story of how we were so in love that we couldn't wait to be together. Two weeks after our honeymoon, she lost the baby. Then later we had Zak and the rest is history.

"We're broken people, Charlie. We make mistakes. And sometimes it just takes years to mop up the messes they leave behind."

"But you learned from them. I just keep spinning out of control, hurting my mother, consuming myself with things that don't matter, and running back to Jeffery for reasons I don't understand. And I don't know how it all happened, Mac. I came from a loving home. I was raised to love God, respect purity, and honor my family. Instead I've shamed them all." Charlie's skin felt hot with embarrassment. With a desperate need for something cold she reached for the glass of ice water that was resting precariously near her elbow. In one quick swoosh of her hand the glass went flying, spilling the cold water across her lap before it crashed on the floor next to her feet.

Mac rushed to help her as she bolted out of her chair looking shocked and bewildered. He wrapped her in his arms and held her while she cried. "Charlie, it's just a small spill, we can clean it up later."

"I know. I don't deserve you, Mac. I don't deserve anything. Maybe it would be better for you to just cut your losses and run out that door and never think about me again."

He slipped his hand under her chin as his lips pressed against her forehead. "I love you, Charlie. And nothing you've done before we met is ever going to change that."

All the fear, and guilt, and stress she'd been carrying melted in his arms. "You're a good man. And you need a woman who will never leave you again, or hurt you, or embarrass you with the leftovers from her grimy past. You need a woman who won't come between you and your son."

"What I need, Charlie, is *you*. I need you and all your complicated ways. You make me want to buy flowers and truffles. You've turned me into the kind of guy who finds himself staring at his closet searching for something to wear. You make me worry about how my breath smells and whether or not I'm using the right fork at the table. I love you. I loved you before I knew your story and I love you more now. I've spent eight years running from girls who had their minds set on marrying a doctor. Then I saw you and all I could think of was, '*how can I win the love of this incredible woman*'. You're worth more than you think you are, Charlie. Don't ever let the Jefferies of this world tell you otherwise. And don't worry about Zak. He's eight! He loves anyone who loves soccer and ice cream. You do love soccer don't you?"

Charlie wiped her nose with her napkin and laughed apologetically, "I don't. But I'll give it my best shot."

He put his arm around her shoulders and led her to the sofa where they could sit together and without a table between them. "What about the abortion, Mac. What do we do about that? How do we get past that?"

"We look at it for what it is – a misguided decision that left you with a heart full of shame and regret. I see it all the time, Charlie. Women do all sorts of things they don't really want to do because they're afraid of being alone. Abortion, is what it is - the thief that keeps on stealing. And frankly, if Jeffery hadn't been the selfish brat that he is I doubt you would have ever walked into that clinic. Right?"

"I think so. No. I know so. But I still did it. And I agreed to it because I was afraid of losing him. How stupid is that?"

"Pretty stupid. But remember, we're broken people and broken people do stupid things. We're both prime examples of that." He held her face in his hands as he handed her a blessing she never felt worthy to receive, "Thank you for trusting me with your heart. I promise I'll do everything I can to not break it."

"Trust hasn't been easy for me." She reached up and webbed her fingers through his. "But, I trust you, Mac. I'm not very good at God talk, but I think – no I know, God brought us together for a reason. As I've been reading my mother's journals I've discovered what an amazing prayer warrior she is. I've heard that term so many times but it never made sense to me until now. My mother prayed constantly for me, now all the answers are raining down and she can't even see it happening."

"Who's to say what she sees and doesn't see? The mind is a mystery, Charlie. We can look into it and we can see all the waves of activity going on in it. But we can't see what it's thinking or what it's seeing. We're limited that way. So maybe your mother knows more than what we think she does. I wish my mom could meet her though because they would have a lot in common. That woman's been on her knees every day asking God for someone, just like you, to come and rescue her son from becoming a monk."

Charlie nestled her head into Mac's shoulder trying to savor the moment while her brain felt like a book that had been wiped clean of words. "I'm sorry, Mac. I'm so tired right now that I can't think of a thing to say. So I'm either going to just sit here and stare at your wonderful face or I'm going to have to kiss you. Which would you prefer?"

"I choose the latter."

She planted a series of kisses on his cheek explaining each one as they were delivered. "That, Doctor Mac, is for being such a great listener. This one is for looking past the terrible things I've done. This one is for loving me. And this one is to tell you that I love you back."

Blessed are all who fear the Lord, who walk in His ways.
You will eat the fruit of your labor; blessings and prosperity will be yours.
Psalm 128:1-2 NIV

Chapter Twenty-Six

Mac touched his face with the back of his hand as he drove home. The tenderness of Charlie's lips against his cheek aroused a host of thoughts and feelings he'd kept buried since the day Irene walked out of his life making him a single-father and sentencing him to a life of loneliness and celibacy.

He was drawn to Irene's dangerous kind of beauty. He slept with her in a fit of uncontrollable passion. And when she got pregnant, he married her out of a noble sense of duty. And yet love, real love, the kind of love that makes a man want to rise up and be a better man, was never part of the equation. I will never touch you, Charlie. I will never cross the boundaries with you. I will never ask you to do anything to compromise your well-being or leave you feeling ashamed and used. We're walking into a new thing. The kind of thing our parents wanted for us since the day we were born.

Parents! Sheesh I totally forgot! My mother is going to have my head on a turkey platter. He pressed the button on his steering wheel and waited for Siri to greet him through his Bluetooth. "Hello Mac. What can I do for you?"

"Call Charlie for me."

"Thank you, Mac. I'm calling Charlie now."

Charlie answered on the first ring. "So, miss me already?"

"I miss you all the time. But you discombobulated me so badly that I completely forgot to ask you a very important question."

She responded as calmly as she could while Mac remained completely unaware of how his unasked question would drive her imagination into fantasies about diamond rings and wedding dates. "Discombobulated, huh? And there you go again."

"I blame you. You inspire me. So listen, my mother would like you and Cheri to come for Thanksgiving dinner next week. She's setting the table already. She's crazy that way."

"Oh, Mac, I'd love to, but it's not just me and Cheri. I've got Bernie to think about."

"Bring Bernie too. Bring whoever you want. Seriously, Thanksgiving is like a high holy day for Mom. The more places she can set at the table the happier she is. So, you'll come?"

"I can't think of any place I'd rather be than in the home you grew up in with the people who taught you words like discombobulated."

He headed home with fantasies about diamond rings and wedding dates dancing in his head.

Cheri shook the box of Crunch 'n Munch then sifted through the crumbs to find the last few kernels of caramely, buttery, crunchiness. "Oh my gosh, I can't believe I ate the whole box."

"I know. I'm stuffed. But, good job on the jammies." Charlie picked a piece of the sticky corn off her new pink flannel pajamas, decorated with silhouettes of poodles and Eiffel Towers, and plopped it in her mouth. "I think we'll need to save these for nights when all we want to do is hang out, eat bad stuff, and talk about life, love, and men. Speaking of men, we're going to need to find you one. There's got to be one around here somewhere."

"But I'm not looking. I like being single. Single is good. Really. Really, really, good. Sure, someday it might be nice to have someone to fuss over and who thinks I'm gorgeous in my sweats, but for now I'm just happy to be who I am, doing what I'm doing, and not having to think about what I'm gonna fix for dinner or if I shaved my legs."

Charlie rolled her eyes. "Yep! We definitely need to find you a man before you end up on the news dressed in bib overalls, with crazy hair, and crying because animal control is taking away all your cats. So, tomorrow morning

I'm going to head over to Walmart and get you a man."

"You're a very mean girl, Charlie. I would never stoop to buying you a man at Walmart! Wawa maybe, or Food Lion, but never Walmart. Anyway, from the looks of things I'd say you managed to find the last good man on the planet."

"I did, didn't I? It's not like I did anything to deserve it. Honestly, look at me. I'm a mess." Charlie wiped the crumbs off her mouth. "I've got more baggage than Paris Hilton on a slow day. And in walks Mac McKenzie, with those blue eyes and a dimpled grin, and all his hokey phrases, and suddenly I'm hearing wedding bells ringing in my future."

"You think he's going to ask you to marry him? If he does are you going to say 'yes'?"

"Yes and yes, and it scares me to death because he's already been hurt once. And behind that smiling face of his, he's a trusting soul. I don't want to be the one who hurts him again. And then there's Zak. I can't wait to meet him, but if he doesn't like me, then what? I'll be left at the altar before I have an altar to be left at."

"Oh, come on Charlie, what's not to like? You're totally hip and groovy. Besides, what eight-year-old boy wouldn't fall for a thirty something girl who loves shoes and hates sports?" After her words had a chance to sink in, Cheri retracted. "Oh, yeah. You're totally doomed."

"Do you suppose I can find a book on soccer for dummies?"

"Hey, Bernie! Oh man, that pie smells awesome! Driving to Dover is going to be pure torture. How long have you been sitting here in the cold?"

"Just long enough to let the thought of sharing a Thanksgiving meal with a whole table full of family to send me tingling right down to my toes and feast on sweet memories. I can see them like it was yesterday. All of my brothers fighting over who gets the drumstick and Mamma skedaddling the dogs out the door with her broom. Good times. They were surely some good times. Makes me miss them all on days like this. Mamma, George, Jake, Samuel, and my sister Milly. Those were some mighty good times."

Thirty five minutes later, with a couple of wrong turns and a stop for gas, Charlie turned into the MacKenzie's circular driveway. "Wow, that's quite a house! It's huge! It makes our beach house look like a cabin." All three women stared out the window, half expecting a chauffeur named James to come and park their car. "I feel like I need to go back home and put on a ball gown."

"Now, Charlie girl, it's just a house with a lot of rooms. So let's just go in and see what kind of people fill them up."

"You're right as always. After all, it *is* just a house. Of course, it's as big as the White House, but it's just a house. So come on girls, let's scrape the sea gull droppings off our shoes and go in and eat us some vittles."

Before Charlie had the chance to ring the bell, the women were greeted by a tall man with greying red hair and just a hint of Irish flowing through the rhythm of his words. "Well, you must be our hungry guests! Come on in and shake the cold off of you. I'm Les and if I look old and tired it's because I'm the head of this whole crazy clan. Enter at your own risk."

The sound of footsteps pounded on the hardwood floors and soon Mac and a Mac look alike joined his dad with their hands ready to take their coats. "Sorry Charlie, we usually try to beat Dad to the door before he has a chance to dazzle our guests with his subtle charms." After everyone's coats were hanging on the rack near the door, Mac began the introductions.

"This is my dad, though most people call him Les, but we often call him More because, quite honestly, with Dad less is always more. And this ugly guy is my brother Casey. He's older than me by about 16 months, which is like a decade in dog years. My mom's in the kitchen basting the bird and my sisters are fussing with their hair. They're twins. And when I told them we were going to be sitting at the table with three super models they ran back upstairs and we haven't seen them since."

Bernie, Cheri, and Charlie, moved in wordless wonder as Mac escorted them to the living room. Soon the girls came to join them and before long they were all chatting away as if they'd known each other since birth. Though the home was a picture of perfection, the atmosphere couldn't have been more warm and engaging. Family pictures sat perched on every flat surface of furniture, luring Charlie around on her own while catching glimpses of the MacKenzie kids at all their most adorable and awkward stages of life. She soon found herself in the dining room standing in front of a large framed picture of their family tree. The aging parchment bore the family coat of arms with each name, picture, and birthdate nestled into oval cut outs spaced evenly among the branches. A scripture from Matthew 19:6, calligraphed in sweeping letters: *"What therefore God hath joined together, let not man put asunder"* rested proudly along the base of the frame.

While Charlie stood mesmerized by the MacKenzie Family Tree, Mac's mother walked in wiping her hands with a kitchen towel. "You must be Charlie."

Charlie turned to face the mother of the man with whom she was falling completely in love. "Yes, I am. And you must be Mrs. MacKenzie."

"Yes, I must be, though there are times when I wonder. But please call me Marlene. I see you've found our claim to fame. Don't we all look just so angelic and almost dignified? When the house starts rumbling with the hoof beats of hungry kids I like to stand right here and gaze at all their calm faces smiling at me. And then, of course, someone screams, falls, or breaks a lamp and the spell is broken." Marlene whispered in Charlie's ear as if she were letting her in on a family secret: "And just in case you're wondering, I am the only one who isn't Celtic. And that my dear explains just about everything."

Charlie felt a hand wrapping around her waist. "So, I see you've met my mother. She's Scandinavian. But we try not to hold it against her." Mac handed Charlie her coat. "Zak just texted me. He's waiting for us in his fort."

The snow crunched under their boots as Charlie and Mac walked hand in hand into the backyard, stopping short of the three story playhouse surrounded by an ice covered moat. Wow, that's more than a fort Mac. It's a fortress!"

"I know. Many a battle has been won right here in Zakland. This is what child psychologists would call a gross attempt at overcompensation. But really, it's just dad and I living out our own fantasies through Zak. It took us three years to build and a bunch of weekends of garage sales for Zak to fill it up with what he calls, 'the plunders of piracy'."

A voice from inside the fort bellowed. "Hark, who goes there!"

"It is I your humble servant most exalted king. And I bring with me the fair maiden Charlie."

"You may enter."

Charlie ducked as she entered the fort through the draw bridge. The inside of the fort was less imposing than the outside. Star Wars posters covered the walls and the floor was littered with candy wrappers. Zak presided over his small kingdom from his tattered throne upholstered in green velvet. Books lay strewn across an old coffee table and a large rubber sword, with a red plastic medallion stuck in the center of the handle, hung above the head of the little boy king.

"King Zak, this is the Lady Charlie who has come to your kingdom to share in a meal of most noble delicacies of bird and dressing."

Zak's smile slid to the left forming a dimple deep enough to hold a small handful of M&Ms.

Charlie curtsied. "I am so happy to meet you good, King. The news of your excellence has spread far and wide across our land."

"I like her Daddy! She can stay!"

Before they had a chance to catch up on the latest exploits of Zak's army of six the dinner bell clanged and the entire household rushed into the dining room, circling the table while looking for their names in the small silver frames perched in the center of each plate. Once everyone found their designated place, they held hands as Les prayed.

"Lord, we thank You for this home and for every person who has gathered here today to share the abundance of Your extravagant blessings. We thank You for Your generosity to us and we ask You to preside over this meal as You take your rightful place at the head of this table. Come, Lord Jesus, and enjoy our thankful hearts. Amen."

A reverent hush prevailed over the rowdy family as they all turned their attention toward the empty chair at the head of the table and whispered amen in unison. Once they were all seated Les picked up the name plate from the empty place and read, "Yehoshua – Jehovah God is our salvation."

He then picked up his own. "Les. A fine Celtic name meaning from the fortress. *The Lord is my Rock, my Fortress and my Deliverer; my God is my rock, in whom I take refuge.' Psalm 18 and 2.*"

Without missing a beat Marlene followed her husband.

"Marlene. A lovely Hebrew name meaning highly praised. *'I will praise You forever for what you have done; in Your Name I will hope, for Your Name is good.' Psalm 52:9.*"

The rest of the family joined in as if they had performed this same ritual a thousand times before.

"Morgan. An Irish name meaning of the sea. *'Who then is this, that even the wind and sea obey Him.' Mark 4:41.*"

"Keela. An Irish name meaning poetic beauty. *'For we are God's workmanship (His poema) created in Christ Jesus to do good works, which God prepared in advance for us to do.' Ephesians 2:10.*"

Casey smiled in Cheri's direction giving her a wink before he began reading. "Casey. A charming Celtic name meaning a brave and aggressive warrior. *'Long ago you spoke in a vision to your faithful people. You said, 'I have raised up a warrior. I have selected him from the common people to be king.' Psalm 89:19.*"

Mac elbowed his brother. "Remember, Mr. Charming, the warrior isn't you, it's Jesus." Mac then turned his eyes to Charlie as he read with pride, "Mac. A sturdy old Gaelic name meaning simply – son. *'My son, if your heart is wise, then My heart will be glad; My inmost being will rejoice when your lips speak what is right.' Proverbs 23:15-16.*"

Zak wiggled in his seat anxious to read his name plate all by himself without any help from the gallery of adults watching him. "Zak. A Hebrew name meaning God remembers. *'Remember your word to your servant, for you have given me hope.' Psalm 119:49.*"

Everyone at the table clapped causing Zak to scrunch down into his seat. "I'm not a baby. I know how to read! Dah!"

All eyes turned to Charlie. Fearing they could hear her heart thumping through her ears she cleared her throat and did her best to speak without stumbling. "Charlie. Strong and courageous from the meadow. *'But the people who know their God will display strength and take action.' Daniel 11:32.*"

Cheri smiled back at Casey. "Cheri. Beloved cherry tree. *'She is like a tree planted by streams of water, which yields its fruit in season and whose leaf does not wither, whatever she does prospers.' Psalm 1:3"*

Les turned to Bernie, "Well, Miss Bernie, it's all up to you now. Finish off this little ceremony of ours so we can eat before the food gets cold."

"Now don't you go rushin' me. I'm an old woman and I'll take my time if I need to. 'Bernice. One who brings victory. *'He holds victory in store for the upright, He is a shield to those whose walk is blameless, for He guards the course of the just and protects the way of His faithful ones.' Proverbs 2: 7- 8."*

"Now I think this was just about as close to the Heavenly Feast as a mortal soul can get. So if you don't mind I'd like to take this sweet frame home with me so I can keep it on my table and remember this day until Jesus comes to get me."

Charlie looked around the table as the food was passed back and forth to hungry men and girls who gave up trying to count the calories. And so this is family.

The sun went down long before Charlie, Cheri, and Bernie packed themselves and their bags full of leftovers into the car and headed back to Bowers Beach.

Bernie rubbed the edge of the silver frame with her thumb. Her stomach was nicely stuffed as her thoughts buzzed with homespun intuition. "Now that was one of the finest Thanksgivings I've had since Mr. Levi Mason first brought me home to meet his mother. I knew the minute I stepped inside that house that I found a place in their hearts where I belonged. And by the looks of things, I'd say history's repeating itself. And not just for you, Charlie Girl, but for you too, Miss Cheri. So you just mark my words - there was a whole lot more goin' on at that table than turkey and stuffing. A whole lot more."

Without giving the girls a chance to respond, Bernie just leaned her head back and let her laughter rise up to heaven, "Yes, Jesus, You're surely up to somethin' good now, aren't You? And won't it be fine when it all comes together?"

A good woman is hard to find, and worth far more than diamonds.
Her husband trusts her without reserve, and never has reason to regret it.
Proverbs 31:10-11 The Message

Chapter Twenty-Seven

No sooner had the sun gone down on Thanksgiving Day when the lights of Christmas began to twinkle through the streets of Dover. Cheri and Charlie moved into Charlie's apartment near The Green and began the long process of drawing up the plans for remodeling the Beach House, interviewing architects, and developing a project plan from start to finish. And while Cheri was consumed with details, details, and more details, Charlie was distracted by all things Mac and Zak.

"Okay, Charlie, I need you to focus on our schedule for today. We're meeting with Ken Burgess at ten this morning to finalize the budget. From there we need to meet with Stanley Kramer and let him know that we want his firm to be the leading architects. I don't know about you but I'm not comfortable with the construction schedule. I'd like to see us begin with the upstairs first, then move downstairs, which will take us into spring. By that time the weather should be stable enough for the major reconstruction of the kitchen, mud room, dining room and expanding the porch outside. So I think if we start choosing flooring, bathroom tile and fixtures, and lighting, it will save us time in the long run. What do you think? Can you handle that?"

Charlie put down the bride magazine and stared at her friend as if she hadn't heard a word she said. "Do you think we can be ready for a June wedding?"

"June? Are you serious? Besides, you don't even have a ring yet. And I don't see that happening until his divorce is final. Sure I think it's coming, but who knows when. And if we're going to be planning a wedding how are we going to stay on top of the Beach House?"

"Mac was hinting about honeymoon spots last night. Of course he didn't use the word *honeymoon* he just kept saying things like, 'I'd give my eye teeth to be sitting on a beach somewhere in Florida, or taking a cruise along the Mediterranean.' He's so not good at fishing. I mean, he actually came right out and asked me, 'if you had your choice between tossing a coin in the Trevi Fountain, or snorkeling in Fiji, which one would you choose?'"

"Again, Charlie, I need you to focus. Look into my eyes and read my thoughts. Am I happy or am I getting frustrated and nervous?"

Charlie squinted her eyes and moved in close to Cheri's face. "Hm, I see a man on a white horse riding in to your future. He has red hair and he's carrying a sword in one hand and roses in the other. And he's smiling. Yes. He's grinning from ear to ear like a goof who's found his ball. His name is - wait, it's coming. His name is Sir Laugh a' Lot. No. His name is Doctor I'd Like to Know You Better. No, that's not it either. What is his name? There's a big C on his chest. What could it mean? Oh wait! I've got it. Casey. That's it. His name is Casey."

Cheri's face flushed with heat. "Really? I've met him once. He's mildly attractive and pleasantly humorous. These two things are not the pillars on which I choose to build a relationship. And, if you will remember, I am not looking for a relationship. I'm here for one reason – you! So if you can come back to planet earth for just ten minutes we might just be able to get started on our day."

"Okay. I am all yours. Lead on. Oh by the way, I want to be baptized."

"Whoa! I mean, that's great. A little A.D.D. but awesome. When did you decide this?"

Charlie tucked her legs under her. "I've been thinking about it for a couple of weeks now. I mean, I know God has forgiven me, and Mac has forgiven me, but I'm not sure that I've forgiven me. So when I think about being baptized it's like getting out of the bathtub and leaving all the crud behind. I need to do that. Leave all the crud behind so I can surrender to my new day."

"Hm. That's beautiful. I'm totally in with it. So, let's go and do what we need to do and then we can stop for lunch and talk about getting you baptized. Weren't you ever baptized before?"

"Yeah, actually I was baptized during summer camp when I was nine. But

I don't think I really understood what it meant. Now I do. And my mother wasn't there to see it happen. So this time I want her to be there. She may not understand what's going on but who knows, it just might touch her in some way that will help her to know her prayers for me have been answered. I want Mother to have the peace of knowing that her daughter is going to be alright. That her song has been finished because her Charlie has come home."

Pleased with their meeting with the architect and happy with the proposed budget for the Beach House, Cheri and Charlie stopped by 33 West for soup and salad. Charlie's mind was swarming with ideas for her baptism. "I know this may seem unconventional, but I would like for you to sing the song Mother wrote for me either before or after I'm baptized. It's like the whole story of my coming home put to music and I think it will reach right through to Mother's heart. What do you think?"

"Well, I think we'll first need to find a church. Then we'll need to meet with the pastor of the church and ask him what he thinks. I don't know why he wouldn't love it, but then I'm not a pastor."

"Right. It's been years since I've even set foot inside a church. I guess it's not like they've been waiting for me to show up and rearrange their services for them. But it's a good idea isn't it?"

"It's a great idea. So what about Mac's church? His family looks like the kind of family that would build their whole week around Sundays. Surely they have a church where they all attend."

"You're right. They do. I'll talk with him about it tonight when he calls. Oh, Cheri, wouldn't it be amazing if his family and my family could be there? I know this might sound silly, but I feel like my baptism is sort of like a wedding between me and Jesus. It's like the wedding before the wedding. Jesus, first then Mac – if of course he ever decides to pop the question."

"That's a beautiful picture. Where'd it come from?"

"I was reading yesterday about being the bride of Christ. And I sat there thinking about what it meant and I realized that I've been planning a wedding with a man who hasn't even asked me to marry him yet. And then I saw a ring sitting in Jesus' nail scared hand offering me His unconditional love. And I said, *yes."*

Cheri propped an elbow on the table and rested her chin on her hand. "Wow. I love that. And I love how when you commit yourself to something, you just jump in with both feet. No half-heartedness. No sitting on the fence. No *I'll give this a try and see what happens.* That's why I love you. I love having a friend whose face lights up when she talks about the things that thrill her. And I love that what thrills you is Jesus. And Mac. But mostly Jesus."

"Yeah, that's a lot of love isn't it? I think I'm still trying to figure out how to handle it all." Just as they were about to pay the waitress for their half-eaten lunch, Charlie's phone rang. "Hey, Mister, how's your day going?"

"It was going great until I got a call from the nurse at Zak's school. He fell playing soccer in the halls with his buddies and broke his arm. I'm in emergency with him right now. It's not a bad break, just a fracture below his elbow, but it will keep him home for a few days. I was able to cancel all my appointments for today, but I'm not sure about tomorrow. Mom's down with a cold and ..."

"What about me?"

"What about you? You've already got a lot on your plate."

"I've never seen your place, so you'll have to text me your address. I can be there by 8:30. Will that help?"

"You're an angel, Charlie."

"Yes I am. Besides, this will give me time alone with Zak. I'd love to get to know him when he's not presiding over candy wrappers in his castle, or stuffing his mouth with turkey. So, what does an eight-year-old boy do when he's home from school?"

"I'm pretty sure he's going to need to sleep a lot. But then he'll want you to watch every Star Wars movie ever made. And he might want to play chess with you. If you don't know how to play chess he'll teach you and hopefully you'll be a better student than I am. I thank his grandpa for that. Dad's waited a lot of years for a boy who would sit still long enough to play chess with him. I think it's all the castle stuff. Zak's into castles."

"So I've noticed. Cheri and I have a ton of stuff to do today, but by to-morrow I'm sure she won't mind getting me out of her hair so she can nail down the things I hate doing."

Cheri scowled at her friend as Charlie said her goodbyes and clicked off her phone. "Well, it looks like I'll have a whole day to get to know my future stepson."

Mac was right. Zak slept through most of the morning groaning when-ever the pain meds wore off. But by noon he was ready for lunch and a Star Wars marathon. While they ate their toasted cheese sandwiches Zak decid-ed to do a little grilling of his own.

"How come you're not married? Do you have a dog? How many Star Wars movies have you watched? What's your favorite flavor of ice cream? How old are you? Do you like my Daddy? Do you guys like kiss and stuff? Are you going to get married? Did you ever meet my Mommy?"

It was that last question that tore at her heart. "No Zak. I never met your Mommy. How do you feel about her?"

"I don't like her. She made Daddy cry and she didn't want me."

The simplicity of his words left her speechless. How could an eight-year-old boy understand the complexities of life? "Zak, I don't know why your Mommy left you and your daddy. Sometimes grown-ups do things that hurt other people because they have problems that are too big for them to handle."

"That's what Daddy says. But I hate her and I hope she never comes back here again. I want a new mommy. I like my Grandma and my Aunties, but I want a mommy who lives in my house with me and Daddy. And I want someone who likes Star Wars and makes me toasted cheese sandwiches and hot chocolate."

If she didn't know better she would have thought that Mac was hiding behind the couch ready to jump up with a black velvet box in his hand. But he didn't. It was just her and Zak talking about life and washing down their toasted cheese sandwiches with hot chocolate. By five-thirty Zak and Charlie had made it through The Phantom Menace, Attack of the Clones, and were just about to press start on Revenge of the Sith, when Mac came home with the smell of fried chicken oozing through a red and white bag. "Hey, Wacky Zakky, how's the arm doing?"

"It hurts too much for me to go to school so I want Charlie to spend the night and take care of me again tomorrow. She makes the best lunches and we need to watch the rest of our shows. Can she Daddy?"

Charlie's eyes grew two sizes larger as she looked to Mac to come to her rescue.

"Well Zak, I'm not quite sure. Maybe we need to ask Charlie about that." Mac turned to Charlie with an impish grin on his face. "What do you think Charlie? Are you up for a slumber party with an eight-year-old with about as much energy as a cage full of monkeys?"

Squinting one eye, Charlie patted Mac's chest and quickly changed the subject. "Why don't I get us some plates for that chicken before it gets cold?"

As they wiped the grease off their faces, Zak looked at Mac and Charlie and announced with persuasive innocence. "I like the way this feels, don't you, Daddy?"

"Yes I do, Buddy. But now you need to say goodnight to Charlie because she needs to go back to her apartment so her friend Cheri won't have to be all alone. And tomorrow your Auntie Keela is coming over to take care of you."

Zak shrugged his shoulders, "Okay, but she better not bring her stupid ro-o-o-mance movies with her."

As Mac walked Charlie to the door he planted a kiss on her forehead. "Now I know what Shakespeare meant when he said, *Parting is such sweet sorrow.* And for the record, I'm with Zak; I like the way this feels."

Charlie walked into her apartment dropping her coat and purse on the table and grinned at Cheri. "I am completely and totally in love with the sweetest man."

"Mac's a lucky guy."

"Yes he is. But I'm not talking about Mac. I have a new man in my life. His name is Zak. And he's perfectly adorable."

Jesus answered him, "If anyone loves me, he will keep my word,
and my Father will love him,
and we will come to him and make our home with him. John 14:23 ESV

Chapter Twenty-Eight

From the time Charlie and Cheri moved into the apartment, sleeping through her alarm became a non-issue. At exactly 6:30 AM the aroma of freshly brewed coffee drew Charlie out of bed with her hand leading her to the kitchen in search of a cup.

"I'd forgotten what an early bird you are and if you didn't make such fabulous coffee I'd hate you for it."

"You know what they say about the early bird."

"Yeah, it's the first to get eaten by the neighborhood kitty. So what's on our agenda today for InCreation?" Charlie yawned while scratching her stomach. "I never did ask you how things went yesterday. Were you able to nail down the construction schedule?"

"We've got a team of five guys from Integrity Construction scheduled for next week. They were totally open to gutting the upstairs first. Greg said the bones of the house are solid so they won't have to reinforce the floors. But we're going to have to go out and look at storm windows today, unless of course, you're going to be spending the day with that adorable new man of yours."

"I know this is crazy, but I'm actually kind of mad at Keela for making herself so available to take care of Zak. I laid awake half the night worrying about his arm and wondering if Mac remembered to give him a pain pill before he went to bed."

"His father's a doctor, Charlie. I think he can handle a little boy with a broken arm."

The phone interrupted their conversation. Charlie's face froze as she looked at the caller I.D. "I need to take this in the bedroom."

Her palms began to sweat as she whispered into the phone. "Jeffery, why are you calling me? You have about two seconds to tell me what you want before I hang up on you."

"I'm sure you've been following the news. I just wanted to hear your voice and tell you that Dad and I are innocent. This is all a bunch of bogus accusations by a couple of cranky women. But there's nothing to worry about. We've got the best lawyers money can buy and once they get the charges dropped, we'll be back in business in no time."

"Listen to me Jeffery, I don't care about you and I don't care about your so-called innocence. Cheri's here and now I know what you did to her. So listen to me very carefully - there aren't enough laws in the books to cover the list of things you've done to me, to her, and to whoever else you've put your grimy paws on. Now, unless you want whatever remains of your reputation to be ground into the dirt you will do well to never contact me again. And this time Jeffery, I mean it."

Charlie felt Cheri's presence behind her. "Yes, it was Jeffery. He's obviously feeling alone and abandoned, and frankly I couldn't care less. He's gone Cheri. He's never coming back into our lives again. Never ever!"

By the end of the week nearly everything on their list was checked off. The permits needed for the upstairs construction were signed and delivered. The gutting of the rooms was in process. The windows were on order along with the crown moldings. And the flooring and fixtures were on their way. Cheri and Charlie had found their rhythm as a design team.

Still left unchecked was a date with Mac and an invitation to join him and his family at church on Sunday. Just as Charlie and Cheri finished sprucing up the apartment before heading off for Old City Paint and Decorating Center, a number she didn't recognize buzzed through her phone. If this is you, Jeffery, I swear I'll find a fork and plunge it straight through your dialing finger. "Hello, this is Charlie."

"Oh, Charlie, I hope I haven't caught you at a bad time. This is Marlene, Mac's mother."

Charlie breathed in the sweet smell of relief. "How could I forget the woman who fed us the best Thanksgiving dinner I've had in years. How are you, Marlene? Are Mac and Zak alright?"

"Everything's fine, dear. I'm sorry for scaring you by calling you out of the blue like this, but it's Friday and if I know my son, and of course I do, I'm pretty sure he forgot to invite you, Cheri, and Bernie, to come to church with us on Sunday. And then we all usually go out for lunch after the service is over. We have a standing reservation at the Country Eaterie. So what do you think? Can you handle another meal with the crazy MacKenzie's?"

Trying not to sound too anxious Charlie paused before answering. "That would be wonderful, Marlene. Thank you so much for thinking about us. Cheri and I were just talking the other day about how we wanted to visit your church, because neither one of us has a church that we can call home. And actually, I'm hoping to be able to talk with someone about being baptized."

She bit her lip realizing she just about told Mac's perfect mother that the new love of his life is a churchless heathen. Way to go Charlie.

"Really? How exciting. I'll introduce you to Pastor Dave on Sunday. So do you think Bernie will join us also? I just love that woman."

"Everyone loves Bernie. She has a little church that she's been going to for more years than I've been alive. But I think she'd love to come along with us. Actually, she's been talking a lot about you and your family. You all made quite an impression on her, and Bernie doesn't impress easily."

"Okay, so I'll expect to see all three of you at about 9:15 in front of Grace Community Church and I'll have the Eaterie add three chairs to the table. And lunch is our treat. No arguments on that, believe me, the MacKenzie's don't take kindly to losing arguments."

Siri led Charlie straight to Grace Community Church with just enough time to find a parking space before meeting up with Mac and his family out front. As soon as Zak caught sight of Charlie he began waving his broken wing covered in neon green plaster at her. "Mercy me, Miss Charlie, by the look on that boy's face I'd say he's got himself a great big crush on you. Now you've got two men fighting for your attention. And if you don't want to be the first woman to break that boy's heart I'd say you better head straight for him first."

As soon as Charlie got within ten feet of Zak she was nearly knocked to the ground by the force of his hug. "Hey, Zak, how's your arm doing?"

"It's great! It's green. I had my choice between orange and green. I chose green because it's cool. I got a pen in my pocket. Wanna sign it?"

Her eyes pooled with love, "I absolutely do. So why don't you sit next to me in church and I'll sign it before the service starts."

It was all Mac could do to not fall on his knees and beg Charlie to marry him on the spot. After all, they were at the church, and the pastor was inside with nothing better to do than to join the two of them in holy matrimony. Waiting to pop the question kept him in a perpetual state of fear. He wanted to do everything right this time. No mistakes. Nothing out of order. One thing at a time. He patted his pocket where his first ticket to wedded bliss was waiting to be revealed.

The music thrilled her soul as the worship team led the congregation in praise. After a few announcements Pastor Dave moved up to the stage and without a note in his hands gave a stirring message from the book of John. The story of the woman at the well confirmed what her heart needed most to hear; there's grace for the broken and forgiveness for the fallen. Charlie had been both. Her desire to be baptized intensified with each passing moment. Once the service was over Marlene walked Charlie up the aisle to where Pastor Dave was giving a comforting hug to an old woman with bluish hair. I like him.

"Pastor Dave, I want you to meet Charlie. She's a new friend to our family. And I've just discovered that she wants to be baptized, so I thought the two of you should meet."

Wow, she wastes no time does she? She just went right for it before I had a chance to say hello. Maybe that's a good thing. Note to self: be careful what you tell Mother MacKenzie.

"Absolutely." Dave's handshake was warm and firm. He and Charlie pointed their cell phones at each other and settled on Tuesday at ten. Baptism on the first Sunday in December. And *yes,* Cheri could sing her mother's song. Today was proving to be a very good day.

The noisy clan of the famished family filled the back of the Country Eaterie. Zak sat on Charlie's right and Mac sat on her left. They looked like bookends closing her in with masculine attention. After Zak filled Charlie in with all the details of how his temporary cast was replaced by his current cast, he hopped off his chair to show off his latest signature to the rest of the family.

"It looks like my son has fallen in love with the Fair Maiden Charlie. Me thinks this could be a problem for the son's father."

"No problem, Sir Mac. My heart has room enough for both of you."

Mac's eyes melted into hers as he lifted the envelope from the pocket of his suit. "I have something for you. It's the first step to what I pray will be a lasting relationship with the most beautiful woman I've ever met."

He watched her blush as she unfolded the letter from inside the envelope. "Is this what I think it is, Mac?"

"You're no longer dating a married man. According to this letter I'm officially single. Actually we haven't been dating have we? I think we need to take care of that right away. How about you and me and candlelight at Magnolia's? I've already reserved us a table for two. That would be two, meaning you and me, not three, meaning you, me, that little flirt heading back to his chair."

Charlie looked down the table to where Cheri and Casey were engaged in a deep conversation that seemed to require a good deal of eye contact. "Are you sure it will be just the two of us, because I'm sensing some flirtations of a different kind taking place at the end of the table."

"Yeah, something tells me the Love Bug is working overtime today."

"The Love Bug? Isn't that like an old movie about a car or something?"

"Whatever it is, I think there's a sequel coming."

The king is pleased with words from righteous lips;
He loves those who speak honestly. Prov 16:13

Chapter Twenty-Nine

"I wish you would just come with me. I know I'm being ridiculous but sitting in an office with Pastor Dave staring at me and asking me all sorts of questions that I am terrified to answer just makes me want to duck and run."

She loved the comfort of sitting across the table, any table from Mac. It just felt normal and right; like two people who were meant to share their lives and their meals together. She loved the way he ordered steak while she headed straight for the shellfish. And she loved the way he stopped eating whenever she started talking. Poor man. He's going to lose a lot of weight with me as his dinner partner.

"You really have nothing to be afraid of, Charlie. He's just a man like any other man - except that he's perfect."

"Oh thanks, I feel so much better. Seriously Mac, I'm not used to all this. I haven't stepped inside a church since before – Jeffery." Her face turned pale at the mention of his name. She pushed her plate back and just sat there looking at her food as if someone came along and covered it in gravy. And she hated gravy.

"I'm sorry. I promised not to bring his name up again. It just seems to creep up every time I feel insecure. Why is that? Why can't I just let that part of my life drift off into the stratosphere?" Mac looked wounded. Again. He stabbed at a piece of his steak but held it on the plate without lifting it to his mouth. She couldn't help but wonder if he was seeing Jeffery's face under the tines of his fork. I've done it again. I've driven him to the dark side. Good job, Charlie.

"You're right. I need to go with you. This thing with Jeffery is no longer just between you and him. It's between the three of us. And I want him out of our story. The same way Irene needed to be out of our story. Except you can't divorce him and I don't know how to fix that." He scooted his steak through the silky Béarnaise sauce while collecting the rest of his thoughts. "Getting baptized is about telling the world that we're no longer who we used to be. It's about old things being put away. But we haven't put Jeffery away. I haven't and you haven't. And if we're going to move forward we have to quit moving backward. There's nothing wrong with needing help, Charlie. And we both need help. So I'll pick you up Tuesday night and we'll go together."

The gravy miraculously disappeared from her shrimp. "I love you Mac."

Charlie's fingers were clamped around Mac's hand so tightly that her knuckles were turning white. Pastor Dave's office was remarkably small considering how large his church was. Though Mac was quick to remind her that it wasn't *his* church – nevertheless he was the one in charge. He was the leader. And shouldn't the leader have a better place to do his leading from? Maybe when we're all done I can come in and do something to give it more credibility. Make it more respectable and worthy of his title. And there I go again – controlling the world with my little book of swatches.

"So, Charlie, tell me why you want to be baptized."

She choked on her "um" while tightening her grip on Mac's hand. "Well, I'm, um, at a crossroad I guess. I mean I went to church my whole life until I – stopped. And then I didn't. But now I'm needing to change all that. I need to – no I want to have a fresh start. Mac and I …"

Pastor Dave interrupted her, "Good. We all need a fresh start from time to time. You and Mac are obviously in love with each other. Right?"

She felt her face turning about thirty shades of red as she looked at Mac who was grinning from ear to ear. "Yes. Yes, we are."

"So, is this fresh start about you and Mac? Or is it about you and Jesus?"

Her nostrils began to flare. "It's about both. It's about Mac and me – or

Mac and I - whatever. And it's about me and Jesus. I started to rediscover who God is at the same time Mac and I met and began to have feelings for each other."

"Okay. Tell me about that, Charlie. I would really like to hear your story before we talk about baptism, because baptism is only as meaningful as your story is."

For the next hour and a half Charlie waded through the various episodes in her life that led her to the chair where she was now sitting. And by the time she finished, her anger with Pastor Dave had turned into gratitude. The thread that had been weaving through her life, tying one chapter to another, brought a new sense of peace to her spirit. "I get it now. I see it. All these things that have felt like obstacles in my life are really turning points aren't they. It's like every one of them has been pointing me back to God. All the while I've been trying to run away from Him, He's been running to me." She let go of Mac's hand.

"Well, I'd say you're more than ready to be baptized. And I'd be honored to be the one to do it for you. But before we talk about the specifics, I'd like to backtrack for a minute or two." Pastor Dave turned his attention to Mac who had been sitting in silence since the meeting began. "Mac, if I were you I think I'd be having a hard time dealing with the other man in Charlie's story. Even though he's out of the picture, he's still sort of in it, because until the two of you are able to reach some sort of resolve, or healing, his name is still going to make your skin crawl the way it did while Charlie was talking about him."

Charlie felt Mac's hand reaching for hers. The tension in his voice brought tears to her eyes. "I hate him."

"Hm. I don't blame you, Mac. I love my wife and if Jeffery had done to her what he did to Charlie, I'd hate him, too. Hating what Jeffery *did* puts you on God's side of the issue of sin. But then there's the flip side of that. Hating *Jeffery* puts you on the opposite side of God. In fact it puts you right in the Enemy's camp, because he hates Jeffery, too. He uses Jeffery. But he hates him. So what are we going to do about that, my friend? How can I help you through that?"

Charlie couldn't have been more stunned than if the earth had split in two right where she was sitting. "Oh, Mac, he's right! We've both been hating the wrong thing. No wonder we can't put it past us." Leaving Mac with his emotions spinning she turned to Pastor Dave. "What do we do about it? How do we change it?"

"I'm so glad you asked. But before I give you the answer I need to ask you a very serious question. And you both need to answer it for yourselves. Not together. Separately. So think about this very seriously and very personally before you respond. Are you ready?"

They nodded their heads in agreement.

"Okay, here it is. In light of all that Jeffery did would you feel like justice would be well served if God sentenced him to an eternity in hell?"

Both Charlie and Mac gasped in horror.

"I didn't think so. And this is what forgiveness is all about." Pastor Dave paused long enough to give Mac and Charlie time to digest his words. "Mac, you're a good man. We've walked through a lot of stuff together. So I know you'll understand me when I say - you need to forgive Jeffery for sinning against this woman. And Charlie, I appreciate how honest you've been with me tonight. I know it couldn't have been easy to unload your story to an *imperfect* stranger. If you're the woman God's chosen for Mac then I have to say, He's done a great job with the two of you. I want you to be free not only to love Mac, but to experience the full joy of following Jesus.

"So I just want to give you a few words from The Word to help you understand the justice of mercy." He opened the Bible that was buried under a small stack of what looked like mail, and began flipping easily to the right place. "If you forgive those who sin against you, your heavenly Father will forgive you. But if you refuse to forgive others, your Father will not forgive your sins."

There was a time when the Word of God would have sent Charlie looking for the nearest bed to hide under, but tonight was different. Maybe because she was different. She turned to Mac and said, "What do we do now?"

Mac's eyes were brimming with raw emotion, "We forgive him, Charlie. We let go of him. And we forgive him."

"Okay. I'm ready."

Charlie was deeply touched by the simple way Pastor Dave approached prayer. No fancy words. No pre-fabricated petitions. No illustrious thoughts sent into the air to impress the hearers. Just an honest heart inviting them to follow him to the Throne as she and Mac together surrendered to forgiveness.

"Such beautiful things are happening with our granddaughter, Charles; such amazing answers to our daughter's prayers. And there she sits completely oblivious to it all. She's missing so much."

"Yes she is. For now. But one day she'll read her story in the books you've been writing. You haven't missed a thing Audrey, and neither will she."

Audrey's hand brushed across the paper of where the words she had been writing were waiting to be finished. "Every time I think of her waking up to see the face of Abba smiling at her, I can hardly wait for her arrival. I can only imagine what it will be like for her when she understands not only how powerfully her prayers have affected the life of her daughter and so many others, but the joy that's waiting for her when she sees herself through heaven's eyes. Sweet things are waiting for her. It's wise of God to not let us in on the *when*, because I would just spend all my time trying to find a clock that beats with earthly time. Patience is easier when all we have to do is watch."

Set me free from my prison, that I may praise Your name.
Then the righteous will gather about me because of Your goodness to me.
Psalm 142:7 NIV

Chapter Thirty

Ellie Mae felt the coolness of water on her skin and the gentle tugging of her hair while she listened to the chatter of voices that seemed to be coming from somewhere far away.

"There, you look beautiful. This is going to be such a good day Ellie Mae. Charlie is going to be baptized this morning and she's saved a special place for you in the front row with Bernie, Cheri, and Mac's family. They're all so anxious to see you. And guess what, your daughter has a great surprise waiting for you." All their efforts to explain their constant fussing were just a mouth full of words. She just stared down at her hands as Jodie wheeled her into the waiting van with Celeste following along and carrying her favorite afghan with the knobby nap.

The cold air stung her cheeks. And yet she sat still and unresponsive until the clashing of metal to metal sealed her into the small space with the strange smell. Her eyes widened as the needles of panic pricked at her senses. Before the cries of fear could escape from the places in her brain that felt such things, the purring of something strong settled in, calming her anxious nerves. Windows surrounded her. She looked for Anne but she couldn't find her. Things were moving too fast. Perhaps Anne was lost. Perhaps she was lost forever.

The church was nearly empty when they arrived. "I'm glad we were able to get here before everyone else comes in. Plunking her into a room full of people she's never seen before might cause her to panic. If it does, Celeste, we're just going to have to wheel her back into the van and head immediately back to Still Waters. Though I'm praying that won't be necessary."

Charlie walked up the aisle of the church carrying a toiletry bag in one hand and the red satin box in the other, with Mac, Cheri, and Bernie following close behind. A wave of excitement, the kind she used to feel right before her mother opened the presents she made for her on Mother's Day, nipped at her senses. Loving her mother was becoming her new normal. She bent down and placed a tender kiss on Ellie Mae's cheek. "Hello, Mommy. I'm so glad you're here. This is going to be a very special day for both of us. In just a little while I'm going to be baptized and it's all because of you. You don't have to worry about me anymore. All your prayers for me are being answered and I'm happier than I have any right to be. And look, Mac, Cheri, and Bernie are right here and they're going to sit with you while I go and get ready. Kisses to you. I'll be back soon."

Liquid faces all ran together in shifting waves of color accented by flashes of gold and silver as their voices whispered words without meaning. Where was she? What was she doing here? Her eyes darted back and forth in search of her window and her friend named Anne. Then she saw it; a large shimmer of glass straight ahead of her. She struggled to steady her focus while a rush of adrenaline sent her fingers swirling over the satin box nestled into the afghan on her lap. Something was happening in her world, something she couldn't grasp hold of and yet something that thrilled her spirit with an unexplainable sense of expectation.

Music began to fill the auditorium, accompanied by the sounds of what seemed like a flurry of angels singing choruses of praise. Her fingers tapped lightly on the red satin box feeling as if she were becoming a part of something lovely, something real. But then it just faded away while a tall man walked in front of her window. His voice was too loud. She wanted the music to come back. But he just kept on talking and though some of his words found a place in her vocabulary the rest just seemed to flit across the room like rocks skipping across the water. When the man finally stopped talking the woman with bright hair rose up from her seat and walked across the room to a large piano.

Ellie's lips trembled as the woman sitting by the piano began to play. The familiarity of the music clicked inside her brain like a key unlocking the prison where her memories sat waiting to be released. She closed her eyes allowing her head to dance freely with the music. Hazy visions of the day the song was born awakened her mother's heart. Charlie's Song. She held tightly to the red satin box as if it would help her to stay in these few seconds of time where she felt real. But without warning the sound of a woman's voice began to sing over the melody. Her eyes shot open. Beautiful words. Words she would have written if she had been so gifted.

Coming home
I'm coming home
I've been gone for so long
Coming home
I'm coming home
I've been gone for so long

Ellie Mae was more alive than she had been in a very long time. And while she wondered how the words found their way to the music, she understood the message with crystal clarity. Each note and each word rained down the creases in her weathered cheeks, grown old long before their time. The hands that had been fingering the notes on the red box rose up in praise. Not a word was lost to her understanding. Bernie, Mac, Jodie, and Celeste sat astounded. A miracle was happening in their midst.

As the last word blended into the final refrain, the curtains on the window opened. Standing behind the glass was her daughter, dressed in a white robe, her auburn curls cascading over her shoulders, and wearing that same look on her face she wore on her first day of school. The man with the loud voice stood next to her. He placed one hand behind Charlie's head and held tightly to her hand with the other. Ellie Mae drew in her breath as the man carefully lowered her daughter into the baptistery. She could feel the cool water closing in around her, squeezing her chest with the desire to breathe. But until her Charlie came up for air she would remain submerged in this moment. Seconds later Charlie rose up from the water gasping for air with her eyes wide open and blinking against the light like a child reborn. And her mother sat gazing through the window where her daughter stood drenched in the grace of her loving Savior. Charlie, her prodigal daughter, was coming home and now she was free to do the same.

As she looked up into the heavens she watched the ceiling peel open like the parting of the Red Sea. Voices beyond the skies were calling her name. In spite of the crushing pressure that weighted against her chest Ellie Mae felt enveloped in peace. With her last breath she looked at the beautiful face of her daughter, still glistening with waters of baptism, and whispered, "Goodbye, my Charlie. I do love you so."

Charlie stood in front of the mirror in the restroom behind the stage, doing her best to dry her hair as quickly as possible. In the glass she saw the reflections of Marlene, Cheri, and Bernie walking up behind her. "I'm almost done! It was amazing wasn't it? The song was beautiful Cheri. How's mother doing? Did she hear the song?"

No one answered. The three women just stood there like statues unable to move or speak. "What's the matter? Why are you all looking at me like that?" She leaned into the mirror to check her make-up. "No globs of mascara on my lashes and no slip of the lipstick tube across my cheek." She turned around and without explanation, she knew. "It's mother isn't it."

"Yes, Charlie, it's your mother." Marlene's voice broke the silence. "I'm so sorry. She's gone, Charlie. It happened so quickly that it took us all by surprise. Mac did everything he could to resuscitate her but there was nothing he could do. The congregation has been asked to leave the auditorium so we could all be alone until the ambulance arrives."

"Honey Girl, your mother is in the arms of Jesus. But you need to be with her. Now you just lean on us and we'll go together."

As Charlie walked into the auditorium she saw Mac on the floor by her mother's wheel chair and cradling her mother in his arms. She ran to him. "I'm so sorry Charlie. There wasn't anything I could do. She just closed her eyes and it was over."

She fell to her knees and held her mother's face in her hands. "Mother.

Please don't leave me now. Not now. I need you to come back to me. Please come back to me!"

The sound of sirens split through her senses threatening to steal these last few moments away from her. "Don't let them take her away, Mac. Please tell them to go back and leave us alone."

"Charlie, I'll go with you in the ambulance while my mother, Cheri, and Bernie, follow us to the hospital. We're going to walk through this together."

There were too many sounds to comprehend and too many emotions to sort through. She just wanted everything to stop. The sirens. The words that kept taking her to places she didn't want to go. And the emptiness of the auditorium that felt very much like a grave waiting to be filled with death. She picked up her mother's hand and pressed it against her cheek. It was still warm. Hoping life would return for one last visit, Charlie stared into her mother's face and gasped in awe. "Oh, Mac, she's so beautiful isn't she? Look at her. Her face is radiant." She looked around at everyone who was standing near her. "Do you see it? Bernie, do you see it?"

"Oh, Girl, I surely do. It's like Heaven came down and kissed her goodnight."

"I never want to forget this Mac. Please don't let me forget this. When I feel like God is a million miles away, please remind me of how my mother's face looked when she saw Jesus."

Therefore, since we are surrounded by so great a cloud of witnesses, let us also lay aside every weight, and sin which clings so closely, and let us run with endurance the race that is set before us, looking to Jesus, the founder and perfecter of our faith, who for the joy that was set before him endured the cross, despising the shame, and is seated at the right hand of the throne of God.
Hebrews 12:1-2 ESV

Chapter Thirty-One

Charlie sat especially close to Mac in the front pew reserved for family and friends of the deceased. Deceased. Her mother was now a check mark on a form. Deceased. A new category in the records of life.

The pages in her hand were smudged with tears, the condensation of pain stored up through days of planning and preparing for this moment of saying goodbye. The church was filled to capacity with friends of the 'lovely Ellie Mae', dressed in their best, funneling in like bees to the honey. Faces of all ages and genders dotted the pews each with a story to tell of the best Sunday School teacher they ever had, or the sweetest woman who taught them how to play piano. And there in the middle of the sea were Dr. Sorenson and his wife. And further down the center aisle was Jed the mechanic that kept Mother's old Buick running for about a thousand years. Six women, maybe seven or eight, all huddled together in the back passing tissues to each other. Mother's prayer group. The rest were unfamiliar to her, maybe because she never thought to turn grocery clerks and waitresses into best friends. But Mother did. *Friends are like Jello, Charlie, there's always room for more.*

You weren't at all unremarkable, Mother. All these testify to that. You've touched them all with your kindness and your refusal to make a spectacle of yourself by flaunting your gifts and talents. Instead you treated all of them like they were your closest friends. I'm so proud of you. Do you know that, Mommy? I'm proud of you! And I miss you. Every part of my body aches to feel your hand in mine, to hear you say my name in that sweet way of yours, and to sit next to you for one more song at the piano.

The sheets of music stored in the Red Satin box gave Charlie the sense that her mother was sitting right there with her as the flurry of activity settled into a reverent hush. The large screens on each side of the platform lowered slowly while an old photograph of a young Ellie Mae Mondary filled the screens. Mac squeezed Charlie's hand as the video of her mother's life began to play. It had been a busy week for everyone. Especially Mac's sisters who worked round the clock scanning Charlie's family pictures into their computer and laying Ellie's music under them. The result was a living eulogy of a life beautifully lived to the glory of the God who reigned through their family tree.

"None of us starts from nowhere," Bernie whispered in her ear as the video played on. "Look at them all, Honey Girl. All those faces smilin' down on you. Yes, Lord, heaven is surely close to us today. Praise you, Jesus."

Bernie was right. The story of her life was tucked inside every picture beginning with her great grandmammy Eleanor Hamilton, her great grandparents Esther and Wesley Charles St. Clare, and Gramma Audrey and Grampa Charles – all faithful couriers of the gospel to future generations. Just as her heart began to crest with the pain of loss, the playful pictures of Basil I and Basil II rolled in providing some comic relief preparing her for the face of the man she never stopped missing; the noble Lt. Colonel John Lawrence Mondary looking so fetching in his flight suit and holding his helmet in his left hand. The screen faded to grey as new pictures emerged with Ellie Mae St. Clare standing next to John Lawrence Mondary, looking like love had come and caught them both by surprise. A series of snapshots of life after marriage followed. There was Mother holding her hand over her swelling belly and laughing. And Daddy holding his daughter for the first time. Family walks along the shore. Family dinners. Pictures of Christmas trees and those all- important trips to visit Santa. All sweet reminders of the legacy that wove her past into the present.

She wished she could crawl into the screen and hold them all and stay with them forever. Pastor Dave walked up to the clear acrylic lectern. His words were simple and kind as he welcomed everyone who came to pay tribute to the quiet life of Ellie Mae St. Clare Mondary. The list of dates all ran together until she heard her name being introduced to the congregation. Mac breathed into her ear, "Are you sure you can do this?"

"No. But I'm going to. I have to."

Her legs felt heavy as she walked up the steps to the platform. Breathe, Charlie. Just breathe. It's not about you. It's about Mother. She prayed for strength to do the impossible. Her hands trembled as she laid her script on the flat surface of the lectern and swallowed the wad of fear that threatened to undo her.

"Thank you all for coming this morning. You are all a sweet example of what true friendship and Christ-like love looks like. You are the love letters written into the story of my mother's unassuming yet remarkable life, and I'm so grateful that we can celebrate her Homegoing together. I've written a letter to Mother and I pray that as I read it to her and to you, we will find the comfort we need as we press on in this amazing story that is our life.

"*Dearest Mother,*

"*I can't believe I'm standing here holding these words of goodbye. I find myself closing my eyes and trying to imagine life as you know it to be right now and I wonder - did you hear the angels singing and calling you to come home? Did you surrender with joy to their call, knowing your daughter was safe and that your work of prayer was finished? Did the longing to see Daddy once again thrill your soul? Did your heart leap for joy when you saw that petite woman with the feisty spirit waiting for you with open arms? Did the pleasure of calling her Mother for the first time make you want to write a new song just for her? When your beautiful eyes opened in the light of Eternity did you fall into Jesus' arms and cry for happy? Did all of heaven welcome you home to the place where you belong?*

"*Your battle with Alzheimer's has been won on the other side of the river. The silence and the confusion of these last few months have been broken and you're free, to speak, to sing, to think, to explore, and to treasure every dimension of what defines Heaven. You have left a legacy of kindness, and mercy, and wisdom, for me to follow. You have shown me by your example how to live, and in these last few months you have shown me how to die. You will be forever my teacher, my prayer covering, and my dearest friend. I miss you terribly. I don't know how I will ever learn to live without you here. But your absence draws me nearer to Jesus. So until I see you again I will send you on your way with those sweet words that sent me off to school every single day; 'Remember, Charlie, whatever happens today, I just love you so.'"*

Her hands hurt from what felt like a never-ending stream of handshakes. Bernie, Jody and Cheri stayed close while Mac, Les, Casey and Pastor Dave hovered over them. Marlene and the twins buzzed around the hall making sure the coffee pots were filled, the punch bowls never went empty, and the food never looked like a band of birds had picked it to death. The reception went on for what seemed like hours until Mac wrapped his arm around Charlie and took command. "It's time for us to leave, Charlie. It's been a long day and you haven't eaten a thing since this morning. Mom has a pot of soup in the crock pot and she's invited all of us to come to the house so we can just sit and have some time to be quiet."

"You mean a-l-l of us? Like everyone here?" The thought of moving the crowd to a new location nearly took what little emotional reserve she had left away.

"No, Charlie, not all-l-l-l of us - just our family. Which means you, Cheri, Jody, and Bernie, and the gang of MacKenzie's."

"Where's Zak? I haven't seen him since the service ended. Is he okay?"

Mac's face warmed at the sound of Charlie's maternal hovering. "He's fine. He asked me if he could go home with his friend Caleb. His mother will bring Zak by as soon as we get back to the house. I don't want you to go straight to your apartment without having a buffer between the graveside, the service, and the reception. You need a soft place to land before I kiss you goodnight. By the way – you've been beautiful today. You've made your mother proud."

"I hardly remember a thing. It's all such a blur. I didn't say anything stupid did I?"

"You were perfect."

"So were you. I don't know how I could have made it through all this without you, and your crazy family. I've always wondered what a houseful of family would feel like. And now I know – it feels like home."

Let love and faithfulness never leave you; bind them around your neck,
Write them on the tablet of your heart.
Then you will win favor and a good name in the sight of God and man.
Proverbs 3:3-4

Chapter Thirty-Two

Christmas was drawing near with all its cheery invitations to parties and holiday concerts and a trazillion ways to lure shoppers into their stores to save money by spending it. Yet for Charlie each day was a mirror of the day before. She was numb to the touch and cold to the bone. The simplest things felt like monumental tasks and if it weren't for Bernie's smothering, Cheri's optimism, and Mac's ridiculously ill-timed attempts at humor, she would have lived under her covers until spring. Marlene tiptoed into her life with spontaneous phone calls just to say she was praying for her. Mac's sisters sent her flowers with a Starbucks gift card tucked inside the envelope. And Sunday lunch at the Country Eaterie after church filled the empty places in her heart with a much needed sense of belonging. And somehow it all made her feel close to her mother.

Her love for the Beach House drew her in while her passion for re-modeling it waned. She knew she should begin the process of purging and cleansing but the thought of removing the things her mother loved felt like the worst kind of betrayal.

Cheri walked softly while following behind Charlie with her clipboard containing their lists of things to do before the contractors arrived to strip the upstairs of warped woodwork, windows painted closed, doors that stuck, and claw marks from dogs and kittens that used the hallway to chase tennis balls and mice stuffed with catnip. "Tell me how I can help you. If you want to put all this on hold I'm totally good with that. The contractors will understand and the house will still be here when and if you're ready to plunge back into it all again."

"No, Cheri. Nothing is going to change tomorrow. The house will still be a mess and so will I. I just don't know where to start. I can't think beyond the moment. Everything I touch speaks to me of the man who built these walls, and the child who never knew what it felt like to look into the eyes of her mother. Her little fingerprints are hidden everywhere. I know they've been Windexed away a hundred times over but they're still here. I used to think this place was a like a tomb where the memories of everyone we loved were buried."

"And now?"

"And now it's an open book where the lives of my family live and breathe through the pages. They whisper to me from these walls. Everything I touch brings them closer to me." Charlie sank into the overstuffed chair that held her during countless sleepless nights after Ellie Mae moved to Still Waters. She began picking at the spot where Princess Leia slept until a small wad of fur stuck to her fingers. "I even miss that dysfunctional cat. I don't know how to do this, Cheri. I don't know how to do this at all."

Cheri sat in the chair next to her friend searching for a way to help her work through this season of grief without rushing her into places where she wasn't ready to go. "Charlie, what if we invite Bernie and Marlene to come over on Saturday. Maybe the three of us could help you go through just one room upstairs, like the guest room, and sort out what you want to store and what you want to give away. We'll do all the lifting and packing and all you'll have to do is decide where you want everything to go. We'll stop when you're ready to stop and then we'll come back when you're ready to start again."

After giving Cheri's suggestion time to digest, she blew PL's fur out from between her fingers. "I like it. I think I can do that. If we start with the guest room and the bathroom I might feel like I can move on to my room, the extra bedrooms, and then Mother's room. You're right. I don't have to get rid of everything. We'll store the things that really matter and then we'll take the rest and give it all away. I don't want to sell anything. I don't need the money. I just think it would please Mother to give her things away to people who need them."

Satisfied with the plan, Cheri and Charlie left Bowers Beach and headed back to the apartment. "So, I'll call Marlene and Bernie and invite them over for Saturday. Until then you just take the time you need to rest while I gather up boxes. And if I remember correctly there's a certain doctor who is supposed to be picking you up for dinner tonight. And frankly my dear, you could use a new doo and a nail job."

"Only, if you come with me. And by the way, your subtlety is highly overrated."

The girls were nearly giddy as they walked into the apartment after a full day of hair, nails, and a trip to the mall for ice cream and new earrings. After dropping their coats and bags on the sofa they looked at each other, admiring their makeovers. "Seriously, Charlie, I don't know why we've kept our hair long for all these years. I don't know about you but I feel like I just dropped five pounds. It's not too short is it? I mean I don't want to look like I'm trying to be someone I'm not."

"You mean you're hoping Casey will like it. So when are you two going to stop talking on the phone and go out on an actual date somewhere? You know, like real people do when they are in-like with each other."

"One love story at a time, Charlie. I'm not in a hurry to start picking the petals off flowers and playing *he loves me - he loves me not.* And speaking of love, Mac's going to be here soon. So you just go get into something slinky and I'll put our stuff away."

An hour later the doorbell rang. Cheri poked her head through the bedroom door, "He's here, Charlie. Do you want me to get the door?"

"Yeah. I just need another minute or two. Just dazzle him with your new hair. If he likes it Casey will love it."

Charlie heard her padding to the door. A few minutes passed but there were no voices coming from the kitchen. She ran her fingers through her hair but they stopped short of her shoulders. This is going to take some getting used to. She picked up her new pair of shoes and sat down on the edge of the bed ready to decorate her feet with strappy purple leather. But before she slipped the first one on Cheri reappeared. "You need to go and open that door right now!"

"What?" Charlie held the shoe in suspended animation and looked at Cheri with a mixture of skepticism and annoyance.

Cheri put her hands on her hips. "Seriously, Charlie, put the shoe down."

"Should I be scared?"

"Yes. Yes you should. But go anyway!"

"Is it Mac? Is he okay?" But the look on her face hinted that a good kind of surprise was waiting for her. So she rolled her eyes, trudged to the door with her shoe in hand, and opened it. No Mac. But down near her feet was a basket with something shaking it from within. She picked it up carefully and then looked back at Cheri, "It's heavy. And it's like…alive. What am I supposed to do with it?"

Cheri shouted back at her, "Open it, for Pete's sake." She grabbed it from Charlie's hands and placed it on the table. "There. Now untie that ribbon and open the stupid box."

Charlie pulled tentatively on the end of the ribbon until a ball of white fur splotched with several shades of brown, pushed its nose through the lid and nearly jumped into her arms. "Oh my! It's a…it's a puppy! Why is it a puppy?" She picked it up and held it out at arm's length. "What am I supposed to do with it?"

"I think you're supposed to love it. Look, there's a box hanging from his/her collar." Feeling like an intruder in what was obviously leading up to a special moment, Cheri backed up from the table. "Um, I think I need to go to our room and give you some alone time with your new friend."

"Don't you dare leave me." Charlie handed the dog over to Cheri while she fidgeted with the box that was tied securely to the squirming bundle of fur. She opened the box only to find another box resting inside. She looked up at Cheri whose eyes were brimming with excitement. "I don't know what to do. I think I know what this is but what am I supposed to do with it?" Cheri cleared her throat and pointed her finger in the direction of the door that was still standing open. Charlie turned around. Mac was standing in the doorway. Stars seemed to spin around her like a scene out of Cinderella. "Oh, Mac, what have you done?"

"Nothing yet."

She felt as if her heart had stopped beating as he walked up to her and took hold of her left hand. This was the man whose face had filled her dreams since the day they first laid eyes on each other. She struggled for breath as she watched him bend down on one knee and looked up at her. "I love you, Charlie, and I want to spend the rest of my life building a family with you, a place where there's a father, and a mother, a son, and a dog. I want to give you sisters and a brother and a mom and a dad. When I bought this ring I wanted you to wear it because I couldn't imagine spending my whole life without you. But I am offering this ring to you today because I can't imagine you going your whole life without me, and Zak, and Basil III. And so I'm here with Bernie's blessing, Zak's permission, and in the presence of this witness, to ask you to marry me. So Miss Charlie Mae Mondary, will you put me out of my misery and be my wife?"

Charlie crumpled to the floor and sat eye level in front of him while visions of the video played at her mother's memorial service filled the room with unseen guests all clapping in approval. "Who are you, Mac? Who thinks of things like this? I've been struggling every day since Mother passed to find a way to understand how it's possible for a grown woman to be an orphan. I've felt like the book closed on my family's story and left me with nothing but *The End.*" Cupping Mac's face in her hands she looked into his eyes, "I love you, Mac MacKenzie. I love Zak. I love Marlene and Les and Keela and Morgan and even your crazy brother. And I love Basil III, though I have no idea what to do with him. This is an apartment after all."

Pointing to her left hand with her right index finger Charlie smiled, "I believe the ring goes right here."

Though one may be overpowered, two can defend themselves.
A cord of three strands is not quickly broken.
Ecclesiastes 4:12 NIV

Chapter Thirty-Three

Charlie walked into the living room yawning, stretching, and scratching her scalp with her fingers. She felt the tug of her hair caught in her ring. Ouch! And then it hit her; oh that's right. I'm engaged. She held her hand at arm's length and wiggled it as the perfectly cut diamond caught the morning light and reflected it back to her.

"Hello, Cheri. How are you on this fine and beautiful morning?"

Looking up from the mass of drawings, contracts, and project schedules, that lay sprawled across the kitchen table, she chuckled, "I'm fine, but it looks like I'm not as fine as you are."

Heading straight for the coffee pot, Charlie grabbed her zebra striped mug from the cupboard and filled it to the brim with caffeine. "It was a beautiful night wasn't it. Isn't he just the most romantic man? And that sweet puppy. Not only did he buy me the sweetest St. Bernard ever, but he named it Basil. Basil III. How adorable was that?"

"Pretty adorable. I'm just happy he brought it back home with him before all that water he lapped up ended up on the carpet, if you know what I mean."

Ignoring her comment Charlie dreamed on. "And to think he actually drove out to Bernie's place to ask her for my hand in marriage. I'll be talking to her about that this morning. So I was thinking, how soon do you think we can get the house finished? Because it would be a lovely place for a wedding, don't you think?"

"Lovely."

"So what's up with you, Miss Grumpy Face? How can you not be happy with all this love floating in the air?"

"I'm not grumpy. And I am happy. I'm happy for you, Charlie. I mean really, really, happy. So happy that I got up early so I could go over all our plans and try to see where we are and how much we can accomplish by, say April or May at the latest. And it looks like we can make it if we can get started right after Christmas."

Charlie sat down on the chair next to Cheri, folding her legs under her while sipping the freshly brewed coffee. "Hm. You make the best coffee. But don't let little Megan find out or she'll be completely devastated." Her words bit into her with a sting of fresh pain. She covered her ring with her hand. "I'm never going to visit Still Waters again, am I? I hated driving there. I hated being there. But now all I want to do is hear Megan chirping on about her latest concoction of coffee beans, and see Jodie rounding the corner with that cheerful face, and Celeste efficiently caring for Mother's needs."

"And your mother sitting by her window and telling you all about Anne and her great big puppy." Cheri put her pen down and gave Charlie her full attention. "It's grief Charlie. It will come crashing in on you like huge waves. But then the day will come when they'll hit with less and less force until they just wash quietly over your feet. And then, just when you think you've got a handle on it all, a giant sneaker wave will roll in on you out of the blue, and you'll wonder, 'where the heck did that come from'? And it's all okay, Charlie. I think it's just God's way of keeping us connected to Heaven."

Stabbed with regret, Charlie shifted her focus to Cheri. "I'm so sorry. I've been so wrapped up in my own stuff that I've completely forgotten how much you've lost since you left college. But you handle it all so well, like it was something that happened a long time ago in another place in another land."

"Not so long ago. And not so far away. The waves still take me by surprise like that day when we saw Jeffery's face on television. But it doesn't change the truth that God has been God over all of it, and that my parents are with Him, alive and real. I feel their presence with me in the sweetest ways. Like this morning. I got up early because I had something I needed to think through. And as I did I felt Mother standing over me and cheering me on."

Cheri's eyes lit up as she strategically changed the course of their conversation. "So here it is. I want to take over the whole project of the Beach

House. I mean everything. That will set you free to spend time with Mac and Zak and training Basil to be an indoor dog. And it will give you the freedom you need to concentrate on your wedding. I promise I won't make any changes to what we've decided without consulting you first. But, Charlie, I want to do this. I can do this. So, whad'ya think? Can you let go and let me?"

The waves of grief rolled back into the sea. "It's perfect. It's like the best gift a friend could ever give. Thank you. Thank you, thank you. It's all yours. Have a blast." Charlie got up and wrapped her arms around Cheri's neck. "You're the best friend a girl could ever have. And you're going to be a beautiful maid of honor!"

Cheri turned in her chair, trying not to be too honored, "Are you sure? Because this isn't something you can say to me and then take back after you've thought it through. This is real isn't it? You're getting married and I'm going to help give you away." Without waiting for an answer she surrendered her hands to the air, "I accept!"

"Thank you for your enthusiasm. And I accept your acceptance. But be warned, Miss Maid of Honor, it's going to be your job to keep me from going all Bridezilla on everyone. Especially Mac. Now, I need to get dressed and head back to Bernie's to show her my ring."

"So, when did he do it, Bernie?"

Bernie pulled the dish towel off her shoulder and began drying the dishes as she and Charlie chatted. "Oh, Girl, that man of yours sure knows how to do things right. He came driving that fancy Jeep of his right up to my stairs. And then I watched him go over to the other side and pick up a great big pie and in no time at all we were sittin' around my table smackin' our lips over the best chocolate pie I ever tasted. By the time we took our last bite he asked me for my blessing on your marriage. So I asked him why he was comin' to me with a question like that. And you know what he said?"

It was all Charlie could do to remain patient while Bernie purposely drew her story out to the longest yard possible. "No, I don't know what he said, but I'm hoping to hear the answer sometime before my next birthday."

"Well aren't you the sassy one this mornin'? Now this is my story and I'm gonna tell it the way I'm gonna tell it. So you just pull up a chair, sit yourself down, and eat one of those muffins."

Resigning herself to the long version of Bernie's story, Charlie sat down in her favorite chair, grabbed an oatmeal muffin and began slowly spreading a large knife full of butter over the top. "Okay I'm sitting so start talking."

"Well, that man just looked at me with those blue eyes of his and said, 'Bernie, I did everything wrong the first time around and I'm trying hard to not repeat the mistakes of the past.' Then his eyes drifted off to Loveland and he says, 'I love Charlie. I mean I *really* love Charlie. And with her father and mother being gone, I just can't treat her like an orphan who belongs to no one. You're the only family she has left. And that's why I'm here today, Bernie, to ask you for your permission to marry your Charlie?'"

"He really said all that? So what did you say?"

"I'm getting' there. You don't need to go pushin' me from behind." Bernie took a big bite of her muffin and chewed it slowly before taking up from where she left off. But the playfulness was clearly gone as she looked at Charlie with weepy eyes. "You know you're like a daughter to me, especially now. I miss your mamma so much my heart hurts inside my chest. I walk around this house cryin' out to heaven, tellin' her to get herself right back down here. But then I see her lookin' straight into the face of Jesus and I just want to jump up and join her. The truth of the matter is - I feel like I've got no more purpose left in me, Honey Girl. My Mr. Levi Mason has been gone a long time. My arms ache for my little Elijah. Your mamma's gone, and I want to see Jesus. I'm missin' my Jesus somethin' fierce."

A flood of compassion rolled over her as Charlie watched her dear Bernie struggling to fit more pain into a life that already had more than its share. "Oh, sweet Bernie, how could you even think your purpose is almost gone. As long as I live you will always have a purpose. You're not just my friend; you're my sanity, and the only mother I have left. I can't do this wedding without you. In fact, I didn't come here this morning just to hear your story, I came because I need to ask you something. It came to me last night while

I should have been sleeping but couldn't because I was a little *preoccupied*."

Charlie curled her hand over Bernie's and looked into her face with as much sadness as there was joy. "Bernie, I want you to walk me down the aisle on my wedding day. I know it's a little unconventional, but I can't think of anyone I'd rather have at my side. So, what do you say? Will you give my hand away in marriage?"

"Well now, doesn't that just beat all?"

"So back to Mac; what did you say?"

"Well, I said *yes* to him as sure as I'm sayin' *yes* to you. Now you're not planning to put this big old body in a tuxedo are you? Because that will surely change the whole look of your wedding."

The months flew by as plans for the wedding and plans for the Beach House kept Charlie and Cheri running at full speed and feeling much like two ships barely passing in the night.

By March the upstairs was finished and ready for Charlie's flair for all things lovely. The sand colored walls accented by cream moldings gave uniformity to the whole while the varying accent colors in each room provided individuality to her design. She saved just enough of her family's treasures to preserve her heritage without cluttering them up with outdated trinkets that served no purpose. She felt life coming back to her with the completion of each room and she had Cheri to thank for making it all happen.

The wedding date was set for June 26th and as the guest list continued to grow Charlie realized her dreams of Beach House nuptials was out of the question. But the church that was quickly becoming home to them was perfect for both the ceremony and the reception. She and Mac agreed to keep the event elegantly simple. Marlene jumped right in organizing the reception while Keena and Morgan shadowed Charlie around helping her make decisions on flowers, cake, and bridesmaid dresses. Even Zak joined in the process by designing a fun room so the kids would have a place to go after the wedding ceremony was over.

"It's gonna be awesome! Jakob and I are gonna build a huge cardboard castle and we're gonna have a long Lego table and then there's gonna be another place where we can play WII games. And Conner's big sister is gonna make a whole table full of things kids like to eat, like those little pizzas and cupcakes and stuff. And Daddy's going to help us make this really cool drink that smokes!"

Charlie's love for Zak sunk into the deep places of her heart in ways she could never have expected. He was becoming a son to her and she couldn't have loved him more if she had birthed him herself.

He reveals deep and hidden things; he knows what lies in darkness,
and light dwells with him. Daniel 2:22

Chapter Thirty-Four

Mac hardly spoke three words to Charlie as they drove to the church for their last pre-marital counseling session. Normally she would fill in all the empty spaces with stories of Cheri's adventures in beach house remodeling and shopping trips with Bernie to find her a dress that didn't make her itch and shoes that wouldn't kill her feet. But the air in the Jeep was chilly to say the least. As Mac pulled into the parking space, Charlie blinked back tears and cleared her throat. "Mac, something's wrong. Are you going to tell me about it before we go in or are we going to have to pretend everything's fine when it isn't?"

Mac stared into the night. "I'm fine. Let's just go in and get this over with."

Swallowing her scream she reached over to touch his shoulder but he pulled away. "I'm sorry, Charlie. I know I'm scaring you right now. I just don't know how to tell you what I need to tell you. I just need some space."

Charlie twisted her engagement ring around her finger wondering if she would need to slip it off and hand it back to him. "Space? Mac, you don't get to have space right now. Isn't this what we've been learning from Pastor Dave? To keep the doors of communication open, especially when we're angry?"

"But I'm not angry. Not with you. Never with you. Something happened the other day that I don't know how to deal with." He turned to Charlie and wiped a tear off her face. "I'm so sorry, Babe, I . . ."

"Mac, I'm not going anywhere. Remember what you told me when I was battling through the worst of my grief, 'there's no you and there's no me, there's just us'? Well, there's just us, Mac. Just us."

He reached reluctantly into his suit pocket and pulled out what looked like a postcard. "I got this in the mail a couple of days ago. It's from Irene."

Charlie took the card from Mac. The postmark was from Argentina. She turned it over and stared at the picture on the back. "Um. Wow. I don't even know what to say. Which one is Irene?"

"The woman on the left holding the Margarita glass."

"Then who's this woman on the right?"

"Well, that would be her new wife." Mac turned to Charlie, his pulse pounding in his jaw, "What am I supposed to tell Zak? 'Here's a postcard from your Mommy, Zakky. And no she didn't ask about you. She just wanted to drop us line to say, *Hey! I'm married. Be happy for me.*' What am I supposed to do, Charlie? How do I tell an eight-year-old boy that he now has three mommies but he really only has one because his birth-mother doesn't care enough about him to even mention him by name?"

If Charlie had learned anything about her fiancé over these last few months it was that he rarely ever expressed anger unless he felt helpless in the throes of injustice, a fact that both comforted her and worried her.

"You don't. Someday maybe. But not now." Charlie cupped her hand under Mac's face and spoke softly to him. "This really doesn't change anything, Mac. I love you. You love me. And together we're going to build a life for the three of us, and of course, the whole crazy MacKenzie clan, and Cheri, and Basil, and Bernie. Life doesn't get much richer than that. Right?"

"I know you're right. But being right doesn't take away the ghosts of the past. I feel like Irene and Jeffery are waiting in the wings like terrorists ready to blow up our lives when we least expect it. And I don't know what to do about it. I can't prepare for it and I can't control it. Which scares the heck out me because how can I protect you and Zak if I don't know what they're going to do next? It was easier when she was just a phantom ex-wife. But now she's back. And I don't know what it means."

Charlie chewed on her lip while her mind whirled with answers that had no meaning. "I don't know what it means either, Mac. All I do know is that I love you. And I want that to be enough."

His breath tingled down the length of her neck as Mac pulled her close to him. His grip was tight and almost desperate. "It's enough, Charlie. It's more than enough. I don't know how I ever lived this long without you. I can't wait to whisk you away from here and have you all to myself. I can't wait to feel you falling asleep in my arms and to see you waking up in the morning with all this beautiful hair, albeit shorter hair, sweeping across your pillow. Don't ever leave me, Charlie. Please don't ever leave me."

She wrapped her arms so tightly around him that he felt the pain of the last two days exhaling from his chest. Two people, broken by life, yet joined together in hope. And though they felt it would kill them to separate they pulled away from each other, breathless with desire.

"We're late." Mac straightened his jacket while smiling into Charlie's eyes, "As much as I want you right now, I will want you more when we say *I do.* I promised God, and you, and Bernie, that I will wait until the last piece of cake is served, the last toast is made, and the marriage certificate is signed, before I carry you off to our future. But know this, Charlie Face, it isn't at all easy."

"Thank you, Mac, because I haven't an ounce of strength to resist you right now."

Make haste, my beloved,
And be thou like to a roe or to a young hart upon the mountains of spices.
Song of Solomon 8:14 KJV

Chapter Thirty-Five

The sun rose up bright and beautiful on the morning of June 26th. Charlie opened one eye to see if her dearest friend in all the world had slept as little as she did. "Good morning. So, are you ready to help me get married?"

"No. No, I'm not. This apartment is going to be miserably depressing while you're off romping around a deserted island somewhere. I can't believe that whole family of his is keeping his secret. Aren't you dying to know where he's taking you?"

"Actually, I'm just dying to say *I do*. Everything after that is frosting." Charlie sat up and propped up her pillows behind her. "So, Cheri, here's what I've been chewing on all night. The house is almost done, right?"

"Right," Cheri said through a long yawn.

"I know this sounds crazy, but I really don't want to live there." Charlie put out her hand to squelch Cheri's objections before she had a chance to voice them. "No, hear me out. Zakky is going to be nine soon and by September he's going to be heading off for third grade. He's got a whole tribe of well-established friends. If we move to Bowers Beach he's going to have to change schools, which means everything in his life is going to feel strange to him. Strange house. Strange school. Strange friends. Strange mommy. And there's Basil to think about. We've been shifting him from Mac's place to my place to his mother's place and back to my place. That poor dog never knows where he's going to wake up in the morning. It's too much, too fast."

"So, what are you thinking, Charlie? You've been so excited about the progress of the house. I can't believe you don't want to move into it."

"That's just it. I *don't* want to move into it. Now that it's almost finished

I feel like I've, actually *you've*, done what needed to be done. But it's not my home anymore, Cheri. Mac and Zak are my home. So, I'm thinking that we'll spend the summer there, you know, like a vacation home. That will give us time to find a house near Marlene and Les and Zak's school and he will be close to his castle, and his friends, and Basil will have a yard all his own. And when September comes we'll be all moved in and ready to be a family, in a real neighborhood, with a very big dog. So whad'ya think?"

"It makes beautiful sense. But what about the Beach House? It's been in your family for so long that I can't imagine what it will be like for you to give it up."

"Well my friend, I won't have to give it up. I want you to have it."

Cheri climbed out of bed and wandered around their room in circles trying to digest Charlie's words. "Charlie, I love your generosity, but you can't give me a whole house. Besides, it's not like I can't afford to live on my own. I have a pretty sizable bank account you know. Not as big as yours; but enough."

"It's not about money, Cheri. It's about keeping the family home in the family. And you're my family. You and Bernie. She's going to need you after I'm married. Besides, we can use part of the house for InDesign. So whad'ya think? It's a great plan isn't it?"

"What I think is that you have a wedding to go to and we can discuss this later. Much, much, later."

Bernie stood next to Charlie as she looked at the bride looking at herself in the full length mirror. "Oh, my Honey Girl, you couldn't be more beautiful if the angels came down and kissed you with the stars of heaven." Opening up her beaded handbag, she pulled out a shimmering string of pearls and fastened it around Charlie's neck. "This necklace was given to me by my Mamma. She gave it to me on the day I married Mr. Mason and I always dreamed of passing it on to one of my own children. You're all I got left now and so I'm prayin' this necklace will mean as much to you as it does to me. And someday, when your Zak gets married maybe you can pass it on to him. Because that's what love does Miss Charlie, it just keeps on givin'."

Charlie ran the tips of her fingers across the smooth pearls. "It's beautiful Bernie. Thank you." She turned and gently hugged her friend while trying not to let her tears ruin her make-up. "How can I ever thank you for all the things you've done for me?"

"Oh, girl, you've blessed me with more love than this old heart can hold. Now I know you're feelin' both pain and pleasure right now, but Baby, I want you to know what God's been showin' me today. He told me that your Mamma and your Daddy are smilin' over you with pride. Yes, they are. And so am I. So now, let's just go and get you hitched to that handsome man out there. Now you hold on tight to my arm so we can keep each other from fallin' over the hems of these beautiful dresses."

As the Wedding March began to play, Charlie slipped her arm through Bernie's, tightening her grip on her bouquet, and fixing her eyes on the man standing on the platform looking mighty fine in his ivory tuxedo while the soft coral rose bud set in a tiny spray of Baby's Breath smiled at her from his lapel. You're a beautiful man, Mac MacKenzie. I only hope I can make you as happy as you make me. Soon, my darling. Soon.

The aisle to the altar seemed to have grown longer since the rehearsal the night before. Her bridesmaids bloomed like a row of spring flowers along the base of the platform on one side, while the groomsmen stood guard over a very focused and very nervous groom. Pastor Dave's voice boomed through the congregation as Bernie and Charlie reached the pink stickers on the white runner stopping them just short of the bridal party.

With his open Bible balanced between both hands he called for someone to declare consent for the wedding to proceed. "Who gives this woman in marriage?" Without hesitation Bernie proclaimed with the dignity her Doctorate deserved, "Her mother, Ellie Mae St. Clare-Mondary, her father, the Honorable Lt. Colonel John Lawrence Mondary, and I, Bernice Adela Mason, do hereby offer our blessings to this most perfect union." She planted a kiss on Charlie's cheek and whispered, "This is the day the Lord has made, now go and rejoice in it."

Charlie handed her bouquet to Cheri and walked to Mac's side. The thrill of this moment made her dizzy with delight. Pastor Dave's sermon floated through the air like clouds drifting off to sea until the final words struck a familiar chord and brought her back to the moment. "Love is patient, love is kind, love bears all things, believes all things, hopes all things, endures all things. Love never fails." Lord, let me never fail. "Let us pray."

A cacophony of amens rippled through the congregation as Mac and Charlie joined their hands together and looked thoughtfully into each other's eyes. "Do you Lester Mac MacKenzie take Charlie Mae Mondary to be your lawfully chosen wife? Will you love her, care for her, protect her, defend her, and encourage her in every way possible to live according to the predetermined will of God? And will you remain faithful to her until death separates you?"

"I will."

"And will you, Charlie Mae Mondary take Lester Mac MacKenzie to be your lawfully chosen husband. Will you love him, care for him, protect him, defend him, and encourage him in every way possible to live according to the predetermined will of God? And will you remain faithful to him until death separates you?"

"I will."

Her knees were dancing to the rhythm of her heart as Zak walked proudly up to the platform, who from his tux to his dimples was a microcosm of the groom, carrying the rings tied with ribbons onto a satin pillow. He wiggled himself between Charlie and Mac - a symbol perhaps of things to come.

"So how about it, little Zak? Do you think we should let them have their rings so I can pronounce them husband and wife?"

"Yeah! But they're not going to get all kissy are they?"

"I'm afraid they are, but feel free to close your eyes." Pastor Dave took the rings off the pillow and handed them to the bride and groom.

Mac slipped the diamond crusted ring over Charlie's long and slender finger. "Charlie, with this ring I marry you, and with this covenant of love I surrender you my heart to hold, my material goods to possess, my body to cherish, my future to share, and my faith to lean on for all the days of our lives. In the Name of the Father, the Son, and the Holy Spirit."

Audrey, Charles, Esther, Eleanor, Lawrence and Ellie Mae gazed through the window that joined earth to heaven and heaven to earth, treasuring each word of promise spoken through tears as Charlie slipped the simple gold band over Mac's finger.

"Mac, with this ring I marry you, and with this covenant of love I surrender you my heart to hold, my material goods to possess, my body to cherish, my future to share, and my faith to lean on for all the days of our lives. In the Name of the Father, the Son, and the Holy Spirit."

"And so it is with great joy I pronounce that you are indeed man and wife. May what God has approved through the joining of your lives together be protected from all harm." Bending down to Zak's level Pastor Dave gave a quick word of warning to the freckled face little man who had been about as well behaved as a boy could be. "You might want to head back over to your seat, Buddy, because I think we're about to witness a record-breaking display of unrestrained smooching."

Zak's face twisted like a pretzel as he scurried over to the groom's side of the aisle and buried his head between the back of the pew and his grandfather's arm.

"Mac, you've been about as patient as a man in love can be. So have at it, man! Feel free to kiss your wife."

Shouts of praise and peals of hearty applause filled the space between time and timelessness. Though he felt like he could kiss her forever without stopping, Mac released his bride and the two turned to face the congregation before heading down the aisle as husband and wife. "Friends and family, it is with pure pleasure that I introduce you to Dr. and Mrs. Mac MacKenzie."

Ellie Mae blew a kiss through the portals, her mind as clear as the diamonds on Charlie's finger and her heart as strong as the promise of resurrection. "All is as it should be, my precious daughter. Now go and live your new day. Your Mommy loves you so."

Epilogue

Yet God has made everything beautiful for its own time. He has planted eternity in the human heart, but even so, people cannot see the whole scope of God's work from beginning to end. Ecclesiastes 3:11

Ellieanne sat along the river's edge swishing the water with her feet and watching how the gentle splashing's reflected through the air like tiny crystals. The coolness of the water satisfied her. Everything here satisfied her. She loved discovering the wonders of Heaven. She never grew complacent in the joy of living in the presence of Holiness or tired of knowing her mind would never again be held hostage by disease. She would always be free to enjoy the pleasures of Eternity - this place where she could sing and dance, and express her praise without fear of drawing critical attention to herself. It wasn't possible here. Jesus was in all, and through all. He was the Center of all things.

The story of her life, narrated through Audrey's words, lay next to her. She had been reading for what in earthly time would have been days, but here it felt like only moments. Tears of gratitude fell like rain refreshing her spirit as she stared into the water seeking to absorb her life in pages. She felt the presence of someone coming up behind her and as she turned her head she saw Him. Messiah. Jesus. The Lover of her Soul. The Famous One. Abba Incarnate. "Oh, Jesus, I see it all and yet I feel like I don't see it all. It's so deep that I wonder if I will ever be able to grasp the whole of it."

"You have plenty of time to explore the depths of Abba's love for you, Ellieanne."

Jesus sat down next to her, took off His sandals, and dipped His feet into the water. "So, what do you think Ellieanne, now that you've seen your life through Heaven's eyes?"

She breathed in the fragrance of celestial air and smiled with delight. "I think I might have wasted a lot of time feeling less than I really was. I always felt so small and insignificant, like a clam stuck inside its shell. I never doubted how much I was loved. Daddy, and Gramma Esther, saw to that.

But still there was a sense of missing stirring deep inside me. I missed my mother. The only place I felt truly close to her was at the piano. It was like I was searching for her in my music, wondering what Heaven was like, and what she was doing. I wondered if she could hear me and see me and if she missed me as much as I missed her.

"And then Gramma Esther left, then Daddy and then Lawrence and the missing only intensified my longings for Heaven. Sometimes at night, I'd look out over the water to the horizon, and I felt as if I could see them all standing there waiting for me. And I'd picture myself just walking across the ripples of the water and falling into their arms like an exhausted child. I think I always felt like I was living somewhere between two worlds - Eternity and Bowers Beach. But no matter how deeply my heart ached for all of them, there was always that one thing that kept me from stepping off the sand and letting the waves carry me Home."

"Charlie."

"Yes, Charlie. She was so much fun and so full of life. In her eyes I could see bits and pieces of everyone I loved. She had her father's noble pride, my mother's gift of words, Daddy's strong will, and Gramma Esther's tenacious spirit. She's a lovely portrait of our family tree."

Jesus picked up a stone and tossed it across the water, counting how many times it skipped the surface until it sank into the bed of the river. "And what about you, Ellieanne, where do you see yourself in this amazing daughter of yours?"

The sound of that name still felt foreign to her. "It still surprises you doesn't it? That you and Anne are one and the same."

"It overwhelms me, Jesus. Anne was my secret friend who lived outside the window at Still Waters with her dog and her piano." Ellieanne laughed at her own words, "It sounds impossible now, but it was so very real to me at the time."

"Aha, but Abba is the God of impossible things."

"But why? I don't understand why I was able to recognize her and not my own daughter."

Jesus brushed a wisp of hair back from Ellie's face and rested His hand along her cheek. "I think the answer to all your questions is in your answer to Mine. How did the girl in the window make you feel, Ellieanne?"

Ellie drew circles in the water with her toes as she went back to Still Waters to relive her time with the girl in the glass. "Hm. She made me feel alive. She broke through my deadness and brought life to me. I loved the way the wind would blow through her hair and I loved watching her dance through the grass with her bare feet. She had such a freedom about her. I loved the way her fingers would flit across the keys of her piano alongside the lake. She had such beautiful hands."

"Like yours."

Ellie looked at her hands. "Yes. They were just like mine. Her hair was just like mine. Everything about her was just like me. But she was so free. I still don't understand it."

"Ah, Ellieanne, people seldom ever see themselves as they really are. Their humanity hangs like a veil over their spiritual eyes blinding them to their true worth. They wander through life looking to find themselves but they never really do until they surrender their search to Me. Their worth is in My love for them. And even after they surrender to My love they struggle to accept the freedom that My sacrifice purchased for them on that tree."

"But why Anne, Jesus. Why was I seeing myself? Why didn't I just see You?"

Jesus looked through Ellie's eyes and into the depths of her soul. "You always saw Me, Ellieanne. You saw Me in My Words, in the eyes of hurting people, in the lives of your family, and in the world around you. Your love for Me never lost its childlike trust. But you struggled to see yourself through Me. You saw all of your flaws. You counted up all your inadequacies as if they were written in My Book like a bad report card. You looked in your mirror and you saw all your sin, but you didn't see how My love covered you with My glory."

Ellieanne bent over the water and stared into the face that was looking back at her. The sun shimmered over her reflection with the glory of heavenly light. "Oh, Jesus, You're right. I understand. It all makes sense doesn't it? In seeing Anne, I was seeing You. You in me."

Jesus bent over the water to join His face with hers. "Yes Ellieanne. Now you see why Abba chose to reveal to you the mystery of this great exchange.

My life for you. My life in you. My life - your glory.

"Your mother called you Anne and your father called you Ellie. But I call you Ellieanne because you are now complete in Me. The fullness of My Spirit has made you whole. You are My Poema, Ellieanne, a masterpiece of My design. And here you will discover more and more of how your worth reflects the glory of Abba's Throne. But for now let me show you the place where music flows. Trust Me, you're going to love it."

"He called me His Poema, Mother. Isn't that just so beautiful?"

"Everything He says is beautiful, Ellieanne. And you are a poem. You are the beautiful work of His beautiful heart." Audrey's eyes gleamed with maternal pride as she smiled into her daughter's face. "And your daughter, Charlie, is so much like you. Her sensitive spirit, her love for beauty, her desire for home and family, and her struggle to see herself as Abba sees her. She's untamed right now, but watch with me and you will see your prayers for her bearing fruit that will astound you. But for now, my lovely daughter, we have work to do. I know you have a heart full of songs waiting to be born and I have an endless supply of words just waiting to fill them with lyrics. You and I are about to make glorious music together. Trust me, Ellieanne. The journey has only just begun."

Coming Home

Charlie's Song

Words and Music by Bonnie Knopf -
Worship leader, musician, writer, speaker, friend.
From her album, *Do Not Fear*

http://www.youtube.com/watch?v=5Q6AYtxWfxA
Visit Bonnie at her website
www.bonnieknopf.com

From the Author

It all happened one day while I was curled up in a blue mood. Pain, the kind that moves in to rearrange your life and mess with your head had just about done me in. I was living in The Land of the Un's; Unnecessary, Unloved, Unwanted, Uninspired, Unable, and Undone. Then it happened – I saw a woman, Ellie Mae Mondary, lost in the world of Alzheimer's, sitting by a window and watching a little girl romping freely through the grass near the lake. And within fifteen minutes the scattered bones of Ellie's Window came to life. Seriously, the whole story was sitting in front of me like a puppy in a pet store. The cast of characters, the backstory, the present story, and the end story were all in their places with come hither faces.

I wasn't looking for a novel idea. I wasn't looking for anything but peace, and security, and a fresh wind to blow away all the bad stuff. But when I saw Ellie Mae sitting all by herself with no one to tell her story, I knew that I had been summoned to the Throne for a one on One visit with the God who takes great pleasure handing over unexpected assignments to unsuspecting people.

But before I could dive in and start writing:
I needed to learn how to write Christian fiction. *Study*
I needed friends who would read what I was writing. *Humility*
And I needed to work at it every day. *Perseverance*

Thank you for coming along with me on this journey. I pray that Audrey has given you a glimpse of Heaven, that Charles has inspired you to allow pain to chart a new course for your life, that Esther has encouraged you to love your children with truthful resolve, that Bernie has given you the courage to speak well of the God who loves you, that Charlie has taught you how to come back Home to the heart of God, that Mac has helped you to wait for God's best, and that Cheri has blessed you with her quiet and gentle spirit. But most of all, I pray that Ellieanne will live beyond these pages to remind you that in God's eyes, you are a finished work of art, a poem, a masterpiece, and oh, so very remarkable.

May *Ellie's Window* cause a flurry of "what if's" to burst through the boundaries of what our limited imaginations can comprehend.

What if - Heaven is more than what this story portrays?

What if - Our gifts and talents are being honed on Earth for Eternal use in Heaven?

What if - God is not bound by the limitations of time, and space, human failures, and even disease?

What if - Our stories are being written down for all Eternity to read?

What if - Those who have gone before us have, know us still?

What if - God is bigger than we can fathom?

Until we meet again in story,
Love and joy
Sandy
www.sandysnavely.net

About Sandy Snavely

Sandy Snavely has been married to her best friend, Bud, for fifty years. She has two grown children Annette Marie Snavely and Dean Ellis Snavely, one daughter-in-love, Kim Snavely, and two grandchildren, Morgan Elizabeth-Anne and Jakob Ellis Snavely. At home Sandy and Bud are owned by their two cats, Murphy and Spinelli. Their days are spent serving each other, loving their family, enjoying their neighbors, sitting by the pond, writing, studying, cooking delectable meals, and flying Space A around the world on military cargo planes.

Sandy Snavely has been speaking to women for over thirty years throughout our nation as well as in Africa, Bolivia, and the United Arab Emirates. Her first book, Called to Rebellion – The Key to a Single Hearted Love for Christ, was published by Multnomah Publishers and is available on Kindle. Other works include: two Bible Studies for Women, Still the Ever Present God and Becoming Ruth, as well as contributions to three volumes of Stories for the Heart. Sandy began her working career in retail management, marketing, and became a local radio talk show personality for five years in Portland Oregon.

You may contact Sandy Snavely by visiting her website www.sandysnavely.com, friending her on Facebook and Goodreads, or email her at sandy.snavely@frontier.com.

Congratulations, you've finished Ellie's Window.
Before you go ...

Tweet/share that you finished this book
Rate this book ★★★★★

Review this book through: Amazon.com
and/or Goodreads.com